Wyndham

CW00351932

Diploma

by

Roger Bland

For Bob,

Roger Bland

About the Author

Roger Bland has spent most of his adult life in trouble spots over-seas, in commerce, journalism, university lecturing and in the Foreign Service, mainly in the Middle East and in those parts of Africa most prone to power cuts, floods and civil unrest. Back in UK he practised as a psychotherapist before deciding that writing novels might be a less harmful occupation. He has been kept moderately sane throughout by his warm-hearted and cool-headed wife, whom he captured in the Congo several revolutions ago.

ROGER BLAND

Diplomatic Corpse

**Wyndham
& Chilters**

Published by Wyndham & Chilters
4 Wyndham Lea, West Chiltington, Pulborough,
West Sussex, RH20 2NP
Email: chiltfulus@btinternet.com

The Author asserts the moral right to be
identified as the author of this work

ISBN 978-0-9554142-0-6

Printed and bound by
CPI Antony Rowe,
Eastbourne, East Sussex

Acknowledgements

I am grateful to Tony Ingledow, late of HM Diplomatic Service, for advice on pidgin English; to Stephen Somerville for lending me his wide expertise in several fields; to John B, John S, Mike A and Alp M who read and commented usefully on the manuscript; to A N Other for certain specialist guidance; and to my friend Kay Boothby for much sound advice. I also wish to acknowledge the valuable and imaginative input (including much necessary surgery) by Simon B of the *Wyndham and Chilters* editorial team. Thanks must also go to Bridget and Katie, both of whom have slaved over a hot computer in my interests.

My good friend L has advised me on certain military matters and language and kindly allowed me to subsume elements of his (distinguished) career into that of my Military Attaché. Anne, my patient and multi-talented wife, has – as with my earlier works – constantly sustained my morale and been of immense practical help. It wouldn't have been half as much fun without her.

For Philip of Holborn

Ah, with the Grape my fading life provide,
And wash my body whence the Life has died
And in a Windingsheet of Vineleaf wrapt,
So bury me by some sweet Gardenside.

The Rubaiyat of Omar Khayyam

List of Characters

Bernard Brathby	His Excellency the British Ambassador
Cuthbert	The Ambassador's ancient Steward
Eventide	A boy. Cuthbert's Assistant
Ogolo	The Ambassador's Driver
Polly Pym	The Ambassador's PA
Colonel Jack Squires MC	Military Attaché at the Embassy
Jenny Squires	Jack's wife
Octavius	Jack and Jenny Squires's Steward
Francis Paynton	The Embassy's Head of Chancery
Moses	Paynton's Steward
Violet Tryam-Jones	Paynton's PA
Bert Woodley	Embassy Information Officer
Harry Fieldhouse	Third Secretary in Chancery
Tom Muckle	Intelligence Section Clerk
Trevor	Embassy Archivist
Lydia	An Officer in the Commercial Section
Unnamed	The (boring) Embassy Commercial Counsellor
Bill	The British Consul
Edith	Bill's wife
Jane Paige	The lovely Vice-Consul
Antoun Elias (*aka Greaseball*)	An Embassy Chancery Officer
Bertha	Elias's deplorable wife
Cyril Ellison	Embassy Admin. Officer
Sodham	An Embassy Security Officer
Fred	A competent Embassy Security Officer
Dr Ali Karim-Bux	Embassy Doctor
Nurse Tayla	Karim-Bux's (close) Assistant
Philippa Brainbridge	Embassy Intelligence Officer
Richard Cardenas (*alias Berridge*)	A Security Service Officer seconded to FCO
Joe Singleton	Local Manager for London-based United Mining Company (Uminco)
Oswald Obunga	Protocol Officer, Ministry of External Affairs
Commissioner Zalomo	The Chief of Police
Inspector Ferdinand	Zalomo's Secretary and confidant
Sergeant Omobi	An unsubtle policeman

Part One

1

The stink of rotting fish and fresh human excrement wafted across the swamp, penetrating the Embassy's primitive air-conditioning system.

From his office window Bernard Brathby scanned the sluggish grey river as it meandered its way towards the sea, hoping to pick out one of the alarming number of bloated corpses making their one-way trip to the Bight. His monthly wager with the Military Attaché over the number of bodies to be spotted from their respective windows was not going well, even though he had banned Squires from using his army issue binoculars.

He sometimes wondered who they could be, these water-borne wretches. Surely they couldn't all be thieves - *tiefmen*, as they were called locally - lynched by upstream villagers and tossed into the river. Nor could they all be criminal suspects over-enthusiastically interrogated by the local police.

A macabre game for a macabre country, Brathby reflected, and he now wished he had not agreed to it in the first place. It suited the edgy mood of the place, but in an unsettling, menacing way. This was a part of the world where high spirits could turn to violence at any time, where sudden death was commonplace – as he had already discovered in his first few months here as Her Britannic Majesty's Ambassador. A little longer, and perhaps he, like others before him, might lose his curiosity and even his compassion. Standards might disintegrate. Moral rot might set in. He sincerely hoped not, but he could not be sure.

Old hands in the Foreign and Commonwealth Office described the country as 'the arsehole of Africa', and the post was notorious for its habit of ruining the reputations of ambitious and upwardly-mobile diplomats. Frustration, apathy and drink were the main culprits, and his predecessor, whom he had met briefly in London, had been brought down by a cocktail of all three.

In spite of the reputation of the place, Brathby was actually happy to have the posting as his first ambassadorial appointment. After some tedious times in Europe, he was ready for a change, and a challenge.

His main task, he had been briefed in London, was to defend Britain's strong economic and strategic interest in the country's generous supply of minerals, as exploited by the London-based United Mining Company, better known as UMINCO. And then there was the cut and thrust of the Cold War, averting the Communist threat and so on. Not that Brathby took that too seriously. In his view, West Africans were natural capitalists. They believed in God, family and money. No danger of their swallowing any of that Marxist garbage, except for short-term profit. Still, the old East-West rivalry did make the continent a market place for arms sales, and that was also in his brief to exploit on behalf of Her Majesty's Government.

The Ambassador shifted his bulky figure away from the window and broke the silence in the room. Although it was only nine in the morning the cloud cover was eerily low. 'Difficult to be certain in this atrocious light, but I think I can spot another one, just over there, on the other side of the path.' He pointed towards the swamp, seeking another corpse, despite himself. 'You see where I mean, Polly, near those two women there, one with a pink bundle on her head?'

Polly Pym joined him at the window and he glanced sideways at the vivid auburn hair which he found so alluring, before calling himself to order and resuming his seat. He knew she didn't really approve of the game, but felt a need to involve her in things other than work.

'Anything I ought to see before Morning Prayers?' Brathby asked, forcing his mind to office matters and briefly wondering who had thus christened the Ambassador's weekly staff meeting. He gestured unenthusiastically towards the thick folder of telegrams which Polly had brought in. 'Let's hope that nothing serious blows up and that I'll be able to finish getting the various personnel problems sorted out.' *Including my own*, he added silently. 'We've been damned lucky to have our first few months here free of serious bilateral issues – apart from this wretched Ayumba business, of course.' He looked up. 'Anything there I should read?'

Polly riffled expertly through the sheaf of telegrams, stripping out five of them with a practised flourish and in one smooth movement laid them out on the Ambassador's desk in order of importance. Brathby watched her delicate fingers as they flicked through the papers – quick, accurate and unfussy, like a bank teller counting notes.

'You're wonderful, Polly,' he said, in such a way that she could interpret the compliment as purely professional, if she wished.

Polly was the perfect PA for this dump; reliable, cheerful, discreet, supportive and radiating a quiet energy in inverse proportion to her height. And at just turned thirty she was a good age for a tough African posting, with the right balance of professional experience and youthful enthusiasm. Brathby had done well to persuade her to come with him when he had been transferred here from his last tedious posting In Europe.

At first he'd doubted whether Polly would thrive in this very different environment, but he needn't have worried. She'd taken it all in her stride: power failures, armed robberies, pot-holed roads, and the desperate unreliability and unpunctuality of the host country's officials. She remembered everybody's name and had all the right papers to hand at the right time. She knew when to speak and when to be silent. But what he most admired about her was a quality, rare among Europeans in West Africa: she never took the easy path of blaming the locals for the incessant problems and frustrations of life, not even for using the land around the Embassy compound as a public latrine.

No, Brathby reflected wryly, he couldn't have done better. Except for one most uncomfortable fact: his admiration for her was fast developing into consuming desire. Which she showed absolutely no sign of reciprocating.

'Well if there's nothing else Polly, you can leave me to get on with this stuff now and perhaps bring coffee in later. Thanks'.

He lowered his head towards a file as if to read, but lifted his eyes in time to see her walking briskly to her adjoining office, provoking in him a spasm of mixed lust and tenderness. He asked himself yet again if perhaps she were a lesbian; surely not, and yet she appeared to show no romantic interest in her many admirers. She loved formal ballroom dancing and often partnered Tom Muckle, his Intelligence Officer's clerk. Muckle, a short and slim, almost weedy, young man was as silkily smooth on the dance floor as the bulky Brathby was shambolic and ungainly. But her interest in Tom went no further than that, he was sure. Well, nearly sure.

Muckle was a rough fellow in many ways but the Ambassador had a soft spot for him. One of the young Welshman's peculiarities was

3

that he invariably addressed him as *Buster* – this unusual pronunciation of *Ambassador* might have seemed impertinent but he knew very well that there was no disrespect implied. Besides, it rather tickled him.

'Morning, Tom,' called out Trevor, the amiable Embassy Archivist.

'And to you too, boyo', Tom Muckle returned cheerily as he walked past the stacked files and safes and began work on the first of three combinations necessary to gain him access to the office of the Embassy's Intelligence Section, sited in the most remote and secure area of the building. He had first to open the grille and the steel door, and then finally the light wooden privacy door.

Once settled and locked in, Muckle started work on developing the secret writing in a letter which had been passed to him by a contact earlier that morning. He carefully removed the dripping sheets from the tray and hung them up to dry. That's the easy part, he muttered to himself. The real bugger was that with Philippa Brainbridge, his Head of Station, on leave, he himself would have to concoct a report from this information to send to London and to show to the Ambassador. He wasn't much good at that sort of thing.

Tom then turned his attention to his most pressing concern. Lowering his trousers and with the aid of the Station's large magnifying glass he carefully examined his penis. He didn't like the look of it. Sure, it *could* just be wear and tear – after all it had done some heavy work in recent weeks – but on the other hand ... Damn, damn, damn. He did *not* want to go to Dr Karim-Bux, the Embassy doctor – couldn't be sure of the man's discretion. A tricky fellow, and his contract soon due for renewal. He might well try to curry favour with the Ambassador by tipping him off about an errant member of his staff.

Not that his Buster would over-react, Tom felt sure. He was a really good bloke who cared about his staff and the job he was there to do. Not like most of those poncey bastards in the Foreign and Commonwealth Office who didn't give a toss about the juniors, especially among the Intelligence staff, whom they ironically called *The Friends*.

And where was Buster himself having it off? Wife at home in UK, some sort of scientist it appeared. There was no doubt that Brathby fancied Polly Pym – it stood out like a turd on a tablecloth – but Tom's nose told him she hadn't yet succumbed. Why not, he couldn't imagine. Tom himself fancied her something rotten but he knew his chances were slim. All right, she didn't mind going dancing with him, especially to those crazy expat evening competitions, but his tentative advances had been gently refused. But as far as he knew she wasn't getting it anywhere else. So what was her problem, he wondered? He could hardly bear to think of those splendid tits in bed on their own – what a waste. Well, maybe she'd see the light one day. Meanwhile he'd consolation near at hand, hadn't he, just across the path, in the Embassy annexe that housed the Consular and Commercial sections. Not to mention the saucy hostesses at *The Welcome Pussy* ... Even so, he told himself, I've been bloody careful where I've put it – got to be in Africa – so maybe it's just an honourable wound I've got. So perhaps he needn't go to see old foxy Dr Pox.

The main thing was to keep out of trouble. Lie low for a while, if he could. There'd been that violent incident soon after he arrived, although he'd come out of that rather well, local hero even. Bit more worrying was the warning he'd had from his boss for bringing porn in through the diplomatic bag – and the scorn that had greeted his weak excuse that the Station should have a supply in case of demand by agents. It certainly wouldn't be healthy if it leaked out now that he was actively playing at home and away as it were, Embassy annexe and *Welcome Pussy*. Not healthy at all.

Tom shuddered. The thought of being posted home sent a chill through him. No more field work, no agents to run, no travel – just ghastly commuting to some dreary job in Finance or Supplies, and no overseas allowances. Ugh! Didn't bear thinking about – he'd done that sort of crap for long enough at home and now he was proving himself at the sharp end. Better watch your step for a while, he told himself, and of course continue to handle *Operation Carrot* securely – that was of supreme importance.

So, boyo, unpin the dried sheets now and do your best to cobble together an accurate report. Then tackle the Station accounts. After that it would be time for the routine weekly electronic sweep – his responsibility was of course only for the Intelligence Station premises, not the rest of the Embassy, and it was virtually impossible for an intruder to get in here. Still, there was also his absent boss's front office in the Embassy's Chancery corridor to think of – as usual he'd have to sweep that too.

The senior staff should all be in the Ambassador's meeting by now.

6

So, he'd check out Philippa's office, come back for a fag and write that damned report. Then he'd better get cracking on *Carrot*.

He left the back room, closing the privacy door, the steel door and the grille behind him, twirled the dials and walked out through Registry to the Chancery corridor.

*****

The door to the Ambassador's office opened slowly and Tom Muckle stepped in quietly, holding a single sheet of paper.

'Ah, Polly, could you take these up to …' Brathby stopped short and looked up in surprise as Muckle approached his desk holding his finger to his lips. During normal office hours, only Polly ever entered without knocking or being announced.

'Good Morning Buster', said Tom unfolding the sheet of paper and holding it up in front of the Ambassador. 'I'm sorry to disturb you so early in the morning, sir, but I wondered if you would like to come and have a look at these new pictures we've got for the Chancery corridor and give them your approval?'

Brathby's astonished gaze moved from Tom's face to the large block capitals written on the paper in front of him: *YOUR OFFICE POSSIBLY BUGGED. AGREE TO COME OUTSIDE WITH ME - NOW.*

'Yes, Tom … er … good morning. Of course, the new pictures … I should be delighted. Lead on, dear fellow.' Brathby pushed back his chair, swallowing hard, and moved awkwardly towards Polly's office. Tom held open the outer door, gesturing to Brathby not to close it and ushered him along the corridor into Philippa Brainbridge's front office, where Polly was already waiting, looking puzzled and anxious.

Closing the door to Philippa's office, Tom exhaled and grinned broadly at the Ambassador and his secretary. 'Sorry about all the cloak and dagger, Buster. We should be all right in here. I've just swept this room and it's clean, but while I was doing the routine check I heard something very strange on my headphones and I'm pretty sure there's a listening device in your office.'

Brathby and Polly stared at him, speechless, as if afraid to talk out loud. 'Sorry, Buster, I know you'll have lots of questions, but number one priority right now is for me to find the bloody thing and deal with it. I'll explain everything later.'

Tom picked up his monitoring apparatus, slipped on his headphones and, with an apologetic smile, opened the door to the corridor. 'Oh, by the way, Buster', he said, looking back briefly, 'you were very natural, very convincing back there. If you ever wanted to join our lot …' And he was gone.

Antoun Elias heaved himself out of his perfumed bath, dabbed himself dry, applied a liberal dusting of talcum powder, and donned black silk socks and monogrammed underpants. He gave his cut-throat a final strop, drew the large expanding mirror towards him and carefully began the pleasurable morning routine of shaving his plump olive chin and jowls. A strong face, he told himself, one to instil confidence. Certainly not at all bad for his age. True, his treasured moustache, which he would trim in a few moments, was showing a speck or two of white but that could be remedied. No problem there.

From long practice Elias could exclude any worries, however pressing, from the sacred ritual of his morning toilet. Time enough for that later in the day, when he would be in demand everywhere.

A final examination of his fingernails – manicure needed again soon, he reminded himself – a splash here, a dab there, a generous application of cologne to his now glowing face. Then a sprinkle of hair perfume on the ivory-backed brush, bought on his now distant visit to London; the spreading of his few remaining hairs across his shining pate and he was ready to dress. His mind turned to the selection of suit, shirt and tie.

'You are late this morning, Tun-tun,' were Bertha's opening words at breakfast. 'And today is the Ambassador's meeting, yes?'

Without replying he spread a thick layer of butter on a piece of toast and took up the newspaper. He was unsure which infuriated him the more, her use of the hated diminutive or the painful reference to Morning Prayers.

'Or do they not invite you still?', she continued suspiciously. 'I thought you vill *make* this new Ambassador invite you, *nicht wahr*?' She noisily poured the tea. He shrugged, face buried, and she drove on, her voice even shriller, 'So just what is the problem, Antoun? You said you vill insist on it so you vill get promotion before you finish. We need the extra money, *don't* we? *Don't* we? Or we must stay here in this foul country when you vill retire, *shan't* we, *shan't* we? How you like that, with no Embassy to protect you any more?'

When he still said nothing she rose, messily flinging down her bread and jam, and advanced on him, her finger wagging in his face.

'*Schwein! Schwein!*' she shrieked. 'I cannot and I vill not stay in this horrible country, do you understand? I vill *not*, I vill *not*, I vill *not*.'

Words, that's all they are, just words, he told himself. Just stay calm and in a few minutes I'll be on my way to the Embassy, where I am at least respected. Even if not often invited to Morning Prayers these days, he bitterly added to himself, His Excellency having regrettably allowed Head of Chancery to have his way in this matter. However, by arranging to arrive late today he'd give the impression that he'd attended an important outside meeting and thus been unable to attend H.E.'s meeting. Yes, he thought, and to give substance to that he would in fact call at the Police Commissioner's office and leave an invitation to lunch with him one day next week. In fact, he would …

'Listen to me; I vill make you answer, you, you peeg.' She stepped up to him and grasped his tie with her sticky fingers. '*Say* something, you coward.'

The second he felt her hands on him he lost control. Fury, fear and hatred swamped him as he pushed her away and then backwards.

'Shut up, just shut your fucking mouth you fat, ignorant, Kraut bitch. What do you know of all I have to do to feed your worthless carcase, idling here all day, stuffing your face and swigging beer?'

He shivered with rage and stared into her eyes. 'What have you done since I pulled you out of the gutter all those years ago? Nothing but *eat* and *complain.*'

He knew it was unjust but he desperately wanted to wound her as deeply as he could: 'and you couldn't even produce a child, you barren creature.' He pulled her earlobes. 'Could you?'

'Take those stinking hands off me. You think I not *know* how you get your money. You think I am stupid. Touch me again and I tell the Ambassador about the men you bring late at night here … oh yes and your business with them. Oh you think I hear nothing, you foolish man. I know what you do. I can *ruin* you – *verstehst du*?'

His anger was just as intense but now cooler and he looked at her with contempt. 'My grandfather had camels with more brains than you. These matters are for men, not ignorant women like you.'

He opened the window, cleared his throat noisily and gobbed heavily into the garden. 'Now I have work to do, even if you don't'.

He went to his room, chose a clean tie and walked out to his car.

With luck the meeting would last an hour, thought Polly - especially after the earlier excitement of being bugged and everything - and the Ambassador might be away even longer than that. He would often drop in on one or two of the staff afterwards. There was so much for her to catch up on and Tom had said that it was all right for her to use her office again now that everything had been "debugged". He had shown her the deactivated listening device, which looked quite harmless to Polly and which, absurdly, seemed to use the same sort of batteries as her electric toothbrush. The thrill of it all had rather worn off after that.

Bernard was a sweetie really, such a kind man to work for, very considerate and appreciative. Could explode in anger, usually at injustice or stupidity, but this was never directed at her. He clearly had a soft spot for her: after all he had arranged to have her transferred here with him from Europe and that wasn't easy to fix. It hadn't been just because they worked well together, had it? Yes, she knew all right, it was useless to deny it: he did feel something for her.

But where was it all leading? Nowhere. Not because of his wife Louise: that certainly wouldn't hold her back. If the silly woman insisted on putting her work before her husband she couldn't expect to hang on to him, could she? But if Polly did let Bernard know how much she liked him then certainly he would want to … And then it would all collapse because anything like that and the past came rushing back and killed it off.

Better push it out of her mind for the moment and take the chance to catch up on some routine work. She opened her shorthand book and began to type up a preliminary draft of Bernard's impressions of his first few months at the Post, which he had dictated to her the previous day in the Safe Speech Conference Room.

The telephone rang. 'Hello Missie Pym, this is Oswald, you know, Oswald Obunga from Protocol'.

'Of course, Mr Obunga. I know your voice well; how are you?' You bloody creep, she added silently, remembering how he had patted her bottom while making a courtesy call on the Ambassador soon after his arrival.

'Fine, fine. Tell me now, is Mr Brathby free on Friday in morning please?'

'Er, I'm not sure; I'd have to find his diary first.' It was of course open in front of her. 'What did you have in mind, Mr Obunga?'

'You remember those *tiefmen*, the ones who killed the British workers in Eastern region and some others too – well Friday we shoot them. Ambassador invited at ten-thirty for eleven.'

Polly felt slightly giddy. 'Er, ten-thirty for eleven?'

'Yes at beach police barracks. Guests are asked for drinks at ten-thirty for killing a little later. Dress casual. Sorry about short notice; they took some time to volunteer full confessions. Your Mining Company representatives will be present, naturally, but Minister also think British Ambassador maybe want to see the bad men punished. What you think?'

'I'm sure it is very considerate of the Minister to invite the Ambassador, but I've found the diary now and I'm afraid he is busy with appointments all day.' Polly knew that however unorthodox Bernard was in many ways, there was no possibility of his wishing to attend that particular event.

'Pity. If he like to send someone in his place they very, very welcome. Perhaps Mr Francis would enjoy it? Or the Colonel perhaps? Please let me know.'

Polly had got through another couple of paragraphs when Trevor, the Archivist, put his head in at her door. 'Mail for you Polly, just in. Where's the Old Man then? Still yacking at the meeting, I expect.' He was gone.

She riffled through the mail. Bank statements, *Come Dancing* magazine, circular from her old school … what was this one then? Writing familiar but … good Lord, her aunt, that woman indeed. Stirring things up, she expected. She'd put it aside until she felt better able to cope. Anyhow, got to get this draft done. Back to the shorthand book.

The wretched phone rang again. Dr Karim-Bux this time. How was dear Miss Pym? Fine, thank you. And was her esteemed Ambassador in good health? Yes, excellent. Had he been reminded that Dr Bux's contract with the Embassy was soon due for renewal, presumably this was only a matter of routine but nevertheless …? Yes, Polly was sure that the Ambassador was aware of this but no, she regretted that she did not know exactly when he would attend to it. Yes, she would let him have any news.

Draft finished at last. Aunt's letter could surely wait; it must be years since she'd heard from her anyhow. She'd just glance at *Come Dancing*. Goodness, just look at the photo there of the National Semi-Finalists. White tie and tails, long sweeping dresses. *Not* the local scene here, although Tom did sometimes go so far as to sport a jacket if the air conditioning was working.

She couldn't put it off any longer and summoned the resolve to open her letter, using the paperknife which Bernard had, somewhat unimaginatively, given her at Christmas, a few weeks back.

7 Fir Tree Close
5 February 1980

Polly, my pet, [how *dare* she?]
For a long time now I've not been at all well. I put off seeing the doctor as long as I could but now I know the worst. He says an operation wouldn't help but that I shouldn't give up hope quite yet. The pills he's given me make life more bearable, but I don't know how long I've got.

So Polly I want to say sorry before it's too late. I never knew exactly what went on, you must believe me, and you never complained – but I was wrong, I know I was. Of course it meant he didn't bother me. I was never keen on that side of things. But he never did more than sort of get you to play with him, did he? Please tell me that.

If I meet your mother on the other side, and I believe I shall, I shan't know what to say. I loved you when you were little and there were just the two of us, but when I married him it was all so different. Oh Polly, please forgive me.

When you left home so young I was sad you didn't trust me enough to tell me your plans, but I suppose I can understand. It was a shock at first when you left and of course he was furious but it was all for the best. I hardly ever see him these days, you know. He has a place in London, paid for with my money all that time ago, and stays there most of the time, I think. If he speaks of you it is to call you an ungrateful whelp, as he puts it. I hate him really, I can see that now. I'd like to think that my passing will make him sad, but I don't expect so. He never loved me.

What he doesn't know is that I've left this little house to you – I don't expect you'll want to live here but the money from it will give you a bit of security. It's the least I can do.

Please write, Polly, and let me know you've got this letter. If you can, try to forgive me.

Then she'd signed off as Polly's loving Aunt. Which was hard to take.

5

Head of Chancery. Head of Chancery indeed! An appropriately absurd title for an absurd position; well, for a man of his abilities anyhow.

Francis Paynton laid down his slim gold pencil exactly parallel with the virgin notepad, stroked his soft hair, steepled his hands, and allowed himself a few moments of reflection.

He'd been doing the job now for a year and a half and was as near bored with it as it was possible to be. The administrative tasks were risibly simple, although the drudgery was to some extent compensated for by real work in the form of some of the political reporting and a certain amount of cultivation of key local officials. That latter task could be tedious, but at least it ensured that he had some personal input into the local Personalities List so beloved of his second-rate Ambassador.

Then there were some really shitty tasks he'd been allocated, such as trying to persuade the Education Minister (an ex-Army colonel prominent in the previous military *régime*) to pay the rates on his large house in London which were being demanded by the local council. Worst of all, he was supposed to be drawing up an outline programme for a possible visit by the British Prime Minister. That was most unlikely so soon into her term of office, Brathby had said, but the Ministry of Defence were pushing for it, by 1981 at the latest. The idea was that she might tip the balance towards the UK for an arms contract for which they were competing with the French.

*****

Five minutes until the morning meeting. Paynton slid into his inside jacket pocket a very interesting letter just received by bag. A good friend in the Office was tipping him off, in the greatest confidence, that a particularly desirable UN job was coming up, one for which Francis was clearly eligible. It would mean escape from this dreary routine, an independent command, fat allowances and the chance of a golden future. All the things which he deserved in fact.

If his name were put forward, it would be important that the Ambassador did not oppose his appointment. Above all, there must be no scandals, no problems at Post for which he could be held accountable. That was crucial. Perhaps Brathby had already been asked for his views.

Francis had a list of half a dozen points to bring up at the meeting, and had briefed himself on a number of other issues which others might raise. But he had written nothing on the notepad – it was all recorded in his splendid memory. He stroked the gold pencil, slipped it into his jacket, and left the room.

6

Colonel AFL Squires, MC, always known as Jack, was badly hungover. Not so badly that he hadn't been able to get himself to the car to be driven to the office and not so badly that he failed to acknowledge the greetings of the Embassy gateman, and of the Security Officer at the front desk.

But badly enough to dread the effort that would be required to attend Morning Prayers and put up an acceptable performance. What a stupid officer I am, he muttered to himself. His eyes were sore and his mouth tasted of sour milk. He was too dispirited even to look out of his window and do the morning corpse count.

The door opened slightly and his amply-built middle-aged secretary eased her way in, bottom first, placing on his desk a tray with tea, water and Alka Seltzer tablets.

'Good morning, sir', she murmured. 'Just over forty minutes before the meeting'.

'Thank you, Dorothy, m'dear.' He managed half a smile. 'What a good trouper you are. Just the rations one needs.'

Damn it, last night should have been no problem. After dinner he had asked his Steward Octavius to bring him a very weak whisky ('tall one Octavius, him colour of tap water with trace of cat's piss'), settled down at his desk and had begun to draft the latest Arms Procurement Report for the Ambassador. That was when the damned woman had pranced into the room and started banging on about money again. Everything from the extras needed by the children at their private schools to the subsidy needed to keep her mother in the nursing home. There wasn't enough rent from the house in UK to cover the mortgage, there were all these bills still outstanding and what were they going to do about it all ... she went on and on like an artillery barrage.

'The money, Jack, that's the point, the money; where's it to come from? Are you being deliberately obtuse? Why won't you talk about it? It's really only the overseas allowances that are keeping us going now, isn't it?' Her voice became shriller and shriller.

Yes, he thought, and we both know that you wouldn't be here at Post with me except that it boosts those allowances; and that we can't afford for you to live separately in UK.

But she was right of course: they did have a serious problem. They had many times, and with varying degrees of acrimony, chewed over the problem of how to manage if posted home, especially whether they could keep the children on at their expensive schools. He was searching for something neutral and conciliatory to say when she ploughed roughly on:

'So exactly what are you going to do about it? Are you going to get your promotion and are you going to get another Post with the Diplomatic? We're due to finish here in three or four months, aren't we? *Then* what do we do?'

She left the room before he could answer, but in any case he had learned that the best way to survive the flak was by keeping his head down and his mouth shut. Don't provoke another salvo; just sit it out, Jack.

Christ, he'd muttered as he poured himself a huge single malt, the miserable woman can't even slam the door – that would be too unladylike, too bloody real. Yes, that was the problem with her. She entertained well, was a good manager, never let the side down in public, all that stuff. But a man needs more than that, course he does. But she'd never been much of a one for bed, no definitely not. Not even in the early days.

Unsatisfactory woman, in that respect anyhow, yes most unsatisfactory. Really he should have some water with this stuff. Can't be bothered to fetch it. Just one more small one and then bed. On his own, of course. As usual.

But her analysis of their financial situation and the need for him to be promoted and get another overseas job was spot on. Couldn't fault her on that. Important to be fair in these things, not to allow ... where was he, yes, important ... well, something or other.

One must say this stuff is slipping down well. Another one, Colonel? Well, since you press me old chap, yes I'll take a small one.

What she didn't yet know was that he'd been short-listed for the Liaison Post in Washington with the American Special Forces. The position would be available towards the end of the year. The timing would be perfect since they were due out of here in a few months. As for the job, it was just up his street, he could do it off the top of his head. His background couldn't be better: counter-insurgency in Cyprus, the

Malaya Emergency, Borneo, even an attachment with the SAS in Arabia. A spot of regular soldiering of course, in Korea – where he'd got his MC – and Germany a couple of times. But mainly skulduggery of one sort or another.

Perfect for him, that would be. Worth killing for. It would entail automatic promotion to Brigadier: the rank went with the job. And with the extra pay and the substantial Washington allowances and the certainty of the FCO continuing to pay the school fees, he'd even be able to leave Jenny in UK.

And that would suit them both.

*****

Well, at least you made it to the office, Squires, present if not correct. The old hangover formula still worked: shit, shave, shower and shampoo. But not the day for the shaft and champagne. Right, now what is one supposed to be doing, apart from staying awake? Oh yes, preparing for Bernard's meeting. Feel like death, and probably look like it too. But the second cup of tea was helping. Should one risk a cigarette? The splendid lady had brought in two new packs – should keep him going all day. Need one badly now, but is it worth it? Come on Squires, live dangerously.

He struck a match – one's hand really quite steady – and gently inhaled. A sharp jar behind the eye balls and then a slow agreeable warmth.

Ten minutes to go. Better check up what's going on. He picked up the phone: 'I'm alive now, m'dear, thanks to you. Anything I ought to be doing or know about?'

'Mr Elias called from Police Headquarters. Said he had a snippet of news for you and would call in hoping to see you before lunch.'

What would he want, Jack wondered? Always hanging around, currying favour, smiling, rubbing the side of his villainous nose, stinking of Eastern perfumes, hinting at his supposed wonderful connections, promising that bit more than he could produce.

Mind you, the man had been very useful with one or two of the arms deals that Jack had set in motion. When it came down to the nitty-gritty of advising a salesman what would be needed to oil the wheels between

19

buyer and seller Antoun Elias could get a lot nearer to the bone than it would have been proper for Jack himself to do. He might perhaps have made a few bob out of it himself as well, Jack admitted to himself. Fair enough – you wouldn't expect anything else of his sort; and the Embassy probably didn't pay him enough anyhow. Not that that excused it.

Anyway there was no doubt that Antoun, however useful, was certainly a slippery bugger. Jack remembered one like him, up on the Thai border when he'd been on secondment to the Malayan Special Branch hunting down insurgents, Communist Terrorists they called them. Yes, they'd used a local Chinese lawyer as an interpreter and recruiter; he came into the jungle with Jack's men and was brilliant at persuading any captured CT to change sides and go back in. This had to be done very fast too – if a chap returned to his group after being missing for more than twelve hours he would be executed, however good his explanation, on the assumption that he'd been turned by the security forces. No use his claiming he'd been lost, even if true.

Hard men, Jack thought admiringly, but we beat them in the end. He'd have some tales to tell his American friends all right, that is if he got the job.

He glanced towards the cupboard. A nip before the meeting? No, not that far gone. Certainly not. Moreover it might smell. Good moral and practical reasons to abstain. When the two marched side by side they were probably right. Where had he learned that now? Can't remember, not important.

So straighten the back, Jack Squires and get on parade.

7

It was Bernard Brathby's habit in the few minutes immediately before Morning Prayers to clear his mind of any business likely to arise at the meeting, and concentrate on something else. He found this left him fresher for the meeting and more open to new ideas. He privately felt that the exercise was mildly pretentious, even eccentric, and so had never mentioned it to Polly. But she seemed aware that he should be left quiet at this time and would only interrupt him for something urgent and serious; yet another example, he realised, of her special quality, her very … No, that was certainly *not* the subject to occupy these few minutes.

Despite the troubling discovery of the listening device in his office, he found his thoughts turning to his faithful Steward, Cuthbert. This last couple of weeks or so the old chap had seemed unsettled. Just when everything should have been fine.

It must have been about a month ago, Bernard calculated, that a supper party to which he had been invited had been cancelled at the last moment. His host, the French Ambassador, had himself phoned to explain: 'Bernard, *mon cher collègue,* I am vairy sorry to annul this dinner at the last moment but a *tragédie* has struck and it would be indecorous to proceed. The wife of our *Attaché Culturel* was multiple *violée* this afternoon by a gang of what we call 'ere *tiefmen*. You comprehend, *cher collègue*?'

Bernard proffered sympathy on behalf of himself, his Embassy colleagues and Her Majesty's Government, and agreed that it would of course be indecorous to proceed with the party. Privately he viewed with pleasure the prospect of some time to himself. He'd wandered into the kitchen to get himself a beer. Slightly to his surprise he found Cuthbert there; he'd given him the evening off and assumed he'd have gone off to his room by now. On reflection, Bernard realised, the kitchen was of course where Cuthbert was most likely to be – after all, if anywhere was his sitting-room, this was it.

Gesturing to him not to get up, Bernard found his drink and joined him at the large kitchen table. He now realised how little he knew of this man who lived in such intimate proximity to him, cooking his food, ironing his shirts, watching for his comfort. He had of course consulted

21

such sketchy pay and personnel records as the Embassy kept on Cuthbert. His age, not unusually, was unknown. He himself didn't know, but Bernard reckoned at least sixty-five. Cuthbert had worked for the British as a domestic servant since distant Colonial days, starting as *Small Boy* and working his way up to be Steward at the Residence. The file contained many testimonials to his loyalty, discretion and capacity for hard work. Also to his courage – while on tour with a previous Ambassador he had disarmed a drunk who had threatened them with a machete at a remote petrol station. There was on file a Minute recommending he be considered for a medal when he eventually retired. The box on the form for next of kin was empty, and there was no mention of any family.

After a preliminary exchange of courtesies Bernard had gently, and as tactfully as he could, asked Cuthbert whether after so many years of faithful service, he might perhaps like to consider retiring reasonably soon. He would certainly have – Bernard had worked out – quite a healthy pension to live on. He carefully did not mention what they both knew, that Cuthbert was slowing down and in a year or two would have real difficulty in performing his duties satisfactorily.

Cuthbert's reaction was immediately tearful. 'You no want me, Master?'

When he had first served in Africa Bernard had found this term, with its redolence of the Deep South, somewhat distasteful, but soon learned that it was the common form of address by all servants in anglophone Africa to their employers.

'No, no, Cuthbert, I'm not saying that at all. But you've worked hard and well for many years and have earned the right to retire, to spend time for yourself doing what *you* want to do, perhaps with your family where you'd be well-off and much respected ...' He tailed off.

'When I no fit work, *den* I stop. Dis place my home. Here I get fine room at back and dis kitchen for sitting. Master, I know I old now, but you no send me away please..'

'You have nowhere else, Cuthbert, no village, no relatives ...?'

'When I piccin de bandits come, in de time of troubles. Dey kill my people and burn de village. Dey hurt me but I run away. I get here to de city, hungry and wid nuttin. One kind man find me, one old Steward, long time dead now, he give me *chop*, bring me here to help him.

22

All dis happen long time now.'

'I'm very sorry about your village, Cuthbert. Do you have any family at all?'

'You mean piccin, Master? At all! I try wid three four womans dey no fit done born piccin, so I pack um. When de soldiers take me dey do tings … may be dat my problem, Master. I happy here, you no send me away. Please, I beg you.'

Bernard had regarded him with awe, shame and tenderness, fighting to contain his tears.

'Cuthbert, you can stay here till you die. I promise. And I will write this promise in the Embassy book and tell the big men in London.'

'Tank you, tank you Master.' He rested both hands on Bernard's. 'Now I too happy.' He got up and poured Bernard a beer he didn't want.

'Thank you, Cuthbert.' But as he hesitated Cuthbert spoke.

'You tink soon I too old for *all* de work? Dat wot you tink, sah?'

'Yes, Cuthbert, something like that.'

'I tink all same ting.' He beamed: 'So I get Eventide.'

'Er, I see, or rather I don't. Er … Eventide?'

'He be small boy. I teach um. He for dis house and he fit help me. I now teach um every ting, make whisky-drinks, make ice wid boiled water. Soon udder tings, iron de clothes, choose de shirts for Master. Many, many tings.' He was glowing. 'Den, one day he serve drink at party, start wid de small people, den de bigger ones'. He was swept up with excitement. 'Den …'

Bernard interrupted him, 'Er, what about accommodation and wages … I'll have to ask.'

'Money? Oh no, Master. No need, not yet. He too happy to get *chop* and learn. I give um small cash for de sweets and smokes. He sleep in my quarter, on de floor. No, no, for now I teach um, like de old Steward teach me. I tell um dis ting I learn um long, long ago: *Oh Cuthbert, oh Cuthbert, it is a dreadful sin, to put tonic in de whisky or soda in de gin.* So many tings, Master, so many tings.' He was shining with happiness. 'Eventide, he like son for me, I teach um every ting.'

'Well Cuthbert, I suppose it might be possible.' His mind reeled at the thought of how many Embassy employment regulations they were cavalierly ignoring. 'But tell me Cuthbert, where did he get his name from? It is … er … slightly unusual, isn't it?'

'That simple, Master. It was eventide when I find um, by de river.'

'You *found* him! You mean … in the same way that …?'

'Na so. He scape from home. Fader done die. He be *tiefman*. People catch um and burn um. Mama bad, bad woman. She make jig-jig to get de hot drink, she beat um all de time. Den one man want um for bumboy. So he scape. He tink better he die. I find um sleeping by de river.'

Within a couple of weeks Eventide's situation had been more or less regularised. Bernard officially entered him on the Embassy strength as 'unpaid trainee junior Steward' and also, at Bernard's insistence (and, unknown to Cuthbert, at Bernard's expense) the boy was now attending school every day.

The lad had been formally introduced to Bernard one afternoon; he'd been marched in, terrified and pathetic in a pair of cut-down white shorts. Bernard had solemnly shaken his hand, welcomed him to his staff and just avoided his voice wavering. Since then he had glimpsed him a couple of times in the compound, kicking a football which Polly, who clearly adored him at first sight, had given him; and once Cuthbert had allowed him to bring in Bernard's morning tea. Otherwise he was mostly in the background.

Everyone seemed happy with the arrangement. The lad himself clearly loved his new home, Cuthbert was revitalised and glowed with pride. Bernard found Eventide, whenever permitted to see him, to be a delightful lad. He was even giving thought to the boy's longer term future.

Then, recently the joy had seemed to run out of Cuthbert. He became anxious and clumsy and when asked if anything was troubling him would only answer unconvincingly that all was well. It was strange and disconcerting.

Now Polly had slipped into his office and he turned his mind to the present.

'Time to go?' He smiled at her. 'Yes, Ambassador. Here are the papers you'll need.'

8

Colonel Squires smothered his cigarette in the sand tray outside, automatically checked that the dull green entry bulb was on, pushed up the long wooden handle and stepped into the over-lit and virtually featureless Conference Room.

Even when one had a clear head the room was bad enough, a cross between a bank vault and a submarine. But in his condition this morning it was purgatory. He didn't know what he hated the most: the stark neon lighting, the antiseptic tang of filtered air or the glaring whiteness of the walls and low ceiling. Or possibly the cord carpet in a colour the Colonel could only think of as dog-vomit yellow.

At least the place was big enough for its purpose, with room for at least ten of these uncomfortable tubular steel chairs each side of the long rectangular deal table. No telephones of course; they would defeat the whole aim of making the room unbuggable. At least he would be spared the risk of their trilling noise.

With a muttered attempt at a cheery 'Good morning, all' to the half dozen or so already there Squires made his way to the far end of the room and gingerly took his customary place on the right of the Ambassador's seat at the top of the table. He rested his eyes, looking up from time to time as the opening and closing of the door marked a new arrival. Another cigarette might just help his head – or make it worse of course – but no point thinking about that. Brathby himself had an occasional cigar but out of consideration for the non-smoking minority had banned smoking in the confined atmosphere of the Conference Room. Quite right too, Squires reluctantly admitted to himself.

While waiting for the Ambassador to arrive and start the meeting the staff were as usual catching up on news and discussing minor points of business. Squires only wished they could do so more quietly, and on less stupefyingly boring matters.

'So what fun items have you got for us today?' Harry Fieldhouse, the dark-haired young Chancery Third Secretary, cheerfully sang out his weekly challenge to Bert Woodley, the usually taciturn Information Officer, who was shuffling cuttings from a selection of the day's newspapers.

'Nothing out of the usual run, I'm afraid, ' Woodley replied drily;

then, sensing disappointment in his audience, he added slowly: ' …
although the obituary page of *The Tribune* records with "ineffable sad-
ness and many sorries, the untimely and sudden demise in a ghastly
motor accident on the Yulelere Road, of Josiah Olutandifi Oragbemi, of
the National Electricity Power Authority"'. He paused. 'Then it goes
on to express the wish that perpetual light may shine upon him.'

'Apart from that', he continued when the laughter had died down,
'*The Sketch* has a report of a beautiful young woman from Bogitaku
village whose nipples vanished while she was at the butcher's. She's
blaming the incident on witchcraft'.

'Good thing we get *our* meat flown in from Kenya, eh Jane?' Harry
blurted out, attracting a frown from Francis Paynton and a deep blush
from the newly-arrived young Vice-Consul. Jane Paige was attending
her first Morning Prayers, determined to look alert and serious. Harry
was evidently not helping.

'And there's an important report here too, in *The Daily Democrat*',
announced the Information Officer, pulling out another cutting. 'When
the police in Surunami village caught a *tiefman* he turned himself into
a goat. It seems that to trap him they offered the animal a cigarette but
it ate the whole packet. Then …'

At this point the door opened, conversation died down, those seated
rose to their feet and the Ambassador entered.

'Good morning, ladies and gentlemen. Please sit down'.

Morning Prayers were underway.

*****

Brathby smiled at his assembled staff and glanced at his notes. He
had already decided not to bring up the matter of the listening device
until he had been properly briefed by Tom Muckle, and managed to put
it to the back of his mind.

'As usual we have a good deal of internal business to discuss. But
before that I thought it would be useful to update you on the Ayumba
affair, which has now evolved into a serious impediment to the maintenance of good relations between ourselves and our hosts, which may
also involve trouble for us locally. 'That last bit certainly caught their
attention. He continued.

'As you will remember, three months ago Joseph Ayumba, the Minister of Mines, failed to return home from a routine visit to London. Minutes before he was due to board the aircraft at Gatwick he suddenly changed his mind and returned in some agitation to his house in Regent's Park. A week later the government here announced that an attempted *coup* had been suppressed and its ringleader, the Deputy Chief of the General Staff, and a score of other senior officers, had been arrested.'

Colonel Squires looked up suddenly and grunted: 'Almost all certainly innocent, of course, Ambassador. Innocent of treason anyhow.'

'Quite', continued Brathby, 'as you usefully informed me at the time.' Jack was looking pretty rough this morning, he noted. 'The Military Attaché', he continued, 'has also learned that most of these unfortunate fellows have already been hanged.'

He glanced briefly around the room and continued: 'It was claimed that Ayumba was the political front behind the alleged plot with the plan being to install him as President. However it is a puzzle why Ayumba, who had already made a fortune and is indolent by nature, should have risked all for the dubious pleasure of becoming Head of State, especially as the real power would have been wielded by the military plotters. There seems little sense in it.'

The Chancery Officers and the MA were nodding their agreement. How much of this the others were grasping, the Ambassador was unsure.

'Much remains unclear. What is obvious is that Ayumba learned, just in time, that the conspiracy had been uncovered. Hence his decision to stay in London. As you know, his government immediately demanded his extradition from the UK, on grounds, almost certainly justified, that he had embezzled from the State by corruptly awarding contracts for personal gain.'

The Colonel stirred again: 'Fifteen percent was his usual cut; he overdid it, you see. If only he'd confined himself ...'Perhaps Jack was just demonstrating that he was awake. Brathby hoped there wouldn't be too many such interruptions.

'Naturally HMG refused the extradition demand. If he'd been sent back he would have been in serious danger of ill-treatment during questioning'.

'Yes they'd probably have started by ...'

'Thank you Jack, I don't think we need the detail'. There were times when his well-informed Military Attaché could be mildly irritating. 'A refusal was doubtless expected and perhaps in some quarters welcomed.'

'Why welcomed, sir?' Harry interposed.

'Because of the precedent it would establish. Many leading figures in the regime have properties in London and would hope for asylum there if they fall from favour. Unless you feel I'm being too cynical,' he added.

'Is it possible to be too cynical about this government, Ambassador?' the Consul contributed quietly.

'A good point, Bill', Brathby said, smiling at him. My God, the man looks tired, he thought. Understandably so, of course. The post of Consul in a country like this was extremely demanding; his badly-understaffed department not only had responsibility towards all British subjects in the country but also had to sift, and then grant or refuse, visas to the thousands of importunate applicants pressing to visit the UK.

'The Ayumba matter might have been allowed to die down quietly with the Ministry of External Affairs here occasionally renewing their formal request to extradite the man and us responding by "taking note of their concerns", and in fact doing nothing,' the Ambassador continued.

All still awake, he wondered, glancing quickly around the room? Lydia Gates, his Second Secretary Commercial, was a little detached, he noted. Perhaps what he'd heard about her and Muckle was accurate then, although she must surely be nearly twenty years older than Tom. And what a pretty girl the new Vice-Consul was. Not in the same generously-endowed way of course as his dear Polly – he really must *not* think of her at such a moment – but she looks as if she'll bring some sparkle to the Embassy. He'd seen that bumptious Harry looking at her a couple of times. Well, better that than fall prey to the predatory Muckle.

'Then ten days ago,' Brathby continued, forcing himself to concentrate on the matter in hand, 'Ayumba seriously exacerbated the situation by openly calling for the overthrow of the *régime*. It appears that we are legally powerless to silence him. The Minister of External Affairs has privately made clear to me that while an inactive Ayumba might eventually be quietly forgotten by the government, an Ayumba making bellicose noises in London is quite another matter.'

The Ambassador took a sip of water and went on: 'Now perhaps the Head of Chancery will summarise the possible practical consequences for us here. Francis?'

'Thank you, Ambassador.' Francis Paynton stroked his beautifully groomed hair. 'The most obvious concern is the possibility of a rupture in diplomatic relations. But the chances of that are remote. There are too many interests on both sides, including the obvious ones of *Uminco's* mining activities, military co-operation and the Police Training Scheme. Another possibility is the withdrawal of Ambassadors, but that seems unlikely if only because their recently-installed Ambassador in London is the President's cousin and close friend and is happily settled there.

'It is more likely,' the Head of Chancery went on, 'that our hosts will express their displeasure by covertly encouraging demonstrations against British property. The most likely targets are this building, the adjacent Consular/Commercial section and the Residence. Precautions already in train include the tightening up of our fire drills – as you know we can in emergency draw water from the old sewers beneath the building – and the shredding of non-essential files to reduce the volume of paper that would have to be destroyed in an emergency. The Archivist has this in hand.

'Concerning personal security outside Embassy premises,' he continued, 'there is little to add to standing advice. It is unlikely that the locals bear any personal grudges against British individuals as a result of this business.'

'What about the Police?' asked the Admin Officer. 'Would they come to our aid during a demonstration?'

The Consul looked at him across the table. 'More likely they'd have been given the job of arranging it in the first place. Wouldn't you agree, Ambassador?'

'You may be right, Bill; there'd certainly be no demonstrations without government encouragement or, at least, approval. But it's all very hypothetical at present and there's no immediate cause for alarm.

Moreover we would hope to get advance warning of any "spontaneous" demonstrations.'

'Doubtless from one of greasy El's copper chums,' the Third Secretary interposed.

'I don't think that that sort of speculation is helpful, Harry,' the Ambassador rebuked him quietly. 'Now I know that the Consul has something to say about the manning of the Immigration Section. Before he speaks I should say that the Office and Home Office Immigration Department in London are fully aware of his concerns over this.' He gestured Bill to go ahead.

The Consul spoke briefly about the staff shortage, saying little new. There were murmurs of sympathy from all and, from the Commercial Counsellor, an offer to lend Bill one of the part-time locally-engaged Brits who was working on a long-term project in his department. 'We could manage that for a week or two, couldn't we, Lydia?' he asked.

'Oh yes, of course, yes I'm sure we could,' she replied eventually.

Yes, mind on other things, thought the Ambassador.

The Admin Officer, who was next to speak, regretted that the next plane delivery of frozen meat from Kenya had had to be postponed by a week. But the good news was that the American Embassy had kindly agreed to lend them their refrigerated lorry to collect the consignment. As usual at the time of such deliveries Admin Section would arrange to top up fuel supplies for home emergency generators in case of power cuts.

After a number of other minor administrative matters had been aired the Ambassador spoke again.

'Before we come to other matters you should know that a junior diplomat from the Italian Embassy has recently been sent home for black market currency dealings. I must remind you that I should take an equally firm line in the event of any such activity in this Embassy.' It sounded a bit pompous, but it *was* a serious matter.

Brathby looked at his watch. Time now for others to air matters of importance to them. 'Perhaps the Commercial Counsellor would like to bring us up to date on …

The door of the Conference Room slowly and silently opened.

In the doorway stood Tom Muckle, dressed in white overalls.

'Sorry to interrupt your meeting Buster, but I have some more news about what we … er … discussed earlier. Can we have a word?'

'Of course, Tom, we'll speak in the corridor. Would the rest of you please wait here until I come back?'

*****

'Meeting suspended, eh?' Jack said sleepily across the room to Paynton. 'Wouldn't mind slipping out for a fag but of course one doesn't know when the Ambassador may be back. All very rum.' But his head was improving: no doubt about that.

'So what's going on, do you think, Francis?' asked the Vice-Consul excitedly. 'What could Tom want?'

'I don't think it profitable to speculate,' Paynton replied primly. 'Doubtless we shall soon be enlightened.'

'Perhaps Philippa's run off to Moscow,' called out the Third Secretary. 'Or maybe Tom didn't get his usual gross of condoms in the diplomatic bag; now that'd be a *real* crisis.'

Lydia managed to look simultaneously cross and embarrassed, Squires noticed. 'I'm sure Tom wouldn't have burst in without good reason. There must be some trouble – perhaps a demonstration.'

'If it was that,' said the Consul, 'H.E. wouldn't leave us here in ignorance, and he'll be back soon anyhow.'

'I say, I know what must have happened: Tom's killed another intruder in his flat and can't find Greasy El to fix the police.' It was the Third Secretary again.

'What do you mean, *another* intruder? Tom didn't really kill anyone, did he?' Lydia looked around the room for re-assurance. 'Is this one of your horrible jokes, Harry?'

'No, no joke, Lydia; well certainly not for the *tiefman* he clobbered. Happened soon after Tom arrived here, in the middle of the night. As I expect you know', Fieldhouse paused insinuatingly, 'Tom lives on the ground floor in the President Yombo block; the intruder fellow had got in by yanking out the outside air-conditioning grille and crawling through the hole. Tom woke up, wandered sleepily into the kitchen and lo, there was this chappie, seven foot tall, bottle of scotch in one hand, bloody great chopper in the other – of the steel variety, of course – '

'I'm not sure that this ought to be so openly …' the Head of

Chancery was protesting.

Prissy idiot, thought Squires, since almost everyone already knows the story.

'So what happened then?' Lydia was asking 'Poor Tom!'

'By the time our Tom had finished with him, it was poor *tiefman*. He started to go for Tom but luckily was so pissed or drugged that he fell over a chair. Tom took his chance, threw the nearest heavy object, which happened to be a radio, straight in his face, snatched up the chopper from the floor and nearly cut the bloke's head off.'

'Well done, Tom, I say.' The Colonel had temporarily forgotten his need for a cigarette. 'Had a corporal like that once, in Korea. And Tom tidied it up neatly by ...'

'Yes, very neatly, indeed,' put in the Third Secretary, rather rudely, Squires thought. 'He phoned Greasy El and told all. Within half an hour Greasers was round there complete with two hairy coppers and official wagon. Tom expressed his appreciation in the time-honoured way and the late *tiefman* was removed to play hide and seek with the crocodiles. Greasers helped Tom mop up, stayed for a scotch and all retired to bed. That was the end of it. Moral is: don't go round to Tom's house unless you're invited.'

'May I please make it quite clear to you all,' the Head of Chancery was saying 'that what happened that evening is still classified *Confidential*. The incident was never officially reported to London, although the Deputy Under-Secretary was informed verbally. But it could be embarrassing if it became public knowledge in UK that a member of a British Embassy had killed a man and then had the body disposed of.

'Satisfactory in all ways; no doubt about it,' Squires said firmly. Surely nobody here was so wet as to argue that point.

The door opened and the Ambassador re-appeared.

*****

'I'm sorry you've been kept waiting,' Brathby said. 'Let me first assure you that nobody is ill, nor are there demonstrations going on against us. No, what has happened is less serious than that, but perhaps more intriguing.'

Then, realising that he was keeping his listeners on tenterhooks and, worse, that he was enjoying doing so, he quickly added: 'Muckle came to report on a listening device which he discovered in my office earlier this morning, and to tell me what he had done about it.

The Head of Chancery was looking puzzled. 'But what was he doing in your office at all? Nosing around, was he?'

The others remained silent and waited for the Ambassador to continue. 'We should be grateful that Muckle made this discovery,' the Ambassador said pointedly. 'By doing so he has undoubtedly limited the damage, which at the moment seems likely to be very small'.

'So what happened, sir?' the Consul asked, glad perhaps to have something to take his mind off his Visa Section problems.

'It is part of Muckle's duties that twice a week he does an electronic sweep of the Intelligence Station's offices and also of Miss Brainbridge's front office, just across the corridor from mine. He is not of course responsible for any other parts of the Embassy, or for the Consular/Commercial building, which are all looked after by the visiting sweep teams from London.'

'And who were here only a week ago,' contributed the Head of Chancery, 'and made a thorough search of your room, sir, and all the others. But now Muckle …'

'While Muckle was in Miss Brainbridge's room, using his monitoring device, he very clearly heard through the headphones the sound of Polly and I talking. So he switched off his machine, went into Polly's room, gestured to her not to speak, took her across to Miss Brainbridge's office and briefly told her what had happened. He then returned to extract me from my office.'

'That was quick thinking,' said Lydia.

'Yes, indeed', the Ambassador continued. 'Muckle has now removed the device, which was a wooden box about the size of a large hardback book that had been lodged behind the bookcase near my desk; it is a crude device with wires protruding from it and powered by four batteries. He did it in such a way, he assures me, that whoever was listening to it may deduce that it has merely ceased to function. Muckle disconnected the batteries and the device is now in a safe in his back office, preparatory to being sent home by bag.'

The Third Secretary could apparently contain himself no longer: 'Exciting stuff, sir!' he said. 'Pity we couldn't have left it there and fed the Russians lots of false information. Too late now, I suppose.'

'Yes, too late now, Harry,' the Ambassador smiled tolerantly, 'and that sort of thing is very difficult, I'm sure, unless you're trained for it. Anyhow this is not wartime and I'm not sure what lies we could profitably feed the Russians, if indeed they are responsible, and we don't know that they are.'

'So what do we do now, sir?' Paynton asked.

'Firstly I should say that whoever was responsible for having this microphone planted in my office will have gleaned little of interest. Any secret business is always discussed in this room, which is purpose-built to ensure totally safe speech, rather than in my office.'

'A very good rule, too, Ambassador', put in Squires. 'So what action is now needed?' Whatever it was he probably wished they could get on with it, so that he could escape and have a cigarette; the Ambassador recognised the symptoms. But he'd have to wait a few more moments.

'The most inconvenient and potentially disruptive aspect of this incident,' Brathby went on, 'is that we are required by Diplomatic Regulations to report the matter immediately to London, and until they reply, to take no action to find out who was responsible, however straightforward that might be. Unless we are very lucky they will send out an FCO Security Department man or, worse, someone from the Security Service.'

Aware that he had perhaps aired his feelings on this subject a little too freely, Brathby added: 'Of course if an investigator is sent we shall all welcome him hospitably and co-operate fully, whatever the disruption to normal work. And for the moment I must ask you all not to discuss this matter outside this room or with anyone not now present.'

They all murmured agreement and Brathby asked them to leave, retaining only Head of Chancery to help him draft the necessary telegram to FCO.

*****

Ten minutes later they had concocted a message which, without actually suppressing any of the facts, might, Brathby hoped, persuade the Office to leave the Embassy to carry out its own investigation.

'Well, fingers crossed then, sir.' The Head of Chancery was moving toward the door to open it for the Ambassador.

'Yes indeed, Francis.' He paused to choose his words carefully. 'But there is just one other thing, an exception to what I told the others about keeping this to ourselves: I'd like you to brief Antoun Elias on what has happened and see what he has to say.'

The Head of Chancery appeared less than enthusiastic: 'Of course I *can* do that, sir. But I'm unsure what we have to gain.'

'I know you don't much like the man but he is the most likely of any of us to have seen or heard of anything unusual that could cast light on what has happened. Equally importantly he is going to learn about the incident very soon, whether the Office sends someone or whether they let us carry out the investigation ourselves. Not to have told him in advance will look to him like an obvious lack of trust.'

'Very well, sir.'

He wasn't sure how convinced Paynton really was. 'But ask him not to take any action or make any enquiries until you or I say so. Is that clear?'

'Yes indeed, Ambassador.'

9

'To the Embassy, Mr Elias?' asked his driver woodenly, as Elias climbed into the back of the old Embassy Vauxhall. As usual it stank like goat but at least the man had remembered to start up the rudimentary air-conditioning in time to cool the vehicle for him.

'Good morning, Samuel', replied Elias. 'No, we go first to Police Headquarters.' He knew the man was unhappy to have been allocated to him. They were all the same, he understood, they all wanted to drive for the senior men, the white men. But this boy was at least competent. Most importantly he had brought the local newspapers.

'How are your family, Samuel?' enquired Elias, forcing himself to give an example in civility.

'They all right,' was the only reply.

As they moved towards the main road and Samuel began the daily battle first to enter the choking and sulphurous congestion of traffic and then progress through it, Elias settled back and began his daily ritual of examining the country's many vibrantly outspoken newspapers. Several were still reporting the government's demands for the return of Ayumba but, he noted, with little editorial support. Plenty about the local elections soon due in the Eastern Province ... usual letters and articles about the electricity breakdowns ... long-sought bandits killed in gunfight with police ... reprimand of surgeon for negligence (amputated both legs instead of just one) ... religious riots in the North ... more graves desecrated here in the capital and body parts stolen ... 35,628 people calculated to have died over last four years in traffic 'mishaps' ... Ah yes, here was something that could be useful: *The Sketch* offering some scraps from its correspondent across the border, including an offer of joint manoeuvres, with preliminary staff talks to plan details. Yes, a timely report on that, a specimen offering from his notional Head Agent-designate, was a definite possibility. With Philippa Brainbridge soon due back from leave, that could fit in neatly.

'Can you see what the problem is?' asked Elias; the traffic had been stationary for five minutes.

'I look', Samuel grunted, and got out to join the other drivers who were straining to see what was happening.

A pock-marked old man with one leg limped through the traffic to offer lucky charms. His crutch appeared to be made from an old packing case, padded with cast-off rags.

As Samuel went to cuff him away Elias called sharply: 'Don't hit him. Give him this coin and ask him what is happening'.

A gabble of words and Samuel turned to Elias: 'He say one big mammy wagon got smashed by lorry. Many bleeding in road.'

'You believe him?'

'Oh yes, he try to sell me fine handkerchief from one of the bodies. I no want.'

'Tell him thank you and give him the coin please. Also this cigarette.'

The driver asked: 'Now what we do, Mr Elias? You got cigarette for me also?'

'Here, take one. We'll try the road through Egushi village, if you can get us to the turn off by the petrol station.'

The driver looked appalled. 'Through Egushi?'

'Yes, try it.'

Samuel shrugged in acceptance and the traffic began to inch forward. A match vendor who had been trying his luck among the stalled traffic was knocked down by an ancient Ford but struggled to his feet and disappeared.

Elias knew that Samuel feared a repetition of the problems they had encountered the last time they had gone that way. The road, even by the untaxing standards of the capital, was dreadful. Some major potholes – now fenced off by the desperate municipality – contained foetid rubbish varying from household refuse to drowned animals. Others, starting as modest cracks, had been ingeniously deepened and widened by cheerful bands of street urchins who hung around waiting to rescue, at a price, any vehicles that fell in. There was also, Elias remembered, a notorious stretch of road alongside which lay the remains of recently necklaced *tiefmen*, and a heap of tyres ready for the next victims. Close to this area was a vast, heaving meat-market, the stench of which wafted over half the city. Elias would avert his eyes and hold his scented handkerchief over his face as they passed it.

'Today we lucky', Samuel was relaxed enough to offer as they eventually emerged from their diversion and joined the road which would take them to Police Headquarters. 'Soon there.'

They crept along behind an ancient pick-up which was spluttering acrid smoke from its cracked exhaust. The heavy sky looked much the same disgusting colour.

'Stop one moment,' commanded Elias, stepped out on to what had once been briefly a pavement and dropped some coins in the bowl of a crippled woman holding up a hollow-eyed baby. Poor wretched soul, she'd probably have it taken by her man – if she had one – for beer; but he couldn't just ignore her.

'Why you give *dash* for dese trashy people, Mr Elias?' asked Samuel. 'Dat one go die soon anyhow.'

'Keep quiet and get on with your job.' Elias replied tersely, and crooked his neck to see if there was any break in the approaching blanket of rain.

Then it hit them like an artillery barrage and all the traffic stopped again as even those vehicles with functioning windscreen wipers temporarily admitted defeat.

A brief lull in the storm and Elias took out his comb and re-arranged his hair. Much of this morning's toilet destroyed – but he was still respectable, he reassured himself.

'Good morning, it's Bisi isn't it?' They had eventually reached the guard post at the Police HQ gates.

'How you, Mr Tony?' the guard replied cheerfully, lowering his gun and taking the proffered packet of cigarettes. 'The Iron Man is on seat, also your friends in Traffic and Border.'

'Thank you, my friend.'

Elias was unsurprised to learn that Commissioner Zalomo was already at his desk. He worked damned hard but he had to with that gang of apes to supervise. Tough bastard, block of black granite. Clever too, Elias acknowledged. But it was said that he took no *dash*. This was incomprehensible to Elias: the man was perfectly placed to make a fortune from bribes. But the only thing he could be tempted with, it seemed, was good information. This was the commodity – he had heard the Commissioner say it himself – which kept him on top of the toughest job in the country. Apolitical and uncorrupt, he had survived two changes of *régime*. A difficult man to understand. Dangerous to cross too but a man Elias felt he could continue to do business with. He knew how to manage the Commissioner, although it required great care.

Today he might or might not actually call on Zalomo. Anyhow he would drop in on a few other contacts first. The Inspector in the Diplomatic Protection unit, of course; Elias had good news of his sister's application for a course at the British Council ... then the Criminal Records man who owed him a favour ...

A constable for whom he had once done a good turn came over to the car park with a vast umbrella. 'Come wid me, Mr Tony. Dis way you no get wet.'

'Thank you, my friend.'

He stood in the main concourse amid the noise and the bustle. Time to get to work.

*****

'I swear um, Commissioner, I swear um. I beat um only small small. Like usual, sir.' The fat policeman, crumpled uniform stained with sweat at armpits and crotch, was trembling as he stood, at a parody of attention, in front of Zalomo's desk.

The Commissioner, who had been in his office since dawn and wanted his coffee, looked at him with contempt and pity. The material he had to deal with these days – oh dear God.

'Then why, Sergeant Omobi, if you only beat him "small small" is he very dead? Who was this wretched man? Not a *tiefman* or ravisher, no?'

The policeman shifted awkwardly and tried to explain.

'He be de cook. In house of one Master, one big Oga, who make complain.'

'Complained of what, his cooking?' Now that would be a fine story for the next Hendon Police College reunion.

'De Oga come to Station, pulling dis man by ear. He say dis man he take his daughter and make um son.'

'Did what? Explain yourself, man.' He had a thousand things to do and here was this wretch gabbling rubbish.

'One day de Master's girl, she ten year old, she shout um so cook make bad ju-ju and now she be boy-piccin, spout and all. So she run away. Cook den say he can find dis boy-piccin and make um girl-piccin again if he get big *dash*.'

The Commissioner struggled against the wave of the desperation that assaulted him from time to time.

'And you believed this?' He turned to his secretary, the young, smart, Inspector Ferdinand who was sitting at a small desk in the corner, and signalled for coffee.

'Yes Commissioner, sorry Commissioner.'

Zalamo closed his eyes for a few moments. He needed to make a quick decision and get on with the other problems waiting their turn.

'Right, Sergeant, this is what will happen. You will go to this man, this "Master" and tell him from me to bring here one year's wages for the cook. To that you will add one month of *your* wages; you will then take all the money to the cook's village and give it to his family. You will bring here to me a paper, with signatures or thumbprints, showing they have received the money. Got that, Sergeant?'

'Yes, Commissioner. I understand, Commissioner.'

'Good. Because if you fail I shall personally change you from man Sergeant to woman Constable. Now get out.'

*****

'Right, Inspector Ferdinand my friend, over here with in-tray and book. Half an hour, that's all I can spare for bumf. Feed it to me chop-chop as they say.' He smiled briefly at his protégé. Could do with more like him, just here in the capital, let alone up-country. Might get them too, if he could get his fists on the money for his training programmes. No problem finding the raw material, just in knocking it into shape.

They worked away steadily.

'Promotions list to Chief Inspector. Fifteen names. Needs your approval. All recommended by their district Supers.'

'You'll have looked through them, I take it. Any funnies?'

'Just one, sir; an Inspector in Ibodi. Competent but very young. Governor's nephew, however. Which might have something to do with it. What do you say?'

Zalomo thought about it for a moment. 'I'll accept it. But write to the Governor, from me, letter to be delivered tomorrow, congratulating him on his nephew's promotion and inviting him to support a bigger Provincial contribution to the new training plan.' He put that out of his

40

mind. 'Next?'

'A dozen invitations for various receptions, including three National Days.'

'Refuse all. Next.'

'This is the speech I've written for you for this afternoon's passing out parade for new Traffic Officers.' His secretary passed a slim folder across the desk.

'Thank you, I'll read it in the car. Put it in my briefcase. Anything else?'

'Plenty, sir.' He poured more coffee for them both. 'The Ministry of External Affairs have a complaint from the West German Ambassador; apparently yesterday we towed away one of their diplomatic cars, which – I have learned from Traffic – was blocking the exit from the *Independence Hotel*.'

'Did the removal gang damage the car?'

'No.'

'Pity. Ignore the protest.' He paused. 'No, better than that. Teach them a lesson. Get Traffic to draw up a questionnaire for the Embassy about the incident, everything from date and place of birth of the car's driver, date of arrival in this country, purpose of his visit to the hotel, registration number and make of car, engine serial number, you know the sort of thing, several pages long, to be submitted in triplicate in German and English and taken personally to the Traffic Department Complaints Section by the registered diplomatic owner.'

'That should do the trick, Commissioner. Shall I add "on a Saturday morning"?'

'Perfect. And remember to tell the Ministry of External Affairs that we are carrying out a thorough investigation of the incident. What's next?' They seemed to be making progress.

'The Head of Prison Services is pressing for us to lend him more men, immediately. Two prisons in the East have had serious riots in the last month and every prison is undermanned.'

'Can't be done; we ourselves are short-handed. Make sympathetic noises but promise nothing. He'll have to borrow soldiers instead, and God help the convicts. Next.'

'I don't think it's quite as simple for us as that, sir. Apparently he's discussed all this with the Interior Minister, who supports his request.'

41

'Oh does he! Then that useless streak of Northern piss will have to unsupport the request.' He thought for a moment. 'On second thoughts arrange for me to see the dear Minister, will you. At this afternoon's passing-out jamboree perhaps. You could tell his office that the admiring cadets are clamouring for him to attend the parade. Next?'

'Detailed report from the British Embassy on each of our students on the UK training courses.'

'Good. Anything out of the ordinary?' This was something close to his heart.

'Not much. One, who hadn't shown much interest in his work anyhow, has gone missing – and we had some doubts about him at the beginning. And there are two they would prefer us to withdraw, i.e. they've been sacked.'

'Right. Arrange it.' He paused. 'Yes, I've got it. Have the two of them brought home immediately and transferred to the Prisons Department; and I'll tell the Minister we've withdrawn two of our best men from London to help him out. That'll keep everybody happy. Any more?'

'The same letter from the Embassy also suggests a review of arrangements for protection in the event of violent demonstrations.'

'Right Ferdie, tell me what all that's really about. I'm sure you've got some thoughts.' This young man might one day have his job, Zalomo knew. So accustom him to working out the angles.

'Well, sir, they know how much we need the training and of course are genuinely concerned for the Embassy's protection. So they are linking the two, not all that subtly however.'

'We train your chaps; you protect ours. That what you mean? Yes, you're probably right. And do they have genuine cause to fear demonstrations?'

'Well, sir, there's another message there perhaps. They know that serious demonstrations would require official approval, if not encouragement. They will be aware that some factions in government want to use the Ayumba affair to break or weaken the link with the British and that others want nothing of the sort. The Embassy may think that your reaction to their suggestion may give some idea how the land lies.'

'Possibly; you're using your nut. Now …'

There was a knock on the door. The Secretary wondered who had

42

had the nerve to ignore the *Do Not Disturb* sign and opened the door.

It was the senior officers' coffee-boy. 'Always tell you one time if he come.' He spoke straight to the Commissioner, ignoring the frowning Secretary.

'If who come?' he asked gently. He treasured this old man, who could neither read nor write but had been there for ever, and was utterly reliable.

'Dat oily brown man who work for de British. He now wid Traffic. Before dat he talk with friend in Public Order.'

'Thank you Efemi, you did right to tell me. You may go now. No, wait a moment, take these with you.' He handed Efemi a packet from a carton sent to him at Christmas by the American Embassy. He himself did not smoke.

*****

Twenty minutes later he got up to stretch his huge and tightly-muscled body. The in-tray was empty.

'When can I fit in a game of squash today, Ferdie? I'm beginning to feel slack.'

His Secretary did not need to consult the diary. 'Six o'clock would be a good time, sir.'

'Right. Phone the Akoya Club and book a court. That's if they've got one available.

'I don't think we'll encounter any problem there, sir', he heard his secretary reply drily, 'and I'll phone round regular partners to find who'd like a game, shall I?'

Yes, it'd be good to get the body moving a bit. He'd won the students' Open Squash Competition the first year he'd been at Hendon. The plaque to prove it was on the wall behind him. By God, he'd been good then.

He caught himself practising backhands and straightened up. 'Go and find my friend Elias, will you, and ask him if he could spare a few moments to call on me. I think you'll find he can.'

*****

'Come in, Antoun my dear fellow, come in. Please, do sit down. I hope you have time to take coffee with me on this delightful morning?' His words coincided with the beginning of another brutal downpour as he ushered the bowing and slightly breathless Elias towards a corner of the office which contained a low coffee table and a number of orange-coloured plastic chairs of obscure origin.

'Good morning, Commissioner. Thank you, Commissioner. Yes, I'd be delighted to have coffee. I had not intended to disturb you personally, Commissioner, not without an appointment. I know you are such a busy man.'

'But never too busy to see a good friend, such as yourself,' Zalomo replied.

Time now to get down to business. Which was always a challenge with Elias, the scheming, greasy, corrupt, Levantine arse-licker. But enjoyable, because he liked the man and because however subtly Elias thought he was playing the game Zalomo reckoned he could anticipate the moves. Elias respected him, and to some extent feared him, Zalomo knew, but he was sure that Elias also to an extent despised him. Couldn't help it, of course, it was bred into him. For generations his people, Lebanese or Syrians or whatever, had had rich pickings from Africa; they thought that could continue indefinitely. Well, in this particular case Zalomo was getting the better of the bargain, he was fairly sure.

But all that was irrelevant. The important thing was that Elias was useful in a dozen ways, and if the price was to help him out from time to time, well that's how it had always been between them, ever since he'd been a young Inspector and Elias had been a very much lowlier presence in the Embassy than he was now.

'Is there any way in which I can help you, Commissioner?' Elias asked. 'You know I am anxious to be of service to you.'

As well you might, Zalomo replied silently. His disposal of Muckle's dead *tiefman* had put Elias heavily in his debt. Not that what Zalomo had done was particularly unusual, but the resulting credit which Elias would have acquired with Muckle, and consequently Muckle's boss, must have been substantial.

'Yes, Antoun, there is a small thing. The Minister of Health has two "nieces" to whom he has promised long-stay visas in UK. Can that be arranged?' For a man in his late fifties, the Minister's sexual stamina was remarkable.

'That should be no problem, Commissioner. I'll have a word with the Consul. Who, by the way, was very grateful for your recent help over crowd control at the Visa Section of the Consulate. Shall we put the Minister's young ladies down as "higher education students"?'

'Yes, Antoun, that'll do fine.' He handed him a folder with the applicants' details. 'More coffee?'

'Thank you so much, yes. May I ask you a blunt question, Commissioner?' Elias took a clean handkerchief from his jacket pocket and dabbed at his moustache, then mopped his forehead. Zalomo wondered why the wretched man didn't take his jacket off. Perhaps he thought it showed extra respect to keep it on, or he could just be ashamed of his pot belly. Who could tell with these people?

'You can try.'

'I can …? Oh yes I see.' He laughed heartily. 'The question, Commissioner, if I may put it this way without offence, is how quickly and how effectively would your riot control people react if there were serious demonstrations against the Embassy. Our Head of Chancery has written to you about this but obviously it would put the Ambassador's mind at rest if I could give him your personal assurance …'

'You can tell Mr Brathby from me that the Embassy will be adequately protected at all times.'

'That is most reassuring, Commissioner. I am emboldened also to ask …'

'Yes, Antoun?'

'It would be most helpful to have your own esteemed *personal* assessment, Commissioner, whether or not any demonstrations are likely to take place in the near future, in view that is of …' He raised his now damp palms gently towards the ceiling.

'In view of the understandable disappointment of the populace at the continued British refusal to extradite the criminal Ayumba perhaps?'

'Yes, exactly, Commissioner, exactly. One could put it like that.' He mopped his forehead again.

'Let us say, Antoun, that it is too early to judge the mood of the people. But I imagine that any popular discontent, if it were to overflow, would most likely be manifested by a medium-size demonstration, with

45

a good deal of shouting and waving of placards and some light stone-throwing until my men arrived to reinforce your normal protection unit. Also ...' he added, tiring of all this double talk, 'if it's going to happen, I'll let you know in good time.'

'Tell me, Antoun' he said when Elias's fulsome thanks had subsided, 'how is our friend Muckle coping on his own? He *is* on his own, isn't he, with your lady witch doctor away on leave?'

Elias shifted uncomfortably on the sticky sofa. 'Really Commissioner, you know I always wish to help you but the internal workings of the Embassy ... and anyhow I don't really understand what you are asking.'

'You understand well enough, Antoun; you even do things for that section yourself, don't you my dear fellow, just to be helpful? Many Embassies here have these people. Which is fine by me, just so long as they don't interfere with *our* politics. Play games with others but not with us.'

'I'm sure they – if they exist here, I mean – I'm sure they wouldn't dream of doing anything against this country ... no, certainly not.' He stumbled to a halt, but then after a moment continued; 'Moreover, Commissioner, there have been no recent arrivals at the Embassy so that there is nobody, as it were, who might be replacing her on a temporary basis if indeed ...'

'Thank you, Antoun, that is helpful. Now is there anything else I can help you with?'

'Just one thing, Commissioner. I've heard of possible joint army manoeuvres with the forces across the border and wondered if you could confirm that.'

'The coming joint manoeuvres are no great secret of course.' He glanced at the wall clock above Elias's head. In another few minutes he ought to start his daily round of the departments. He hoped Ferdie had managed to fix a game for him. Time to throw Elias a bone.

'What you may not know, Antoun, and if you pass it on do not attribute it to me, is that there is some talk that the *Air Forces* of both countries may also take part in the exercises.' Which should be good news for Colonel Squires, who would be ready as always to offer replacements for the machines invariably flown into the ground on the rare occasions they were actually used.

'Thank you, Commissioner. Most interesting.'

'It is not certain, you understand: Just "some talk."'

'Certainly, Commissioner.' Elias unstuck himself from the sofa and stood up. 'I must thank you for your time, Commissioner; and I'll be sure to look after the visas. Probably bring them back myself; and perhaps leave them with your secretary?'

'Yes, give them to Ferdie. Now go carefully, Antoun - in all respects.'

10

'Good morning, Mr Sodham', Elias greeted the grumpy and di-shevelled Security Officer on entering the Embassy. 'Well, better than it was, anyhow', he added with a smile.

'Oh yes, good morning.' Sodham allowed his attention to be briefly distracted from *Penthouse* as Elias walked through the lobby. Why that bloody wog was allowed into the Chancery area was quite beyond him; he wouldn't trust the slimy turd further than he could piss. Idle bugger too, creeping in here half way through the morning when the others had been in since eight. He's the one Paynton should be keeping an eye on instead of spending his time fussing about the cleaning register and asking him who he'd let through in the last few days. It was all in the log, well most of it anyhow. He couldn't keep an eye on everything at once, could he? What did Paynton expect?

That reminded him and he called out after the disappearing Elias: 'Head of Chancery said you must go to his room when you arrived.' Perhaps it was connected with whatever this flap was, not that anyone had admitted there was one. Well if Elias had anything to hide that poofter would get it out of him. No flies on him. No, not a poofter, but *something* weird about him. Couldn't put his finger on it. Flies and fin-ger, clever that … reminded him of a story Tom Muckle had told him in the Club last week.

'Head of Chancery *asked* to see me.' Elias gently corrected him.

'What I said weren't it?' His head was back in the magazine. Oily bastard. Who did he think he was?

*****

Elias opened the door and entered the Chancery area, just as Fran-cis Paynton emerged from the Ambassador's office.

'Ah, Elias could you spare me a few moments of your valuable time? In my room, perhaps.'

'Of course, Mr Paynton. I did get your message and was just com-ing to see you as requested …' Elias trotted along the corridor behind him.

'Right, here we are. Do sit.' Paynton watched Elias's face closely as he went over the microphone story. Not that the man was likely to have initiated such a clumsy business himself, too smart for that. But he might have been involved in some way or another.

'So keep your ear very closely to the ground and report anything you learn which might be relevant.' Paynton said as he finished. 'But on no account make any enquiries until instructed either by me or by an investigator from London, if they send one out.'

Paynton stood up. 'Is all that clearly understood?' One really had to be very firm with this man. Quite likely to take some unauthorised initiative unless restrained.

'Oh yes … er … quite clearly understood, Mr Paynton.' The man turned to go.

'Did you learn anything of interest at Police Headquarters, by the way?' Paynton asked. Elias often did pick up useful snippets, it must be admitted.

'Nothing worth occupying your valuable time, Head of Chancery,' Elias responded after the briefest pause, and left the room.

Pretty sure he *did* have something, the cheeky devil, Paynton thought. Probably saving it up for the ghastly Muckle who would then tart it up as secret intelligence, from a 'reliable source whose identity needs protecting', or some such twaddle.

Well, if he'd done nothing else in his time at the Embassy at least he'd got Elias excluded from Morning Prayers and caused H.E. to think a little more carefully about the man's loyalty. Of course one had to consort with all sorts in the Diplomatic but consort with didn't necessarily mean trust. Now, if he got this UN Post …

*****

'Certainly, Polly,' the Ambassador called out cheerily, 'tell him to come in, and coffee for us both please.'

'Good morning, Your Excellency.'

'Good morning, Mr Elias. Sit down. Coffee's just coming.'

'Most kind, sir, most kind. I just … er … wanted a brief word …'

'Did Mr Paynton brief you about the microphone?'

'Yes indeed, Your Excellency.'

'Here, take a look at where it was found … just here behind the bookcase. It wasn't even pushed very far in. Not very professional was it? Oh, thank you Polly, I think we'll have it at the desk then.' He looked back to Elias. 'So you wanted a word ...'

'Yes, sir. I called on Commissioner Zalomo this morning. It seemed to me that it might be useful if I ... er ... gently raised the question of possible riots and police protection for the Embassy.'

The Ambassador listened carefully until Elias had completed his account. 'This is interesting and valuable information, Mr Elias. I just want to be quite clear on your last point – that Commissioner Zalomo has promised to warn us of any planned demonstration and to ensure adequate protection for the Embassy? Yes? Good, very good, well done, Elias.'

'Thank you, Your Excellency, most kind, Your Excellency.' He took a sip of his coffee and smiled appreciatively.

'Did you mention any of this to the Head of Chancery by the way?' the Ambassador asked.

'No, sir. He seemed, well ... er ... very busy. Not of course that you yourself are not – I'm sorry. I didn't mean ...'

'No, that's fine.' Paynton might have an exceptional brain but, Brathby was beginning to realise, he occasionally lacked a sense of balance. Surely one could simultaneously harbour doubts of a man's loyalties and at the same time listen to, and assess, the worth of that same man's information. Of course Elias, conscious of an approaching decision about his future, was no doubt glad of the chance to report directly to him. Paynton had clearly rubbed the man up the wrong way.

'So, Mr Elias,' the Ambassador continued with a half-smile, 'what did you have to give or promise in return for this very welcome pledge that the Commissioner has given us? You do trust him to keep his word, by the way, don't you?'

'Oh yes, Your Excellency, I have never known him break a pledge.'

'And in return ...?' Inevitably there'd be something: it was the way this country worked. Most countries for that matter.

'Two visas, no questions asked, for his Minister's ... er ... "nieces". I have the applications here, sir, if you would like to see ...' Elias replied, handing them across the table.

'They look pretty enough.' Brathby smilingly commented after a cursory glance. Do you want me to have a word with the Consul about this?'

'No need, sir, he'll be happy to do this.'

'Two visas, doubtless useful to the Commissioner but surely not enough to make him stick his neck out quite so far for us …'

'It's the training, Your Excellency. The courses in UK. He values them highly and is always angling for us to accept more candidates. His work is all he cares about. He does not even take normal *dash*.'

Brathby put aside for later speculation what the difference might be between normal and abnormal *dash*, and concentrated closely on the nuances of what Elias was saying:

'So it is very important indeed to the Commissioner that the training continues, Your Excellency, especially on the favourable terms that we offer. He also said something which I did not really understand, about … er … taking up the Black Man's burden. I think it was some sort of joke between him and his secretary. So yes, Your Excellency, the training is very important to him.'

'Yes, and so?'

'Perhaps he fears that the Ayumba problem may worsen and that if his government makes any move against us we should retaliate by cancelling the training programme.'

'You wouldn't have put that idea in his head now, Mr Elias, would you?'

'Oh no, Your Excellency, it would not be my place to suggest such a thing.' Elias seemed to about to stroke the side of his nose with his forefinger and then desisted. 'I should never take the liberty of acting in such a way without instruction.'

'No, Mr Elias, I'm sure you wouldn't. Anyhow thank you for your information. Since I am now *au courant* with this business please continue until further notice to report on it to me directly.'

'Certainly, Your Excellency.' He stood up to leave.

'So how is Mrs Elias, these days?' asked Brathby, also rising. 'Well, I trust? Perhaps we can find a mutually convenient date soon for you to bring her to the Residence for supper.' He shuddered inwardly at the prospect of an evening with Bertha, but it was time he had them round. Perhaps Polly could come, and he'd also ask that cheeky Third Secretary – yes, he'd put him next to Bertha, that'd keep him quiet.

'Yes, very well indeed, Your Excellency.' He hesitated before continuing. 'Bertha is a little unsettled at the moment of course.'

'Unsettled?' The Ambassador wondered what was coming.

'It is the uncertainty, Your Excellency. She keeps asking me ... er ... how much longer I shall be permitted to carry on working, and whether we shall be able to afford to live elsewhere, out of the country that is, when I do retire.'

'Your own preference being an extension for at least a year, if I've got that right, Mr Elias?'

'Yes, Your Excellency, I would be most honoured to stay on and serve under you.'

'Well', replied Brathby, firmly rejecting an unbidden image of Polly serving under him, 'this is a matter to which I am giving active and sympathetic consideration at present.' My God, he was beginning to talk like ambassadors he had once mocked.

'Yes, Your Excellency. Thank you, Your Excellency.'

'But, Mr Elias, you must be quite clear that even if I *do* recommend an extension for you it will be the FCO who will make the final decision. At the risk of indiscretion, I can tell you – you probably know already – that you have both supporters and detractors there. But I think we might just carry the day unless some new factor weighs in against you.'

'Thank you, sir.'

'I should also say, Mr Elias, in case you still harbour hopes in that direction, that the chances of a further promotion for you are virtually nil. I did take some tentative soundings in that direction but it is now clear that there is no chance.'

'I understand, Your Excellency; the chance of being able to serve a further year is more important to me.'

'Right Mr Elias, I will let you get on your way; I know you have other calls to make. Anything you hear of possible demonstrations, come straight to me. And if I'm not here or upstairs in the Residence then Polly, as always, will know how to get hold of me.'

*****

Tom was arranging the bundles on the large office table when he heard Elias's distinctive tap on the privacy door.

Shit, he'd have to count that last batch again.

'Hold on a sec, Antoun old chum. Won't be long.' Wouldn't do for old Greasers to see that mountain of money; wouldn't do for anyone. Guard this secret with your life, he'd been told. It had been made quite clear that running operation *Carrot* securely was by far his most important duty.

Muckle moved the bundles into the Station strong room and covered up the few secret papers which he had out in the office. Only then did he open the door for Elias. 'Come in Antoun, sorry about the delay. Security rules and all that, you know. Same for everyone; the Old Man calls on me, or the Colonel, same drill for all of you. As for our deeply-esteemed fart-faced Head of Chancery, I won't let the bugger in at all; and you know what they call buggers who can't get in, don't you?' Had he told him that one before? No, he didn't think so.

Elias sat down on the indicated seat. 'No, but … er … I'm sure you'll tell me, Tom.'

'Frustrated, that's what. Now Antoun, what have you got for us today, my friend. Pinched the Cabinet Minutes, have we? Nice if you've done that, boyo. Coffee, yes? Kettle's just boiled. Just filthy proletarian nescaff as usual. Hope it's okay in a mug. I put the fancy cups away when the boss went on leave in case they got broke. So, fire away old chum.'

'Well, Tom. I went to see our mutual friend this morning. The one who makes bodies … er … disappear in the night. We talked about the security situation, bi-lateral relations, that sort of thing. I've already told H.E. in some detail – more his area than yours, especially with …'

'With Philippa away? Yeah, sure.' He handed Elias his coffee. 'What else did he have to say, my old copper chum?' He didn't want to hurry the invaluable Elias, but he was rather busy.

'He was anxious to know if your people had sent out someone from London to provide leave cover for Philippa. I protested that I couldn't comment on such matters, but he insisted, so I told him no, that you'd been left in charge.'

'So you told him the truth then! That's one for the record book!'

'Please, Tom, that's not a nice thing to say.'

'Only joking, boyo, only joking. And I'm sure you did the right thing; he knows I work for Philippa, probably suspects you do too, don't you think?' It was time to get a move on. 'Anything else?'

'Just a small thing, Tom. I heard from another ... er ... friend at Headquarters,' – he paused to rub his finger gently along his nose – 'that the head barman at *The Republic Hotel* is very ... er ... sharp. Keeps his ears and eyes open, sometimes picks up information of interest. He co-operates with the Police, of course; has to in that position, but they don't pay him. If you don't already have someone there ...'

Sounded worth following up. 'Could be interesting, Antoun my friend. Can you get his name and some details of his background: place and at least approx date of birth, the usual stuff? Then we can check him out and Philippa will let you know if we want him approached.' Unknown to Elias, well at least as far as the Station knew unknown to Elias, *the Republic's* manager was already on the books, but that needn't rule out recruiting his barman.

'Anything else then, Antoun? Don't want to hurry you but I've got a few things ...'

'Yes, Tom.' He took a tiny sip of coffee, leant forward and lowered his voice. 'You'll remember that Philippa asked me to find some ... er ... helpers among the ...' he mimed a soldier firing his gun, 'across the border.'

'Yeah, know all about that. Got a whiff of something there, have you?' Old Greasers had got his extra-conspiratorial look on, rubbing his nose and hooding his eyes. Could be complete bullshit of course, but Tom doubted it. He must make sure he understood exactly what the man was saying.

Elias gave another glance round the room as if to reassure himself that no eavesdropping enemy had miraculously and spontaneously concealed himself there in the last few minutes, and continued in a near whisper: 'The man I had some hopes of to give us a start, as I mentioned to Philippa ...'

'You mean the potential Head Agent?'

'Er ... yes. I suggest we give him the working pseudonym *Blunderbuss*, that's one of your old rifles. Is that all right?'

'Fine by me. But doesn't this chum of yours have a name? Would be handy if we are to check him out, like.'

He had spoken more sharply than he had intended because the sore on his penis was starting to hurt again.

54

'You know me, Tom. If I had a name I would give it to you imme-diately. But he came to me, this was about a month ago, through a con-tact who has now left the country, and who himself did not know the man's name. Do you follow me, Tom?'

'No problem. Sounds fairly standard. So what happened?'

'He'd wanted to meet somebody from the Embassy, he said, some-one not too senior. At first he talked in general terms about the politi-cal situation over there and especially in the ... er ... military.' Another glance round. 'This man, this ... *Blunderbuss* ... wondered whether the British Government was properly informed about the situation. If not, perhaps he could help ...'

'In other words, boyo, he volunteered his services. A walk-in, like.' Shit, it was itching. Better get this bit of business nailed down fast.

'I can see you haven't a great deal of time, Tom, so I'll be brief. Or we could ... er ... discuss it some other time.'

'No, please carry on Antoun.' Tom replied, duty, curiosity and am-bition temporarily triumphing over discomfort.

Elias leant even closer to Tom, exuding an odour of what seemed to be a mixture of sweat, cologne and aftershave with a slight overlay of corpse. He certainly got around, did old Greasers. 'I told him that we might be interested if he could offer us a sample of useful ... er ... in-formation. I think he must work in some form of military administra-tion section, but he wouldn't give any details. Understandable Tom, surely, until he learns to trust us.'

'So where have you got to with him?'

'He can only get across the border to visit every two or three weeks. He came over again last night. I'd asked him to bring me some docu-ment, any confidential document, to show he was serious. But he did-n't bring any papers – said he hadn't yet had the chance to copy anything interesting – but ...'

'But ...?' Inevitably more nose-stroking and eye-hooding.

'He said that the matter was still confidential but the ... er ...joint manoeuvres with our lot here are now going to include an Air Force el-ement from both sides.'

'And if true ...'

'If true, *Blunderbuss* said, this would prove he was genuine. Next time he comes across, Tom, he'll try to bring some confidential documents about a new special army unit which is about to be formed. A cousin of his works in the Central Military Bureau and said ...' Elias lowered his voice even further, 'there's a rumour that the Cubans are involved.'

'Sounds promising, Antoun. I'll report it all to London. And Philippa will be all agog, I'm sure. Not so long now before her leave's up. So that's it then till your *Blunderbuss* chappie comes back? Anything else?'

'Just the matter of expenses and whisky, Tom. I thought it would show confidence in him if I repaid his travelling expenses – I gave him the three hundred he asked for – and also I *dashed* him two bottles of duty free whisky.'

'How would he account for duty-free whisky if challenged?' Tom knew that that was the first question Philippa would have asked.

'You can buy it here on the black market, I regret to say.'

Oh can you, thought Tom disapprovingly, I wonder who's selling it. It could be someone from any Embassy; just hope it wasn't someone from ours. It's one thing lying and fiddling for your country, but very different doing it for personal profit. That was wrong. A twinge from his penis terminated that train of thought.

'Fine,' said Tom, fetching his cash box. 'You're also owed other expenses if you remember. Now, let's just run through this ... yes, and that ... that's it I think. No, there's this as well.' He checked his work on the calculator. 'Do you mind adding the old moniker there? Makes 780 in all.'

'Also', added Tom, as Antoun scribbled his signature, 'London said to tell you that from next month your special salary, the one paid direct to your account in Cyprus, will go up by ten percent. Sounds as if old Philippa's been putting in a word for you in London.'

'Tom, that is most welcome. Please express my appreciation.' He carefully put the notes into his jacket pocket and stood to leave. 'Now I must go and see the Consul over some visas, and then the Colonel with a small piece of information not worth troubling you with, and then the Admin Officer and so on. There is, as you say, no peace for the wicked.' He pushed away his half-finished coffee with an apologetic smile. 'And I hope, Tom, that whatever is troubling you soon disappears. A pain in the stomach perhaps. And thank you again for this.'

He tapped his pocket and left.

Tom filed the receipt and was moving towards the strong room when he heard a gentle tap on the door.

'Yeah, who is it?' he called irritably.

'Your dancing partner,' came the reply.

'Oh Polly,' he opened the door and smiled. 'What can I do for you, my lover girl?' Not that she is or ever likely to be that, he reflected. Nor would he want her to be until he'd got this damned problem sorted out.

She curtsied. 'His Excellency the British Ambassador Mr Bernard Brathby requests the almost unimaginable pleasure of the company of his lowliness Tom Muckle for drinks at 6.30pm, this evening. Scruff order, no other guest.'

'Trouble, or what, do you think?'

'Tom, my dear, I have no idea. Really. I'm not just being discreet.'

'Right, tell the Old Man that if nothing better crops up I'll drift along as suggested. Now I really must get on with some work. Thanks, love.'

11

Early that evening Brathby heard Cuthbert open the outer door of the Residence, and laid aside his papers. 'Come in, Tom', he called down from the study. 'Oh yes, and Cuthbert, bring Mr Muckle a beer will you, and one for me at the same time.' He looked around. 'Now, Tom where will you be most comfortable? Over here perhaps', he gestured; 'choose your chair. The air-conditioning is working well for once, so you'll soon be cool enough.'

'Good evening, Buster,' Tom replied, and 'Oh, thank you, Cuthbert,' as he received his beer a few moments later.

Looks apprehensive, poor fellow, thought Brathby. Probably wondering which of his sins have come to light.

'Your good health, Tom.'

'And yours, Buster.'

They both drank and were silent for a while.

'Tom, the first thing I want to say is how much I appreciate what you did this morning.'

'It were nothing, sir, just routine like.'

'Perhaps just routine, but conscientious routine, carried out by a conscientious person. The Russians, or whoever were responsible for planting the device, won't have learned many secrets from it, I don't believe; but it could have proved embarrassing if it had stayed there for any length of time. That it didn't I have you to thank, and I shall send a Personal and Secret Note to your Head Office to that effect.'

'Thank you very much, Buster, that's very good of you.' The young man looked pleased, but still apprehensive.

'Well, you deserve it. Now let me get you another beer.' He disappeared into the kitchen.

'Be in trouble with Cuthbert for doing his job, if I'm not careful,' he said lightly as he returned with the drink.

'Thank you Buster. How is he, sir, and that lad of his?'

'Been a bit quiet recently, Cuthbert that is, as if he's got something on his mind. As for young Eventide, he's fine, growing in confidence every day, doing all right at school, learning to play football as well.' He paused. 'Tom, there is one other thing I need to discuss with you.'

'Er, yes Buster?' He was nervously tapping his coat pocket.

'Do smoke if you wish, Tom.'

'Something you want me to do, sir, perhaps?' asked Muckle, lighting up.

'No, it's not that, I'm afraid. The fact is that I've been reliably informed that you've recently been frequenting *The Welcome Pussy* nightclub. Which, as you know, is out of bounds for UK-based staff.' He paused to consider. 'Now, Tom, if you tell me that you have good professional reasons for visiting this place, tracking down straying Hungarian cipher clerks or whatever, then I'll accept your word; although in that case your boss really should have cleared it with me in advance. I should then have been better prepared how to react when I was told of this. It's for just such a reason that the local clearance system is in place.' For the second time that day Brathby admonished himself for pomposity. Although what he said made excellent sense, he knew.

'No Buster, it were nothing like that, I'm afraid. It's just that, well, the girls in that place, they've some right crackers there. Two of them are really special like; and some new ones expected too, from ...' he petered out and Brathby noticed what could have been a twitch of pain across Muckle's face before he continued: 'But Buster, I know I shouldn't have gone there. I'm sorry, specially if it's put you in a difficult spot like.' He stubbed out his cigarette. 'I'll not go back again, sir.'

'Good. You can perhaps confine your attentions to a little nearer home, but,' he added smilingly, 'without breaking any hearts among my staff please.'

To Brathby's surprise Muckle coloured at this. He gulped down half his beer before saying despondently: 'Philippa's not going to be overjoyed when she hears about it.'

'I've been thinking about that, Tom. So long as you stay away from the place from now on there's no need for me to tell her. Philippa would not necessarily take a harsh view but might feel that she had to include it in your annual report. That wouldn't help your career, and I don't want you to suffer disproportionately for an infringement that any young man might have been guilty of.' What a mouthful indeed, but it was how he saw it.

'That's really very kind of you, Buster, very kind', said Muckle, seemingly in some discomfort again.

'Tom, is something troubling you? Something physical? I mean,

59

have you got a pain?' Brathby was sure something was wrong.

'Er, oh no, sir, I …' He stopped. 'Well, actually Buster, there is … well, it's difficult to explain, like.'

'Take your time.' Poor fellow was sweating, despite the air-conditioning. 'I'll get you another drink.'

By the time Brathby returned, Muckle seemed ready to talk. 'Yes, Tom?'

'It's my cock, Buster. Sorry, sir, my … er … penis.' He finished half the new beer in one gulp.

'Yes, I know what a cock is. Have you damaged it in some way?' Goodness knows what games they played at *The Welcome Pussy*.

'Well, not really damaged, like; I've got a sore place, only looks like a pimple but stings you know. Of course I'm wondering if it could be …'

'If you've caught a dose, is that it, Tom?'

'Yes, sir.'

'Does it hurt you to pass water?'

'No, sir, not at all.'

'Any discharge, of pus or blood?'

'Oh no, nothing like that, Buster.'

Probably not gonorrhoea then, thought Brathby. Syphilis? Surely not? Perhaps, knowing him, it could just be over-use; but still worrying for the poor chap and best sorted out soon, and professionally.

Muckle was looking at him nervously.

'So what do you think, sir?'

'I think you should see Dr Karim-Bux tomorrow and have a proper examination. Oh, yes and please don't tell him that I advised you to consult him. All right?'

'Yes, Buster; and I'll let you know what he says.'

'Fine, try not to worry, and just in case it's something contagious perhaps it'd be better, I'm sure you'll agree, if you didn't …'

'Don't worry, Buster. I'll lay off like. It can get uncomfortable in this condition …'

'Quite.' It was clearly time to bring this to a close. 'Right, Tom, I think you'd better be on your way now, and I must get back to my papers.'

At the door Muckle turned and looked at Brathby. 'You've been very good to me, Buster, very good. I don't deserve it. Goodnight, sir.'

12

Cuthbert, his neatly-darned white shirt and baggy blue trousers protected by an ancient apron, was at the kitchen table, polishing the silver. He heard a tap on the door. The Ambassador entered, gestured to him to sit down and took a chair.

What does he want, Cuthbert wondered, straightening his spectacles and scratching his grey hair. Of course, the Master would sometimes come and sit in the kitchen and talk with him and Cuthbert enjoyed that. Always so interested in everything; what life was like in the old days, did Cuthbert believe in God, how was the special yam dish prepared, did the market mammies give all their monies to the men to buy beer, where did the gate guards sleep when they were not on duty? Many, many things, and, of course, since Eventide had come they talked often of him, and how they could help him. A good man, this Master, a good man whom they all respected, you could see that. He had so enjoyed those friendly palavers and felt he had helped the Master to understand many things about his people. It was all good.

But now Cuthbert had spoiled it all. How could he talk happily to the Master with this weight on his soul? What a terrible choice it had been, between his love for Eventide and his duty towards – yes, and love for – Mr Brathby. Perhaps all would yet be well and no harm done – except, Cuthbert knew, to his own honour, to which he attached a fierce ancestral pride. But at least that so-called 'cousin' had now gone and had promised not to come back. He hoped the promise could be relied on. He doubted it. The man was evil.

The Master was looking closely at him. In kindly fashion, as always, but also suspiciously, Cuthbert felt. Oh God, why had he done that terrible thing, perhaps Eventide could still have been saved …?

'Are you all right, Cuthbert?' the Ambassador was asking him gently.

'Yes, Master, of course. Jus I tire, small.' That at least was true.

'Good. You'd tell me if you had a problem? I am here to help, you know.'

'No problem, Master.'

'Well, what I came in to say is that I don't need you any more this evening, so why don't you stop work now and rest? All I'll need are

62

the sandwiches you've made up for me and put in the fridge.'

'Yes, sah, dey for fridge.'

The Master seemed to be hesitating as if uncertain whether to speak or not. 'There is one thing I'd like to ask you before I go, which you may think unusual and curious but in which I'm very interested.'

This did not sound good; and if the Master did ask the question which he feared, Cuthbert wouldn't be able to lie – in fact it might be a relief to get it out, like the vomit that the witch doctors in the old days would call forth to cure the mind-pain.

'Sah?' Quickly: get it finished quickly, he prayed.

'When we talk together, Cuthbert, or when you talk to other members of the Embassy or, say, to my friend Mr Singleton when he comes here for supper, you speak in English, in pidgin, whether you are speaking of food and drink or of God or the weather, don't you?'

'Na so, Master.' Cuthbert could only stare at him. This was strange talk but at least it wasn't about the other thing. Usually the Master had good reason for his questions.

'But what is the language you use to *think* in?' the Ambassador continued. 'Is it your own tongue, Angala, which you then translate in your head into pidgin, or what? What language are you thinking in now?'

'This hard question for me, Master.'

'Take your time, Cuthbert. It's a hard question for anybody.'

What does he want me to say, wondered Cuthbert, bewildered but deeply relieved that it was not the other thing. Then he realised that he must not find words just to please the Master but he must find true words. The question was difficult but slowly the answer was forming.

'When I speak wid anudder in English, like now my mind tink in English, but …'

'Yes …?'

'Dis wot I tink often more clever dan de words I use. No, not clever, dat not be right word.'

'Subtle?'

'Ahaa! Na so. How you say, sutal. Sometimes in de head is many fine dishes but all dat comes out of mouth is piece of bread. Dis too vex me.' He paused. 'Maybe dis because I never learn book when piccin, jus de letter and number when I start work for de British, so I tink clever but de thoughts come out pidgin. But if Eventide do well in de school he no have dat problem.'

'Let us hope so. His teachers say he's a bright young boy.' He stood up. 'Now I must go back to work. Thank you for helping me with my problem.'

Cuthbert felt puzzled but pleased because he knew that in a way he *had* helped the Master. But mainly happy that the Master seemed not to know of the other thing.

'Good night, Cuthbert; don't sit up late polishing; leave something for our young lad to do tomorrow.'

'Good night, Master.'

*****

But it was still too early for sleep, especially with this bad thing in his head. First he would check that Eventide was sleeping peacefully and then come back to the kitchen he loved, and listen to music on his radio while he finished the silver. The Master did not seem to understand that he *liked* working; and what else had he to do anyhow?

He opened the back door of the kitchen, kicked off his old brown sandals and shuffled down the ill-lit narrow corridor to the servants' quarters, where he had lived for so long. With the Master's approval and help he had cleared out what was really no more than a small old box room, and made it into a bedroom for Eventide. He had scrubbed it out, the Embassy handyman had white-washed the walls and the Administration Section had found a child's bed from somewhere. Roughly stuck to the wall, and the room's only decoration, was a large picture of the England football team, donated by that nice friend of the Master, Mr Singleton, the big *Oga* of the mining people.

The door of Eventide's tiny room was wide open so that a small fan, sitting on an old box in the corridor, could provide some cooling. The boy, smiling even in sleep, lay at an angle across the bed, the sheet bunched around his shoulders. His football and his satchel, ready for school in the morning, lay neatly on the floor beside him.

Cuthbert returned to the kitchen, turned on the radio to low volume and laid out the silver that still remained to be cleaned. He decided that the next time he was asked to help out at a party he would take Eventide with him. Not to be paid, naturally, but to start to learn how things are done in different houses. He could help with washing-up of glasses, only if they were hired of course; he couldn't trust him with the special ones.

Perhaps he would take Eventide when Mrs Squires gave her big party. He would ask the Colonel. He was sure to say yes. The Colonel was a good man but, Cuthbert shook his head sadly, he liked the hot drinks too much. A kind man but could be fierce as an Angala, it was said; his Steward had told how the Colonel had nearly struck the night-watch for forgetting to lock the compound gates; his eyes had come out of his head with fury. He had also heard from the Steward that the Colonel had won a medal fighting the Chinese when he was a young man. When his gun was empty of bullets he had picked up a wounded enemy soldier and thrown him into the trench he was attacking, before bayoneting the soldiers there. Yes, a dangerous man if angry, as Cuthbert knew he too could be, like all his tribe.

But at heart the Colonel was a kind man. Not like that Mr Francis, oh no. Always correct, Mr Francis, sometimes even smiling. A clever man also, others had said. But underneath he was cold, cruel, like the men of the North. Cuthbert remembered a time he had been offering drinks before dinner. When he held out the tray to Mr Francis, who was talking to another man, Mr Francis appeared at first to pay no attention and then suddenly took two glasses from the same side, so that the tray would have over-balanced if Cuthbert had not quickly adjusted it. Mr Francis had said: 'Whoops Cuthbert, you'd better be careful', and smiled at him. But he'd meant to cause an accident, Cuthbert had no doubt about that. And this in Cuthbert's first week with the new Ambassador. It would have looked bad.

The person Mr Francis had been talking to at that time was Miss Philippa, 'The Secret Lady', the Stewards called her. Now *she* would never do a bad thing like that, or if she did, it would happen as she wanted it. A quiet lady, always listening, everyone respected her. Away now for leave; back soon, he hoped. Somehow everything felt safer when Miss Philippa was here. Maybe he could even ask her about that bad man …

Or Mr Tom, Cuthbert thought, putting away the cutlery and starting to polish the large silver tray. He was almost certain that he worked in the Secret Section for Miss Philippa. Twice he had seen him come to the Residence in the middle of a party he had not been invited to, and speak to the Master, who soon afterwards had spoken quietly to Miss Philippa, who had then left the party. Mr Tom seemed a peaceful man, Cuthbert thought, although he had slaughtered that *tiefman* who came into his house. He had once told Cuthbert that he came from a small but fierce tribe in the West of Britain; this was a joke to make Cuthbert laugh, he knew, and after a few hot drinks Mr Tom sometimes spoke pidgin to him. And the Master liked him; but – Cuthbert nodded and sighed slowly – the Master liked most people. He really needed to be warned and protected, even told such simple things. For it was as clear to Cuthbert as the creaking of the ageing ceiling fan that Mr Tom had a stiff one for that lovely Miss Polly but that *she* looked only at the Master. But also she have something wrong inside; her eyes were sad – perhaps outlaws came to her village when she small, like they came to mine. Cuthbert, you old fool, you talk nonsense – such bad things did not happen in England.

Why did the Master not take her to warm his bed? His wife had not wanted to come here with the Master. Same as running away. Must be bad woman. Miss Polly much better.

This tin of Silvo nearly finished. Time soon for bed. Maybe tomorrow he speak to someone about the bad man. That Mr Antoun? Yes, perhaps. Could keep a secret, that was sure, and had many friends at Police Headquarters, he'd heard from the drivers. Might be able to tell him about the bad man. Think about it and decide tomorrow. Mr Antoun was a kind man; but would he help, if asked, and not tell the Master?

On his way to his room Cuthbert stopped to look at Eventide, still fast asleep but now with the football in the bed with him. No, he could do nothing to endanger the boy. But then if he didn't speak and was still caught out …?

13

The gate guard and Cuthbert exchanged their usual greetings as the Steward left the Embassy compound in the early morning on his way to the little fish market. This was set up across the road twice a week, selling mainly to the Embassies in the area, and to the houses of such big *Ogas* (*tiefmen* without machetes, as Cuthbert thought of these local rich merchants) as lived nearby.

The fish mammies, jovial brawny women in their colourful head-ties and vividly printed cloth, operated from a primitive tin shelter over which they exerted long-established customary rights. It was open on all sides with the fish displayed on newspaper and spread on two rusty iron tables. Under the tables lay a profusion of ice-boxes, pink, blue, some with their original handles, others now looped over with rope. Also a scruffy puppy which recognised Cuthbert long enough to stop playing with a fish head and wag its tail at him. The area rang with the bawdy banter of the mammies.

Cuthbert, impervious to the powerful stench that pervaded the market area, slowly made his way past the other dozen house servants who were arguing and bargaining until he reached the mammy he usually bought from. When she saw Cuthbert she shouted at her small daughter to stop teasing the dog and bring over the special pink box; the baby on her back slept imperviously through the racket of fish being chopped, prices being disputed and insults traded.

'Welcome, how you dis day, Mr Cuthbert? Fine, I hope,' she greeted him.

'Yes, fine tank you missus. You look good. And de piccin?' He had known this woman's mother when it had been she who had stood here. Yes and the generation before that. They did not speak Angala and he had always used pidgin with them rather than their own language.

Formalities over, the ritual battle began. And for real too because this was the Master's money he was spending. Even after what had happened he must get the best price. In fact it was more important now. It was his duty and his love. How he despised those servants who stole from their Masters, paying one price and telling another. This of course made the Masters pay their servants less, who then stole more. What a mess. What trash they were.

'So you get fine fish for my Master, missus?' He turned over the fish she had displayed on the table, then leant down to shout at the puppy, which was gnawing his sandal. 'Dis one no look good to me.'

'Well dis udder one fine'. She pulled it out of its box by its tail and slammed it on the table. 'He sweem into my house dis morning, he so fresh.'

'Dis fresh! How you say dat? Dis fish so-so rottin. Show me udder ones.'

Five minutes later he had settled on what he wanted. Now to settle the price. He automatically laughed at the sum she first asked for and made to leave without buying.

'How you no pay proper price?' She shouted after him, pausing to hoik her baby to the front and latch him onto the breast. 'You want me *dash* you? Ah-Laa. You too mean, you Embassy people. You get fine *chop* and plenty beer and we people fit starve!'

'Look your belly missus, you too fat na. All same like fat pig. And dat fine baby full for milk.'

'Don't give me dat fool-talk, you stupid old man. You want de fish or no?' As he hesitated she added: 'How much you pay den?'

Cuthbert knew that the fish mammy valued the face she got from selling to the British Embassy and that eventually she would lower her price to what he was prepared to pay. Besides she had other fish to sell and the sun was getting higher.

Agreement eventually reached, Cuthbert asked politely after her mother, that once strong lady whom he remembered well.

'Mama fine for head but de legs no good. She too old now and she stay for house all day. She fit cook, and mind piccin when I go for out.' She smiled at him while automatically shifting the baby to the other breast. 'And how is *your* piccin, Mr Cuthbert, dat Eventide boy? Next time, you bring um for market. I teach um pick fine feesh, proper.'

Cuthbert laughed. 'Eventide have no time for feesh. Not yet. He for school, learn plenty tings. 'Bye now missus. Tell your mama I greet her.'

Cuthbert put his well-wrapped purchase in his string bag and moved down the road, sandals flapping, in search of sweet potatoes. The puppy followed him friskily for a few paces and then skipped back to the fish market.

It was good to be out of the compound for a while; he could almost put that other thing out of his head.

14

Colonel Squires was sitting clear-headed and relaxed behind his desk, his eyes for once resting on the silver-framed photograph of his wife. Not such a bad old stick, really. At least she does her duty, spends hours listening to dull old farts, says the right things to them, smiles when garrulous guests from UK start boring on about their bloody children; some of them even producing snapshots of them, for God's sake! Doesn't smile much these days when it's just the two of them at home but then does one really expect it after so long married?

They'd now talked things over, without rancour, assessing their financial situation objectively and discussing the future. He'd briefed her about the Washington post he hoped to get. As he'd told her, he was sure that Bernard Brathby, whose views would doubtless be sought, would at least give him a fair wind. Yes, fine man Bernard. Of course he hadn't mentioned to Jenny the possibility, more of a hope really, that Bernard might put him up for a gong. Perhaps indeed had already done so. That, plus the promotion that would accompany the new job if he got it, would be a good package. Brigadier AFL Squires, CBE, MC – a good ring to it, one felt. He could visualise it standing out boldly as a name-plate on his office door, or printed in the Washington Embassy staff list or on a card marking one's place at a Regimental Reunion Dinner.

He pulled himself up – this would not do. Not at all how one should behave. Bad luck and bad form. But by Jove he felt well. Hadn't touched a drop last night – truth to tell that hadn't been too difficult after the excesses of Sunday evening – and after supper he'd caught up on some reading and then done a recce of the compound to see that all was in order. The new nightwatch was shaping up well. Good fellow and alert, but armed only with the ubiquitous *machete* – quite absurd these Embassy regulations against firearms; what century do they think we're in? Then he'd smoked a cigarette with the man, given him the rest of the packet and checked that Octavius had issued him his supper. The nightwatch was a Northerner of course, tough but loyal, quite good soldiers some of them. Wouldn't do to have local guards, who'd soon be corrupted by the *tiefmen*.

A tap on the door heralded the familiar sight of his PA's ample posterior opening the door as she brought in iced water and coffee for two. No need for Alka Seltzer today, he thought with satisfaction.

'Mr Armitage is here, sir, your favourite arms salesman. A few minutes early, he says, and apologises.'

'Never mind that, m'dear. Show him in.' He stood up as the man entered. 'Take a pew; let's sit over there in comfort, shall we. Now black, white, sugar how do you like it? Take your jacket off. You must be soaking, need to get some cool air round the armpits and all that.' He paused. 'Now tell me how it's been going.'

'Quite well.' Armitage swallowed his glass of water and picked up his coffee. 'Several quite promising developments, mainly follow-up stuff with my predecessor's contacts, you know ...'

He went into considerable detail but the Colonel doubted that any of it would come to fruition.

'But the best chance of getting anything nailed down seems to lie with that chap you so helpfully introduced me to at dinner on Sunday,' Armitage continued. 'Yes, Bonzo as he's asked me to call him, is very friendly and says he wants to help the thing along a bit, if you see what I mean.'

'Yes, I'd heard that the two of you had an amusing evening together at *The Republic*. Need to be a bit careful with the female company there, however, so one has been warned in the past.'

Armitage seemed to be looking at him with both embarrassment and admiration. 'I say, how on earth did you ...'

'Well, one keeps an ear to the ground.' What a useful fellow Elias could be at times.' But good to know that you and he are getting on well.'

'Yes, on that subject, Colonel, well ... er ... Jack, point of detail really. Back in the office, in Leeds you know, we understand that when one of the locals helps out, like Bonzo seems keen to do, then obviously a certain reward has to be considered, as it were ...'

The Colonel stiffened. Of course what the man was saying made sense, everyone knew that a large backhander would be expected. But one just did not discuss these matters openly , certainly not with a senior member of the Embassy in his office.

'Question is, Jack, where do I pitch my offer? He's asking for at least ...'

'I'll think we'll leave it there, Armitage, if you don't mind.' The Colonel was on his feet. 'It would be improper of one to listen further, certainly here in the Embassy.' He put out his hand. 'But do give a call before you leave the country and we'll fix up to have a drink at my house perhaps, if you'd like to do that. Meanwhile the very best of luck.'

After showing Armitage out his PA put her head round the door.

'Small piece of good news, Colonel.'

'Aha, details please.'

'While you were with Mr Armitage your young friend from the Air Training Team called in to see you. He couldn't wait but asked me to tell you that yesterday "another red bird went crunch." He said he'd learned this from a contact in air traffic control.'

'Excellent, excellent, although of course one is feeling a pang of regret for the pilot.' He paused for two seconds. 'Ah yes, the regret's wearing off already.'

'Shall I cross out another one then?' His PA approached the chart. 'That'll leave only four.'

'No, not yet, my dear. Better wait for some collateral, just to be absolutely certain.' He lit a cigarette, amazingly only the third of the day and it was late morning already. Quite a reformed character really. 'So what's next on the menu?' he enquired cheerfully.

'There are some papers here that you will wish to see before your meeting this afternoon at the MOD. Including the list of questions about the Air Force which you asked me to prepare – the Annual Review is due soon.'

'Yes, dammit; I'll have to see what I can do about that. But the most important aim of today's visit is to find out a bit about how the Army views this Ayumba business. H.E. wants to sniff out what I can.'

'Do you need me any further then, Colonel?'

'No, off you go for lunch. Tell you what, take this packet of nasties with you and leave it on your desk out of temptation's reach, please. If I get through the morning on only three that'll be a record.'

Good to test one's will from time to time, he thought, as she smilingly departed with his remaining cigarettes.

A day on which it feels especially good to be alive. Improvement on the home front, got the demon booze under control, work going well.

All could be set fair. Of course that microphone business may cause a few ripples if the FCO insist on sending someone out – having an investigator from London would be uncomfortable for Brathby of course, and he'd be sorry on that account, but it could hardly affect oneself, could it?

Right, no need for lunch today. Do him good to miss out a meal and anyhow he'd be obliged to eat one of those dreadful cakes when he got to the MOD. He'd better study these papers. He looked round automatically for his cigarettes. Of course … oh well, that's why he'd put them out of reach. So, forget them: not so difficult is it?

He drew the top file towards him and began to read. What an abstemious officer he was being.

*****

Paynton silently handed Moses his jacket and tie, kicked off his shoes, and sank back in the cane chair. He nodded a faint acknowledgement for the jug of iced lemon juice and soda which his Steward had prepared for him and placed on the side table. The air-conditioning was working effectively – as indeed it should do with him as the Admin Officer's line manager. Payton was going to enjoy these ten minutes before his shower and he supposed, rubbing his jowl with the side of his hand, what would have to be his second shave of the day, despite his fair hair and complexion. The penalty of being so virile.

'Master want *chop* at house or go out?' The man was back, filling his glass and removing his shoes for cleaning.

'Out, Moses,' he replied expansively. 'Out in order to savour the almost unimaginable delights of feasting at the Ghanaian Counsellor's virtually compulsory luncheon for his Commonwealth colleagues, among whom I have the honour to number myself.'

'Right, out.' Well he'd clearly grasped the gist. What trash these people were. 'No want me more?'

'No, dear Moses, disappear to wherever you disappear to. Until this evening.' As the man padded away, Paynton wriggled his socks off, unfastened his watch – just after twelve, he noted – and allowed his eyes to close.

Considering this was bloody Africa he was well set-up, he thought.

The flat was large and had a fine view of the swamp; and his grade and position had ensured that it was furnished comfortably and functionally. He hadn't risked bringing many of his own prized possessions out here, but he had included in his heavy baggage two daring modern paintings by artists who were admired by his friends in London, but whose names he doubted would be familiar to his Embassy colleagues, even to his Ambassador. Additionally, he had shipped out a set of black silk cushions, a large and handsome silver gilt mirror, a fine Damascus coffeepot and a scattering of his less expensive Persian carpets.

He had spent a fairly tedious morning. First he had assembled copies of all the data which he could visualise might be needed by any investigator London might send out – Duty Officer and cleaning rosters, staff lists with dates of engagement for local staff and dates of arrival for the UK-based; standing orders on physical and personnel security. Even leave dates and salary scales. He had asked Brathby if he should include copies of the staff's Annual Confidential Reports but had been told firmly no.

Paynton sat up, poured himself a second glass of lemon juice and soda and slumped back again. All this preparation for something which *Inshallah*, God willing, would not be required. He was sure that he and Brathby could sort this out between them and preferably without the involvement of the bone-headed Colonel, who thought the sun shone out of the Ambassador's posterior. His nose told him that the unreliable Elias was very likely to have been involved in this one way or another. Pity that Brathby was so blind about him – well perhaps not totally, but still irritatingly inclined to give the man the benefit of any doubts.

But how very satisfactory it would be if it became apparent, even in the absence of hard proof, that Elias must have been complicit in this microphone affair. If Francis were able to play a full role in the investigation then this might well happen – a combination of treachery by Elias and negligence by the revolting Sodham, which would be easily provable. Yes, that looked like a good solution. But he would have to be careful. Brathby clearly didn't like the way he handled Elias; he'd have to watch that. The man was too soft by half but Paynton couldn't risk antagonising him now, not with this splendid UN job on the horizon.

To keep on the right side of Brathby, Paynton always forced himself to be agreeable to his Ambassador's dreary PA, Polly Pym. Oh dear, what a woman. Conventionally good-looking of course, mass of auburn hair and well-rounded enough if you liked that sort of thing but too, too obviously ... how should he sum her up ... well ordinary, straightforward; no spark, no unexpected twists, no fun to be had there, too damned clean-minded. But Brathby had his tongue hanging out for her, that was clear enough – another sign of his soft-headedness. Paynton's own PA, another from the same boring mould, was chummy with Polly and had let it slip out that Polly *knew* Brathby was very fond of her. But, it seemed, Polly found his interest confusing and worrying rather than anything else. He shuddered as he imagined their girl-talk.

He himself hadn't the slightest intention of risking a local entanglement but if he *had* to pick an Embassy woman with spark and promise then he'd go for the lively Vice-Consul. She was arousing a good deal of interest already, he could see that. That upstart Third Secretary was targeting her. He hoped she wouldn't be easy meat for him; yes, the thought of meat reminded him, that *had* been a cheeky remark at Prayers yesterday morning. The boy definitely needed controlling. He hadn't been too happy this morning when Paynton had gone over one of his drafts with him, line by line, sarcastically cutting it to pieces on grounds of fact, logic, balance and even grammar. In fact, the draft hadn't really been too bad but it must have been salutary for him to suffer a little. Everyone had to learn. Certainly when he left Paynton's room the young man's shoulders were satisfactorily slumped and he was biting his lip.

Time now to get ready for this regrettable lunch party. What a pity he couldn't change places with his Ambassador, who seemed to *enjoy* the company of Commonwealth diplomats, even the hairy-arsed Australians, po-faced Canadians and earnest Indians. Whereas he with his perfect French, a lot better than Brathby's, would have shone at the French Embassy. Oh, well.

He shaved carefully and took what passed for a cold shower in this perpetually sticky country.

As he was drying himself he glanced out of the bathroom window. On the ledge, just the other side of the security grille, he could see a green and orange lizard sunning itself, mouth open to ingest any passing insect. What a piece of luck. Quickly he tiptoed into his bedroom, picked up a shoe and returned. Yes, the creature was still there. Very quietly Paynton eased open the window, just managed to fit his arm through, and positioned the shoe. It still hadn't moved. Now! Crack! Got it, the back part anyhow, enough to send it squirming, still alive but its insect-eating days now definitely over, down onto the balcony floor. It was squirming there. Most satisfactory. He went out and stirred it with his foot. He felt ready for lunch now.

Minutes later, clothed and carrying his jacket, he stepped out to the waiting air-conditioned car. But seeing tiny specks of blood on the right hand shoe he told the driver to wait and to pass him a cloth.

All was in order now. 'To the Ghanaian Embassy.'

15

Through the open door to Polly's room – the air conditioning there had broken down again soon after lunch and she was sharing the cool output from his – Brathby heard the Duty Communicator open her outside door and speak:

'*Immediate* for the Old Man. Reckon he's not going to like it much. See you.' The door banged shut and he was gone.

'All right, Polly', he called out. 'I heard that. Let's see the worst.' FCO had taken their time replying, he grumbled to himself. More than twenty-four hours since he had reported about the microphone. Still, the Deputy Under-Secretary would have needed to arrange a meeting, no doubt, and that would have entailed complicated arrangements.

Here it was now. He read it quickly. The communicator had been right. Blast. 'No Polly, it's not the answer we wanted. However ...'

Polly was seated upright across the desk from him, book on her crossed legs, pencil in hand, bespectacled and smiling up at him, all attention. God, she's wonderful. He wrestled his focus back to the job in hand. 'We need to arrange a meeting fairly quickly. I'll want Head of Chancery of course, and the Colonel. Better have the Commercial Counsellor along; he might be a bit miffed to be left out.' He paused. 'Anyone else?'

'Tom Muckle perhaps, Ambassador; after all ...'

'Yes, of course we must have Tom.'

'The Consul, sir?'

'No, Bill's got too much real work to do. One of the others can brief him later. We'll use the Conference Room. See if you can tee it up within an hour or so, will you Polly. Is everybody we want here at the moment, do you know?'

'The Colonel's at the MOD, sir, but due back soon.' She scratched her shoulder with the blunt end of her pencil and smiled apologetically. 'Everyone else is here, I think.'

'Thanks, Polly.' He quickly eyed her underarms before glancing again at the telegram. 'Do you think they're joking with this ripe choice of codeword for the investigation, or is it a hint of what's going to happen to us all as a result?'

Polly seemed uncomfortable at this: 'I really couldn't help on that

77

point, Ambassador.'

He kicked himself hard in the left calf. What an idiotic thing to say to her. The sort of juvenile remark that Harry would make. Which reminded him. 'Add the Third Secretary to your list please; he can take a Note at the meeting.'

He vainly tried to resist watching her take the half dozen steps back to her room. He was sick with his need for her.

Part Two

1

'Thank you for making yourselves available at short notice.' Courtesy towards subordinates was deeply ingrained in Brathby. That nothing short of an earthquake would have justified non-attendance did not affect the principle of the thing.

Brathby glanced around the room. The Commercial Counsellor looked irritated to be there at all – so much for the tactful decision to include him in the meeting. The Head of Chancery was looking respectful but was doubtless reflecting how differently and better he himself would handle such a meeting; the Colonel was all attention but probably needing a cigarette; the Third Secretary seemed excited and keen; Muckle appeared relaxed.

'By now,' Brathby continued, 'you will all have seen a copy of the relevant FCO telegram. It is disappointing that we ourselves are not to be permitted to clear up this matter, this ... er ... *Stuffing* as it has been code-named. However we must accept the decision with good grace and give all the help we can to the investigator whom they are sending, this Mr "Berridge", as we must call him. As you will have noted from the telegram he is referred to as *recently seconded from the Security Service to a senior position in the FCO Security Department'*.

The Third Secretary commented: 'Full-blown spook, then.'

'Yes indeed, and since we are not to investigate this matter ourselves it is, in my view, just as well to have a professional on the job. However,' he continued, 'I must admit to being uneasy about the apparently routine inclusion in the FCO telegram that Mr Berridge *in addition to his main task of investigating the microphone attack, is also authorised to carry out a brief security review of such aspects of Embassy procedures and duties as he may deem relevant to the avoidance of any future security breaches, either physical or concerning personnel.'*

'In other words, sir, one must conclude that he has *carte blanche* to ferret wherever he feels inclined.'

'Yes, Jack, that seems to be it.'

'Sorry, Buster', said Muckle, 'but I can't have this Mr Berridge poking around in my offices, not without authority from my people in London. Sorry, sir, but I'm just not allowed.'

'But isn't he just another spook, like you Tom?' the Third Secretary put in unhelpfully.

'Perhaps you'd confine yourself to keeping the record, Harry, and leave me to run the meeting.'

'Sorry, sir.' The Third Secretary looked chastened but Brathby doubted if he was. He didn't want him *too* chastened but the young man must learn when to keep quiet, as he himself had had to learn.

'But to answer your question, it appears that Berridge is a different sort of "spook", as you call it, from Tom Muckle and anyhow he's now working for the FCO.' He turned to Muckle: 'Tom, you're within your rights to refuse him admission, unless authorised by your Head Office. But it might be tactful, if he asks to see you, to invite him into your office – although clearly not into your strong room – after you have removed all your papers; in the same way as I have on occasion been invited to visit Miss Brainbridge there. However the decision is yours.'

Muckle smiled his thanks.

'I don't suppose, sir, that you have any idea how long all this is going to last?' asked the Commercial Counsellor, a little peevishly Brathby thought. 'My department *is* rather busy at present.'

'No doubt we shall *all* be pleased when this is over', Brathby replied in a more agreeable tone than he felt, 'and I imagine anyhow that work in the Consular/Commercial building will be virtually unaffected by Mr Berridge's enquiries. Unless you are unwise enough to find a microphone in your office.'

The Commercial Counsellor smiled thinly and Brathby continued: 'Now, to the allocation of duties. Francis, I'd be grateful if you would meet Mr Berridge at the airport tomorrow and bring him into town. Take the most reliable driver from the pool and my car with the bullet-proof windows. We don't want him killed before he gets here.'

'Yes, sir. Shall I take Elias to ensure there's no problem at Immigration? Not that there should be with a passport describing him as *British Government Official*.'

'Yes. Francis, do *ask* Mr Elias for his help with that matter.' He turned to the Colonel: 'Jack, may I impose on you and Jenny to have Berridge to stay, and will you bring him into the office on Thursday morning?'

'Of course, Ambassador. We'd be delighted.'

'Thank you. You'll have noted from the telegram, Jack, that Mr Berridge requires only a light supper and to be early to bed.'

'No problem, sir. That'll suit us very well.'

The Third Secretary was smiling tactlessly. To be fair to him, the vision of a happily abstemious Colonel did have its comic side.

'Thank you, Jack.' He addressed them all. 'The details of Mr Berridge's programme can wait until tomorrow morning. He will doubtless have his own agenda with which we must all fall in as best we can without total disruption of normal business. Any questions?'

A chorus of 'No, sir', and a 'No, Buster,' and the meeting was over.

*****

On his way back to his office Brathby visited Elias's room, braving the acrid fumes of his Latakia cigarettes, and brought him up to date on developments. 'It is possible that Mr Berridge may wish, discreetly, to involve the local police. But do nothing for the moment. Mr Berridge will doubtless wish to consult you early on anyhow. All right?'

'Yes Your Excellency, thank you for telling me this, Your Excellency. I will of course do anything I can to help.'

It will be interesting, Brathby reflected as he left the room, to see what Berridge makes of Elias. He hoped the latter would show his better, and extremely effective, side, not the caricature of an oily Oriental which he seemed to adopt when nervous. Perhaps in some way we drive him to it, he reflected.

Back at his desk Brathby could see Polly through the open adjoining door bending over as she tidied some papers. His basic desire to possess and protect her suddenly eclipsed all thought of Berridge, *Stuffing*, his job and everything else. What should he do about it? If he spoke out she would almost certainly reject him; and then she could scarcely continue to work here with him, could she? Whereas if he succeeded in resisting what was surely a doomed course of action, was it just possible that whatever was inhibiting her would one day disappear? The more he chewed it over the more confident he was that she had no lover. Certainly not Tom; no, that was nonsense. She *had* once been married of course, but for less than two years, he knew. Once he had

81

gently tried to get her to talk about it but she had abruptly changed the subject. What had gone wrong, he wondered.

By the time Polly came in, bearing a clutch of files and evidently in a hurry, Brathby had most of his mind back on work.

'Thank you, Polly. Anything of interest while I was at the meeting?'

'There's another *Top Secret and Personal for Ambassador, Decipher Yourself* telegram just in, sir.' She paused. 'It's probably what you were waiting for – Mr Berridge's real name. Shall I unbutton it?'

He noticed her glance very discreetly at her watch and then remembered. 'No, Polly, it's this evening that you and Tom are in the dance finals, isn't it, and you're going off early to get ready. Yes?'

'Yes, but I'm quite …'

'No, Polly, very sweet of you but it's time you were away. You can … er … unbutton it tomorrow first thing – it can wait till then. I'll put these files away in my safe when I've finished. There's nothing else I need.'

He stood up. 'So off you go and good luck.' He suddenly put his hand out to shake hers, savouring its warmth and softness but holding on a second or so longer than he decently should have done, he told himself in irritation. And what was he doing shaking her hand anyhow? How absurdly he was behaving; how would she interpret it? Oh damn, oh damn, oh damn. Did the minx mean anything by 'unbutton'? Did he himself?

He was flooded by desire so powerful that he collapsed trembling into his chair as she left the room. Something must break, and soon.

2

The tea on his bedside table was cold but Brathby drank it never-theless; he must have slept through Cuthbert's morning greeting.

From the size of the growing lake between the Residence and the front gate Brathby realised that it had been raining most of the night. Good thing he'd closed that window. He hoped that the recently-re-paired roof at Polly's block of flats had withstood the onslaught. Oh Polly.

Then he remembered the previous evening. It was today that he had to do it. He'd written it down: there was no escape. He was uncertain whether he was more frightened or excited.

Calling now to Cuthbert for fresh tea, Brathby made his way to the tiled area with antediluvian fittings that passed for a bathroom. The primitive shower contraption was working well today, producing a healthy stream of brownish warm water. He washed carefully, soaping and then rinsing first one limb, then another. When he'd been taking a shower soon after his arrival at Post the water had trickled to a halt while his whole body was covered in soap. He'd had to search out Cuthbert; who of course, bless him, had spare buckets of water in the back corridor for just such an emergency. Similar supplies were ready in the Residence's three modern lavatories for those frequent occasions when the water supply failed. Indeed one might almost have been bet-ter off, Brathby had thought, with an old-fashioned thunder-box. There was one still around somewhere in the rambling Residence annexe, he believed. He'd look for it one day.

As he dressed, Bernard turned over his decision of the previous evening. He'd got home reasonably early after dutifully attending var-ious functions. First a drinks party at the British Caledonian manager's house. From there to the National Theatre to view what the pretentious invitation card had billed as *The Official Opening of the Exhibition of Works of Assorted Bulgarian Artists sponsored by the Ministry of So-cial Development, Youth, Sports and Culture in Collaboration with the Embassy of the People's Republic of Bulgaria.* After greeting his hosts and obtaining a glass of warm beer, he had spent some minutes gazing glassily at huge ill-painted canvases portraying scenes of "socialist re-alism". The event was sparsely attended and the guests were outnumbered by Embassy guards, standing at regular intervals along the walls, arms folded across their ill-fitting blue suits. Brathby assumed they were there to foil imperialist plots to steal the precious exhibits. He made a mental note to send Francis to the next Bulgarian function, abandoned his beer behind a huge portrait, and took his leave, having had his fill of valiant workers defending the Motherland from counter-revolutionaries.

Seated in the back of the comfortable and efficiently air-conditioned Ambassadorial Bentley on his way to his next appointment, Brathby formulated Diplomatic Circuit Law Number Two, for later transcription to his private diaries: that the likely interest and benefit from a diplomatic function is in inverse proportion to the size of the card on which the invitation is written. (Law Number One stated that the drink you took at home before starting out was the best of the evening.)

Then to a reception by the Japanese Ambassador in honour of an expressionless, verging on faceless, visiting metallurgist from Tokyo. Well at least the Japanese served cold beer, and in the scrabble for seats at the buffet supper he had managed to manoeuvre himself next to the amiable Egyptian Ambassador. But it had been a close-run thing; Brathby had just left the buffet, a plate of unidentifiable delicacies in one hand and a beer in the other, when he discerned the Japanese Counsellor signalling him to sit on the sofa next to the metallurgist. Brathby avoided his eye, plunged to his left and with a lift of the heart saw the Egyptian grab a spare chair and gesture him over to join his table. Brathby would do most things for the Queen but eating in armchairs or on sofas was not one of them.

The Egyptian sounded out Brathby about the chances of the British government extraditing Ayumba. Virtually nil, Brathby had replied, and in turn asked him how far he thought the locals would go in trying to put pressure on the British on this issue.

'So, Hikmat, should we expect a mob in front of the Embassy, demanding the return of the treacherous Ayumba?'

'That would not surprise me, Bernard, but I *would* be surprised if it went much further than stone throwing. I doubt that our mutual friend, Commissioner Zalomo, would permit it. Incidentally *Saturday* is a good day for riots here, I'm told, makes a fine start to the weekend.'

'Very interesting, Hikmat.' Brathby smiled his thanks.

'One other tiny thing, Bernard,' as he was acknowledging a wave from the other side of the room, 'and I'd better be quick because I fear our Indian friend is about to join us.'

'Yes?'

'The beach executions on Friday. As you know the condemned men include the rapers and murderers of your *Uminco* lady. Well I've heard that the Ministry will feel badly slighted if you don't send a representative – they understand that for some absurd reason of protocol you yourself cannot attend; but if you were to send somebody else, perhaps the Military Attaché … ?'

Brathby nodded, smiled and stood up. 'I'm aiming to leave this party early so I'd better start circulating. I can conveniently leave this chair for our Indian *cher collègue*, whom I see approaching. See you soon, Hikmat; and thanks. Many thanks.'

*****

A quarter of an hour later a young Japanese Attaché, holding an enormous umbrella against the pounding rain, ran off to find Brathby's driver and bowed the Ambassador into the back seat of his car.

Brathby had a question for the driver but knew better than to distract him until he had safely negotiated the first stretch of road. It suffered from numerous pot-holes, which could usually be avoided, but after long periods of continuous rain were barely distinguishable from the rest of the flooded surface.

'Well done Ogolo,' called out Brathby when they emerged on to the main road, 'but careful on this part also please.'

'Road block coming ahead, Ambassador,' the driver said a moment later, 'but they real police, belong to the Iron Man, not *tiefmen*. No problems. They know our flag.'

A cheerful exchange of greetings at the barrier, an unsolicited revelation from the officer in charge that his brother was studying English in Brighton, an unanswered request for cigarettes from the sergeant, and they were through.

'So Ogolo, while you were waiting for me at all these places this evening, did you hear any talk from the other drivers whether the people are angry about Ayumba being in London?'

'Ambassador, sah, they say he just 'nother *tiefman*. So against the Embassy, there is no big anger, only small. And they know that the Iron Man will protect us.' He broke off for a moment to squeeze the Bentley past a burnt out car in the middle of the road. 'Two of the drivers at the Japanese house ask me for scholarships for England, Ambassador. I tell them go to office of British Council man.'

'Quite right, Ogolo, quite right. Did you get *chop* at the Japanese house?'

'Yes, plenty *chop*, they not mean those Jap people.'

'Good *chop*?'

'All except the feesh: they forget to cook it.'

*****

Against orders, Cuthbert had been waiting up for him. Brathby shooed him off to bed, changed into pyjamas, got himself a beer and stretched out on his favourite cane chair in the study. Ten minutes to unwind and review the evening, and then early to bed. The next few days were going to be busy.

How wonderful he thought, stupidly allowing his thoughts to stray in that direction, if only Polly could sometimes accompany him to these events, sharing the fun and the boredom, and dissecting it with him afterwards. He was sure that she'd enjoy life if she could only break out from this shell, this constraint, this … what was it? You damned old fool, just because she's not rushing towards you with open arms – and you're too cowardly to speak out – that doesn't mean there's anything wrong with *her*. Be logical. Make an assessment according to the known facts and the statistical probabilities; be professional. She views you as an amiable old buffer. Forget it, Bernard, forget it.

The telephone ringing on his desk startled him.

'Brathby here. Yes?'

'Duty Security Officer, sir. Just done my round of the compound and saw you had a window onto the front balcony open. If the wind gets up the rain'll get in and flood you.'

'Thank you, Fred. I'll fix it. Otherwise all in order is it? Good. And even the gate guards awake, you say! Well spotted with the window. Good night.'

When the phone had rung he had experienced a wild moment of hope that Polly would be on the line, calling him to go to her. How he longed for the chance to save her from danger; he fantasised throwing himself between her and some foul assailant – or she was drowning in the creek and he was plunging to her rescue. He lusted to be of service to her, to be her gallant knight. Bernard, what is this adolescent rubbish? You're in your mid-forties, supposed to be mature and responsible; and even – by some miracle – an Ambassador. So grow up.

When he had located and closed the window, Brathby fetched another two beers. Since he clearly wasn't going to be able to sleep yet he might as well work.

For twenty minutes he was able to exclude Polly from his thoughts as he sipped beer and ploughed through a backlog of newspapers, absorbing, analysing the material, making the occasional note.

He worked on steadily until abruptly derailed. From a leading article on education in *The Sketch* the word *polytechnic* leapt at him. He tried in vain to ignore it. But she was back. If you wish to sleep tonight do not think of her, Bernard. Do not think of her hesitant smile, her concern when you are worried, her goodness. Above all do not think how her breasts lift when she stands, do not think of her little ears when she pushes back that wonderful hair, do not think how her hips move, do not think … Oh Polly, oh Polly, I love you, I love you, damn you, I love you, but there's nothing, nothing I can do about it.

He stood up angrily. Correction, Bernard: be honest even if you are weak. Do not lose all self-respect. The truth is that all options seem unpromising; therefore you are *choosing* to do nothing about it. At least acknowledge that.

Well, do something positive, Bernard. Put an end to indecision. Take action – now. The answer was simple. He would telephone her, this moment, and tell her that he loved her. He sat at his desk and pulled the telephone towards him. What time was it? Eleven o'clock. Late, but not too late. But he couldn't just blurt it out like that – she would think he was drunk. Was he, a little? He wished he were. No, it was too crude. Nor could he sink to inventing a professional reason for needing her at such an hour. Nor could he drive over to her block of flats without half the other occupants, all Embassy staff, knowing that he had called on her so late. So that was impossible.

But his mind was made up. He would definitely declare himself –
he smiled at the old-fashioned expression – tomorrow. First thing in the
morning, without fail, he would invite her to the Residence for lunch,
tea, whatever – and then, when they were alone, he would speak.

Polly might laugh at him but at least he would have the relief of
having acted. Probably it would end with her going away – but he
would no longer have to bear the pain of his constant failure to take the
necessary risk.

So that was decided, at last. Yes, decided. The next step must be to
confide this decision to his diary. It would be a pleasure to do so. And
also an insurance against his courage failing him in the morning.
Brathby had kept a diary since joining the Service, at first with the aim
of one day publishing a heavily bowdlerised version, *Memoirs of a
Diplomat*, or similar. That idea had faded but he had continued the
diary out of habit and because it was a useful mind-clearing process.
And since the decay of his marriage, who else had he to confide in? It
was both a comfort and a discipline. The diary now numbered nearly
a dozen volumes of plain paper notebooks. In them were recorded his
earliest impressions of life in the Office, his changing feelings for his
wife Louise, the deterioration of their relationship, his opinion of colleagues both overseas and at home, and everything else that was important to him. Most recently he had spilled out there his tormented
feelings for Polly.

Time to fetch the current volume then and take the irrevocable step.
Brathby finished his beer and made his way down the corridor that
eventually brought him to an old wooden door. Taking a venerable iron
key from beneath a stuffed elephant's foot (Cuthbert had said that the
key had always lived there and he had not questioned the point) Brathby
let himself into the now disused storeroom that had been part of the old
Mission. He carefully negotiated the half-flight down of creaky
wooden stairs. The room, lit by a single bulb suspended on an ancient
flex, was dusty home to the discarded rubbish of generations – broken
cane chairs, a rusty old iron bedstead, a lidless trunk, stuffed birds in
cracked glass cases, the broken and rotting leather scabbard for a cer-
emonial sword. Also bizarrely, and a mystery until Cuthbert had explained, were a number of cricket balls around the room – apparently
one of Brathby's more eccentric predecessors had conducted an exper-

iment, the results of which were now lost in the mists of time, to learn in which part of the room a ball first became totally covered in mould.

Brathby had found in this room the ideal place to keep his diaries – in an ancient tin box, on the very top of an old wardrobe, the lower part of which held hundreds of rotting old books and magazines.

A good thing the beer in this climate doesn't stay around long enough to make you unsteady, Brathby thought, as he climbed the rickety old ladder. He reflected that Cuthbert must use this same ladder if he needed to change the light bulb. Definitely not safe for the old boy. He made a mental note to replace it with a proper set of steps.

Brathby descended, clutching the current volume of his diary and replaced the ladder against the wall, giving a wide berth to the remnants of a rotting wooden staircase that led down to some now useless area at ground level, once presumably another storeroom. The floor boards around the opening to the stairs were also rotting.

On the way back to his study, delightfully cool after the sweaty old storeroom, Brathby collected another two beers. They, together with an hour's work on the diary, should suffice to let him sleep. If he were lucky.

His first task was to set on record his decision to speak his heart to Polly. Once on paper the decision would be irrevocable. His need for self-respect would insist on it, even if his courage seemed like failing and he started weighing up the pros and cons all over again.

Brathby picked up his pen.

3

Polly began her morning routine of preparing for the Ambassador's arrival in the office. First things first, get the percolator going. Of course Bernard would've had coffee already upstairs, in the Residence, prepared by funny old Cuthbert; but he liked to have a cup with her as soon as he came down.

Next: his desk and chair. The cleaners would have been in but they couldn't be trusted to be as conscientious as she was. All right, today there wasn't a speck of dirt anywhere, she could see that, but she wasn't going to be deprived of her morning ritual. Her hand lingered for a moment on the back of his chair.

This, she thought, this is the only way I can look after him. I don't love him, I won't allow the word, not really love him – if I did I would want his arms around me, all right, but then inevitably that would lead to … But I can look after him, make his life easier and, when he's not actually here, but just about to be here, or just left, then I can perhaps allow the word love to creep in. But in his large, ungainly physical presence, love was too frightening a possibility for her to consider. She would never be able to explain that to him; but then why should she ever need to? Surely he was no more than just fond of her. How presumptuous, and useless, to think otherwise. Anyhow, she preferred it that way. She had to.

Ink-pot full. Good. Both his fountain pens in the right place. Clean blotter. Better check that Cuthbert has refilled the fridge with beer. Fine. Now …

The telephone rang. It was the Ambassador's external line. Bit early, surely?

'Yes, Mr Obunga, I *do* recognise your voice. Fine, thank you. And you?' She listened for a moment. 'No, I'm sorry but I'm not free to come out for a drink with you any day this week but thank you for asking nevertheless.' When was he going to come to the point? 'Certainly I passed the Ministry's invitation to His Excellency. Of course I will remind His Excellency. Thank you for calling. Yes, and all good wishes to you as well, Mr Obunga.'

Polly made a mental note to tell Bernard about the call. Now, what's next? Today was the day that "Mr Berridge" was arriving, although he wouldn't be in the office until tomorrow. She'd got the relevant papers for that. Goodness, how stupid she was! She hadn't yet deciphered the telegram giving the man's real name. That would be the first thing Bernard would want to see. What was she thinking of!

She spun the dials to open the Ambassador's personal safe. From it she extracted the telegram folder labelled *Top Secret and Personal for Ambassador. Decipher Yourself,* and took out his personal cipher pad and code book and set to work on the message.

Thank goodness there were cipher machines, operated by the Embassy communications officers, to deal with the bulk of the incoming and outgoing classified telegraphic traffic. She was glad she didn't have to get involved in any of that. But if a message was not to be seen by anyone but the Ambassador himself (which is why London would have been upset if they'd known of her involvement) then it was sent using the personal cipher. Polly knew that there were only two copies in the world of this particular cipher pad, one in London and the one in front of her now. It was called a one-time pad, and consisted of pages containing blocks of numbers.

Polly set to work, first writing each of the incoming four-figure number groups under a corresponding group of numbers on the Ambassador's pad. Then she subtracted the bottom line from the top one, to produce a third set of numbers. She remembered that when Bernard had first showed her the procedure, she had found it difficult not to add or carry tens. Forget the tens, he had said; this is arithmetic made easy. The originator of the message adds his cipher numbers to his text, not carrying; you simply take them off at this end, and are left with his original numbers. Look them up in the codebook and, hey presto, you have the text.

Easy Polly, isn't it, he'd said. For example the sender adds four from the cipher pad to nine, which is what he wants to send, making thirteen; but there are no tens in this game so he sends three. Then at this end we take away the four from the three he's sent and we get the answer nine (in no tens arithmetic, as he called it). We do this in groups of four, he showed her, and then look them up in the book.

Polly had never been absolutely sure of the theory behind it but it worked and she could manage it.

The incoming message that faced her now was short and the subtraction didn't take her long, leaving her with the third string of numbers, neatly divided into groups of four. That was the difficult bit over. Now to look up the resulting numbers in the old blue codebook, which was common to all in the Service who needed personal ciphers. This book contained a few hundred commonly-used words and also listed the number group equivalent of the letters of the alphabet, so that the sender could spell out any unusual words, and of course proper names.

Pencil in hand Polly looked up the first number: 3692. She ran her finger down the page. Yes, *NAME*. That made sense. Next: 1774. She knew that one without looking it up, it was *OF*. Now: 6250. She didn't know that one and quickly scoured the 6000 columns, *VISIT*. Then: 2289. She recognised that one, *OR*. So some clever clogs had got round having to spell out all the letters of *VISITOR*, which wasn't in the book. Next word: 3245. She knew that, *IS*. The next two words were predictable enough, *I SPELL*.

Dealing with spelled out words was more fun and Polly, humming as she worked, amused herself guessing what the next letter would be. 4192: that was *R*. So what might the name be, *RALPH, ROBERT, RUPERT*? 1391: the letter *I* ... So, *RIORDAN, RINGO, RICHARD*. Then *C* ... with ... *RIC* it'll almost certainly be *RICHARD* – *not* her favourite name. Check it out; yes, *H ... A ... R ... D*. Yes, *RICHARD* it is. Stupid to feel like that over a name which is common to millions of people; but even so she didn't like to hear it or see it written down. You're a nincompoop Polly; stop thinking, and get on with the task in hand.

Now to the surname. First letter, 7673. That was *C*. Well, so what, on its own that means nothing, does it? Polly looked up the second letter, 1131. A quick glance showed this was *A*. She was feeling just a little sick, but surely from re-awakened memories rather than from current fear. After all there must be several letters of the name to go. She was just being weak and pathetic. She continued ... so *CA* ... do it quickly, girl. Next letter, *R*. Her throat dry, her heart pounding. This is nonsense. It doesn't have to be him, he's not even in the Office, and she'd have known if he had been. Not him, please God not him. She stumbled to Brathby's private wash-room, splashed her face, forced herself back again. *CAR* ... but what next? Do it, do it quickly. Two more letters: *D ... E ...* Oh, no, oh God no, I implore You. She was shaken as by fever, a swirling pain behind her eyes.

A half-run to the toilet bowl, and the vomiting brought her some relief.

Calmer, almost resigned, nearly detached from what she was doing she continued the message. It had seemed inevitable a few moments ago but maybe the man was named *CARDEW*. Why not? Or some other names that started *CARDE*. She found that she could look at the next group of numbers but couldn't make her fingers turn over the pages of the codebook. She felt herself thinking of the *tiefmen* who were to be executed on Friday. She envied them. Their demons would die with them – hers were flooding and poisoning her soul.

She had no real hope left. To give herself resolution she thought of Bernard, of how strong and caring he was; of what that shrink in England had said long ago, that it was both normal but absurd for her to feel this sickening guilt. Come on then, where's your grit? Get it done. There's no hope, no last minute reprieve. Here the letters come: *N* ... *A* ... *S* ...

There were a further few words. Numbly she decoded them. They explained much and removed her last shred of hope that there could be someone else with that unusual and, to her, dreadful name.

She was trying to write out the full decoded message for Bernard's folder, but could not control her hand. She staggered to her room, rolled a sheet of paper into her typewriter and tapped out the text. Bernard would be here very soon. She must strive to be normal for him. But how could she be? In her weakness she could hardly stand. What was she going to do? Bernard was a wonderful man but he must never know, never; she could not bear to think of it.

Moving like a condemned prisoner Polly tidied up, shredding the incoming telegram and her workings on it, replacing the unused sheets of the one-time pad and the codebook in the safe. She cleaned the washbasin and put out a fresh towel. Then she slumped behind her desk, staring numbly at the wall and awaited the Ambassador's arrival.

*****

'Good morning, Polly', Brathby called. 'The coffee smells good. Are you going to pour for us both?'

He was nervous, no denying that, but he wasn't going to say anything now was he, nothing that committed him; he was just casually going to ask her to come upstairs for lunch today. Casually? Well, not so casually that she might think it unimportant and refuse. If she did refuse, then what? He could suggest drinks this evening, he supposed. Damn it, he'd asked Karim-Bux round for six thirty. Well he could be put off anyhow. That'd be easy enough if the doctor's phone was working although it often wasn't, in which case he could always send a message …

All right, you're nervous and wittering internally. But be calm and normal to Polly. Women like men to be resolute. His father had told him that many years ago. He must stay calm.

Where was she? Normally she'd be straight in, with a cheery greeting, and pour out the coffee.

Ah, here she was. He looked up and was immediately alarmed: she was pale, trembling, silent. 'Good heavens, Polly, what on earth's the matter. You look as if you've seen a ghost.' He was quickly out of his chair and round the desk to help her into a seat. He found he was holding her hand. Brathby quickly leant back across the desk, grabbed his suit jacket and wrapped it around her.

'Polly', he cried, 'Are you ill? What's happened?'

'No, sir,' he leant over her to catch her words, 'it's just … just some woman thing. It's nothing serious. I suddenly felt weak. I'm so sorry. Perhaps I've been overdoing things … I oughtn't to do that, ought I?'

He briefly left her side to pour coffee for her, adding a heavy ration of sugar. 'Here, drink this.'

'Thank you, I'm so sorry …' She took a sip and Brathby thought she seemed a little less distraught. It even appeared that she was attempting a weak smile. What a wonderful woman. He craved to show her how he much he thought of her. Perhaps this was the moment, this was his chance. His heart was thudding, concern, desire and discretion battling for possession of him.

'Is that what it is, Polly, overwork and this … er … female thing? You look as if you've had a shock.' A sudden thought. 'Did something happen last night? At the dancing competition? Were you attacked, or anything like that?' What a damned stupid question, he realised as the words left his mouth. He wrapped the jacket even more tightly around her.

'No, sir. Nothing happened there.'

'Not any trouble with Muckle, was there?' An equally stupid question, which served no purpose except to betray a jealousy which he knew to be unfounded.

She answered his question with a slow shake of the head.

Brathby was confused and uncertain. He was struggling against the urge to bend down and hug her to him. But he could not take advantage of her in that way, although he longed to hold her, to crush her to him, to have her melt into him. He quickly retreated to his side of the desk and refilled her cup. Brandy would be better, he thought, but there wasn't any to hand, and he didn't want to leave her, not in this condition.

She had found a tissue and was wiping her eyes. 'That Obunga from Protocol telephoned earlier.'

So was *that* what had upset her? Insensitive young brute, joking no doubt about the executions and causing this distress. He'd like to see *him* tied to one of the posts in front of the firing squad. By God, if he'd said anything out of order Brathby would ruin him. But he was leaping to assumptions. He must keep his head. What was important now was to help her. 'Did he say anything which shocked you?' he asked gently.

'No, nothing.'

'Just wanted to remind us about Friday, no doubt?'

'Yes, that was all. I told him we would let him know. He didn't say anything upsetting.' She then added as if straining to sound normal: 'Have you decided what to do about it?'

'About what?'

'The executions, sir.'

'No not yet.' Perhaps talking about Embassy business would usefully distract her for a while. 'I'm thinking of asking the Colonel to attend. I can't go myself; it'd send all the wrong messages and get me into trouble with the Office, not that it'd be the first time. More importantly I'd find the thing distasteful. We can't even be sure they've got the right men, not just for the *Uminco* murder but ...' he tailed off. Enough of this. 'Just what is wrong, Polly? Are you going to tell me?'

Was he getting through to her now? She was looking alternately at her hands and at him, as if deciding whether or not to tell him something. Then she slumped back in the chair, shrunken inside his jacket as if the little remaining life in her was draining away.

He was out of his chair again and at her side. 'Tell me what I can do to help. Please, I *know* you're in trouble. Why in God's name not tell me what it is? I'd do *anything*. But you must let me help, don't you see?' With a great effort he made himself speak slowly and more calmly. He was desperate to help her, but how could she be so infuriating, so illogical, so unresponsive, so downright bloody thick? No, that was not fair; perhaps she was protecting *him* in some way. But if so, from what? He crouched beside her, placed his hands on hers and tried to will her to look at him. But her eyes were dead. She gently detached herself, sat up in the chair and shrugged out of his jacket. 'It's really nothing serious, although I appreciate your concern, sir.'

There couldn't be many cooler ways than that of telling him to keep his distance.

'It's just the normal thing, perhaps a little more severe than usual, and that on top of last night's dancing and being a bit tired recently.'

He had to accept it; he supposed that it might just be true. 'I'm sorry if I've been overworking you. I must have been. I can be a bit of a brute, can't I?'

She was gently shaking her head in disagreement; she looked desperately pale, yet still desirable. He paced round the room while he thought.

'So what would you like to do, Polly? Of course you must go home. I can send you straight round in the car to Dr Karim-Bux, or I can arrange for him to visit you at home if you prefer. But obviously go now and rest. I'm worried about you, Polly, do you understand?'

'If I could just have a few days off, perhaps that would help. But no need for a doctor, just some sleep I think.'

'Of course, take as long as you need.' He smiled rather nervously at her. She seemed to be a little more relaxed. 'But who will look after you? I can send Cuthbert over with meals, if you need them and of course I can keep you well supplied with books.' Probably the last thing she'd need but he couldn't think of anything else to offer. 'You'd better leave your car here in the compound for the moment. Have you got all the basics at home, bread, milk that sort of thing? I think it'd be a good idea if Violet went back with you to get you settled in, that sort of thing. '

'If your car could take me to the flat I'd be very grateful, but there's no need for anything else. Fatima, the maid who looks after Vi and me, will be around; and with Vi next door I'll have everything I want. No need for her to come home with me now; she'll look in on me later, after work.

'Well, I suppose that sounds all right. You *will* let me know if you want anything sent over, won't you?' Brathby thought to suggest that he visit her later in the day. But that might upset her rest and she might think … it wouldn't do. He could of course go over there with someone else. But who? No, better leave it. If she needed anyone around it would be another woman. Of course if she invited him to go round …

This was still flickering in his head when she said: 'While I'm away, sir, Vi can look after you, if that's all right.'

'Yes, that's fine. The Head of Chancery will have to use the typing pool.' How like her even in her distress to be thinking of his needs. Then he blurted it out. 'When you're better would you like to come for lunch at the Residence one day? Just the two of us; you can tell me what you've been reading and I can recount how I managed to survive without you for so long.'

'Not all that long; I hope to be back to by Saturday.' She still sounded very low.

'Right, Saturday it is then, if you're well. Now let me help you to your room to collect your bag and things. I'll go and fetch Violet. By then the car will be at the door for you.' He went to help her to the door, but she stood up on her own and handed him back his jacket.

'One good thing from all this,' he said, 'is that I'll have to stop being lazy, and unbutton my own personal signals. Starting with last night's of course!' Not that that's what you really want to unbutton, an insistent voice was telling him. And perhaps that's what's really wrong with her is that she's been denying her own nature. My God, I could put that right fast enough, given just a hint of encouragement.

'It's already done, sir; it's there on the desk in a sealed envelope, and the deciphering material is back in your safe.' Her voice was very shaky.

'Wonderful, thank you.' He gently took her elbow and steered her towards the room.

'I'll be fine now. A quick word with Vi, and I'll be on my way. Thank you for being so kind. I only wish …'

'Wish what Polly?'

'I don't know. I'm confused as well as everything else. I'll see you on Saturday for lunch, then. I'll look forward to that. I … er … thank you.' She turned away and went slowly to her room.

*****

What was really wrong with her? Perhaps he should have insisted that Karim-Bux be allowed to give her the once-over. It could be that she really was ill, maybe got a touch of malaria – but he was sure that she took her Paludrine tablets like everyone else, so that was unlikely. Or blackwater fever? No, not these days. Or some female thing, as she'd claimed. But it hadn't happened before. No, he didn't believe that either – something had shocked her badly, he felt sure. He'd find out what it was sooner or later, and if it was within his power to even the score then he would enjoy doing so.

Suddenly he realised the significance of what had happened. He'd done what he'd promised his diary. Moreover he'd told her that she would be the only guest, and she hadn't objected. What a pity it was not going to happen until Saturday – or was he relieved to have three days to prepare himself? Three busy days however, with this "Berridge", whoever he was arriving this evening.

Yes, who is this man they're sending? He opened the sealed envelope and read the name. Oh no, bloody hell, of *all* people they had to send that poisonous little shit Cardenas. Why not somebody from Security Department? He looked again at the signal and read: *recently seconded to us from the Security Service.* So the man had sent himself. This was *not* good news.

Despite his foreboding, disappointment and sense of being ill-used by the Office, Brathby forced himself to think professionally, to allow his sense of balance to kick in. He must be fair, objective. Perhaps what he'd heard of Cardenas, from colleagues who'd run foul of him, was exaggerated; and his own strongly unfavourable impression of the man from a brief encounter during his pre-posting attachments could also be wrong. Just possible, he told himself. But he smelled like trouble. Should he warn Paynton and the MA? He considered this carefully. No, he decided, the man must be given the chance to do his job without prejudice. Brathby just hoped there wouldn't be any collateral damage from this piffling investigation, one that he could so easily have carried out himself.

He would miss having Polly here to chew over how Cardenas's enquiries were going, and to discuss tactics with her if the man started to make a nuisance of himself. Roll on Saturday.

4

'Good morning, sir. May I have your ticket please? Ah yes, Mr Berridge; now let me see …' The British Caledonian Ground Stewardess consulted her chart for the First Class cabin. 'I've put you here, sir, in A9, port side window; and, unless we have a last minute booking, the aisle seat beside you will be vacant.'

'Right.' He watched carefully as she labelled his suitcase and despatched it on the conveyor belt. 'A9 is in a no-smoking area, as requested?' How ugly she was; and worse, fat. He hoped for better things on board.

'Yes, Mr Berridge. The row in front of you and the three seats to your right are also non-smoking. Also I think you'll find the ventilation system satisfactory.'

He hoped so. 'Do you have a copy of the menu for the main meal you will be serving? You'll find that I requested that when booking.'

The concourse behind him was a mass of humanity, most of it black, cheerful and shouting. Behind him in the check-in queue were an African couple obviously on their way home after a shopping trip. He was slim and nervous-looking, wearing a sober, conventional European-style lightweight suit. His wife was several inches taller and wrapped in robes of vivid and clashing colours; and with a huge headdress of startling complexity. Her thick lips were slashed with crimson and her gold earrings hung down to her shoulders. She was precariously balanced on white high-heeled shoes, and smoking a Black Russian through a pink cigarette holder. Two trolleys, piled high with suitcases and packages, were beside the couple.

'Hey, yo', she called out to Cardenas with a massive smile, 'you finish with de lady now so we udders can get checked in? Man, my feet am killin' me.' And as he raised his eyebrows slightly and looked at her coolly she said something to him that he did not understand, although it was clearly uncomplimentary.

And as he moved away wordlessly from the desk he heard her laughing to her husband: 'Joseph, I could eat dat man for breakfast. He one really tight arse.'

Africa certainly begins at Gatwick, Cardenas reflected, stopping on his way to passport control to watch the activity at the economy class check-in desks. At a conservative estimate most passengers must have had at least half as much again as the permitted weight allowance, some much more. It seemed that anything short of double the permitted allocation was ignored; presumably because otherwise with the ensuing disputes the system would eventually seize up. It was clear from the amount of intended hand baggage – some pieces clearly too large to fit into the lockers – that the regulations in that respect were also being disregarded. He noticed that several passengers, presumably fearful of being challenged at the desks, had left hand baggage items with friends and relatives who came to see them off, and then collected them between check-in and passport control.

As the aircraft reached cruising height Cardenas leant back comfortably and signalled the air hostess to refill his water glass. Yes, a much better specimen this one, with quite a neat little rump. He settled down to think. All was now peaceful. That outrageous woman he had encountered at check-in had bustled past on her way to the toilets, the aisle scarcely wide enough for her skirts, but was now safely asleep several rows ahead of him. The other first class passengers were quiet, well-behaved and concentrating on their free drinks.

Cardenas removed the airline vomit bag from the back of the seat in front of him and carefully stowed it in his briefcase. A useful addition to a collection which he had started as a young man. He derived satisfaction from his strong stomach and excellent head for heights; these things flowed naturally, after all, from his superior will-power and physical condition, qualities matched only by his brilliant and incisive intellect.

Because he had won an open scholarship to Cambridge in Modern History and was fluent in a number of European languages, including his paternal grandfather's native Spanish, he had been accepted for his National Service by the Royal Navy, although this entailed his serving for three years rather than the two years demanded by the Army. He had expected to be taught Russian, and then employed on routine Intelligence tasks; but after basic induction and further assessments, he was, to his surprise and pleasure, chosen – with only three others at the time – to learn Cantonese. This involved a six-month course in England and a year's intensive training in Hong Kong. While there he came to appreciate the cool but thorough way in which the Chinese cultivated the pleasures of the flesh; he liked the range of carnal possibilities which he found were open to him and the way in which they were presented without hypocrisy. His life there was so agreeable that when, towards the end of his service, he was offered a position with a British trading company there he was seriously tempted to stay on. He was also offered a permanent commission in the Royal Navy with the assurance of at least a further two years in Hong Kong. However, he turned down both offers and returned home to take up his scholarship, confident that his chosen course would offer equally attractive opportunities in the future.

He had taken a Double First at Cambridge. That had not stretched him unduly; what had really pleased him was that during this time he had managed with discretion to refine and indulge his private tastes. Even before his obvious academic brilliance had been confirmed in his Finals he was refusing offers of Research Fellowships from several colleges, including his own, as well as one from the Modern History Faculty at Harvard. He also knew that he would have been readily re-admitted into the Royal Navy and could have made a successful career there, if he could have adapted to an ethos that esteemed leadership qualities and raw courage over brains and cunning.

But he had known since before leaving school that his natural and obvious destination, for which he was indisputably well suited – and now in terms of experience and languages exceptionally well-qualified – was the Foreign Office. The Commonwealth Office, in those days a separate Government Department, did not hold the same attraction for him; it employed too many obvious second-raters and was widely viewed as less prestigious.

Cardenas's application to join the FO was warmly welcomed there. He passed easily through the preliminary stages, a powerfully well-qualified applicant; he was even able, through long practice, to simulate in interview, a degree of warmth to complement his indisputably effective mind.

And then the bomb had dropped.

The FO had found out about his membership of the club off the Fulham Road. It was a small, exclusive establishment which catered perfectly to his predilection for certain pleasures of the flesh, the legality of which even the most open-minded would consider questionable at best. He had been careful to register there in a false name, and it was only by the most cruel of coincidences - a man in Personnel Department who knew him and who also knew that the establishment had an evil reputation chanced to see him emerging from there one evening - that the FO had discovered his secret. He had quietly, but firmly been invited to withdraw his application.

The disappointment and humiliation had brought Cardenas to his lowest ebb. He had coldly considered the merits of suicide versus the pain of continuing to live in a world where what he wanted most, what he needed and deserved and had been all but promised, had been wrenched from him with the brutality of an unwanted abortion. The debate in his mind of whether to live or die had been finely balanced, but anger finally prevailed over despair and his growing need for revenge allowed him to overcome this moment of weakness. He would live and by God he'd make them suffer. Who did these people think they were! And he'd perfect and enjoy himself on the way. That club? Nothing to what he'd find in the future. His brain raced. How could he have thought of killing himself? It was absurd. The fight was there to savour.

For three years after withdrawing his Foreign Office candidature he had worked as a lecturer at Harvard, discharging his duties competently and building the foundations for a successful academic career, should he decide to continue in that line, either in the States or back home. But more significantly for his future he had at the same time learned a good deal about economics and investment. He returned to the UK and had applied to, and been rapidly accepted by, the Inland Revenue. With the added dimension of knowledge from working in this field, and very occasionally by using privileged information from his work, Cardenas began very slowly and carefully to play the stock market. Both money and power were going to be essential, he had realised, now that the immediate shock of his failure to join the FO had faded and been replaced by a long-term need for revenge. And money of course was necessary for the other main interest in his life: namely the safe indulgence of his refined leisure tastes.

'Are you sure that I can't tempt you, sir? To a glass of champagne?'

'Thank you, no. I never touch alcohol. But perhaps you could show me how to adjust the foot rest.' Clearly the setting was for a giant, not for someone of slightly below average height like himself.

As she bent over to show him how to shorten the footrest he had to use all his will-power to resist stroking her beautifully-engineered rear. He closed his eyes and commanded his hands to remain motionless and his memory to file the shape. She must be at least thirty, he reckoned, but still had the tight buttocks of a teenager. As she straightened up he congratulated himself on his control; he also consoled himself that Brathby's Vice-Consul was said to be a particularly attractive young lady, on her first posting. Doubtless he would need to interview her.

In a self-satisfied reverie he recalled the woman he had selected to marry: plain and retiring, but rich. She was a widow, and guardian to her young niece. A self-disciplined choice.

He had begun discreetly to cast around for a wife soon after starting work for the Inland Revenue. One aim was to obtain the capital to support his increasingly successful forays into the markets. He also wanted the appearance of respectability that marriage would bring; he had by then decided that after a spell in the Inland Revenue he would transfer to the Security Service, a more challenging arena for his very special talents and ambitions, and eventually offering, he hoped, opportunities to compensate himself for the FO's failure to accept him.

Cardenas remembered how perfectly Althea had fitted the requirement. By chance a colleague had asked him if he could provide financial advice to an acquaintance, a woman whose husband had died leaving his complex affairs in a muddle.

That she was plain was unimportant and her clear preference for staying in the countryside to tend her garden rather than spend time with him in London was a positive advantage. She quickly succumbed to his charms – he remembered with a shudder the deeds he had been expected to perform in those early days – and she savoured the stability that he brought to her life. She happily handed him control of her assets, the exploitation of which in his skilled hands grew into a considerable sum, most of it eventually in his name. A few months after their quiet wedding, Cardenas had exchanged his small flat near Victoria for a large and comfortable apartment in Chelsea. Althea never visited him there, sensing she would not be welcome. To be doubly certain that she would not one day descend on him in London he told her that sometimes his investigations of serious tax evasions required him to pose as a well-to-do bachelor, using a different name. Her presence, whether planned or spontaneous could prejudice these activities. She accepted the story without question, as she did his frequent absences from their country home at the weekends. She was happy enough with her garden, her bridge, her few local friends, and, in a desultory way, looking after her orphaned young niece whom she had adopted. The child made an attractive nine-year old bridesmaid when she remarried; her increasing prettiness as she grew older was an embarrassing contrast to her aunt's drab appearance.

It was soon established that Cardenas slept in the spare room when in the country. The placid Althea had accepted his explanation that stresses and strains at work had reduced his physical needs. The truth was that he could not tolerate, especially with her, the physical rituals of conventional marriage. Even sharing a bedroom was distasteful. Cardenas had correctly divined that however much he distanced himself from her she would not seek a divorce; she was comfortably housed and provided for, and any sexual appetite she might have had had seemed rapidly to have withered.

A whiff of perfume at his side.

'Have you decided what you would like to eat, sir?' Ah, the bum was back.

'A plate of smoked salmon with very thin brown bread and butter, and a glass of chilled lemonade.'

'Nothing else, sir? There's some excellent steak if you'd like that …' she bent over to point it out to him. ' … and of course a choice of fish for main course.'

'I've told you what I want.'

'Very well, sir.' She rapidly straightened up. Yes, even more attractive when angry. And the way her skirt was tailored: delicious!

In the lavatory Cardenas removed all his clothes and washed as thoroughly as the limited space allowed, concentrating on sponging the thick black hair that grew so profusely on his chest and in his arm pits and crotch. He viewed his genitals with satisfaction, trying now to remember the name of that girl, the daughter of a soldier, who had so gratifyingly compared his erect organ to an anti-aircraft gun well dug into thick brushwood. What a satisfying young lady! When she had told him that for obvious reasons she really ought to call him Dick

105

rather than Richard he had responded that he preferred the latter appellation; after all, he had said, Dick is short for Richard but Richard is the long for dick. She had laughed heartily and then kneeled prettily, asking if perhaps all his ammunition were not yet fired. Delightful, but very expensive. She of course, like others at that and similar establishments, never knew his surname – he had learned that lesson long ago in Fulham.

Back in his seat, and savouring his fresh linen, Cardenas consulted his black notebook to refresh his memory about the Embassy staff and what he had learned about them. He would doubtless rapidly uncover who had been responsible for planting the microphone. More interesting, in view of his belief in the near universality of human weakness, would be to see how the denizens of this murky African pond measured up to their responsibilities and – most importantly – how effectively they suppressed imperfection. Here, if anywhere, he would uncover and expose the hypocrisy of the much-vaunted Diplomatic Service.

'Your smoked salmon, sir,' the voice was cooler than previously. 'And your lemonade.' She placed it at his table, and quickly moved on. Not quite cheeky enough for him to lodge a complaint against her; and anyhow that would be complicated since he was travelling under alias.

He ate the first of his sandwiches, took a sip of lemonade and returned to his notes.

Amb. What Cardenas had learned about Brathby over lunch with Hathaway, the Head of West Africa Department, had reinforced his own personal impressions. A management style that was loose-reined but paternalistic. Slow in manner but could be impetuous. Relaxed, well-liked but slightly suspect on that vital quality of 'soundness'. Had been involved, at University, in protests over the Suez invasion not, interestingly enough, on grounds of morality but because of the (as it turned out well-founded) belief that British influence in the area would suffer sharply as a consequence. Married, but unaccompanied; not unusual in that part of the world. His PA was named Penelope Pym; she had overlapped with Brathby for a few months at his previous Post. He had somehow persuaded Personnel to let her accompany him to his new position. Clearly it was possible that Brathby had a personal interest in the woman. But the idea of Brathby as an Ambassador, for God's sake! And, no doubt, demanding his *droit de seigneur* from some plump apology for a PA.

Another note in his book under the heading of Brathby read simply: *Cuthbert, age.* The set-up sounded like the familiar story of a servant kept on too long, afforded too much licence, probably corrupt in several ways. His continued employment was in itself irregular; he must be well over the age limit. Probably Brathby didn't even know his age. But a servant in his position could be a useful source of information on the Ambassador and the other staff. Worth talking to.

Next: *Col S.* Against him the words: *Washington, drink.* It hadn't taken Cardenas long in the MOD to learn that Squires was generally considered to be doing an excellent job in difficult circumstances, and that he was a serious candidate for a top Attaché job in Washington. Barring a recurrence of a drink problem, now under control, he would almost certainly get the position. Yes, Cardenas said to himself, and then doubtless start drinking again when he had what he wanted. Obviously Squires was a typical representative of the more useless echelon of the military caste. Cardenas despised and distrusted drinkers although that hadn't stopped him bringing the good Colonel a bottle of single malt whisky as a present. Certainly not.

Cardenas took twenty minutes off to perform a number of seated exercises which he had perfected over the years. He then rewarded himself by reliving and, by the application of severe mental control, doing so without allowing physical arousal, a number of his most recent sexual experiences. How, he reflected, could he yet further refine those moments of essentially unshared bliss. Perhaps they could only be further enhanced, if at their culmination he were able, he fantasised, to monopolise the act by injaculation rather than ejaculation. Therein would be perfection, the utterly self-contained act of pleasure.

Time for work again. Next on the list: *Elias.* The man was neither fish nor fowl. Why should he be trusted? Even if not involved in *Stuffing* he was likely to be compromised in one way or another. His value to the Embassy was probably exaggerated. No doubt given too much rope by Brathby. These people were obviously living in the days when Elgin was Consul in Constantinople and Cromer High Commissioner in Cairo. *Who do they think they are?* Elias obviously needed his serv-

107

ice terminated. Interestingly, it appeared that his entitlement to a full pension was technically not absolutely watertight, although 'morally irrefutable' (whatever that meant). He wondered if Elias knew... Clearly a point of leverage there.

H of C UN? Cardenas liked what he had heard about Paynton. Cool, efficient, ambitious. Unmarried but no scandals. No known weaknesses. Whether he actually had any or not was unimportant to Cardenas, so long as the man was clever enough to *conceal* them. Hathaway had told him, in confidence, that Paynton was the front-runner for a plum job, on loan to the UN. He believed that Paynton was the man for the job but he would welcome Cardenas's impressions, particularly of his moral fibre.

Intell: PB and *TM? Op.* At a hastily arranged meeting with an MI6 contact who owed him a serious favour Cardenas had got a run-down on Muckle's background. He was the son of a policeman who had been shot dead in the course of duty. As a young man he had been charged with affray while defending a young tart from her pimp. This had not deterred MI6 from recruiting Muckle as a clerk. Muckle was in charge of the Intelligence Station while his reputedly formidable boss Philippa Brainbridge was on leave.

Hathaway had hinted at something which the MI6 contact had not told him, in fact almost certainly did not himself know, that the Station was running a very delicate operation on behalf on the CIA. Hathaway knew no details but doubted that there'd been any political approval granted. Most irregular, Cardenas thought. If an operation receives political clearance then it goes ahead. If it doesn't then it ought not to be happening at all. But if it *is* happening but has not been cleared (the parallel in Cardenas's mind with his own irregular pleasures was obvious) then no outsider should know about it. But Hathaway did. This anomaly was worth looking at. If he, Richard Cardenas, was not to expose this disgraceful conspiracy with the Americans – of all people – then who was?

Cardenas glanced at the rest of his notes. Hathaway had had nothing of interest to say about the Commercial or Information Sections. There was a bright young man in Chancery but Hathaway knew nothing about him. The Consul was an old sweat who, supported ardently by Brathby, had been nagging away for more and better trained visa

108

officers. In response to the Consul's insistence, Hathaway was arranging to send the Consul an official from the Immigration Department in Dover; the formalities were nearly complete. This was a man born in Cyprus of Turkish Cypriot parents and who was brought to the UK as a small boy. Had a most charming Welsh wife and two young daughters. 'Of course,' Hathaway had added, apparently oblivious of Cardenas's lack of interest, 'he's only on secondment to the FCO but it's encouraging for those who are working towards getting greater racial diversity into the office.'

'Better watch out,' Cardenas had replied in what he felt was the humorous tone which Hathaway would appreciate, 'he sounds like a smart young man who will transfer to the Office and finish up as an Ambassador.' Hathaway had laughed, chaffed him in that dreadfully matey way of his that he must have been overdoing the lemonade, and then told him something of real interest: that through some aberration of Personnel Policy Department an extremely attractive young lady had been posted there as Vice-Consul. 'But the Consular and Commercial Sections are in a separate building from the Chancery so you won't need to investigate them so thoroughly, will you!' Hathaway was a ghastly man, but usefully indiscreet.

The aircraft was beginning its long slow descent, heavily buffeted by a tropical storm. The seat belt sign was switched on and passengers asked to return to their seats. The lady with the voluminous robes and an insolent tongue was happily ignoring instructions, and pulling down an enormous suitcase from the overhead rack. The hostess with the lovely rump persuaded her to sit down and fasten her belt. She then took her own seat for landing.

Cardenas wiped them from his mind. He was going to enjoy himself. He had a mission to fulfil: a chance at last to get revenge for the personal disgrace of all those years ago, by exposing the gross inadequacy of those whom the FCO had thought fit to send out here.

5

As he emerged from the aircraft Cardenas saw a plump, immaculately groomed Levantine holding a placard labelled "Mr Berridge". He noticed disapprovingly that some of the other first class passengers were also being similarly met on the tarmac, in what was surely a zone which should be restricted to officials. The man was also *smoking*, as were most of the airport workers …

'Good evening and welcome, Mr Berridge', the man said, treading out his cigarette and offering a warm hand. 'My name is Antoun Elias, Second Secretary at the Embassy. His Excellency sends his warmest regards and hopes you had a good flight.' The man sounded nervous? Doubtless he had much to be nervous about.

'Now keep close to me please, Mr Berridge', he was continuing, 'and I'll soon have you through all this.'

Which task Elias managed admirably, Cardenas had to admit, as the man negotiated their way through the threatening and near-chaotic immigration controls, the apparent lottery of baggage collection and a customs point which would obviously be a tedious and expensive barrier to the uninitiated. But a smile here, the mention of the name 'Zalomo' once, the flashing of a couple of bank notes and they were soon emerging from the air-conditioned cool of the Arrivals Hall into the humid main concourse, his stamped passport safely in his pocket and his suitcase carried by a slightly puffing Elias. No wonder the man was out of condition; a smoker, and from the look of him a drinker as well.

A tall fair-haired man accompanied by a uniformed driver, was waiting for them.

'Richard Berridge? My name is Francis Paynton.' The man looked relaxed and in good shape. 'Welcome to Africa.'

'I think Africa began at Gatwick' replied Cardenas, lightly shaking the man's firm, dry hand and feeling an immediate warmth towards him. Most unusual. What was it about the man?

Out of the corner of his eye he saw the large lady from first class getting into a car and was reminded of what she'd said to him: 'Tell me Paynton, what does "Don't give me dat grammar" mean?'

Paynton laughed. 'It depends on the context – let us say that it is a forthright way of suggesting that you drop any ideas you may have of superiority based on culture, colour or social position.' He turned slightly: 'Would you agree with that Mr Elias? You're the expert, after all.'

'Yes, Mr Paynton, that is a good translation.' He handed Cardenas's suitcase to the driver. 'Good evening then, Mr Berridge. I shall perhaps see you in the Embassy tomorrow. Good evening, Mr Paynton.' Elias disappeared into the crowds.

The driver carefully manoeuvred the car onto the main road from the airport and the two men sat back to enjoy the effective air-conditioning.

'That Elias man was helpful. Seems useful. Got me through without fuss.' It could be valuable to get a feel for the relationship between Elias and Paynton.

'Well, it *is* his job. After all these years it would be scandalous if he couldn't arrange these things.'

'Yes, point taken. Why isn't he travelling into town with us? Got his own car?'

'I brought him to the airport with me'. Paynton didn't seem to resent the question. 'He'll find his own way back. There are sure to be contacts at the airport he'll want to visit first anyhow.'

'Of course.' Perhaps Paynton had made it clear to Elias that he wasn't welcome on the trip back. Quite understandable.

'Now, Berridge, your accommodation. We have arranged for you to stay with the MA, Colonel Jack Squires. You'll be well looked after there. Jenny, Jack's wife, can be relied on for that. In the morning Jack'll bring you into the Embassy. H.E. is busy this evening but is looking forward to seeing you tomorrow.'

Perhaps he is, perhaps he isn't …

Night was falling fast now and those cars with working lights had them switched on. They made their slow and difficult passage along the potholed road. The driver spoke up: 'Look Mr Francis, over dere, on the right, anudder *tiefman* done quench.' He was pointing to what Cardenas at first thought was a pile of black rags underneath an old tyre. Closer examination showed it to be the charred remains of a corpse.

'Translation and explanation, Paynton?' This was proving to be an interesting country.

'*Tiefman* is the pidgin English for *thief man*. What we have just seen is the result of so-called "necklacing". Invented in South Africa,

I believe. One or more tyres are secured around the victim's neck and he is then soaked in petrol and set alight. Officially the government deplores the practice but nobody is ever arrested for it. In an under-policed country such rough justice is both unsurprising and useful. Of course you can never be absolutely sure that the mob gets the right man …'

Cardenas noted approvingly that Paynton was talking as coolly as if lecturing to an evening class. 'But presumably the police themselves catch some of these *tiefmen*. What do they do with them?'

'They shoot them. After due process of law; there is never any doubt about their guilt – for some reason they always confess.'

Was that a note of cynical resignation in Paynton's voice? Or relish?

'Interestingly enough,' Paynton was continuing, lowering his voice with a warning glance at the driver, 'there are going to be some official executions here on Friday. The victims include *tiefmen* who took part – more accurately, who have *confessed* to having taken part – in the rape and murder of a *Uminco* employee's wife a couple of months back.'

Cardenas had heard nothing of this in London.

'The locals are keen for us to be represented' he said quietly. 'Difficult decision for H.E.. Clearly he can't go himself. I imagine he'll send Jack Squires. That'd be a neat solution; *en poste* he's technically a diplomat, but if the Office makes a fuss we can point out that his parent organisation is the MOD.'

'Or I suppose Bernard Brathby might send you, Paynton. How would you feel about that?' Taking his cue from Paynton, Cardenas was also speaking softly.

'I should go of course, if so ordered. But I wouldn't enjoy it. Not that the criminals are getting more than they deserve, even if not technically guilty of the specific offences for which they have been convicted.'

The voice was devoid of emotion. But 'enjoy' was an interesting word to for him to have selected.

They rode in slow but companionable silence for a while, the road dissecting a sprawling shanty town on the approaches to the outer suburbs. It was Cardenas who spotted the next body, a man on the pavement lying on his back, his bare arms swollen and facial features melting. 'Another *tiefman*?' asked Cardenas.

'Not dat one' the driver spoke up. 'Him killed in accident. He dere long time. Nobody claim him. He be dere till he go bang.'

'I believe the technical term for his condition', interposed Paynton, 'is deliquescent.'

'He lucky' the driver said. 'He go to heaven in one piece. Sometimes de witch doctors cut off head to make medcin.'

Ten minutes later and Colonel Squires's night watchman was unchaining the compound gate for the car.

Squires was coming forward to shake his hand. Cardenas saw a rather tall, red-faced, oyster-eyed man with a gingerish moustache.

'Welcome to the humble abode, Berridge. Octavius here will take your bag. Come on in.' He addressed Paynton with a throaty cough, 'How about you, Francis, you staying for a drink?'

'Thank you Jack, but I have a reception to attend, so I'll take the car straight on there. Goodnight to you both.'

Once inside Cardenas looked around him with interest. After what he'd seen on the road the obvious comfort of the house was a welcome surprise. And now here was his hostess – middle-aged, thin-faced, and plain, he noted – approaching to greet him.

6

Night was closing in rapidly. Brathby got up from his desk in the Residence study to stretch. He looked out of the window. For once it wasn't raining and something faintly resembling a sunset could be seen over the compound gatehouse.

For the past hour Brathby had been ploughing through the backlog of work that Violet had loaded into his briefcase when the Chancery had closed. Most of the papers she had included he certainly needed to read, or at least skim – a monthly review of Commercial Department's activities, exchanges of telegrams with the Home Office over visa applications, an updated summary of the Ayumba affair as seen from London, a report on religious tensions in the North, half a dozen local newspapers. But there would have been others, routine administrative matters and other such ephemera, of which Polly would either have prepared a summary for him to read in the morning or just fed through the shredder.

A mistake to be thinking about Polly if he wanted to get through any more work before Dr Ali Karim-Bux arrived. She had been on his mind all day – poor girl, she had looked so sick, so shattered this morning – but he had successfully resisted telephoning her. Through Violet he had sent her some books and a cake and a message that she must let him know if she needed anything, and that he hoped she would soon feel better. He had allowed himself to speak of her with warmth and concern, as was appropriate concerning a valued colleague, but not in such a way, he was sure, that Violet could detect that his feelings for Polly were a good deal stronger than that.

Brathby put his papers away, picked up the beer which had sat untouched on his desk all this time and retired to his cane chair. While waiting for Karim-Bux to arrive he would think about whether he was going to recommend that his medical contract with the Embassy should be renewed.

In his favour was that Karim-Bux was well-qualified and was a good clinician. He had a large practice in town, but was always readily available if the Embassy needed him. His surgery plate proclaimed him as 'Medical Adviser to the British Embassy'; the *cachet* was certainly worth more to him that the accompanying modest retainer. His main loyalty was doubtless to himself (and perhaps to the extended family in Pakistan who lived on his remittances there). But, Brathby reckoned, Karim-Bux also had some genuine liking for, and loyalty to, the British. And one never knew when one might need a discreet and reliable doctor.

On the other hand – a final thought as he heard the door bell over the noisy air-conditioning – there was always the chance of minor embarrassment to the Embassy if Karim-Bux's less orthodox medical activities came to light. Brathby was aware that he occasionally performed skilled but totally illegal abortions for young women from rich Muslim families; he was also an expert at the arcane art of repairing hymens for intended brides – known in the trade as 'revirginisation.'

A tap on the door and Cuthbert shuffled in:

'Doctor done come, sah. Say he have appointment.'

'Show him in, Cuthbert.' He walked over to greet his guest. 'Good evening, Dr Karim-Bux. Now what can Cuthbert here get you to drink?'

'And good evening to you, Your Excellency. You are so kind to be receiving me. Most kind …'

'Do sit down doctor. Now, to drink …?'

'Well, Your Excellency, you know I am usually abstemious, my religion you know, but perhaps in view of the abnormal weather …'

'Cuthbert,' Brathby interrupted. 'I think the good doctor would like a large ginger ale, half of which should be whisky.' He turned to Karim-Bux. 'A Lahore ginger, I believe it's called.'

'Most kind, Your Excellency, not that I often …'

'Of course not.'

'Your good health, Your Excellency', Dr Karim-Bux said, taking his first large swallow a minute or so later. 'I am saying that both conventionally and medically.' He gave a little laugh.

'And yours, doctor.'

'I am hoping your staff are all being well at present, Your Excellency. Are you having news of that person we had to be sending back to the United Kingdom?'

'The young man from the Information Section who caught malaria? Yes, he's doing well, fully recovered I hear.' And not yet replaced, dammit, he added silently.

'I am pleased to be hearing it. It is so very important that the precautions are being taken against the catching of these pesky tropical diseases. In particular the need to follow the rules over the regular ingestion of Paludrine tablets to counter the malaria cannot be over-estimated, Your Excellency.'

'Yes indeed, doctor.' The ginger ale seemed to be fuelling the doctor's volubility.

'You have nobody in the Embassy sick at the present, I trust, Your Excellency?'

'I believe not, not seriously I mean, or of course you would know.' After a moment he added: 'Actually my PA is taking a few days off, feeling slightly under the weather – one of those female things, apparently. I impressed on her to call you if she felt at all concerned.'

'Oh, Miss Pym not so well, I'm so sorry. To be telling you the truth, Your Excellency, I am seldom trusting a self-diagnosis of menstrual complication if there is no history of such matter. Better, I think, Your Excellency if I am calling on her to give her once-over. Perhaps after we are finishing our talk this evening ...'

'No, doctor.' Brathby cut in. 'Very thoughtful of you, but the decision must be hers. I am sure she will call you if necessary.' The last thing he wanted was for Polly to think he was interfering.

The Ambassador took a sip of his beer and changed the subject. 'Dr Karim-Bux, the main reason I asked you over for a chat this evening is that Miss Pym said that you were asking about the renewal of your contract with the Embassy.'

'Yes indeed, Your Excellency. Is there any news yet on this matter?'

'Nothing definite, I'm afraid, doctor. I think you are aware that the Foreign and Commonwealth Office has taken over direct responsibility for such matters. All part of the latest economy drive, it seems.'

'Yes, Your Excellency, I am understanding, but I am sure that the FCO will be according great weight to your recommendation.'

'Perhaps.' Brathby replied. 'Am I am right in thinking, doctor, that you plan to stay on in this country until you retire?'

'Most definitely, Your Excellency, oh yes most definitely. I could not be affording to leave my good practice here, of which of course an esteemed element is your Embassy.'

Cuthbert appeared at the door. 'Scuse, sah. De Colonel's driver he come. Say dat de man from England done come. He at Colonel's house. De telephone, he go quench. And I breeng dis udder hot ginger for de doctor.'

'Thank you, Cuthbert. Please tell the driver to tell the Colonel that I have received the message and look forward to seeing Mr Berridge in the morning.'

When Cuthbert had left the room Dr Karim-Bux took a small sip from his second drink. 'There is one other delicate point, Your Excellency ...' he said tentatively.

'Yes, doctor?' Karim-Bux looked ill at ease.

'Am I being right in assuming, Your Excellency, that those establishments in the town, so-called bars but in fact where the low-moral girls entertain men, that you are not permitting your staff to be frequenting these places? In short that they are *forbidden* to be visited by persons from the Embassy?'

Who else but the good doctor could take so long to ask if brothels were out of bounds?

'Yes, why?'

'Of course I would not be mentioning this to anyone else except you, Your Excellency, you can be assured of that. It would not be a correct action. But in view of your position, being in the *loco parentis*, as we are saying, for your young men.'

'I'm not sure I know where this is leading, doctor?' He wasn't going to make it easy for him.

Dr Karim-Bux had both hands round his drink and leant forward looking distinctly uncomfortable, Brathby was pleased to see. 'Your Excellency, it is just that I am worrying that one of your staff may be endangering his health in one of these places.'

'Really?' Would he go so far to produce a name?

'Perhaps I should not be telling you this, Your Excellency ...'

'But you are telling me, aren't you doctor?'

'It so happens, Your Excellency, that this young man is not in the event suffering from a sexually-transmitted disease but he came to me fearing that he did. From this I was inferring his frequenting of what Your Excellency might describe as a house of ill-repute, and he confirmed this.'

117

'A reasonable inference, doctor; and if I asked, you would no doubt tell me the name of this young man?'

'Oh yes indeed, Your Excellency; if you insisted.' The doctor seemed more relaxed now.

'In which case', Brathby replied 'I shan't insist, and I'm sure it will be a relief to you not to have broken a professional confidence.' The Ambassador stood up and moved towards the door. 'So, thank you for calling to see me, Dr Karim-Bux, and be assured that I shall let you know about the renewal or otherwise of your contract as soon as I can.'

'Thank you, Your Excellency, for your time and the refreshment and … I'm sure you realised that it would be only to you that I would ever be talking about the … yes, goodbye, Your Excellency.'

'Good night, doctor.'

'You are sure you don't want me to call on Miss Pym, Your Excellency? I could easily do so.'

'No, thank you' Brathby replied firmly. 'Not until asked.'

The door closed behind Dr Karim-Bux.

A few moments later Brathby went to the kitchen. 'There's no need for you to wait up, Cuthbert. Mr Singleton won't be here until half past nine.'

'Yes, Master. De cold supper here in fridge and de table laid. Wot of de wine; you want new bottle or de leftover from last night?'

'Neither thank you, Cuthbert.' He smiled. 'Mr Joe always drinks beer and I shall do the same.'

Cuthbert pulled his ear in a gesture that Brathby knew signalled frustration. 'Of course he drink beer, Master, of course. I know dese tings but dey sometimes fall from head. I sorry. I too sorry.'

'Cuthbert, it's not important. I'm not angry. Not at all. It is a small, unimportant thing. Do you understand?'

'Yes, Master.'

'But I am concerned, Cuthbert, that these last few days you are not happy, I think. Is something wrong; can I help? Is it something to do with Eventide?'

Cuthbert looked exhausted and Brathby gestured him to sit down. 'No, Master. Eventide fine. Me fine too. No problem for me.'

'All right, Cuthbert. You go off duty now. Mr Joe and I will look after ourselves. Say goodnight to Eventide from me.'

A light briefly flickered in Cuthbert's eyes: 'He fine boy, Master, fine boy.'

'And you are a fine man, Cuthbert. Now go and rest.'

7

When Octavius had brought in the after dinner coffee Jenny Squires announced that she had letters to write, and would take the opportunity of an early night. She thanked their guest again for the presents he had brought, checked that she knew his requirements for breakfast and withdrew, leaving the room with a slightest of glances towards the drinks cupboard, a warning message that her husband correctly interpreted.

As the men resumed their seats Squires glanced around him with some satisfaction. The table, prepared by Octavius under Jenny's relentless supervision, had gleamed with silver and glassware, the latter largely ornamental as it had turned out. The dining room furniture was splendidly polished and his impressive collection of silver trophies, presentation boxes and signed photographs displayed to best advantage.

'Shall I pour your coffee, Richard?' he asked. The ice broken, Squires's guest was 'Richard' – at his request.

'Please, Colonel. Black with no sugar.' Though he himself was not yet 'Jack'. One had one's standards.

The food had been the best available to them – they still had meat from the last Kenyan delivery as well as some New Zealand butter. But as for drink, available in copious quantities, it seemed that this Berridge chappie didn't touch the stuff at all – he had refused a pre-dinner gin, and also wine at dinner. In fact – made you laugh to think about it really – the only one of them to have had a drink at all that evening was Jenny, who had had a couple of glasses of her favourite white.

Squires himself was now on his third day without a drink. As soon as that *Stuffing* device was discovered – and helped by his dreadful hangover that morning – he had gone into battle mode: no drink, easy on the food, take a spot of exercise and keep your wits about you. Over the years he had learned the value of this simple formula. The need to be sober and alert had of course been reinforced when the Ambassador had asked him to host this Berridge fellow.

So, while waiting that evening for his visitor to arrive, Squires hadn't taken even a small snifter. Mind you the way Jenny had batted on about how ruinous it could be for him to be drunk in front of this mystery man had nearly driven him to it. She couldn't take yes for an answer.

So it was a sober Squires that eyed his guest, a rather under-sized, but well-proportioned and obviously very fit, man neatly dressed in white shirt and dark suit, and carefully manicured. Could be ex-Guards? No, too *slick*. And he made Squires feel slightly uneasy, he wasn't sure why.

'Little something to go with the coffee? Perhaps a drop of this fine-looking malt you so kindly brought.'

'Most kind but I never take alcohol.'

'Really! You mean never! Not even a glass of champers at celebrations, that sort of thing?'

'No. However, don't let that deter you, Colonel. I was reliably informed that that particular malt *is* rather special.'

'Oh, I know of it. Absolutely top of the range stuff. I'll save it to take in small doses on special occasions. But nothing now, not that this isn't a special occasion, but one finds that one needs a clear head in this climate, and to knock off the stuff altogether for a week from time to time, you know.' Perhaps he was overdoing it a bit, carrying on like this? He refilled their cups and looked across the table interrogatively. 'You know, small thing puzzling me, Richard.'

'What is that, Colonel?'

'The malt. Did you bring it especially for *me*, or for whoever was going to put you up? I mean you didn't know you were going to be staying here, did you?' A bit puzzling, that.

'No mystery there. I knew from the diplomatic list that there was a senior British officer here as Military Attaché, so I brought the bottle as a mark of respect.'

'Well that's jolly nice, I must say. And very good of you to have brought the other things too – you were well briefed, if I may say so.'

'Not too difficult. London told me that bacon, marmite and the latest newspapers would be acceptable wherever I was staying.'

'Spot on.' Squires looked over at the bottle, half made to rise and then whipped himself back into line. 'Now tell me Richard, how can one help over this microphone affair – fill you in on the background, that sort of thing?'

'Very kind but I think I'll leave that until tomorrow.' He paused: 'But it'd be helpful though to get some sort of feel in advance for what

it's like to live here, how difficult it is to get supplies, the daily struggle, that sort of thing. Whether there's a threat, or a perceived threat,
to life and limb, how you cope with the climate, and so on.' He sat
back.

Squires began to talk. Obviously it would be useful to give this
Berridge chap a spot of historical background, mentioning early ex-
plorers, invaders, slaves, traders, all that. Then he spoke of the climate
and its effect on health, especially on one's energy levels. He briefly
covered the run up to Independence, tribal conflicts, the civil wars, the
successful and failed *coups*. Then how the bureaucracy was riddled
with corruption, what sort of bribes – 'they call it *dash* here' – had to
be paid to secure any contract.

It was refreshing that the chap should show such an interest in these
matters. All too often visitors had a much narrower vision, just wanting to do the business and get out.

'So life in the Embassy can be difficult then, Colonel. Bad climate,
shortages and so on – can't be much fun?'

'Ah yes you're right in a way. But the vital point, one really can't
over-emphasise it, is that *morale* is high. Simple reason – we have a
first rate Commanding Officer.' No harm in putting in a plug for
Brathby, especially when it was true.

'Yes, that must be important. Being Ambassador here must be demanding. Especially, am I right, since his wife is not here?'

'Yes, she's back home sweating away in some laboratory, I believe.'

'But he copes without her, socially I mean?'

'Oh yes that's not really a problem. Jenny has acted as hostess for
him on several occasions, also the Commercial Councillor's wife. Even
his PA, Polly, who is a most competent woman.'

'And a good support to him, evidently?'

'Yes, indeed. Can't do too much for him, absolutely first class. Very
attractive too. Then of course there's old Cuthbert, a great asset.'

'Cuthbert, Colonel?'

'His Steward. Been here since God was a subaltern. Absolutely
devoted to H.E. Excellent man. Getting on a bit now of course, though
it'd be a foolish, as well as a cruel, man who'd give him the push. Until
he wants to go of course. Sort of chap who knows where the bodies are
buried.' He laughed.

'Must be hard work for an old man, being H.E.'s Steward I mean.'

How refreshingly interested in everything this Berridge chappie was. 'Well, matter of fact he's training up a young lad to help him.'

'Oh so there's an Assistant Steward, is there?'

'You mean young Eventide – that's his name! He'd be tickled pink to be called that. No – he's no official status as far as I know. He's just a boy, dosses down somewhere in Cuthbert's quarters, unpaid but never short of pocket money. I think H.E. and his chum Joe Singleton, the *Uminco* manager you know, look after his schooling and all that. Anyhow it works. Brathby's fond of the lad, Cuthbert dotes on him, and he's learning fast. Everybody happy. Now ...' He stood up. 'More coffee?'

'Thank you, yes.'

Cardenas took a sip. 'Tell me, Colonel, the man who helped me through the formalities at the airport, Elias, what is his status in the Embassy? Is he an Attaché, or what?'

'Oh, chum Antoun? Our Mr Fixit. He's in the book as Second Secretary so he must be in the Diplomatic Service, one supposes. Never thought about it, you know. Bit of a rogue of course, typical Syrian or Lebanese or whatever he is, but gets things done – as you found out this evening.'

'Yes, indeed.'

'What's more he's always popping up with useful bits of info. God knows where he gets it from. Seems to know everyone in town – yes, very useful fellow.'

'Well paid for his pains, one hopes?'

'Imagine so, though whether he gets Overseas Allowances, like the rest of us – I've really no idea. Never thought about it. But he lives well. He and that rather strange German wife of his had us round to supper soon after we arrived. Did us very well. Even produced a sound malt. Not as good as the one you brought of course, Richard,' he added with a laugh. He couldn't remember when he'd talked so much before without a few glasses inside him. This Berridge man had a knack ...

'Yes, Elias did well at the airport. In no time he'd got me through all the controls and handed me over to Francis Paynton. Now *he's* a man who's got a tough job to do here, I suspect.'

'As Head of Chancery, you mean? Yes indeed. Responsible to H.E.

for all the general management as well as doing much of the political work. Competent man, I'm sure of that.' Squires didn't like Paynton but that was irrelevant, he wasn't going to run him down in front of Berridge, however well-disposed the fellow seemed to be. And it was true that Paynton, however disagreeable, was effective.

'Well he's going to be even busier now I'm here, delving into the background and so forth,' replied Cardenas, with a half smile. 'But I hope not to disrupt the normal workings of the Embassy too much. I imagine most departments are fairly busy, aren't they? It seems to me, from what I've seen so far, that actually surviving here is difficult enough.'

The chap really was very understanding.

'It must be a great help to Bernard Brathby to have a man of your experience here to advise him,' his guest continued, 'someone who's seen it all before as it were. He must rely on you considerably.'

Squires cleared his throat diffidently. 'Well ... of course there are a number of other old hands he can also look to. The Commercial Counsellor's had several postings in Africa and knows the form. And of course there's Bill, the Consul; he can seem a bit of a grouch at times but he's solid gold all through. Really cares about his work, don't you know. Constantly worried that he's too short-staffed to keep up with the visa work; always on about how the wrong'uns may be getting into the UK and the really deserving people aren't.' Squires realised that all this time they'd been talking he hadn't even thought about having a drink.

'It's a pity', Cardenas said, 'that the Head of the Intelligence Station is not here at the moment. I'm told she's a very bright lady, well-regarded by all.' He looked interrogatively at Squires.

'Oh yes, dear Philippa. They don't come brighter than her, I can tell you. Mind like a razor, always in the picture – and always willing to help out. Nothing to look at, poor woman, but then one can't have everything, can one? A shame you won't meet her, she's not due back from leave for another ten days or so, I believe.'

'It was her clerk, of course, wasn't it, who discovered the microphone I've come out to investigate? Sharp young man, is he?'

'Tom Muckle's a good chap. Bit of a rough diamond, but amusing and competent. Always busy, but always a smile.'

124

'Busy even with the boss away. Is that normal?'

'It seems so. What he gets up to is not my business of course.' And it had been a slightly unusual question for Berridge to ask. He peered into the empty coffee pot. 'I say, I'm neglecting my duties as host. Would you like more coffee or perhaps a cold drink?'

'Just a tonic please, Colonel.'

Squires rang the bell and Octavius soon appeared.

'Yes, sah? Dis coffee done finish. You want I make more?'

'No thank you, Octavius. Time for cold drinks now. Two iced tonics please; you can put them in the study.'

'*Two* tonic, Master? You no want de whisky?'

'*No*, thank you, Octavius.' Did the chap really not understand? 'Just put the drinks in the study and then fall out.'

In the study his guest admired a large photograph in a silver frame. 'May I look? Is there perhaps a younger Jack Squires here somewhere in the picture?'

'Well as a matter of fact – yes. And do please call me Jack. I should have said so earlier. Staff College 1960. Not a bad year, one is told. You'll spot me there in the second row, yes just there on the right.'

'Interesting. Anyone else there I should recognise?'

'Archibald Bruce-Harrison perhaps, Lieutenant-General, now in the War House. Most distinguished man. Then ...' He ran through a dozen or so others who had had interesting and successful careers. Really, this Berridge man was interested in everything. What a companionable chap.

'But you yourself, Jack; done pretty well, haven't you? Prestigious and important job here. By the way, do you retire from here? Or is there another job to come?'

'Well, Richard, one is going to have to move on in a few months. Will be sorry to leave in a way but that's the way of the Service. One goes where one's sent.' Presumably it was the same for Berridge.

'That'll be to the MOD, will it? Senior Post no doubt. Glad to be home after a long spell out here, I expect?"

'Could be, I suppose. Or of course one may be offered another Attaché Post; after all one has the experience. There's a faint possibility that a suitable Post in Washington might be coming up at the right time.'

'You'd like that?'

'Well it wouldn't be altogether unwelcome, shall we say.' That was an understatement.

'So how highly do you rate your chances of getting the job? Have you been sounded out about it yet?'

'No, no, certainly not.' This Berridge seemed a good egg, but sometimes just a touch probing.

'Right, I'm for bed now, if you'll excuse me. An excellent dinner and I've much enjoyed our chat.' Cardenas stood up. 'I reckon Bernard Brathby's been lucky to have had you here to see him in. Perhaps he'll put you up for a gong. I'm sure you deserve one.'

'You're very kind to say so, Richard, but the thought has never crossed my mind.' Not half it hadn't. 'Now have you everything you want? Good, let's turn in then.'

8

'I hope the coffee's the right strength, sir?' Violet was standing rather awkwardly a few paces from the Ambassador's desk.

'It's fine, thank you. Now do please sit down and bring me up to date.'

'Well, the Colonel telephoned about twenty minutes ago to say that he and his visitor were just leaving, so depending on the traffic they should be here any moment.' She paused. 'The overnight incoming telegrams are in the yellow folder. I've also brought in two of the Inspection files you said you wanted.'

'Good.' Though not a word yet about Polly. Was she teasing him? Almost unimaginable. No, more likely being professional, taking the day's business first.

'The Commercial Counsellor would like a word some time, sir. Wants the two of you to get together with the British Council team to discuss developments about the Engineering Books Exhibition planned for April.'

'Really?' Not the most exciting prospect.

'Also the Consul looked in. Wants to extend the Visa Office hours, and also asked if we've got the money to take on another part-time helper? He left this Minute for you.'

'Thank you.' He paused briefly. 'So the telephones were down again last night, I understand.'

'Oh yes sorry, sir; otherwise I'd have called about Polly.'

'How is she?' Come on girl, out with it.

'Difficult to tell really, sir. I mean, I'm sure she's not ill. If she were she'd have called Dr Bux, she's not stupid. More like ...'

'Er, period problems, that sort of thing, do you mean?' He got the words out almost brusquely to cover his embarrassment.

'No, sir, I'm sure it's not that. I asked her and she said no. About the only straight answer I did get from her.'

'So what *is* wrong? There must be something to explain it. I can't believe she's exhausted from over-work, anything like that.'

'She just seems listless and - I know you'll think this strange, sir - it's almost as if she's frightened. I'm worried about her. '

'She *must* have had a shock. I felt it at the time. But from what?'

He found that he had risen from his desk and was pacing up and down. So much for concealing the depth of his concern for Polly.

But Violet had no more news and soon returned to her, or rather Polly's, office to get on with her duties.

A few minutes later there was a tap on the door and Brathby opened it to admit a spruce and smiling Colonel Squires and his house guest.

'Morning, Ambassador.' Jack did look well this morning! 'May I introduce Richard Berridge? Richard, this is our Ambassador, Bernard Brathby.'

'Thank you, Jack,' Brathby responded. 'Actually, Berridge and I have met once before, in London.'

'I say, Richard, you didn't mention that last night.' Jack looked puzzled and slightly aggrieved.

Brathby stepped in quickly. 'Probably Richard decided it would be unprofessional to do so because, as you know, he is here under alias. That was the reason, wasn't it, Richard?'

Cardenas nodded. Squires looked partly mollified and said that if H.E. and ... er ... Berridge would excuse him he'd better be off now to his office to see what awaited him.

'Many thanks, Colonel,' Brathby said, 'we'll have a word when Berridge and I have got his programme sorted out.' Then, as the Colonel was leaving, Brathby remembered: 'Oh yes and would you keep tomorrow morning free in case I need you. '

Squires assured him that he would be available if required, and left the room.

'Coffee, Richard?' He didn't particularly wish to use the man's first name but it seemed both pedantic and faintly ridiculous to address him by his alias.

'Black, Ambassador.' He was on his feet looking, round the room.

'"Bernard" will do, when we're alone anyhow.'

'Very well, "Bernard".'

'Won't you sit down? This is West Africa after all; never stand if you can sit, never sit if you can ...' he faded out. The man was already making him uneasy.

'So where was the microphone?' Cardenas asked abruptly.

'Just here, behind this bookcase.' Brathby was on his feet, pointing it out.

'Was it photographed in place?'

'I don't know. You'll have to ask Muckle about that.'

'Is the man reliable?'

'In what way?' What was he getting at?

'I mean, can I depend on his account of what happened, of how and when he found the device and what he then did with it? Could he have any motive for embellishing his report?' He was now at the window, looking out towards the swamp.

'Muckle is extremely professional. You can rely on his honesty and accuracy.' Brathby was fighting hard to conceal his annoyance at Cardenas's questions about Muckle. He regained his chair and spoke calmly, addressing Cardenas's back.

'Now there are a number of points to settle before I hand you over to the Head of Chancery.' He paused and added more sharply: 'Richard, unless there's something particularly fascinating out there will you *please* come and sit down.'

'Very well, if you insist.' He gave a thin smile, presumably intended as conciliatory. 'Reaction from too much sitting on the flight over, perhaps.'

'Did you have a good flight?' Continuous turbulence with any luck.

'Yes.'

'Everything satisfactory for your reception, I hope?' Beaten up by Immigration, strip-searched by Customs? Stop being childish, Brathby told himself.

'Your man Elias met me. He seems to be on very friendly terms with many officials at the airport.'

It was unclear to Brathby whether Cardenas was speaking approvingly, or the opposite. He wasn't going to ask. 'Paynton was presumably there as well. Did you have a good journey into town?' At all costs he must observe the courtesies.

'Yes. There were no problems. Very properly Paynton didn't discuss *Stuffing* in the car, in front of the driver, but he was interesting and informative.'

'Good.'

'There is one point I wish to talk about, Bernard, before we come to the main purpose of my visit.'

'Go ahead.'

'Henry Hathaway, Head of the West Africa Department, told me in confidence that Paynton is being considered for an important job, where steady nerves are essential.' He paused. 'You know this, of course.'

'Yes, indeed.' But Hathaway shouldn't have discussed this sensitive matter with Cardenas. It had nothing to do with the *Stuffing* investigation

'He said that Paynton was likely to be nominated, that you would probably be in favour, and that all others concerned considered him suitable.'

'So?' Why was Cardenas raising this at all, he wondered.

'Well, mine not to question why,' Cardenas said lightly. 'Hathaway just said that in view of the importance of the position for which Paynton was being considered, he would welcome a further opinion, i.e. mine.'

'Of course Hathaway has a perfect right to brief you in this way although how he expects you to ...'

'In the car yesterday evening,' Cardenas overrode him, 'Paynton mentioned the executions scheduled for Friday, tomorrow that is now. He said there was pressure on you for the Embassy to be represented and that he expected you to send Colonel Squires as an observer.'

'Yes, I've more or less decided to do that.'

'May I suggest that you send Paynton instead? The way in which he comports himself would be a useful indicator of his likely behaviour under pressure.'

Blast the man's cheek. Hateful, interfering little man. But then Brathby's sense of balance swung back into play; it was in fact by no means a bad idea. Yes, and it would do Paynton no harm to be faced by such stark reality. He was half-inclined to accept the idea. Moreover it would spare Jack Squires an unpleasant duty. He made up his mind quickly. 'Right, I'll ask him.'

'*Ask* him?' one of those dark little eyebrows was raised.

'Yes, *ask* him. I'm not going to *order* anyone to attend an execution, more accurately a number of executions.' The man seemed to lack a basic sense of decency.

'Point taken.' Cardenas was essaying a smile, it seemed. 'Though when you're an Ambassador, asking and telling aren't much different, are they? But I hear what you say.'

How Brathby loathed that expression. However, time to press on. 'Excuse me a moment'. He dialled Paynton's number on the intercom, said he'd like to see him briefly later in the morning and would he please keep tomorrow morning and lunchtime free until they had spoken. No, no need to come immediately; wait until he had Mr Berridge launched on his enquiry. He would be bringing Mr Berridge to him in a few minutes.

'What's the problem, Bernard? *I* can tell, er ... *ask*, him when I see him.'

'No, Richard. *I* will speak to him, to *ask* him. Do you understand?' The man was intolerable. Not material for the Diplomatic Service, not even on secondment.

'As you wish, Bernard.'

'Yes ...' He took breath. 'Now the investigation and your programme. Paynton has all the relevant papers, logs and so forth waiting for you, whenever you want them. Miss Brainbridge, as you know, is on leave; we have arranged for you to use her Chancery room, her front office as it were. Here is the key.'

'Yes'. Cardenas took it.

'The staff have all been told to co-operate fully with your enquiries. Obviously the less disruption to normal working patterns the better, but you have your job to do.'

'I have indeed.'

'I expect you will wish to concentrate your efforts on this building but the Commercial and Consular staff, housed in the same compound, are also warned that you may wish to speak to them, either over there or in your temporary office here.' Then a question: 'I don't suppose you have any idea how long it is likely to take you to clear up this business? I wouldn't have thought more than a few days.' Or was this wishful thinking? And how could the man know before he'd even started?

'Two or three days maximum. I'd expect to leave on the Saturday or Sunday flight. These matters are usually quite straightforward.'

'Yes indeed. In fact ...'

'In fact, what?' The man had an arrogant sneer on his face.

In fact why send out this bloody man for a simple task that Brathby could have done himself. But Cardenas was here now; better accept the situation and get it over with minimum damage.

131

'I was going to ask what other facilities you will need. Are you likely, for example, to have much telegraphic traffic to send? Or receive for that matter?'

'There'll be nothing coming in for me and I shall send nothing. I shall keep an outline of my findings here,' he tapped the notebook in his pocket, 'and make sense of it and write it all up in London.'

So that nobody in the Embassy would know what he was reporting. That was obvious. 'As you wish. Do you envisage wishing to see the local police? I imagine it is to cater for such a possibility that you are travelling under a false name.'

'It's unlikely, and I don't suppose you'd welcome it.'

It seemed that for once Cardenas was considering something apart from his own convenience.

'But if I did need to see Zalomo, would you yourself arrange it, or should I get Elias to do it? I understand he knows him well. Very well.'

Cardenas was certainly well briefed. But his emphasis on Elias's relationship with Zalomo was clearly out of order and designed to provoke. Brathby declined to show his anger. 'Try Elias first. He has, *with my full approval*, a good working arrangement with the Commissioner. If he fails, come to me. In the unlikely event that you need to see the Commissioner that is.' It was fairly clear to Brathby that the sole purpose of Cardenas raising this point had been to probe him on Elias's friendship with Zalomo. Time now to get the remaining matters settled and then pass him over to Paynton.

Oppressed by Cardenas's presence, and suddenly swept by a longing for Polly, Brathby moved rapidly to conclude the meeting. 'Now, your programme, outside of your enquiries that is. I had hoped to give you lunch myself today but unexpectedly I have to go out' – how surprised the Sri Lankan Consul would be when Brathby arrived in person, rather than send a representative, for a buffet lunch and photographic exhibition of recently discovered early ship-building artefacts – 'but I shall arrange that my Steward, Cuthbert, prepares a light meal for you upstairs in the Residence.'

'That will suit me. I shall not want to interrupt my enquiries for long.'

'Antoun Elias and his wife Bertha are very keen to entertain you this evening. I thought you'd find that interesting, so I provisionally accepted on your behalf.'

'Yes, that's all right.'

Brathby had been unsure how Cardenas would react to the suggestion but surprisingly he seemed happy enough about it.

'*Bertha*. Wife German is she?' Cardenas asked.

'Yes, but she speaks passable English of course after all these years.'

'No problem anyhow. My German is excellent.'

'Glad to hear it.' He consulted his notes and continued. 'A car from the pool will collect you from the Colonel's house and pick you up again after dinner. I thought you might like to call in at the Residence this evening on your way to Elias's. We're more or less equidistant here from the two houses.'

'Right.'

'Shall we say six-thirty?'

'Yes.'

Was Cardenas being deliberately offensive by these monosyllabic replies or was his gracelessness now ingrained and automatic, Brathby wondered. Anyhow, that was something to think about another time. Meanwhile all the more reason that he himself remain courteous, and try to make allowances, however difficult to do so. He continued: 'I shall look forward to that. Now tomorrow, Friday, I hope you'll have lunch at the Residence. I'll ask Paynton as well and he can tell us about the executions. Perhaps the Colonel will also join us.'

'Agreed. Friday evening?'

'The Consul and his wife would like to entertain you.' After a little encouragement from his Ambassador, that is. 'He'll have his junior staff there too, I expect. Buffet supper, casual evening.'

'That's acceptable. Saturday? If I'm still here, that is.'

'Not yet firmed up. Depends partly on the local situation, particularly the possibility of anti-British demonstrations. Also whether the heavy rains have begun; at the start of the season there are often flash floods and that restricts where one can travel.'

Cardenas for once seemed surprised. 'You mean what I've seen so far, what's happening out there now – that's not "heavy rains" as you call them?'

'Just wait and see,' said Brathby, rising to his feet. 'Now I'll take you to the Head of Chancery so that you can start work.'

As they moved toward the outer door Violet came in, smiled slightly at the two men and placed a sheaf of telegrams on the Ambassador's desk. Brathby opened his mouth to make the introductions but Cardenas, after a cool glance at her was by then in the corridor. Not interested in observing any of the courtesies, it was clear. Four letter man.

9

'I am sure it is obvious to you, Francis, that it is a waste of money and time for me to be here doing what you personally could easily have wrapped up by now. But the Deputy Under-Secretary was insistent I came.' Did Paynton believe this? It didn't matter whether he did or not; just so long as he wasn't weak enough to betray any doubts – that would be disappointing.

'So where would you like to begin, Richard?'

'What do you suggest?'

'Well, first I should show you round the Embassy, inside and out, then give you the rosters, incident logs and so on to read. I shall then be available if you have any questions for me, and to summon anyone you wish to interview.'

'That is satisfactory.'

'Then let's leave our ties and jackets here, shall we, and walk round the estate now while the rain holds off. As you may have been told, the Big Rains could start any time and make such activity extremely uncomfortable, if not impossible.

They started in the courtyard where Paynton explained the basic geography. An hour later they were sitting in Cardenas's temporary office drinking iced tea. Cardenas noted approvingly that the armpits of Paynton's short sleeved shirt were only lightly stained with sweat, despite their recent exposure to high humidity. Clearly a fit man.

'So I'll leave you for a while with this lot', Paynton indicated the files he had brought in, 'and pop along to see H.E. After that I'll be in my room down the corridor if you need me.'

Paynton had done well so far, Cardenas reflected as the man left the room. He had shown no nervousness in front of him although as Head of Chancery his was the main responsibility for physical security, and that had undoubtedly been breached.

Cardenas turned his full attention to the material in front of him. He rapidly filleted the papers, comparing logs, Duty Officer reports and cleaning schedules. He examined the plans of the buildings. It was clear that no intruder could have entered the Chancery area via a window – all were adequately secured. The back entrance to the building, a large steel door in the Registry area, was heavily bolted and barred –

it was for use only in emergency, and there were no signs of its having been recently used. There was no direct access to the Chancery from the Residence. Therefore, the intruder or intruders had entered through the front door of the Embassy, and then via the privacy door into the Chancery corridor. Clearly the perpetrator was not a UK-based member of staff; any such person, working presumably for a hostile intelligence service, would be too valuable an asset to hazard in pursuit of an, at best, transitory gain. The microphone had not even been properly concealed.

Locally-engaged staff then? Possibly, but access to the Ambassador's room would still be needed, even once through the privacy door. A key somehow borrowed and copied? Again, possible. Or someone having rightful access to the key, or on the premises while the door was open.

Early morning cleaners? A distinct possibility although the Duty Security Officer was supposed to oversee them at work; but then the SO was liable to be called away to open the door to any visitor to the Embassy. An accomplice could have arranged for the SO to be thus distracted while the microphone was planted.

Cardenas consulted the files on the cleaners. All were women and had been working for the Embassy for at least two years. If a hostile service had recruited one of these why waste her on such a clumsy operation? Given regular access to HMA's office a properly controlled agent could be trained to plant a far more sophisticated device, one that could be properly concealed, for example in a plug powered by the mains.

What did all this add up to? Cardenas asked himself. What explanation would fit the probabilities? Entrance by the front door, almost certainly by someone with rightful, or traditional, access to the Chancery corridor, ideally someone also enjoying access to Brathby's office either because the door would be open (as for a cleaner) or because he had a key, legitimately obtained or otherwise. Rule out the cleaners for the moment, for reasons already outlined.

Cardenas quickly re-examined the personnel files of the Security Officers. It seemed that one of them, FR Sodham, strongly favoured the 3 am – 11 am shift. This was an official sleeping shift until 5.30 am, apart from the requirement to make one round of the Embassy at 4 am;

and then from 7 am the Duty SO would have to deal with delivery of newspapers, local mail and so forth. From around 8am he would be busy with staff and visitors arriving until he went off shift.

Cardenas dialled Paynton on the intercom and asked him to come to his office.

'Is Sodham that puffy-faced lout now on duty at the desk?'

'Yes.'

'I see from your note here that six months ago you gave him a poor report and recommended that he be sent home unless he improved.'

'That's right.'

'And has he improved?'

'No.'

'Then why is he still here?' Cardenas had an idea of the answer.

'The Ambassador felt he should be given a further chance. The man's marriage is in trouble. He told H.E. that if he were sent home his wife would leave him.'

'Brathby took mercy on him?' He had suspected as much.

'Yes.'

'And you accepted that?'

'Yes, after registering my disapproval.'

'Right. Let's have him in. But one question first. Who apart from the cleaners, the Duty SO, the Duty Officer and his PA would have access to Brathby's office in his absence?'

'Officially, nobody. But occasionally H.E.'s Steward, Cuthbert, will come in to check the beer supplies in the fridge.'

'Using Brathby's key.'

'Yes.'

'You approve of this?'

'No, but when I raised it with the Ambassador he told me that Cuthbert was utterly loyal, and not to be so pernickety.'

'Right. I'll have Sodham in for a chat.'

'Just as soon as I can arrange for someone to man the desk while he's with you. Five minutes at most.'

Cardenas decided to spend the interval toning up his stomach muscles. He'd soon have this silly little mystery solved and be able to concentrate on bigger game.

Paynton continued to shape up well. It would be interesting to see how he handled tomorrow's shootings.

*****

First that little Berridge turd comes sneaking round the lobby with Paynton, not saying anything, just gawping; sitting behind the desk, first in the upright chair and then in the soft one in the corner. Measuring, noting, going in and out of the main door, then in and out of the Chancery corridor. All this with scarcely so much as a nod. He knew Paynton was a hard case but this little bastard from London was worse, cool as a freezer, eyes like chisels – he was downright bloody dangerous, whatever his game.

Now he'd been summoned to Berridge's office, or rather that Brainbridge woman's, and made to stand in front of the desk like a soldier on defaulters. Typical of that type not to let him sit down. As if he hadn't been on duty since the middle of the night. He wrestled with his trousers which were tight against his crotch and riding up into the crack of his bum; he tugged them down only to expose a roll of belly where his shirt button had surrendered. Christ, he was uncomfortable. Bloody man.

So what was he after, this thin streak of piss? Hadn't come all the way from London just to put the frighteners on *him*, surely? Must be to do with the flap, whatever it was, that had started on Monday.

'I see you've been here for eighteen months now, Sodham.'

'Yes 'bout that.'

'Are you enjoying the Post?'

What sort of damn fool question was that? A job was a job wasn't it? 'Well, yes, sort of. You know how it is …'

'I don't. Explain.'

Christ, what was this bloke on about? He shifted uncomfortably and struggled to find an answer.

'You look tired, Sodham. How thoughtless of me to have kept you standing. Sit.'

That was better. 'Thanks. D'yer mind if I smoke?'

'Yes.'

'Sorry. Don't quite understand – d'yer mean I can or can't?'

'Did I not express myself clearly? I'm *so* sorry. I meant yes, I do

138

mind if you smoke.'

'Oh I see.' A weird one here all right. When was he going to come to the point?

This Berridge man was looking steadily at him without any expression of approval or disapproval, but as if he was some sort of object. When was he going to get on with it then? All he'd done so far was to ask him if he enjoyed the Post, damn fool question that was, and stop him having a fag. He fumbled unsuccessfully to fasten his shirt button and waited for the questions. What *was* going on?

Two or three minutes passed and still Berridge said nothing. Eventually Sodham burst out: 'What do you want me for, Mr Berridge? I don't understand why ... I mean what's it about?'

'I'm waiting for you to explain.'

'Explain what? I mean ...'

'I asked you if you were enjoying the Post; you said "Well, yes, sort of" and "You know how it is". I invited you to explain what you meant by that. I am still waiting for you to enlighten me.'

The man was off his head. It wasn't as if there was some sort of accusation he could deny, or admit even. He was toying with words, like a man might play pocket billiards. And him dying for a smoke too. The man's not normal.

'Well, I mean it's not such a bad Post. Got quite a decent flat for a start.' If he wanted this crap he'd give it him.

'Better than your flat in Camberwell, is it?'

'How d'yer ... well, yes it is.'

'What else makes it "not such a bad Post", Sodham?'

'Not sure, really.' If he only knew what Berridge wanted him to say, he'd say it. He didn't like that reference to his home district one little bit.

Cardenas pulled out the SO Incident Book for the previous week and opened it. 'You were on the 3am – 11am duty on Wednesday, Thursday, Friday and Sunday.'

'Yes.'

'You clearly favour this shift, taking it whenever you can. Why?'

'Got variety like, quiet times, busy times, yer know.' Sounded keen that did, showed interest, was what people like this weirdo wanted to hear.

Berridge had gone quiet again. He was looking at the Incident Book, then at him, then at the book again.

'There's an entry here for Thursday - "0630 Cuthbert"'.

'Yeh, H.E.'s servant. Old gink comes in to check on the boss's beer supplies.'

'0630?'

'If that's what it says.'

'And out again at 0640.'

'Sounds right.'

'Exactly 0630 and 0640?'

'Near enough. I don't …'

'What does "near enough"' mean?'

'Approximate, like.'

'I see. But I note that earlier the same morning you have the Duty Officer, Mr Fieldhouse, coming in to make his rounds at 0417 and leaving again at 0438. You were exact enough there.'

'Well …'

'Because he checks the times when he arrives and leaves? No "approximate like" with him?'

'No, Mr Berridge.'

'Now Sunday. Cuthbert in at 0645, out at 0650, back in 0655, out at 0700. Presumably "approximate like". Why did he go out and come back in again?'

'Must've forgot the beers. Yeah, that was it.'

'You, Sodham, were doubtless in your soft chair behind the desk in reach of the buzzer to open the front door. With some choice reading matter no doubt. Correct?'

'Could've been.'

'And the door from the foyer to the Chancery corridor propped open, because you can't control the button for it from your corner seat.'

'Well yeah, could be at that time of the morning, with the cleaners about to come in. Not sure.'

'On a Sunday? They don't come in on Sunday.'

'Maybe Cuthbert left it open then, knowing he was coming back with the beers.'

Berridge had paused and was looking at him as if he were a piece of shit. When was he going to come to the bloody point? What was all

140

this stuff about Cuthbert and times in and out and all that?

'So, Sodham. There you are in your chair, reading, pushing the buzzer when the bell rings. You can – that's if you bother to look over the desk from where you are sprawled out smoking and fingering yourself – you can just about see the head and shoulders of anyone you are admitting to the Chancery corridor of this Embassy.'

'Well … er'. What was coming next? Surely not all this just to give him a bollocking for sitting in the wrong chair.

'So Cuthbert forgot the beer?'

'Said he'd be back with 'em,' Sodham replied.

'Which he was, a few minutes later. How did he carry the beer?'

'He had a box on his shoulder, like. Yer know, 'ow all the nignogs carry things unless it's on their heads which is even more stupid.'

'And a few minutes later, a few pages later in your magazine, the man comes out again.' He paused. 'With the box on his shoulder no doubt, on his left shoulder this time?'

'Yeah, think so. Remember now; you're right.'

'And of course, Sodham, you couldn't see his face either when he came in or when he left. Could you?'

'P'raps not very well, but it were only old Cuthbert, weren't it?'

Berridge stood up. Looked like a fighting cock, fierce little bugger. But spoke quiet, that made it worse. 'Your chances of seeing out your tour here are slender. You have only survived this long because the Ambassador took pity on you.'

'Yes, s'pose so.' What was coming next?

'Paynton a good boss is he?'

'Oh yes.' A relief to talk about something else. 'Bit strict like. Don't tolerate no slackness.'

'Good. What do the other Security Officers think of him?'

'Don't like him, much. Too cool. But they sort of respect him. He's not a bloke to try it on with, we all know that.'

'He's not married, is he?'

'Well, no.' What was he getting round to?

'Got a woman here?'

'No. Not that I know of. We'd have heard, the Security Officers.'

'Or a boyfriend?'

'No, sir, not like that either. Reckon he's tied a knot in it.' He snig-

141

gered. Who knows, keep this Berridge man happy, funny questions he's asking, might get out of this trouble, whatever it was.

'The Ambassador's unaccompanied here. You of course know that.'

'Course.'

'What is his sex life?'

'Really Mr Berridge, I can't …'

'Sodham, you are in so much trouble that without my help you'll be back in Camberwell, and without a job to go to before you can say "wank". Got that?'

Christ, was the man using Sodham's own sort of language just to put the shits up him? Better co-operate it seems. Pity, because the Old Man had been decent, that time. 'Well, H.E., he doesn't have any, sex life that is, not as far as we know.'

'Really?'

'Course he's sweet on that PA of his, Polly, everyone knows that. But he's not screwing her, pretty sure of that.'

'Polly Pym. That rather drab, dark-haired girl?'

'No, sir, Polly's a red-head, on the short side; smashing-looking bird she is, great pair of knockers. Off sick now, since yesterday.'

'Ah, thank you. Now I understand.' He went on. 'So who's the other one, working for Mr Brathby at the moment?'

'Violet Tryam-Jones, sir. Normally she works for Mr Paynton.'

'All right, Sodham, you may go now.' The man was almost smiling. 'But be very clear on these points. One: what you told me about Cuthbert's activities on Sunday morning must remain between the two of us for the moment, although the Embassy staff will have to know some version of it later. Two: we did not discuss the Head of Chancery or the Ambassador. Nobody will believe your word against mine. Quite clear?'

Sodham nodded. No way was he going to take risks with this man.

'Because point three is this: one word out of place and I'll crucify you. You'll not only be out of here and out of a job but I'll have your pension entitlements docked for gross dereliction of duty. Clear?'

Sodham nodded. Bloke didn't mess about, did he?

'Now get your flabby carcass out of here. Go.'

He left as quickly as he could. It'd be a relief to have a fag and be somewhere this man wasn't.

10

Cardenas returned to the Embassy in the early afternoon, pleased with what he had achieved during the hour and a half he had spent in the Residence; the exercise of skill and power, whether for personal pleasure or for professional reasons, invariably afforded him satisfaction. He was unconcerned that he had in the process effectively destroyed that bumbling old Steward with the trembling hands and ridiculous grey curls. When *would* officials learn that gross neglect of the regulations just invited disaster? Brathby's Steward should have been retired many years ago instead of being indulged to live a privileged and virtually unregulated existence.

Cuthbert had shown him into a large reception room, and disappeared to fetch the iced tonic water Cardenas had told him to bring. The room was well-furnished and impersonal. Big enough comfortably to accommodate thirty to forty guests, drinking at the expense of the tax-payer no doubt. Did Brathby really need this degree of luxury, he pondered, eyeing the plush furnishings. It seemed that for once the Property Services Agency had shown good taste – a pleasing colour-scheme and good quality fabrics that even Cardenas couldn't fault. No trace here of the overblown flowers and chintz that had accosted him from all sides at the Governor's House in Hong Kong.

On a sturdy table in the corner Cardenas saw an old-fashioned gramophone and a box of records. Surely Brathby could have afforded a proper music system, with his salary and fat allowances. How bizarre. Yet one more reflection of his folksy style, his flabby approach.

Nothing else of interest in here. He would examine Brathby's private quarters later, when he had dealt with Cuthbert.

Cardenas finished his light lunch and rang the bell. He had waved aside most of the dishes which Cuthbert brought in and had eaten only some cold fish and local vegetables. He followed this with a slice of strong-tasting pineapple, so delightful that he had ordered Cuthbert to bring him a second slice.

'Take these things away and come back.'

'You want coffee Mr Berridge?'

'No. Just do what you're told.'

When Cuthbert returned, Cardenas, saying nothing, kept him standing by the table. Soon he could see the man's legs begin to tremble and then his hand reach out to hold on to a chair. An icy look served to make him replace it behind his back. Splendid.

'Wot ting you want, sah?'

'Nothing difficult. Something simple', Cardenas eventually replied.

'Nuddin difficult … wot ting dat?'

'The truth, Steward, the truth.'

'I no savvy, sah.' He reached out again for the back of the chair.

Let him hold it if he needed. Shouldn't be long now, and Cardenas didn't want the man collapsing until he'd extracted the details from him. A few quick questions and he would no doubt crumble. But it would be interesting – no, satisfactory described it better – if he confessed without the need for questioning.

'If you done finish I have work, sah. I go wash de dishes.' He began to turn away.

A little bit of spirit, then. Good. 'No, Steward, not yet. Are you going to tell me, or not?'

'What ting, sah? I no savvy um.'

'I think you do.' He paused. 'It will be easier for you if you tell me.'

He was still clutching the chair, his legs trembling, face grey and drawn. His spectacles had slipped on one side. The creature looked ridiculous.

'You mean de bad man who done come here?'

'Ah.' So it had been possible.

'Tell me about this "bad man", Steward. You look ill. Sit. '

Despite his physical condition and the desperate trouble he was in Cuthbert was clearly embarrassed, perhaps at not continuing to stand in the presence of his superior. Good; that should further disorientate the man. And presumably it was because he felt so diffident that he first covered the seat of the chair with the tea towel he had over his arm.

'The bad man?' Cardenas probed.

'When he first done come he tell me he my cousin, from dat my village long ago. I never know if this be true talk but I give um *chop* and place to sleep.

'Of course.' It would soon come out.

'He go way, maybe two-weeks, den he come again. Den go, then come. I no like um. Eventide no like um.'

144

'Ah yes, your young assistant.' Still very quietly he went on: 'Then after a few visits he began to ask questions about the Embassy?'

'Na so.'

'About the routine, your duties, the keys and other things?'

'I no want to tell um, but ...'

'Go on.'

' ... he tell me dat policemans looking for Eventide to take um back to village. He say I must help um or he tell where Eventide living.'

Within a few minutes Cardenas had extracted the whole sorry story. How contemptible this man was, spindly, old, and useless. Oh yes and smelly too, for he had clearly wet himself just before sitting down. Hence presumably the exaggerated care and the pantomime with the cloth to protect his beloved Brathby's chair covers. What a performance.

So *Stuffing*, or at least the mechanics of it, was solved. The "cousin", in the unlikely event of his ever being found and questioned, would probably not know the nationality of the man who had recruited and directed him. The affair, Cardenas knew, had all the hallmarks of a KGB operation mounted to fulfil some norm, but with little hope of acquiring valuable intelligence. But it would probably never be known for certain who had been behind it.

But that was unimportant. What mattered was that he had uncovered the train of negligence that had made the security breach possible. At one level Cuthbert's weakness and credibility and Sodham's idleness and stupidity. But more fundamentally the responsibility was Brathby's, firstly for continuing to employ the old and vulnerable Steward, and secondly for over-riding Paynton's sound recommendation that the Security Officer be sent home. Plenty of material there.

Cardenas wrote for a few moments in his black book and then looked again at Cuthbert. 'So what will His Excellency say if I tell him these things? He will not be happy.'

'You say *eef* you tell the Master ... you mean p'raps you no have to tell um, sah?'

'I hope not, Cuthbert. Because if he knew what you had done he would certainly send you away. What you did was so bad that it wipes out whatever good things you may have done in your long service.'

'Send me where, sah? I have no place to go.'

'And the boy also, no doubt.' He could see him wince. Really, the man was so soft that it detracted from Cardenas's pleasure in carrying out his duty.

'He also have no place to go.'

'Back where he came from perhaps? You spoke of a village.'

'Oh, no, sah … At all!' He was clearly horrified.

'Oh but yes, I'm afraid.' He paused. 'Also your "Master", as you call him, will also be in trouble if the big people in London learn about this bad thing that you and your cousin have done – the Ambassador is your Chief and responsible for what you do. He also may have to go back to his "village" as you would call it – that is if I write this down in my book for the big people.'

'*Eef*, sah? Eef you tell Master about me, and eef you tell about the Master to de udders?'

'Yes.'

'You no be sure *eef* you tell or not?' There was a flicker of hope in his eyes. There should be no resistance now. Time to get on with the real task.

'No, I have not yet decided.' He paused for a long moment and then continued: 'Listen to me carefully. To save you and Eventide, and maybe your Master also, I must know certain things.'

'And you tink *I* can help?'

'Yes, Cuthbert, you can help.'

So that Cuthbert would think that the cousin was of genuine interest to him Cardenas first demanded to see where the man had slept. Had he left anything behind? No. He made a show of examining the mattress the man had used and then briefly looked at the rest of the servants' quarters.

On a shelf in the kitchen Cardenas spotted a half-smoked cigar resting on a saucer.

'You smoke these things?' he demanded.

'No, sah. Dis be for my Master. One night after supper he come to talk wid me and smoke um. Dis one too fat to throw way.'

'Mr Brathby comes in here to talk to you?' He wanted to get this quite clear.

'Na so, sometime. He sit and ask me about my life and udder tings, like Eventide and his schooling.' The pathetic man seemed proud of this.

'You sit with him?'

'He make me. We seet for dis table.' Deplorable. But all of a piece with everything else he was learning about Brathby. Flabby-minded, self-indulgent, a poor example to his staff. Having such a man as Ambassador here was unsettling and offensive to him – but that situation was not of course irremediable. He already had nearly enough ammunition – time now to acquire more.

'Right. I'll see the other rooms now.'

Cuthbert showed him the spare bedrooms, the dining room, and another reception room.

'Now Mr Brathby's quarters. Quickly.'

'You mean his *private* rooms?' He sounded shocked.

'Yes, of course I do.'

'But nobody ...'

'Are you going to help me to save you and Eventide and your Master or not? Make up your mind, yes or no. I have no time to waste.' Pressure was the only thing an animal like that could understand.

'I show you, sah.'

Cardenas stationed Cuthbert in the corridor outside Brathby's bedroom to give warning should he return unexpectedly early from his lunch engagement. 'And if you betray me, Steward, your precious Eventide will be with the police by tonight.'

He searched the room rapidly and expertly. Books everywhere, mainly about Africa. A large and crudely executed painting of a woman at the river at sunset hung on the wall – a relic of Brathby's time in the Congo probably. A number of garish shirts in the chest of drawers, worn no doubt when entertaining his staff in the evening or hobnobbing with his servant. Ah yes, here was something interesting; tucked away face down at the bottom of the shirt drawer, a silver-framed photograph of a pretty but rather severe-looking woman. Brathby's wife, Louise, presumably. When had she been relegated to the drawer, he wondered? Bedside table: contraceptives? No, disappointingly. Pornography? Not even that. But copies of the Book of Common Prayer, the Koran and *Plato's Republic* and several novels of PG Wodehouse. What weird taste. Sheets looked as if they were clean on today so no point in examining them.

The door half opened. Cardenas immediately adopted the posture of a man buttoning up his flies as if leaving the adjoining bathroom; the, admittedly thin, cover story would be that he had strayed into the wrong area while looking for the lavatory. Brathby might not believe it – the man was not an idiot – but then did that matter very much?

But it was only Cuthbert. 'You finish, sah? No find bad juju?'

So that's what he assumed Cardenas was looking for. No point disillusioning him.

'As it happens I am ready to move on. Mr Brathby has a private study somewhere, does he?'

'Just here, sah.' Cuthbert opened the door.

'Does Mr Brathby spend much time in here?' He turned round in the doorway to face Cuthbert.

'Oh yes, sah.'

'What times of the day and for how long?'

'After de office close he come to sit wid de papers, before *chop*. If he no must go out he maybe sit two hours.'

'Drinking at the same time?'

'Always I breeng de beer but he no drink till after he finish wid de papers.'

Probably hadn't the guts to tell the sycophantic Cuthbert that he didn't want the beer, in case it upset him. Strange man. 'Other times?'

'Before bed he often seet here, I tink.'

'Still "wid de papers" Steward?' Having to bring work home with him – another sign of Brathby's not being up to the job.

'No, sah. De private books.'

'Private? Do you mean reading for pleasure?' But was that a concept that Cuthbert understood, he wondered?

'No, he never read at dat time, he write in de books.'

'What books? Explain?'

'He write about hees life – de real tings and de tings he thinking. Dees books he call um, in English, "dyries".'

'How do you know this, Cuthbert?'

'He tell me, sah. But ...' the wretch was having second thoughts, ' ... sah, I no like dis, what you ask. Dis private ting for de Master, not office ting.'

'Steward', Cardenas spoke softly but menacingly, 'you tell me everything I want and perhaps, just perhaps, you and Eventide and your "Master" will not suffer. But if you hide anything from me you will all have bad trouble. Starting with the boy, who will be taken away tonight.'

'Please, sah ...' The snivelling wretch was starting to plead.

'So you do understand?'

'Oh yes, oh yes, sah.'

Good, he was back under control. 'I asked you how you know about Mr Brathby's diaries.'

'One time after we talk in de kitchen he bringed me here. He tell me that de stories of my life and de old days, he write um for book. He have many books like dat, he say. He call um "dyries" and he have plenty. Den he tank me for dis my help and I go back to de kitchen.'

How ironic that the man's adoration of Brathby should be so transparent even as he was shamelessly betraying him. 'What did this book look like?'

'Wot you mean, sah?'

'What I said. Was it thin, fat, big, small. Tell me.'

'All same, like de piccin's school book. Na thin one.'

'An exercise book?'

'Na so, he go call um.'

'Where does he keep these books when he is not writing in them?' Judging from the rest of Brathby's behaviour he was quite capable of confiding grubby secrets to these diaries and then carelessly leaving the books lying about.

Cuthbert was staring at the floor, preparing to lie, Cardenas judged. 'I never know, sah. I never see um.'

Cardenas took a pace towards Cuthbert and said very slowly 'Will they beat him badly when he is taken to his village, I wonder?'

A few moments later they were outside the old storeroom door. 'One night I see um bring one book in here. Maybe he keep um all inside.'

'Cuthbert, go quickly to the front of the house and check that Mr Brathby is not yet back.'

'Yes, sah.'

Cuthbert was quickly back. 'No, sah. He no come again.'

'The door to this room is locked. Where is the key?'

'I no sure ...'

'Eventide, I'm told, is a pretty boy. Maybe the police will not send him back immediately but keep him for themselves ...'

God, what a stupid place to hide a key. He opened the door and peered down into the sticky, dust-laden room. Now where ... oh yes, up there no doubt ... hadn't even replaced the ladder ... must be ...

'Sah, I hear car. Maybe de Master come back.'

'Right. Replace the key and go the kitchen. And wash – you stink.'

Cardenas was back in the reception room, admiring prints of the local harbour when Brathby put his head round the door.

'So Richard, was lunch satisfactory?'

'Yes.'

'Cuthbert give you everything you wanted.'

'Yes indeed.' He looked at his watch. 'I must return to work now'.

'Fine, so I'll see you at about 6.30 for a drink. I'll look forward to that.'

Why was the damned man so hearty? Yes, damned was the word. He tapped his pocket to check that his black book was in place and left the Residence.

This afternoon he would make a start on Elias and have a first look at Muckle; then a rest before a busy evening.

As he turned the corner to approach the Chancery, Cardenas caught sight of a boy crossing the compound, satchel on shoulder and bouncing a football. So *that* was Eventide, so fresh, happy and attractive. A pity he was the wrong sex. He made a mental note to visit the Consulate before too long and inspect the young Vice-Consul.

11

Weeping with anger, and trembling with fear and shame, Cuthbert crept off to his quarters to shower and change into his best clothes.

When he was ready to go he went to the kitchen to remind Eventide to do his homework before going out to play football.

He found the Ambassador in his study: 'Please, sah, I go now?'

'Oh hello, Cuthbert. Of course, go out. There's no need to ask – the afternoons are yours. You know that.' He had looked at him in kindly fashion, making Cuthbert feel even worse. 'You're very smart today. Going anywhere special?'

'I back for drinks time.'

'Yes, it'll probably only be Mr Berridge here. He's not staying for supper though.' The Master seemed puzzled: 'Are you sure you're all right, Cuthbert? No particular problems at the moment?'

'I be fine, sah.' He did not want to talk.

He shuffled along the cracked pavement as fast as he could, sandals slapping against his leathery feet, his old heart beating furiously. He half-heard two or three people greet him but he pressed on. There was only one place to get help from now, at this terrible time. Indeed it was the worst moment of his life: for had he not stained his honour, the bond of all those years of service? Even in order to save the boy, that was a terrible thing.

*****

'Oh Holy Mary, Mudder-of-God, oh sweet Jesus suffering on de cross – help dis your servant, oh please do dat ting. You know dis man be evil, ee crucify me like dey crucify Jesus.' Cuthbert crouched in a corner pew at the back of the huge and deserted Church of the Rivers. Two enormous ceiling fans gently stirred the stifling air.

'Oh Mary, Mudder-of-God, please give me dis ting I ask; and forgive me no fit kneel now. Forgive dat long time I no come see you.' He peered through the slanting sunlight towards a double life-sized plaster Virgin; a white woman, portrayed in voluminous pastel-shaded robes and clutching a rather plump and somnolent child.

'I remember, Holy Mary, you save me one time before.' He had come to that same pew to tell Her that he was growing old and needed strength to go on working. And lo the next day he had found Eventide, as in the story when they found the baby in the bulrushes. 'First you make a good person come like spirit. I beg you, make you rid dis bad one for me; and for Eventide and for my Master.'

Yes, his dear Master who one evening in the happy days had asked him what language he thought in. Here now in this place he was thinking in the language of the mission school, the language in which he had been taught about mercy and forgiveness. But also, he wondered, who was the Lord who said: "Vengeance is mine"? Jehovah; wont to smite, to slay, who chopped the Malekites in bits, a Lord Avenger such as his own ancestors acknowledged? The same High-one surely? *One* God, cannot be two of dem.

But it was in his native Angala, and not in any prayer-book English, that Cuthbert was muttering as he left the Church and made his way towards a certain group of huts down by the river bank. Oh yes, in body he was old, short-sighted, thin, feeble; but in his veins flowed the blood of warriors. He would give Our Lady two days to do her work – if she had not helped him by then he would find another way to invoke Jehovah's aid, or even manage without.

Clutching his purse tightly Cuthbert told the small girl at the hut door to take him to her grandfather. As he entered he was assailed by smells of blood and putrid flesh, and had to weave his way carefully through nameless dried organs hanging from the ceiling, brushing against his hair and face.

12

Before leaving his small room in Chancery, Antoun Elias replaced the cologne spray in his desk, checked that his hair was neatly spread across his pate and mentally rehearsed the answers to the questions which he expected. He couldn't, surely, be held to account for any security lapses in connection with the microphone. Wasn't the responsibility in an Embassy for such matters always the Head of Chancery's? If anyone was to blame it was Francis Paynton. Berridge wouldn't need to be reminded of this.

During the lunch hour Elias had changed his shirt. Also during the morning he'd refrained from smoking in his office in case the man came to see him there – the look that Berridge had given his cigarette the previous evening had been warning enough.

But instead he'd been summoned to the Secure Speech Conference Room for three o'clock, a venue chosen, Elias suspected, as a subtle reminder that he was usually excluded from meetings in there; Berridge had spent a good deal of time with Paynton this morning and would certainly have discussed him at length.

Although Elias was five minutes early for the meeting Berridge was already there, seated at the head of the table, writing in a black-covered notebook. He did not look up. 'Good afternoon, Mr Berridge.'

'Ah yes, Elias', he eventually said, pushing his book to one side, 'and a good afternoon to you. Do sit down.' His face adopted what Elias presumed to be an attempt at a smile: 'Before we start on our business let me first say that I am looking forward to dining with you and Mrs Elias this evening.'

'And we're both much looking forward to receiving you, Mr Berridge.' He thought fleetingly of the acrimony at home caused by his insistence that the invitation be proffered. And by the problem he'd had making Bertha swear to avoid mentioning a number of specific, sensitive, topics.

'We live quite simply but will do our best for you.' Even if it means a whole evening without a cigarette?

'So, Elias,' said Berridge, 'you must be better placed than anyone else in the Embassy to help me over this microphone affair. Given your long experience here, as well as what I've heard about your general acumen and flair.'

'Very kind of you to say these things ...' Elias recognised flattery when he heard it but it was agreeable nevertheless.

'What is your opinion of the general level of physical security here, compared with earlier years, say five and ten years ago?'

What did Berridge want to hear? Possibly the truth? 'It is at least as good now, probably better, than under any other Head of Chancery. Until this unfortunate business of course.' He hesitated and then continued. 'But there is a small problem ...'

'Yes, what problem?'

'A personnel matter. One of the security officers is not in my opinion up to standard.'

'Which one?'

'Well ...' Better not appear too keen to get the knife in, however much the man deserved it.

'Sodham, Mr Berridge.'

'Tell me.'

'To put it bluntly he is idle, dirty and careless; and, above all, insolent. Not a man to have on the front desk, not a good advertisement for Britain, not at all, Mr Berridge.'

'What have you done about it?'

That was the question he wanted. 'I have twice complained about him to the Head of Chancery.'

'With what result?'

He shrugged. 'None that I can see.'

'The Head of Chancery is a busy man, Elias.'

'Oh yes, indeed, sir' – just the moment for a touch of extra respect – 'I am well aware of that. Not only busy but clever also, a future Ambassador no doubt.' He'd better stop there and see where Berridge was heading.

'You're due for retirement soon, I understand. Are you looking forward to it?' That attempted smile again.

What was going on? This was hardly the moment for social chit-chat. Be careful now. 'In some ways, yes of course. I'm no longer a young man and my duties here are many and onerous ...'

'But on the other hand?'

'I could perhaps be persuaded to carry on for a year or so if the Am-

154

bassador felt that I would be of service to him.'

'And does he feel that?'

'I'm not sure, Mr Berridge but I have hopes ...'

'I can tell you,' the attempted smile had gone and his face was expressionless, 'that the issue is under discussion in London. Also the matter of your pension.'

'You mean increasing it if I am extended for a year or more?'

'No, not that, I'm afraid. It's the more fundamental question of whether you are entitled to a pension based on your length of service. For many years you were only locally-engaged here at the Embassy, and without British nationality. Of course if the lawyers decide that you do not qualify for a sterling pension in the same way as a UK-based diplomat, you will doubtless receive some sort of gratuity as well as a pension in local currency.'

How could this be true? The matter had been settled years ago and he had been assured by successive Ambassadors that he would receive a full pension. And anyhow what business was it of this Berridge man, who was here to investigate a security breach? He forced himself not to look too alarmed. 'So were you asked in London to discuss this matter with me, Mr Berridge?'

'The Deputy Under-Secretary – and essentially it is he who will make the final decision, irrespective of the lawyers' recommendations – told me he would be grateful for any advice I could give, that is if I had time to look into it in the margins of my investigation here.'

'So in what way can I help you in this matter, sir?' His whole future was at stake. Stay here on a pension in the anaemic local currency, cooped up with that dreadful woman? He could taste the bile in his throat and turned aside to cough into his silk handkerchief. He longed for a cigarette.

'One matter of concern in London is to what extent you have been supplementing your FCO salary.'

'Er ... supplementing?' What did they know? Surely Berridge couldn't be referring to his occasional very minor commissions, little more than expenses really, from maintenance contracts.

'I understand, Elias, that over the years you've been helpful to the Service which Miss Brainbridge now represents here. Is that right?'

Berridge should not be talking like this. Even Brathby, who knew that he helped *The Friends*, would never mention these matters. Yet he couldn't refuse to answer since the man had obviously been briefed about the connection. Elias strove to concoct a reply. 'You see, Mr Berridge from time to time there are local people who want to help the Embassy, provide us with useful information, but who are nervous to approach the British, I mean the white British, staff. It can be less intimidating for them to come to me in the first instance– and I am known to be a very discreet man. So yes, in that way, Mr Berridge, I have occasionally been of use to … to that department.'

'And they pay you well.'

Was that a statement, or a question?

'Of course they pay my modest expenses, for entertaining contacts, that sort of thing.'

'And a salary.'

'Yes, a small salary.'

'Paid into a bank outside this country, no doubt?'

'Yes, er …' Where was this going?

'On which you pay no income tax.'

'Well no, naturally not, Mr Berridge. Since we are talking so openly about these things – I see now why you wanted to meet in this special room …'

'Yes?'

'The small financial recognition that Miss Brainbridge's Department affords me for my services comes from what she calls the "Secret Vote". Its purpose is to pay for information.' Did the man really not understand these things?

'Yes, indeed. Money to pay foreign spies. I know all about that. Here, however, we are talking here about official funds, albeit from the Secret Vote, being paid to an already salaried Crown Servant. That is the crucial difference, Elias.'

'But for all these years …'

'I am not saying, and I am sure that the Under-Secretary does not think, that you have knowingly cheated the Inland Revenue. However you have at the very best been seriously misled, and that is unfortunate.'

'But …'

'You are saving now for your retirement no doubt?'

Back to the pension issue? Gently now, Antoun. 'I try to put a little aside, Mr Berridge, but it is not easy.' Better try to steer him away from money matters. 'So is there any way in which I can help you further with regard to this microphone problem?'

But Berridge was not to be diverted. 'What do you mean by "a little" which you "put aside"? Does that include any presents from, for example, local builders with whom you negotiate for work to be done to Embassy property?'

'Mr Berridge, I must most strongly protest against such allegations. There is absolutely no ...'

'I asked you a simple question. Is the answer "yes" or "no"?'

'No. Of course not. Where ...?'

'But you must from time to time have been offered inducements; is this not the land of what you call *dash*?'

'Yes, indeed it is, Mr Berridge but *I* have never accepted anything like that.'

'That is what I expected you to say.' The man made a brief note in his black book and continued: 'You act as the Embassy liaison officer with the police.'

'Yes, sir.' This was safer ground.

'Get on well with Commissioner Zalomo, do you?'

'He is very helpful to me, yes.'

'And you to him, no doubt?'

Pause for thought. 'I'm not clear what you mean, Mr Berridge.'

'A straightforward question I'd have thought.' It was unnerving how the man's face lacked expression.

'I handle some of the administration related to the policemen we accept for training in the UK. He is very keen on this you know, Mr Berridge, always trying to increase the numbers, always wanting to ...'

'I'm aware of that,' the man said, 'but how do we, the British, benefit from this very expensive operation?'

'The locals do pay something towards it.'

'A nominal sum only. What is the answer to my question?'

'Increased influence, I suppose. But it's His Excellency you should ...'

'It is your view I'm asking now. Tell me about this "increased influence"'.

'It is difficult to quantify, Mr Berridge. But for example the Commissioner is keeping us informed about the expected anti-British demonstrations over this business of the ex-Minister Ayumba. I don't know if you are aware of the background to the affair, which started …'

'Yes, fully aware. So Zalomo tells us when he's going to organise a riot against the Embassy. Most helpful.'

'It's not quite …' Berridge was twisting everything.

'Enlighten me, Elias as to the value of all the expensive police training in the UK if Zalomo cannot even protect British citizens here? Where were his trained men when robbers raped and killed that *Uminco* wife? Tell me that.'

While Elias was struggling to find an answer Berridge went on: 'The budget for the training of all overseas police forces is currently under review, as you may know. The Deputy Under-Secretary asked me to let him know on my return how worthwhile I considered the whole project.'

'Very worthwhile, Mr Berridge, extremely so. But His Excellency …'

'Give me an example of Zalomo's being of serious help to the Embassy, apart from his warning you of disturbances which he may well be organising.'

'Really, Mr Berridge, it's not …'

'Just one example, please Elias. Where we got some definite return on our money.'

Could it do any harm to recount how helpful Zalomo had been over Tom Muckle's *tiefman* even if, as Elias suspected, the incident had never been reported to London? And to talk about the matter would show Berridge how open he was being, with no secrets to hide. Yes, it would be a good thing to tell him. He did so while Berridge listened poker-faced.

'Tell me', Berridge said when Elias had finished, 'is it known whether Muckle was sober when he killed his visitor?'

'An intruder, Mr Berridge, a dangerous *tiefman*'.

'We have only his word for it.' He made a brief note in his black book and looked up again. 'Was Muckle alone in his flat that evening? Was there nobody else there to corroborate his story, a woman perhaps?'

'As it happens, no, Mr Berridge.' Where was this line of enquiry going next, he wondered. The man twisted everything.

'What do you mean "as it happens"? It is unusual for him to be alone?'

'He is a young man, Mr Berridge, so perhaps sometimes …'

'It is interesting that you have told me about this incident, Elias. It was never officially reported to the FCO, although I knew about it before you gave the details.'

From that bastard Paynton, no doubt. So it was a good thing that Elias had also mentioned it – that must surely have made a good impression.

'I am staying with Colonel and Mrs Squires.'

Elias blinked at the sudden change of subject. Was this deliberate disorientation? 'I hope you are comfortable there Mr Berridge. They are …'

'Do you like him?'

'Oh yes, the Colonel is always very friendly, very open; and grateful for any information I can bring him about the country's armed forces.'

'Yes, I'm sure.' He looked as if he were carefully formulating his next question: 'When is the best time of the day to call on Colonel Squires, when he is, shall we say, at his most receptive?'

Ah, clearly Berridge had caught wind of his host's problem. He leant forward and gently rubbed the side of his nose. 'Not too early in the morning perhaps, sir, and sometimes not after lunch – around noon is a good time.' There could be no harm in merely confirming what was already known.

'How often are you in contact with Soviet and Eastern European diplomats, Elias?'

Another blink. 'In … in contact with?' He had nothing to hide but this was a disturbing line of enquiry for how could one *prove* innocence in this respect?

'Yes. At diplomatic receptions for example, National Days or while at the Ministries on business.'

'I have always been advised, by our … er … Sometimes they try to talk to me at official functions, the Queen's Birthday Party for example, but I am never more than just briefly courteous.'

'I'm sure you're not.' He tapped his gold pencil on his black book and quietly asked, 'Is Mr Brathby sleeping with his secretary, or does he have another woman for that purpose?'

'Mr Berridge, I must ask you not to …' It was outrageous that the man could talk in this appalling way.'

'Would you prefer that we revert to discussing the doubts about your pension entitlement?'

'No it's …' How could Berridge dare to say such a thing? About the Ambassador himself! But he couldn't just refuse to answer – he couldn't risk alienating him.

'Well?'

'Sometimes Miss Pym acts as his hostess for a reception, as indeed does the Commercial Councillor's wife, but there is nothing improper in their relationship.'

'Other women?'

'Not as far as I know, Mr Berridge. He is of course married.'

'I know.' He made a further note in his book. 'We're finished now, unless you have anything you want to tell me. Do you?'

'Oh no, thank you.' It was so difficult to know what the man was after. 'Mrs Elias and I look forward to seeing you this evening at about 7.30 pm, if that is convenient.'

'I indicated earlier that it is. I shall see you then.' He put his notebook in his pocket and left the room.

Elias followed a minute later, desperate for a cigarette and to analyse this puzzling and worrying encounter. And then he had this evening to get through as well. Tomorrow he must talk to Brathby and seek his reassurance that he would help him if there really were doubts about his receiving a full pension, paid in sterling.

It was all extremely unsettling.

13

That such an obviously unsuitable man as Elias had reached diplomatic rank indicated a lack of judgement by previous Ambassadors; and now, under Brathby, the man not only retained his position but was, disgracefully, being considered for an extension of service. Well, at least Francis Paynton was clear-sighted about him; he had done well to stand up to Brathby and get Elias excluded from the Ambassador's weekly meetings for diplomatic staff.

If he was actually to stimulate a review of Elias's pension entitlements, as opposed to the more obviously achievable goal of sabotaging his extension, he would need to put some flesh on the bones. This evening should offer an opportunity – if Paynton's assessment of Elias's marriage was accurate then he should be able to dig something useful out of the wife.

Now to other matters. Back in Miss Brainbridge's Chancery office he dialled Colonel Squires on the intercom:

'Jack, Richard Berridge here ... yes, fine thank you ... Since I'll have left the house before you get back – I've got drinks at the Residence and then dinner with Elias – I wondered if you'd still be up when I got back, probably around ten; thought we could have a short chat? You're not planning a particularly early night? Good; yes, coffee would be fine.' He'd be twenty minutes late – that should be enough to start the process.

Cardenas placed a large towel on the floor and began his daily exercises, at the same time reflecting on the progress he had made in the Embassy. A little more work and further evidence of Brathby's obvious inadequacy would soon emerge. As for Elias, he was almost certainly as corrupt as his position was unorthodox, and proof should not be too hard to unearth. The thought that Squires could be promoted and obtain an important position in Washington was intolerable; but Cardenas knew how to sabotage that. As for the Intelligence Section, it was outrageous that a man of Muckle's calibre should be left in charge while the Head of Station was on leave. However the clerk's obvious vulnerability would make it easier to identify the special intelligence operation that had been hinted at in London, and which Cardenas, personally and professionally, felt compelled to discover. In fact he would see Muckle now. Cardenas had left him to stew just long enough. Having been the one to find the device he'd have expected to be among the first to be questioned. He should be suitably anxious by now.

But before that he would put his head round Francis Paynton's door, tell him something about 'making some progress on *Stuffing*', and see if he was displaying any nerves about the prospect of attending tomorrow's executions. He liked everything he had so far seen of Francis – a kindred spirit in this world of slackness and openly expressed emotions.

Right. Paynton, Muckle, then a swim in the Embassy pool if Paynton had some swimming trunks he could borrow. Then to Squires's house to change, back to the Residence for drinks – it would be interesting to see how Cuthbert behaved – and then to Elias's for dinner. Then to round off the evening a talk to the Colonel at a strategically chosen hour. A good programme, which should produce results.

14

When Cardenas arrived at the Residence, at 6.30pm, Bernard Brathby fetched him the requested iced tonic water, explaining that Cuthbert was in his quarters, and installed the two of them in the air-conditioned sitting room. He asked him if he had had a 'useful day', expecting that Cardenas would have something to say about his investigation, even if only in general terms. After all, *Stuffing* was the reason why the man was here, wasn't it?

But disconcertingly Cardenas seemed more interested in discussing personalities. Starting with his host and hostess. He said how attentive to his needs Jenny Squires had been, in an agreeably unfussy way, adding: 'I'd have thought she'd fit in well in Washington; that is if she accompanies Jack there.'

'Did Jack really tell you he was being transferred to Washington?' It seemed unlikely.

'He hasn't heard officially yet. But apparently it's more or less "in the bag", to use his expression'.

Could Squires have been so crass as to say that, however flattered or flummoxed by Cardenas? More likely he had mentioned his hopes for Washington and Cardenas had misunderstood. Or Cardenas was knowingly distorting Squires's words. But if so why? What game was the man playing?

'You know him well by now, of course,' Cardenas was continuing. 'You'll be backing him for the job, no doubt?'

'Now, look Richard, I'm not sure this is any of your business.' Brathby paused briefly to control himself. 'Tell me rather, how is the investigation going – are you making any progress? Is there any help I can give you on *that*?'

Cardenas ignored the reference to *Stuffing* and ploughed on: 'Well, yes it *is* my business, Squires's posting, that is. Before coming out here, I was in the MOD's Metropole Building on another matter and called on the officer ultimately responsible for Attaché appointments. He's a Royal Navy Captain named Aufree, whom I'd met once before.'

'And ...?'

'He sent his regards to Squires and asked me to get in touch when I got back to let him know "how things are going", as he put it. Said

Squires was being considered for promotion and a cross-posting, "depending on his health being satisfactory". Seemed a clear directive to me.'

Brathby opened his mouth to reply and then changed his mind. It seemed highly unlikely that a man in Aufree's position would brief a casual acquaintance to report on an Attaché in this way. Another likely example of Cardenas twisting the facts. Nothing seemed clear cut, nothing straightforward. Why couldn't he just get on with his job? Or was he, Brathby, being over-defensive, even paranoid, about Cardenas, too influenced by the man's dreadful manner. 'And your investigations?' That was safer ground.

'Francis Paynton has provided all the necessary back-up, as one would expect from an efficient Head of Chancery. I've been impressed by what I've seen of him so far. But of course we still have to see how he copes with tomorrow's little test.'

For a moment it seemed as if Cardenas was actually smiling. He was anyhow feeling pleasure, Brathby guessed. And he'd again avoided saying anything of substance about the investigation.

'Is there anything useful for me to know in advance about Mrs Elias, Bernard? he was asking. Topics of conversation to avoid, that sort of thing? Can you help?'

A perfectly reasonable request in most circumstances, but Brathby's view of Cardenas was changing fast. He now suspected that any such interest Cardenas lay in the potential to exploit sensitivities, rather than to avoid them. 'No, nothing in particular. Incidentally please give my regards to Bertha.' With any luck she would be in her most mind-erodingly boring form.

'With great pleasure.' Cardenas spoke as if condescendingly handing over a gift. 'I had Elias in for a talk this afternoon, about *Stuffing*.'

Ah, at last. 'He was of use, I hope?'

'Frankly, Bernard, no. But I found him to be a powerful advocate of the Police Training Scheme. As well as being a great admirer of the Police Commissioner.'

With difficulty Brathby managed not to display his anger. 'I am unaware why you should interest yourself in these matters,' he said slowly, 'but you may wish to know that Mr Elias's attitude both to the Training Scheme, and to maintaining close and friendly relations with Zalomo, exactly reflect my own; and what Mr Elias does and says in this respect are at my orders.'

'I'm so glad.' Unabashed, Cardenas glanced at his watch and finished off his drink. 'You are probably anxious, Bernard to learn whether I have made progress on this *Stuffing* matter?'

'If you can spare the time, Richard.' But sarcasm was wasted on this little shit.

'Well, the answer is yes, considerable progress. By lunchtime tomorrow, when you, the Colonel and I meet here to debrief Paynton about the executions, I shall be in a position to give you a full report. Perhaps I could stay on after the other two leave and give you the results of my enquiry.'

With that Brathby had to be content.

*****

As soon as he had seen Cardenas to the door Brathby opened the grille to the balcony and stepped out, to be immediately enveloped by the suffocating tropical heat and the especially heavy humidity that signalled the imminence of the Big Rains. But any atmosphere was preferable to the undiluted company of Richard Cardenas. Brathby was still just about prepared to concede that the man was only doing his duty, but he was increasingly uncertain where Cardenas perceived that duty to lie. It certainly seemed to include grubbing around for information on people's weaknesses. Antoun, and Jack too, almost certainly didn't come up to scratch in Cardenas's book. Possibly not Francis either if he didn't satisfy Cardenas in his reporting of tomorrow's executions. How, Brathby cursed, had he allowed this loathsome man to send Francis to a scene of cruelty for such a purpose.

Cardenas was interesting himself in members of his staff in a way which it was difficult to accept was connected to his official investigation. He seemed to be trying to discredit Antoun as well as Jack Squires. Who else had he got in his sights? Tom Muckle perhaps; Cardenas must presumably have interviewed him today – had he confined himself to discussion of *Stuffing*, or had he tried to put pressure on Muckle to talk about the Intelligence Station's activities? Which would be highly improper but, sadly, quite possible. He'd speak to Tom in the morning and offer him any necessary support.

It was obvious, too, that Cardenas also disapproved of Brathby himself, whom he would see as soft, old-fashioned and too concerned for his staff. It didn't take much imagination to visualise how Cardenas might try to undermine him in London – the implied suggestion of slackness at the top which had led to *Stuffing*, the suggestion of judgement clouded by sentimentality, the pitying shrug, the damning with faint praise. All adding up to serious doubts about his suitability for a Post in which he was effectively only on probation. If he was withdrawn it would effectively mean the end of his career. And he knew that he was cut out for just such work as he was now doing; and success here would lead to other Head of Mission posts in Africa, and the chance to help reshape British policy towards the area. And Cardenas was threatening all that, in addition to menacing members of Brathby's staff, who were entitled to his protection.

He longed to discuss these matters with Polly. Violet had gone home for lunch and called in to see her, reporting to him that she was still somewhat listless but determined to come in on Saturday. 'Bit weird, sir,' Violet had said. 'Almost as if there was something important she has to do that day. And she's begun to show some interest in what's going on; she wanted to know how Mr Berridge's enquiries were progressing and when he would be leaving. That's all really, sir. Of course I'm making sure she's getting enough to eat. Oh yes, she was very pleased you'd sent those chocolates and asked me to pass on her thanks.'

If Saturday meant Polly's return and Cardenas's departure then it couldn't come too soon. But then he thought again of the damage Cardenas could cause once back in London. No, this was no use, Brathby reprimanded himself: you are letting this get out of proportion. All may yet be well.

Before he went about his evening duties – he had a boring reception and then a dinner to attend – he must look in on Cuthbert. He really hadn't looked at all well earlier on, poor fellow. He wondered if Cuthbert would volunteer anything about Cardenas and how he had behaved at lunch. Obviously Brathby couldn't ask Cuthbert directly but the old boy might volunteer something, and Brathby valued his judgement of character.

Then the thought forced its way in – had Cardenas taken the opportunity at lunchtime to question Cuthbert about the Embassy, even about Brathby himself? Surely not. Such would be an appalling breach of protocol. But hadn't Cardenas already showed he was perfectly capable of such behaviour?

But Cuthbert was already asleep, Eventide told him, when he went round to their quarters. Probably the best thing for him, poor old chap, if he were not feeling well. No hurry, he'd have a word with him tomorrow.

15

'Dey give you fine *chop* for dat house?' asked the driver, as they drove back to Colonel Squires's house at the end of the evening.

'Yes, very good,' Cardenas replied. If he were civil the man might produce some useful snippets of information. 'Tell me, do you drive sometimes for Mr Elias?'

'Plenty,' he replied, mounting the pavement to avoid a large pot hole; 'de udders no like working for Mr Antoun but I tink um good man. I happy to drive for um.' Back on the road he threw an arm over the seat and swivelled to face Cardenas. 'You got ciga for me, Master?'

'Watch the road,' replied Cardenas sharply, recoiling from the rich stink of the man's sweat. 'No, I have no cigarettes.'

'Pity; so I fit smoke dis my own last stick,' the man said. 'Dat okay?'

'If you open your window and watch the road.'

They slowed to a halt as traffic both ways competed to shoulder past a lorry bearing the slogan *God is our Support,* which had collapsed onto its axles.

A thump on the backside near window took him by surprise. A toothless, one-eyed man was smiling in at him, his finger tips patting his lower lip.

'Will there be trouble if we ignore this man?'

'No problem. If you no *dash* um he go to next car. But dis ting I go *dash* um.' He shouted to the man to wait and through the window handed him his half-smoked cigarette.

As they inched past the lorry the driver spoke again: 'Dat why de udder drivers no like Mr Antoun.'

'I don't understand …'

'He *dash* de beggars. Always talk to de poor peoples. Even geeve own money to help hospital. Dey tink um stupid. And he not even from our people.'

Conscience money of course, Cardenas concluded. Giving away a small proportion of his illicit earnings would justify his dishonesty to himself; it seemed that he was cowardly and hypocritical, as well as crooked.

Once back in London it wouldn't take Cardenas long to light a fire under that greasy little twister. Not after what he had learned this evening.

The driver, with no cigarette to smoke, wound up his window and restored the air-conditioning. They had reached a main road, comparatively free of pot-holes and hold-ups. 'Maybe ten minutes and we reach Colonel's house.'

Cardenas, reviewing recent events, did not reply.

Elias had been nervous. That was immediately apparent from the way he had received him at the house, over-attentive, gibbering platitudes, apologising twice for the fact that his wife had not yet appeared. He had offered Cardenas iced tonic water – the news of his preference having clearly travelled – and for himself had brought a glass of soda water. Twice he had stretched out his hand towards the silver cigarette box as if temporarily forgetting Cardenas's distaste for tobacco smoke.

'Bertha, Mr Berridge, is not ... how shall I put it, sir? ... not very politically sophisticated; you know how it is with some wives.' He gave an ingratiating smile and stroked his nose. 'She does not really understand my work and it might be better ...' He tailed off.

'If we did not talk business over dinner?'

Elias nodded, smiling.

'Fine by me, I fully understand.'

As he spoke the door opened and *Frau* Elias tentatively entered the room muttering excuses about her lateness and how honoured she was to be entertaining Mr Berridge. The two men stood up.

Cardenas had not wasted time earlier speculating what she might look like but was nevertheless sharply surprised, without of course this showing on his face, which he was forcing into a smile.

She was not only obese but dressed, it seemed, to emphasise the fact, displaying large quantities of her unfortunate body. Slabs of fat were quivering under and around her absurdly short pink halter neck dress, causing Cardenas a spasm of pain at the thought of what her unsupported breasts must look like. Her feet were stuffed into high heeled sandals from which protruded toe nails of the same vivid red as she had applied to the nails of her stubby hands. A jumble of cheap jewellery on her right arm jangled as he shook her damp hand on introduction. He viewed with distaste the sight of her greying and greasy hair, twisted into a juvenile ponytail and draped unattractively over one shoulder.

His nose wrinkled as it detected the cheap and heavy deodorant which reeked from her unshaven armpits,

Her face, its features blurring into each other, could have been moulded in pink Plasticine by an untalented child. Her large flabby lips were smeared with a vivid crimson lipstick. She looked like a cross between a clown and an ageing whore.

For a moment he concentrated on committing the sight and smell of this excrescence to his permanent memory bank. No experience was totally wasted; she could serve as an anaphrodisiac, a vision to summon in the future in the event of an unwanted erection.

Outwardly, he was all admiration. He bent over her hand and in German paid her an extravagant compliment on her appearance. He could immediately detect her responding to him positively, as did most women. This reaction could be useful, especially as it was obvious that Elias was both surprised and displeased by her choice of clothes. Perhaps she had dressed in this fashion in order to irritate her husband, to stir up trouble? In which case the situation had potential.

Over a decent enough *mezze* Cardenas encouraged Elias to talk about his early years in the Embassy. He then went on to draw Bertha out on her childhood in Bavaria. Once started, and lubricated by the wine which she was liberally consuming, she spoke with increasing enthusiasm and freedom, despite her husband's obvious discomfiture; her fast but broken English, sprinkled with the occasional aside in German to Cardenas, dominated the table. By his close interest and questions Cardenas kept her flowing. She must, he realised, be quite unused to a man's attention, especially from such a man as he. Soon, in the glow of his approval, she fast lost all restraint.

As they came towards the end of the meal she moved on to contrast her wonderful homeland and childhood with having to exist in 'this filthy place' as she called it. From the hostile glances she was throwing at her husband it was evident that she held him responsible for her hateful life. She was so blatantly offensive, Cardenas thought, that only such a spineless coward as Elias, inured by the corrupting habit of evading conflict at any price, could have tolerated the situation.

Cardenas deftly encouraged Bertha to indiscretion, and soon she was complaining acidly not only that her husband often left her alone at home in the evenings, but that when he *was* home he was forever receiving disreputable friends, for meetings from which she was excluded, adding – in a muttered aside to Cardenas in German – that Elias was just a mean and greedy pig. Surely the man must have acquired some German along the line? Perhaps she just didn't care whether her husband understood or not.

Cardenas forced himself to continue gazing admiringly at her deplorable bosom, as if it were only her husband's presence that held his lust in check. Clearly she had something of interest to tell him. He turned towards Elias, addressing him now by his first name: 'Antoun, what an excellent dinner we've had. By now you must be sorely in need of a cigarette but I suspect that your courtesy forbids you saying so. Am I not right? So I insist that you go and smoke while I drink another cup of this excellent coffee, and ask Bertha for the secret of how those delicious vine leaves and the tabouleh are prepared.'

Seemingly uncertain for a moment, and then with an ingratiating smile for Cardenas and a warning look at his wife, Elias pushed back his chair and left the room.

How pitifully pliable the man was, his addiction so powerful and his will so weak that he allowed himself to be ordered out of his own dining room. Could such a person effectively carry out his Embassy duties? Obviously not.

As the door closed behind her husband Bertha shuffled her chair nearer to Cardenas's and began to speak rapidly and quietly in German.

'Do you like me, Richard? Am I attractive for you? Oh, *mein Liebling*, I am so unhappy.' Her fleshy hand reached out for his. 'He treats me like filth, vile you, you are so kind.' She suddenly leant over and wetly kissed his knuckles.

With supreme control Cardenas resisted the reflexive urge to snatch away and clean his hand, and with a response of his fingers even managed to convey the message that he welcomed her caress.

He knew he needed to act quickly; soon Elias might finish his cigarette and return, and even before then his own body might revolt and reveal his true response to this slobbering animal. 'Bertha', he said - she had now isolated his middle finger and was fondling it - 'I will come here to you tomorrow morning, when Antoun is at the Embassy. Yes?'

'Oh yes, oh yes.' She held his hand to her cheek.

'Tell me, my dear, in what way is Elias "a mean and greedy swine"?' It was vital she answered straightaway.

'Oh *mein Liebling*, do not talk of him but of what we do tomorrow. This, I mean.' Still holding his finger, she made it quite clear what she meant.

'I will come tomorrow only if you answer my question.' He was holding her away from him by the shoulders. 'You must tell me.'

'Must I, must I, my loved one?'

'Yes, Bertha, now.'

'But …'

He could happily have vomited over her. 'Yes, immediately, my lovely creature.'

'Do you love me, really, Richard?'

'I swear it. Now tell me.'

And she had told him. How very satisfactory.

In the event there had been plenty of time to spare since Elias had not returned at all to the dining room. Indeed to escape the increasing attentions of Bertha, panting to reap immediate rewards for her betrayal, Cardenas had had to plead a bursting bladder, and himself go in search of his host.

Soon after, as he bade the two of them goodnight, detaching his hand with some difficulty from Bertha's meaningful squeezes, he wondered whether Elias's retirement plans included her. He doubted it; but by the time Cardenas had finished with him, he hoped, there would scarcely be the resources for one household, let alone two. A suitable punishment for him, to see that woman every day for the rest of his life.

He, on the other hand, need never see her again.

16

'Good of you to wait up for me, Colonel. I appreciate that.'

'My dear fellow, least one could do. Help yourself to coffee from the tray. Had a spot of reading to catch up with anyhow; and thought one might try an accompanying drop from this bottle you so kindly brought. Can now report that it's absolutely first rate.' To underline this assessment Squires poured himself another tiny one.

'I'm glad it's satisfactory.'

'More than that, I can assure you. You're sure you can't be tempted?' The fellow was good-naturedly shaking his head. 'You've never indulged?'

'Not since I was a very young man; the stuff doesn't agree with me, Colonel.' He gave what Squires supposed was a light laugh. 'So did Antoun Elias and his *Frau* feed you well?'

'Yes Jack, quite adequately. The food was well-prepared and obviously expensive. Surprising they can afford to live like that.'

'Expect he decided to push the boat out a bit, for a distinguished visitor you know. Middle Eastern hospitality, that sort of thing. Probably live on crusts when they're on their own, hah, hah.' He took an appreciative sip of his malt. 'But the great thing is that they looked after you all right, yes?' That comment about the cost of the food was a bit off.

'Mrs Elias is an unusual woman.'

'Yes, one might put it like that. But heart of gold of course.' He hoped Berridge wouldn't make too many personal remarks.

'No doubt.' He paused. 'Tell me Jack, do you think she'd have any reason to tell lies about her husband?'

This shocked Squires and it was only because Berridge was a guest in his house that he refrained from a swift and rude response. He slowly added water to his glass before replying: 'You know, Richard, I'm not sure that that is a proper question to put to me. Elias is my colleague here in the Embassy and Bertha, as his wife, also deserves the same consideration.' He was speaking sternly. 'Now, shall I pour you some more coffee?'

'I'm sorry.'

'Sorry …?'

173

'Yes, sorry that I didn't explain that my question was an official one, connected with the *Stuffing* investigation. I can assure you that I would not otherwise be interested in such a matter.'

'Really. Well, yes that puts a different complexion on matters, I suppose.' He thought for a moment. 'But how is she, or he, connected to *Stuffing*? It seems a little far-fetched ...'

'You'll have to trust me on this, Jack. People have, as you know, to be excluded from as well as included in, circles of probability in such enquiries.'

Sounded complete balls, Squires thought, but Berridge *was* the professional, could see the bigger picture and all that. 'Well, if you can assure me it's official and important ...'

'Oh yes, most definitely so.'

'Very well then. Then one must say ... well, not to put too fine a point on it ... relations between the two of them are notoriously bad; even H.E. finds it an embarrassment to entertain them together. Bertha loathes Antoun, that's clear. But, must say, one doubts she has the imagination to make up stories about him.' He paused. 'There, I don't think I can help any more on that.' He poured himself another tiny one. 'So you're making progress on your investigation, are you? Anything you can tell me?' It would be a relief to get away from personalities.

'I've certainly not finished yet. I'd like to bring you up to date of course but that wouldn't be proper before I've reported to H.E.'

'No, no of course not. I completely understand.' At least in this respect Berridge knew the correct form.

'You mentioned the other evening that you'd had some interesting postings.' Berridge was tactfully changing direction, it seemed. 'Which was the most fun?' He got up and quietly poured himself more coffee.

Fun seemed an odd word in the context, but Squires took it in his stride. 'One's enjoyed them all you know, even Korea. Went out there as a Second Lieutenant and came back as a Captain, largely due to casualties of course.' He looked at the bottle and decided to postpone his next, and definitely last, nip. 'But Malaya was the best, posted there as the Emergency was officially ending – but nobody seemed to have told that to the CT's, the communist terrorists you know. They were still operating in North Malaya and Thailand. My task was to work with the Malayan Special Branch to eliminate the remnants.'

'And of course you were successful, as the whole world knows. Necessary job well done.' He paused. 'But how did you operate, persuade them to surrender? Or did you go out into the jungle and destroy their camps?'

'Bit of both, really.' Unusual these days to find anyone interested in the detail of that vital operation. He poured a very small one, added water, and continued: 'Important factor of course was the reward system. If a commander surrendered he would be paid for the number of men he brought in with him. And then of course, you may have heard of it, every weapon, in fact every bullet, had its price. For example ...'

Think what one might about Berridge he was a jolly good listener and appreciative too of what it had been like up there on the border. After that he wanted to know how the Emergency compared to trying to keep the peace in Cyprus, where Jack had also done a stint. It was a good twenty minutes and two very small drinks later before Berridge mentioned the Embassy again.

'With your background you must be a great help to the Intelligence people here, I'd have thought. Give them a bit of guidance, that sort of thing.'

'Good Lord, no.' Man didn't seem to understand how these things worked. 'Obviously I pass on to Philippa Brainbridge anything that could be of interest to her, but I'd never interfere. She's a great operator, not madly good-looking one must say, but the locals eat out of her hand. She has excellent judgement too. In fact one has nothing but respect for her.'

'And Muckle too?'

'Of course. Reliable, solid chap. Quite bright too. Had a Corporal like him in Korea, did I tell you; whenever I was ...'

'Smart of Muckle to have detected the microphone.'

'Well, yes. But he was probably just carrying out a routine procedure. One can't over-emphasise the importance of remembering the drill. I remember an occasion ...'

'Would Miss Brainbridge allow Muckle to handle an important operation, while she was on leave I mean?'

'Sorry, Richard but I don't think we should be talking about such things. Need to know and all that. Not that I know anything that I'm not saying, 'cos I don't. But ...' He was getting into a muddle. Need another tiny one, with plenty of water, to steady him. It just wasn't right, some of the things Berridge said. He didn't seem to know the form, after all. Disappointing.

Now here he was at it again. 'But Bernard Brathby would know, I assume, if anything very important was going on in that sphere?'

'Sorry, Richard. Don't know and don't want to know. All I can say is that Bernard's a first rate man, excellent commander to work for.' That surely should close the subject.

'Yes, as I've heard you say before.' He paused. 'Which makes it such a pity that his wife is not here to support him.'

'I'm not sure how that follows, and anyhow I don't like ...'

But the fellow was off again. 'His PA is off sick, I understand.'

'Yes, the splendid Polly. Good at her work. Devoted to H.E. Fine woman. Expect she'll be back on parade fairly soon. Maybe in time for you to meet her.'

'What exactly do you mean by "devoted", Jack; does the devotion continue outside the office?'

'Good God, Richard!' This time Berridge had wildly overstepped the mark. It was outrageous. 'I consider your question in the worst of taste. Brathby is a fine man and for you to make such insinuations about him is not right.' And that was putting it mildly. Squires looked pointedly at his watch. 'It's getting late and we both have work to do in the morning. May I suggest that we now retire, that is unless you have any further *official* questions for me, clearly relevant to the business you were sent here to do?'

'I need to be in the Embassy early tomorrow.' Berridge seemed unabashed. 'With your permission I'll take the car in and send it back for you?'

'Yes, do that,' he replied, adding as Berridge made his way to the door, 'Good night, and I hope you sleep well.' He was rather proud of that – even if this ghastly man behaved insupportably one would maintain one's own standards throughout. Even if he was a cad, he was still one's guest...

*****

Now that Squires was on his own he could at least have a peaceful last drink. He needed a substantial slug while he thought over how he was going to cope with Berridge, or whatever the bloody man's real name was.

Yes, that was better. Top it up with water and settle down to think it through. Not easy to continue having the man under one's roof after this evening's business. On the other hand he *had* undertaken to host him, and he couldn't let Bernard down by asking to have him moved, could he? He was just taking a longish swallow when the incongruity of it hit him: here he was mentally slagging off Berridge and debating kicking him out of the house, and yet at the same time drinking the man's whisky. Suddenly the taste of the malt was all wrong.

What to do? Well he couldn't put back in the bottle what he'd already drunk, could he? But he'd get a fresh glass and then for symbolic reasons – yes that was the word, symbolic - open a bottle of his own and sit there quietly for a few minutes. Yes, and he'd fill up the jug as well. Always put plenty of water in the last one. Good rule that.

Squires stood up and tackled his re-supply problem.

Part Three

1

On Friday morning Brathby woke feeling happy, for a moment unsure why.

Ah yes, of course; the previous evening he'd overcome his diffidence and telephoned Polly. She'd thanked him prettily for the chocolates and stressed that she was looking forward to lunching with him on Saturday.

Warm from this, Bernard had fetched the latest volume of his diaries and settled at his desk to confide his hopes for Saturday, even down to what he proposed to say and how he hoped she would reply. Then he had analysed and written up what he had learned about Cardenas and his intentions, and what he felt about him. He took care to distinguish between an objective assessment of the threat that Cardenas posed, and his own strong subjective reaction to such an ill-mannered and apparently ill-intentioned adversary.

Brathby had clearly allowed his growing personal antipathy to distort his judgement. What harm could Cardenas really do? Surely the Deputy Under-Secretary, and other relevant key figures in the FCO, and elsewhere in Whitehall, must know what Cardenas was like and allow for his lack of finesse? And the man was comparatively junior, on secondment and ranked below deputy Head of Department, despite his arrogance; while he, Brathby, was after all the Ambassador. Yes, he'd become unnecessarily alarmed.

But then again Brathby knew himself well enough to realise that he tended to look on the bright side. Was the wish fathering the thought? Quite possibly. Anyhow, it was time to stop chewing it over and get on with the day.

Another good thing this morning was the total absence of even the faintest sour taste in his throat. Brathby had not had a single beer the night before. He liked to have at least one alcohol-free day each week and had instead sipped a succession of herbal teas. No wonder he felt so fresh.

Then he remembered the executions. He shuddered. But it would soon be over for the poor devils, whether they were really *tiefmen* or had just been caught up in a random police sweep. Knowing Zalomo, he could be reasonably sure he'd got it right. Perhaps he should have sent Jack Squires as observer? Too late to change now.

Brathby opened his eyes to find his tea by the bed. Cuthbert must have slipped in quietly just before he woke. Normally he greeted Brathby as he put down the tray. Perhaps he was unwell or, Brathby suspected, worried but not wanting to discuss his mystery problem.

He'd certainly have a word with Cuthbert this evening. Yes, and in the kitchen would be best, where Cuthbert felt most at ease with him.

Time now to rise and get on with the day. He'd get into his office really early – he had work to catch up on.

Things could only get better.

2

Jack Squires was suddenly, and painfully, awake.

He was long familiar with the sensations of slowly coming to in his chair in the early hours of the morning, having nodded off after a glass too many: a slight headache, and a dry mouth. Nothing which couldn't be handled by orange juice, aspirin, a quick wash and slipping quietly up to bed.

This was very different. It was full daylight and he was lying on the floor of his study with a fierce throb behind his eyes and a pain on the side of his head. Maggots appeared to be scampering around his brain. There was a deep sour taste in his throat, and his tongue felt like cloth; but, praise the Lord, no tell-tale smell of sick in the air. He was sore around the crotch where his trousers had twisted in on him. Someone – he himself perhaps, automatically preparing to go up to bed – had switched off the study air-conditioning. He was covered in sweat. But at least he hadn't pissed himself.

After a moment he also realised that someone had placed a cushion for him as a pillow. A cushion now sticky with blood from his head. He must have fallen against the pedestal of his desk. It was all very confusing.

Squires pulled himself up and into a chair. First he must have water; then he could assess the damage.

As if by magic the door opened. It was his plump and smiling young Steward. 'Good morning, Master, I bring drink.'

On the tray was a large glass of iced soda water with a slice of lemon in it.

Nodding to him, Squires drank deeply. 'Well done, Octavius. Good morning.'

'Also dis ting.' He offered a box of soluble aspirin.

Mixing four of these in the remains of the water Squires squinted at him. 'You are a King among Stewards.' He swallowed the mixture, praying for it to take effect quickly. He touched the sticky side of his head. 'How bad does this look, Octavius?'

'I gettum wet cloth.'

'And more soda water,' Squires called after him and slumped back in the chair.

Octavius was soon back and dabbing gently at the wound. 'No be too bad, dis one. Dis one your hair go hide um. After you dress we fixum.'

'Thank you Octavius.'

'And dis cushion, better I burn um?'

'Yes, good idea.' He paused. 'You put it there for me, as a pillow?'

'No, Master, I for quarter. Never know you here. Perhaps de madam done um.'

'Where is Mr Berridge now, Octavius?'

'De small Master? He chop early, just coffee and pineapple. Then he take car for office. He take his suitcase and say he fineesh here.'

So he'd cleared out. That was something, he supposed. 'Give you a good *dash*, did he?' he asked.

'At all! He ask me how many times you sleep for floor or for chair.'

'And ...'

'I tell um you good Master for me. Then he vex and say if I no answer proper he speak bad of me to de Umbassador.'

'Then ...?'

'Den I go make de breakfast. Pineapple he like but not de coffee.'

'Not the coffee?'

'No Master. Dat man no good for we. So I small piss for the coffee. I no do right?'

This was too complicated for Squires in his present condition. Octavius had clearly behaved with commendable initiative in the face of Berridge's bullying. On the other hand ... 'What is Madam doing, Octavius?'

'She no happy, Master.'

'No, one imagines not.'

'She take small breakfast in her room. Say she have headache.'

She have headache, God save us! Memories of the previous evening were trying to return. He shut them off. He could calculate the damage when he felt better.

'Car came back, Octavius, after taking Mr Berridge to the Embassy?'

'Yes, Master. Driver now waiting for you.'

'Had his small breakfast?'

'Yes, you no ready so fit chop.'

181

'You've done well, Octavius.' He stood up. 'No breakfast for me. Not even coffee. Just another big water when I come down.'

Squires slowly pulled himself up the stairs and reached his own room. Delightfully cool: Octavius must have switched on the aircon. Resisting the temptation to lower himself onto the bed he peeled off his clothes and shuffled to the bathroom. He could not remember when he had last felt so low.

Twenty minutes later, however, he was in better order, clean and dressed for the office, headache slightly receding. He reassured himself, with the aid of two mirrors, that his wound was scarcely visible beneath his hair. He would creep down, evading Jenny, and on the way to the Embassy assess what damage had been done. Clearly considerable, even if Berridge knew he'd fallen asleep in the study, but still possibly containable. Bit puzzling why the man had taken his suitcase; perhaps he was planning to take the afternoon plane to London. He patted his pocket; perhaps he'd soon be strong enough for the first cigarette of the day.

Right Squires, time to get on parade. Carefully down the stairs.

As he reached the bottom step a shrill and icy voice attacked him from the sitting room. 'So you've woken up at last, you drunken beast. Have you any, just *any*, idea what you've done?'

'Not now, please. Later. I must get to the Embassy. I am expected. Meeting, you know.' The wretched woman must have gone downstairs while he was showering.

'Why bother?' she said.

'What on earth do you mean, Jenny?' He was puzzled, but went into the room where she had been lying in ambush, her narrow and severe face regarding him with sour disapproval. She'd never before questioned his need to do his duty. That was one of the good things about her – the only good thing, he sometimes thought.

'Sit down.'

He sat.

'Now', she asked, standing in front of him, thin arms crossed and eyes boring into him, 'Just what *do* you remember of last night?'

He lit a cigarette, and after the first moment of nausea replied: 'Last night? Well, after our quiet supper one retired to the study for a spot of catching up on the reading, that sort of thing. You know, you were here.'

'And a drop of whisky no doubt.'

'Yes, tiny drop, while waiting up for this Berridge chap.'

'And then?' she continued coldly.

'When he came in we talked amicably for a while and, yes, I had another small glass or two. He was very interested in one's career, that sort of thing. All very civilised. But then he began to ask some damned impertinent questions. '

'Are you sure? I've found him a nice little man, well-mannered and rather charming.'

Squires snorted disgustedly. 'Of course I'm bloody well sure. He started asking about, well, secret matters, and then about Bernard Brathby's personal life, that sort of thing. He was absolutely out of order.'

'So?' She pursued.

'So one gave him a broad hint that it was time for bed and off he went. Can't think what the FCO is doing, sending a man like that. You'd think …'

'Then you had another few drinks, I expect, to reward yourself for having dealt so successfully with our guest.' Her contempt was unconcealed.

'Well, yes, one felt …' No, he was damned if he'd go on with this; it was time to leave the house instead of sitting here being interrogated by his own wife. Quite ridiculous. He made a painful move to rise.

'Don't get up. Just listen to me.'

'About what for God's sake? You've had your moan, and I'm fully aware that I drank too much last night and that Richard Berridge has decided not to stay any more. Can't say I'm sorry about that.'

'One moment. What was the last thing you remember? Richard had gone up, you said, having been rather rudely told to do so, if I've understood you properly. Then you settled down to finish the bottle.' She gave one of her exasperated sighs. 'You never could do anything in moderation, could you? Like the time, only last month, when …'

'Jenny, please.' He was getting more angry and feeling more ill. 'Just stick to the point.' Unless stopped she'd spend the morning rehearsing his various sins. And he had work to do, however rotten he felt.

'All right. *This* is the point. After Richard had gone up what did you do? Apart from drink, that is.'

'Can remember feeling pretty damned cross with the man. Ran over what he'd said. Thought what a cheek he had. That sort of thing. Then, I suppose, one must have nodded off.'

'Having opened another bottle?'

Suddenly he remembered. Oh God, that must have been what had undone him. He tried to make her understand. 'Felt I couldn't go on drinking *his* malt once I realised what a filthy shit he was.'

'I *do* wish you wouldn't use language like that. It …'

He stubbed out his half-smoked cigarette and stood up. 'That's it then. Better be going.' He started for the door.

'Oh, no you don't.' She had taken a step towards him and he sat down again. 'You really remember no more that that?'

'Nothing, until I woke up and Octavius brought me a drink of water.' What was she on about?

'Nothing? Well, I suppose you wouldn't in that disgusting condition.'

'So what are you trying to tell me?' Why couldn't the bloody woman just come out with it? It couldn't have been anything too drastic.

'In the night, about one o'clock, I heard a crashing sound. I opened my bedroom door. Richard must also have heard it and gone down to investigate. From the top of the stairs I could hear most of what was being said, or rather shouted. It was disgusting. Your behaviour, above all your language.'

He remembered absolutely nothing, but nothing, of this. Was she making it up? Unlikely, he had to acknowledge.

'Richard was presumably trying to help, like the decent man he evidently is, offering you a hand up to bed, it seems. But you yelled at him, swearing like a common soldier, using that horrible word, over and over again. You said you'd be … er … effed if you'd be told by a … effing guest, and an unwelcome one at that, what to do in your own effing house. And that he could eff off back to wherever he'd effing well come from. You also called him a poisonous little runt – it sounded like runt – who needed his effing tongue yanked out and stuffed … well, you can imagine the rest.'

Oh God. He now realised with a sickening jolt who had placed the cushion under his head. Not as a kindly act, he knew, but in order to underline his humiliation. And the shit had turned off the cooling at the same time, of course. It could hardly be worse. He wished a Chinese bullet had got him in Korea.

'You can see what this means, Jack, can't you? Once it gets back to London you're done for. Your drunken stupidity has ruined our chances of Washington.' What a talent she had for stating the obvious. 'Can't you understand what you've done, you thoughtless fool! Now what are we going to do? How shall we manage? What about the children's education? How *many* times have I warned you? You've let us down. Again. You – you – you – you useless sot.' She strode over to the window and turned to face him again. 'You idiot. If only you'd had the sense …'

'For Christ's sake woman, don't go on and on. You're exaggerating.' She wasn't, but he couldn't take any more. 'Now just fucking shut up. I'm going to the office.'

He left the house and walked unsteadily to the car. The thundery light and humid air got the maggots going again.

She was right about the posting. Once back in London that man would do for him. And it was his own fault.

Only a miracle could undo the damage now.

Like Berridge dropping dead.

3

'Morning Tom,' said Trevor the Archivist. 'Early today, aren't we?'

'Morning boyo,' Muckle responded.

'There's a note here for you, Tom: don't look like a love letter, I'm afraid.'

'Thanks a trillion', Muckle replied, putting the envelope in his pocket and moving past the banks of Chancery cupboards and safes. Going to be a busy day, he told himself as he arrived in front of the Station premises. He spun the wheels this way and that to open first the grille, and then the steel door. Finally to the wooden inner office door, with a three button combination, offering privacy, but no more real protection than the members' toilet at his dance club in Swansea, he reflected. But then it isn't necessary, is it? Only UK-based staff ever came in the Registry area and they all knew that the Intelligence Station premises within were out of bounds, even to the Ambassador.

Alone in the Station's outside office Muckle made himself a mug of coffee. Friday, every other Friday to be exact, was a bugger, *Carrot* delivery day. He'd think about that in a moment. Meanwhile he had another purpose for that vital bit of *Carrot* kit, the large magnifying glass.

A minute's careful examination and he was satisfied that old Dr Pox's special unguent was doing the trick. Nearly there. Maybe in action tonight? Lydia had been giving him that desperate look. Nearly a week it'd been now, with her no doubt thinking he was looking elsewhere and he not wanting to tell her what the real trouble had been. Yes, tonight. He'd risk it. He pulled his trousers up and started to open the big walk-in safe in the corner. Annoying that he'd have to close everything down again sometime later in the morning. The note had been from Berridge, saying he'd need to see him again, sometime before lunch. He was a weird one all right. What was his game? He was clearly a copper-bottomed hundred percent shit, cold as frozen coal; disagreeable even by the standards of MI5's boss class. Made sense he'd been seconded to the FCO– probably his own people had been happy to get shot of him for a while.

What was puzzling was how little interest he'd shown in Tom's discovery of the device, let alone in any views he might have on how it got into Buster's office. It wasn't till Berridge had been in the Embassy for more than half a day that he'd first sent for Tom and even then many of his questions were irrelevant to *Stuffing*. He'd had the nerve to probe him on the Station's activities and even asked whether old Antoun did things for them. When he could see that Tom didn't like this line he'd swiftly changed tack and adopted a hostile tone – why hadn't he left the *Stuffing* device in place, photographed it there and sought guidance from London? Why had he sent it home in the bag, without asking approval? When Tom spoke up and said that he'd expected thanks, not slagging off, for doing the FCO's job for them, and maybe they ought to send their sweepers out more often, Berridge had got nasty and said he'd be reporting him for insolence.

And now he wanted to see him again. What on earth for? All right he'd go when asked for because the Old Man had asked everyone to co-operate. But Berridge would have to wait while he put everything back in the walk-in safe and went through the laborious closing down procedure. Which would entail opening everything up again later, sod him.

Tom dragged the first sack of *noisa* notes from the big safe, heaved it onto the long table and emptied it out. Then he set to work. First he separated the many hundreds of evil-smelling notes into the different denominations, mainly tens, twenty-fives and fifties but also including some scores of ones and fives. Tom didn't know where the money came from, presumably bought in London and elsewhere from travellers and businessmen. He didn't care much either: his job was to sort and deliver it.

The real sod about this job was weeding out the unsuitable notes. He had to reject (and then return to Head Office, using special labels, for God's sake) any "seriously damaged" notes, which he interpreted as any likely to fall to pieces if not handled gently; also any which were defaced "in an apparently systematic way", presumably to guard against anyone passing the marked notes abroad to track where they next turned up. "Barium meal" technique, it was apparently called. Whoever feared that happening in this country must be paranoid, thought Muckle. But then everything to do with *Carrot* was treated with extreme care. Philippa and he would sometimes talk about other operational matters in this well-swept office but any discussion on *Carrot* took the form of written notes between them, which were subsequently shredded.

Finally of course Muckle had to spot the forgeries, hence the splendid and useful magnifying glass, used in tandem with the ultra-violet device. He knew he was good at this bit, and quite enjoyed it, but it was time-consuming nevertheless.

An hour later Muckle had made good progress and was on to the second sack. He'd soon have enough bundles to fill one of the cheap and garish locally-produced cardboard suitcases in which the notes completed the next stage of their journey. In the evening, the times varying, Muckle would park a car with plain local number-plates at the far end of the *Independence Hotel* car park. By the time he'd been inside for a beer the suitcase, which he'd left in the boot, would have disappeared. Given the ever-present danger of casual theft he imagined that the case was removed almost immediately after his arrival. He'd never tried to see who took it. He didn't need to know, any more than he needed to know where the money was going and for what purpose.

Shortly before he came out on posting the Area Director had called him to his office and told him what very little he needed to know about his role as bagman for *Carrot,* stressing that whatever else he did or did not do at the Post, he must at all costs keep the operation secure. 'Guard it with your life', he'd said, and Muckle felt he meant just that. In Head Office, the Director had said, only he himself and the two clerks in the mail room who handled the money knew about the operation – and it must be kept that way. Not even the Station's desk officer in London was indoctrinated.

From the way that the Director had spoken, Muckle had guessed that he probably had no political approval for *Carrot*; perhaps because he'd assessed that it wouldn't be granted, but that the operation was important enough to go ahead nevertheless. Not that that aspect bothered Muckle – such considerations were not for the likes of him. Perhaps they were doing this for the CIA in return for heavy favours. The Americans had recently had their fingers badly burned here; a number of their officers were quietly asked to leave and they were keeping their heads down. Yes, that was most likely it.

Anyhow, all that was speculation. Muckle continued his sorting, counting and bundling. Another hour or so and he'd be ready to pack the case.

4

'Good morning, Mr Sodham', Brathby called cheerily as the man pulled himself to his feet, fumbling at his flies and clearly surprised to see his Ambassador so early in the morning.

He'd been dozing in the far corner, behind the desk, Brathby realised, being content just to press the admittance button on demand; his log of events would be unlikely to bear too close an examination. Francis Paynton had been right to recommend his dismissal and Brathby wrong to over-rule him. Oh well, not too late to change his decision. Meanwhile he had other matters to attend to.

For an hour Brathby worked steadily through the mound of paper that Violet had left in his safe overnight. That done he surprised the early Duty Clerk by personally coming to the Registry and collecting the batch of overnight traffic which had been marked up for him. He also took time to put his head in the cipher room and bid good morning to the Communications Officer.

After a quick trawl through the telegrams – too many of them, unfortunately, which he must answer himself – he began to think of the despatch on the boring Ayumba affair, which he really couldn't put off writing any longer. He must get most of it done today, and then add anything relevant following the demonstrations. The first step to grinding through all this was to banish distracting thoughts of Polly.

He'd just about managed it when a slightly flustered Violet put her head round the door. 'Oh, sir, you are early. So sorry I wasn't here before. And you haven't had your coffee yet. I'll fix that straight away.'

'Good morning Violet. No need to apologise; you're not late, I'm early. But yes, coffee would be welcome.'

But before the kettle had boiled Violet put her head in again.

'Sorry, sir. Mr Berridge is here, says he needs to see you straight-away.'

A moment later the man was standing in front of him, refusing coffee – he seemed to have gone off it, he said – and telling him that he'd decided to leave the Colonel's house, and had brought his suitcase to the Residence. 'Presumably that's acceptable to you, Bernard – I'm sure you can make one of your spare rooms available. I had no alternative to moving out. I don't propose to give you details, but I must move.'

Brathby of course couldn't refuse. It would be unthinkable to send the man to a hotel, and he didn't want to inflict him on any of his colleagues. And undeniably there was ample space in the Residence. In fact if he hadn't met and taken a dislike to him in London he would have put him up there in the first place.

'Yes, Richard, I can find you a room.' He paused: 'Won't you sit down and give me some details of what happened.'

'No.'

'No, you won't sit down or no, you won't give any details?' Unsurprising if Jack had thrown him out, the ill-mannered little bastard.

'No to both. I prefer to stand much of the time, as you may know, and being personally unfamiliar with the effects of excessive alcohol consumption, I prefer not to attempt an explanation of what took place at Squires's house.'

Brathby's heart beat faster. Had Jack had a drink too many and insulted Cardenas? If so, he'd been a bloody fool, however much one might sympathise with him. Anyhow, he'd learn more later. But what an unsatisfactory business.

Meanwhile he would maintain the courtesies, whatever the provocation. 'Well, I'll see you at noon then, so that we can together hear how Francis Paynton got on, and to have lunch. I'll have a room prepared and give you a key so that you can let yourself in to the Residence whenever you wish.'

'I already have a key. I told your Steward to give me one. He seemed rather upset about that for some reason, and his manner was insolent.' He moved towards the door. 'Until noon then.'

A moment later Violet appeared with the coffee.

'Please pour for me, Violet.' He was still trembling with murderous anger at Cardenas's last words.

'Thank you.' A moment later he picked up his cup, back in control. 'Now Violet', he forced a smile which soon became real, 'to important matters. Are you coping with the work all right? Any problems?'

'Everything's fine, thank you, sir. And of course Polly will be back tomorrow.'

'Oh yes, of course,' he replied casually. 'How is she today?'

'We had a brief word this morning. I was running a bit late so didn't stay long. For some reason my alarm chose this morning to go on

190

the blink.'

'Yes?' She certainly took her time coming to the point. Could she be teasing him? No, impossible.

'She's much better. If she did have a shock it seems to have worn off. As I said before, she seems, well, sort of determined. It's difficult to explain, sir. As if she's made up her mind about something, or is near to doing so. She certainly wasn't in the mood for chitchat. She said she'd phone this afternoon to let us know how she is.'

'Well, that all sounds promising.' He glanced at his watch. 'Now, Violet I've got a mound of stuff to get through and then an early lunch upstairs. So no visitors please unless their business is urgent.'

Excellent news about Polly.

To the devil with Cardenas.

He drew the papers towards him.

5

Muckle looked with satisfaction at the thousands of notes, neatly bundled, stacked on the table against the wall and ready for stringing together; he was now on the last batch and shouldn't be more than another half hour.

His bladder was getting full – too much coffee, Tom, he told himself. Usually if he was alone in the Station office he'd just use one of the developer jugs and flush it down the wash basin. What nobody knew about nobody cared about, he reckoned. Once, to amuse himself – he'd had a couple of beers at lunch time and Philippa was off seeing Zalomo – he'd stood on the workbench one side of the room and pissed across the gap into the basin. Good five foot carry he reckoned, minus the length of his organ of course.

But today he wanted to stretch his legs so he'd leave the office for a couple of minutes and take the short walk through the Registry and along the Chancery corridor to the gents.

No need to lock the outside grille or steel door: the privacy door would do for the couple of minutes he'd be away.

But as Muckle came out into the Registry area and pulled the wooden door behind him he saw Berridge standing at the counter, making notes from a file which Harry was showing him. He gave Muckle a half nod and continued his work.

That puts a different complexion on it, said Muckle to himself. I wouldn't trust that little sheep-shagger as far as I can spit. Which is about as far as he is now from the privacy door. So he turned and pulled the grille across, locked it, replaced the key in the blister and made his way to the corridor. As he passed behind Berridge his friend Harry rolled his eyes, to indicate that the man was probably poking his nose in where it didn't belong, Muckle guessed.

When Muckle returned the two of them were still at the counter, a different coloured file out now he noticed, and Harry looking less than ecstatic at the time he was having to spend with Berridge. Probably wanted to get on with the file-weeding programme that the Head of Chancery had ordered ahead of the next day's expected demos.

*****

On return to the Registry area Muckle quickly re-opened the grille, swung it back against the outside wall, punched the code for the privacy door and stepped into the Station office. He was turning to shut it behind him when he was suddenly aware that Berridge was at his shoulder, gripping his arm fiercely and pushing him into the room.

Then the man released him, closed the door and faced Muckle. 'That was insulting, what you did now', he hissed, 'coming out, seeing me and then deliberately going back to lock the grille. Who do you think you are, and what are you hiding so carefully?'

'You're not allowed in here. Nobody is. Why did you force your way in?' Muckle was protesting, his voice rising and trying vainly to block Berridge's view of the table. 'I shall report this to the Ambassador. Just leave now. Please. If you want to see me I'll come to your room. You shouldn't be in here, I tell you.'

He knew he couldn't throw him out physically. He wasn't as strong as the little bastard anyhow, and if he laid a finger on a senior man like this he'd be in deep shit. Better to try persuasion instead: 'Mr Berridge,' – he was fighting to control his breathing – 'If you leave now, I shan't complain about this to anyone. But you aren't allowed in here. Against all the rules, it is, don't you see? Please, sir.' It sounded lame and that last word had cost him, but he was getting desperate.

It was too late: Berridge was now by the table and pointing: 'What's this, Muckle? There must be thousands, tens of thousands of – what d'you call them, *noisas* – here.' He advanced, waving his finger and prodding at the piles, knocking down a stack of fifty *noisa* notes. 'Yes, tens of thousands. A fortune.' He swept a great mound of money onto the floor and turned to face Muckle, who at the moment would have killed him, if he'd had the means, as he'd killed that *tiefman*.

'So what's this about, Muckle? In London I asked the Deputy Under-Secretary if you people here, such as you are, had any important operation going here, and he said definitely not. Certainly nothing that had needed political approval. So what is this?' He looked sneeringly at Muckle. 'Yes, this.' His shining toecap stirred the money on the floor. 'Does Brathby know about it? What game are you playing, Muckle? No wonder microphones get planted in this Embassy – the whole place is out of control.'

Tom was trembling. What should he say? His orders had been quite categorical. Nobody, but nobody, must ever know about *Carrot*. He thought furiously.

There was only one way to explain it. 'It's like this Mr Berridge, it's not what you think …'

'What precisely do you mean, Muckle?'

'It's sort of private enterprise, sir. You know, making a bit on the side. There's a group of us, I'm the only one in the Embassy though; the *noisas* are bought abroad, London and places, where they're dirt cheap and then sent back here …'

'So you're a swindler as well as a murderer, Muckle. I see.'

'Murderer?'

'Oh yes I've heard about your drunken escapade with the *machete*, as you call it.'

'It wasn't like that. It …'

'Never mind that now. You're in a mess, Muckle, aren't you? Sure Brathby doesn't know about all this?' He stirred the notes with his foot. 'Not taking a cut, is he?'

'No, no. Impossible. Doesn't know a thing about it.' Was the man off his head?

Berridge was now approaching the strong room. 'What's in here then? Files of your so-called agents, I expect. I think I'll have a look.'

'Get back. Get back now.' Muckle stood between Berridge and the open door. What this man was trying to do was so outrageous, so dreadful that Muckle's brain had almost gone blank with shock. He and Philippa were the only two people in the world who were allowed in there, the holiest of holies. 'Move away now, immediately, or I'll scream for the Registry Staff to break down the wooden door.'

'Dare say they know the combination anyhow, the slack way this place is run.' But he retreated into the centre of the room, gave a final kick at some stray notes and prepared to leave, pausing only to glance at his watch and make a note in his black book. 'I'd start packing if I were you, Muckle. I really don't see you being kept on here once I've reported what I've found out today.' He pulled the door closed behind him.

Muckle sat, head in hands, amid the wreckage. He was ashamed that he had been so careless as to allow Berridge to creep up behind him and force his way in; he was angry, fiercely angry, that this man had

194

– and in the pursuit of what? – violated every norm of accepted behaviour. And he was frightened of the consequences, terrified. If Berridge believed his explanation of the money then he would, as he had made clear, get him removed; if he didn't and reported that an unauthorised operation was taking place, then Tom would be in trouble for letting it be discovered. Perhaps he should have screamed for Harry to have broken in – but even *he* wasn't supposed to know about the money.

Head hammering with pain and confusion Tom began distractedly to gather up the scattered notes. That this Berridge man had actually swept them off the table, had *kicked* them – the anger was like acid in his stomach. For a minute he sat at the table, banging his hands on it and weeping with frustration.

He slowly forced himself to take control. He must *think*, think what to do for the best, take some decisions. He remembered that Philippa kept a bottle of brandy in the strong room. Perhaps a slug of that would help. He was rising to fetch the bottle when he remembered her words, 'It's not for us, Tom, unless we've something to celebrate. It's for *other* people's emergencies. We have *brains* for our emergencies and they're not improved by jungle juice.'

So what would Philippa do? Apart from not being in this mess in the first place, of course. Well the first thing was to get the money organised again and be ready for tonight's drop off. The delivery must go ahead whatever happened.

Next problem: who, if anyone, should he tell about this, and what good would it do? As he knew from the latest Personnel Movements circular, the Director himself was on safari in the Kruger Park, having just visited the Southern African Stations. His deputy, Tom assumed, knew nothing of *Carrot*. Oh God, why wasn't The Brainbox here when he needed her? She was due back soon – perhaps he could invent a good reason to ask for her earlier return. Again, couldn't give the truth of course because the country desk, where the telegram would be received, knew nothing about the operation.

What would she do? Just thinking about her made him feel a little better. Tell the Old Man? It was a good rule at a Station, she'd said, to trust your Ambassador unless he's indiscreet or a fool. Of course it meant admitting to him that this operation, which would have been very embarrassing for him if discovered by the locals, had been going on without his knowledge. But he was a good bloke. Yes that's what he'd do. First get this money ready for delivery again and then go and see the Old Man. Tell him the full story and ask for help. And better do so soon, before he lost his nerve.

6

Friday morning had definitely not gone as Brathby had hoped, and the Ayumba despatch was still unfinished.

He had managed an uninterrupted half-hour before an apologetic Violet ushered in the Consul, who was insisting on seeing him. It was the usual story: his visa people were stretched to breaking point and what could be done? After they had fruitlessly covered old ground Brathby eventually agreed that one of the junior admin officers should help out for two or three mornings a week. Bill must work out the details with Head of Chancery, who would have to accept the idea, like it or not.

The Consul thanked him gruffly, although muttering about the problems involved in training a new hand. But the arrangement should help tide him over until the Immigration Officer from Dover arrived to join the Embassy.

On his way out he asked: 'What's this Berridge fellow like then? Edith and I are having a supper party for him this evening, as you know.' He went on: 'Apparently he's looking in at my department this morning – says he wants to get the geography straight in connection with his enquiry or some such thing. Shan't see him there myself though: got one of these Commonwealth Mission Consular meetings to attend.'

'Well, he won't make serious inroads into your drink supply. His tipple is iced tonic. Hope it goes well.' He'd neither time nor inclination to discuss Cardenas any further with Bill, although grateful that he'd agreed to look after him for the evening.

Five minutes later, when he was just refocused on the Ayumba despatch, Violet was back. 'So sorry, sir, but it's the Colonel. Says he really must see you but won't stay long.' She added: 'He's not looking at all well.'

A serious understatement, Brathby realised, when Squires was sitting opposite him. No self-respecting undertaker would have allowed a corpse to be displayed in this condition. His yellow hooded eyes were flecked with red, above grey sagging pouches. His immaculate turnout of dark suit, highly polished shoes, crisp white shirt and regimental tie only highlighted the man's deplorable condition.

'Won't keep you long, Ambassador,' he began with unusual formality. 'Just that one has a couple of things to say.' He groped for his cigarettes and looked for approval.

'Yes, light up, Jack. Here's the ashtray.'

'Main thing is that one is deeply sorry for having foisted this Berridge person on you. Yes, deeply sorry. I take it he *has* dumped himself on you?'

'Yes, I'm afraid he has, Jack. And the second thing?' God, he did look awful.

Squires had a brief coughing fit and then screwed up his eyes as if the mere act of looking was painful. Perhaps it was. 'More difficult to express really, especially when one's not feeling too well.' He stubbed out the cigarette he'd just lit.

'Take your time.' What he really meant was: spit it out fast and let me get back to my blasted despatch. He'd suggest that Jack went home to bed; he'd never seen him this bad.

'Yes, second thing. Wondered whether to tell you or not. It's that although there's absolutely no excuse for insulting a guest in one's own house – and that's what I'm told I did – one has absolutely no doubt that Berridge is up to no good. Rotten apple, untrustworthy. Sort of officer that deservedly gets shot in battle by his own Sergeant. He's scuppered me of course, that's my own damned fault, but he'll have others in his sights too. You yourself, Bernie, I shouldn't be surprised.'

Exhausted by this, it seemed, Squires nodded off for a moment, recovered, groped for another cigarette and then decided against. 'If you don't mind I'll leave it there for now. Go into detail another day.' He made an unsuccessful attempt at a smile. 'Over a glass of soda water perhaps.' He struggled to his feet.

Brathby had tried to persuade Squires to go home and sleep it off. But no, he had a Mr Armitage coming in to see him in half an hour. 'Got to be on parade. Can't let the chap down.' He moved unsteadily towards the door. 'Oh, and better, I imagine, if I don't show up to this debrief and lunch, if you don't mind. Perhaps you can say I'm unwell. True, actually.'

What had Jack meant by being 'told' that he'd insulted Cardenas? And that bit about being 'scuppered' was a bit strange, wasn't it? Intriguing what he'd said about Cardenas having others 'in his sights'.

But a bit far-fetched. In assessing all this Brathby mustn't be too influenced by Cardenas's ill-mannered behaviour to himself, not so much
to him as an individual, but to the Ambassador. Maybe Jack was exaggerating. But the whole thing was unsettling: Jack was not given to
wild statements and he was clearly not only atrociously hungover but
also quietly very angry indeed. Perhaps it was a good thing that Cardenas had left his house.

Despite all this Brathby had eventually managed a first draft of his
despatch and got as far as dictating it to Violet when Elias had tapped
on the door. If convenient and so sorry for interrupting but, could he
please have a word with Your Excellency, won't keep you long Your
Excellency. More hand wringing. Sorry, Your Excellency.

Was there no peace in this world? Largely his own fault, he knew,
for being so approachable.

When Elias left ten minutes later Brathby was still unsure why he'd
called at all. First he'd raised the question of the next day's demonstrations, but had nothing fresh to report. Then he'd said that the old
hands in the Embassy expected the Big Rains very soon, which Brathby
already knew. Then of all things he started rabbiting on about his pension. Only last month Brathby had assured him that it was totally secure, short of Elias being found guilty of 'gross professional
misconduct'. Then he'd mentioned some perfectly routine matter re-
lating to the Police Training Scheme. If he'd had something important
to discuss, as was implied by his calling without appointment, then he
certainly wasn't producing it. Brathby, who would happily have continued to listen if Elias had had anything of substance to say, found it
very irritating.

Eventually, to get him to go, he stood up, thanked Elias for calling
and said that he hoped that he and his wife had enjoyed entertaining
Mr Berridge the previous evening.

He expected a conventional and anodyne reply from Elias. But no,
he stopped short at the door and turned to look unhappily at Brathby,
saying that regretfully Mr Berridge had not been an easy guest. He had
not been 'as polite as expected', Elias said, and had spoken at length to
Bertha in German, which, as His Excellency knew, was a language of
which Elias had only a smattering. In several unspecified ways she had
not behaved well, Elias was ashamed to say. He was fearful lest she had

taken the opportunity to tell Mr Berridge lies about him.

Or truths, Brathby wondered, and if so, what? He had no means of ever knowing, and was it his business? He couldn't worry about everything.

He murmured a few words of comfort to Elias. The Ambassador doubted that any real harm had been done. Bertha had probably been carried away by the chance to speak her native language. He eased Elias out of the door.

Bertha at her best was not easy company; what she must have been like if even her own husband was complaining about her behaviour - it didn't bear thinking about. Not now anyhow. What for God's sake had got into his staff? Irresolute, fussing, poxed, hungover, fighting with their wives. Listening to an account of Paynton's gruesome morning might turn out to be light relief.

He was just leaving his office when Violet was back: 'Sorry, sir, I've got Tom Muckle here. Can he have a very quick word?'

'Come in Tom,' he called, putting his pen in his pocket and strapping on his watch. 'Is it a quick one? A secret report for me to read, perhaps?'

'No, Buster, something I need to talk about. Bit complicated really.' He was looking flustered.

'Can it wait till after lunch, Tom, or is it really urgent?' God, he hoped the young man hadn't also fallen foul of Cardenas.

'It *can* wait, Buster.' But he looked unhappy.

'Thanks Tom, Violet will let you know when I'm back.'

He left. What a morning, he thought; and now he had the prospect of a so-called working lunch, debriefing Francis about licensed cruelty in the presence of a man who was, to put it mildly, creating unwelcome waves in his Embassy and who needed to be carefully watched.

Who'd want to be Ambassador in a place like this?

Well, he would, so long as he knew he was being useful, and at almost any price.

It was time he started to assert himself a little more.

7

Cardenas let himself into the Residence and swiftly mounted the stairs. He had things to do before the others arrived for Francis Paynton's debriefing on the executions.

He felt at his fittest and most effective; he was doing useful work and enjoying it. The only mild disappointment was that Brathby and his pampered staff were proving so absurdly easy to manipulate. Unsurprising perhaps, given their range of physical addictions. Also that pathetic need to be liked rather than respected; this was manifested most clearly in Brathby's own paternalism and lack of grip. The shake-up certain to follow his return to London would not only afford him technical satisfaction from the skilful exercise of power; it would be in the public interest.

Cuthbert was standing in the hall, at the top of the stairs. 'I show you bedroom,' he said without any other form of greeting. 'Dis way'. He walked slowly down the passage in front of Cardenas and opened a door. 'Dis one.'

It looked comfortable enough although, Cardenas suspected, it was the least grand of the guest rooms. Perhaps choosing it for him was a small gesture of rebellion by Cuthbert; but that could be snuffed out later. Perhaps the ridiculous creature had even hidden some juju object in his room. He'd look tonight. If he found anything it'd be amusing to confront Brathby with it.

His spare suit was hanging up and his other clothes and belongings were neatly laid out. 'Why did you unpack my case, Steward? I did not tell you to.'

'Eet my job. You no want unpack, you lockum case.'

No 'sah' he noticed. Yes, the man had recovered some of his spirit. But he was no sort of threat to Cardenas; and disgrace and dismissal awaited him.

'Leave me now. I'll call if I want anything', adding softly as Cuthbert shuffled toward the door: 'And how is dear Eventide today?' Just a little reminder.

The man looked shaken and left the room without replying. Cardenas showered in the antiquated bathroom and spent a moment in front of the full-length mirror to admire his genitals and his flat stomach – a splendid sight. That young Vice-Consul whose office he had visited this morning had been rather attractive, considering she must be at least twenty-two. Her reaction had not been *obviously* positive when he had made a small move towards her, it was true. But she would be a fellow guest this evening at her boss's supper party. That should give him the opportunity to advance matters; perhaps he would take her back to her flat afterwards. If so, or even if he had to wait a short while longer, his equipment would not be found wanting.

But he mustn't allow such thoughts to distract him from the immediate work in hand; he closed his eyes and summoned the vision of Bertha Elias. That did the trick.

He dressed quickly, made a couple of brief notes in his black book, and prepared to leave his room. With luck he'd have a quarter of an hour before any of the others arrived for lunch. He wanted another look at Brathby's quarters, and also to check that the key to the old storeroom was still in the same place.

But Cuthbert was waiting outside the door.

'What are you skulking here for? Why aren't you at work?' The man had his hand against the wall to support himself.

'Dis my work. Come to ask if you want de iced tonic water.'

Again no 'sah' and a look of what they'd called 'dumb insolence' in the Navy.

'Later, I'm busy; when the others come.' The damned fool still didn't move. 'Now just get out of my path you snivelling, senile, incompetent streak of black shit.' Cardenas was angry with himself; he had nearly lost his temper. 'I'm going that way.'

'Dis no be way to sitting room.'

'How dare you …' He grasped the Steward's bony shoulder and pushed him roughly aside.

'But Mr Francis …' he mumbled, groping on the floor for his spectacles.

'Cardenas stopped. 'What are you talking about, what about "Mr Francis", as you call him?'

'He telephone. He come in one minute.'

Damn. Well, he'd have ample time tonight, or early tomorrow morning, to nose around. It could even be profitable to spend a few minutes with Paynton before the Ambassador arrived.

But no sooner were Cardenas and Paynton ensconced in the sitting room's comfortable upright cane chairs, with their drinks on the glass–topped table in front of them, than Brathby came bustling in. He apologised for not having been there to receive them, and also explained that the Colonel was otherwise occupied and would not be joining them. That was no surprise.

Brathby, although superficially lively, was definitely looking worn. Strange how even a little pressure could tell on some men, especially the emotionally unstable. Paynton, on the other hand, despite his morning's activities, appeared relaxed and fit, with even a touch of colour in his cheeks. He had clearly given his thin fair hair a severe brushing; it was positively glowing. His clothes sat easily on such a slim and well-honed figure. So far, so good.

Cardenas felt an unsummoned touch of warmth towards the man, similar to what he'd felt when first meeting him. He trusted that Paynton would give a good account of himself.

Cuthbert staggered in with a tray of smoked salmon sandwiches and returned with another of drinks. On each occasion, Cardenas noted with amusement, it was the Ambassador rather than his Head of Chancery who had moved to help him. There was a large thermos of iced tea for Paynton, fresh tonics for Cardenas and beer for Brathby. No wonder the man had the beginnings of a paunch, drinking that muck all day.

'I thought we'd be more comfortable in here,' Brathby said. 'I've told Cuthbert he won't be needed any more – he hasn't been too well this last day or so – and if we want more to drink there's plenty in the small fridge over there. We can help ourselves.' He looked around. 'Have you both got all you need?' He started on his beer.

'Now before we come to the main item of business,' Brathby was continuing, 'perhaps Richard would like to bring us up to date on his *Stuffing* investigation. Which I understand has made considerable progress …?' He looked interrogatively at Cardenas. Clearly Brathby had felt emboldened by his subordinate's presence to pester him again, rather than wait until he was ready to explain. But Cardenas had anyhow decided that he would bring up the subject this afternoon; and there was no harm in letting Brathby feel in charge occasionally – he would fall all the harder when the time came.

'Yes', he said, 'I have solved the problem of how the device was planted.'

'You are perhaps going to enlighten us?' Brathby asked, a little peevishly.

'I thought I should tell you first, privately, Ambassador.' Brathby's face softened at the courtesy, as if by the touch of a switch. 'Perhaps I should stay on here for a few minutes after Francis has returned to the office and tell you the full story. Also I hope you will agree that since the lessons to be learned from this are relevant to all the UK-based staff, that we should hold a meeting for me to explain what really happened and why.'

The Ambassador thought for a moment. 'That sounds sensible enough. When would you propose?'

'Since I plan to leave for London tomorrow evening it has to be tomorrow morning. I believe your staff normally work two Saturday mornings a month and that tomorrow is one of them?'

'Yes; it's a semi-official day only, casual dress and no locally-engaged staff present. Then most of us go to the Embassy Club for a drink and a game of darts and I sometimes have a number of the junior staff up here for a casual lunch.'

'Very cosy.' He paused. 'So tomorrow morning at eight o'clock?'

'Too early, Richard. There'll be telegrams to be read and final precautions taken *vis-à-vis* the demonstrations.' He walked over to the window. 'As you can see, the sky is changing; a sign that the Big Rains are very close, as everyone keeps telling me. Is that not right, Francis?'

'Yes, Ambassador. It was exactly like this last year the day before they broke; and the year before.'

'So the staff may have problems getting in, you see.' It was pathetic how the man felt the need to explain – wasn't he after all the Ambassador, however poorly he did the job? 'Half-past nine would be better and that may change depending on developments. But we'll *aim* for half past nine.'

'All right. The Embassy Conference Room at nine thirty; UK-based diplomatic staff only.'

'No', Brathby replied after a moment. 'Downstairs is too formal for a Saturday. 'We'll meet up here, in the Residence, instead. We can all fit into the main reception room; one or two of the younger staff can come early and help bring in chairs and another table ...'

'But security, sir?' Paynton pointed out. 'There's always the possibility of another microphone attack, at least theoretically.'

'Yes, the Head of Chancery has a powerful point there, Bernard,' Cardenas weighed in. 'We really should ...'

'That needn't be a problem. I shall get Tom Muckle to make an electronic sweep of the room before we start, and he will stay in the Residence to monitor the airwaves during the meeting. I shall also need Polly, if she is fully recovered, to take notes. Oh, and when you inform our colleagues, Francis, tell them they can come up here anytime from around nine – there'll be tea and coffee available.' He continued: 'I think that covers everything.'

Paynton said: 'Just one point, Ambassador: I take it you will not be inviting Elias, given the confidential nature of ...'

'I most definitely *do* want Mr Elias at the meeting, Francis. Please arrange it.'

Brathby really was getting above himself, evidently enjoying this petty exercise of authority. But let him puff himself up for the moment. Learning the results of Cardenas's investigations would soon puncture his confidence.

Moreover, on second thoughts Cardenas welcomed the prospect of Elias's presence – it would add a certain piquancy to have him as another witness to the Ambassador's humiliation.

'Now, perhaps we should come to the main reason why the three of us are here,' Brathby said.

For a moment Cardenas considered stepping in to get things going in the right direction with a few well-structured questions, but then decided against. He would permit Brathby to conduct the debrief. How he did it would itself be of interest and probably provide further useful examples of his incompetence.

'Right, Francis,' Brathby was saying, 'we are in your hands. Take your time and go into as much detail as you feel comfortable with, explaining as much background as is necessary so that Richard can see it all in context.'

Whatever that meant, Cardenas thought; and where had Brathby learned to use that sickly expression 'feel comfortable with'? It neatly summed up the man's attitude to his job.

'It is worth making the point,' Paynton began, turning to Cardenas, 'that there was nothing especially unusual about this morning's events, except, from our angle, that the criminals included a number condemned for the murder of a British citizen. Hence the invitation for us to be represented. The police had told us that there were to be twenty executions today, of whom five were to be ours, as it were.' He took a sip of tea. 'When I arrived I was told that "our" *tiefmen* were to be saved until last, apparently as a favour to us, since this would entail extra suffering for them.'

An admirable introduction, Cardenas thought. A solemn demeanour and a sombre tone of voice as befits a tale of human woe. Whatever he might really be feeling.

'So,' Brathby asked, 'you took your own car as we agreed, but used one of the Embassy drivers?' He turned to Cardenas to explain. 'I felt it better not to have a car there with British diplomatic plates. In case the press took an interest.'

Cardenas did not bother to comment.

'Yes, sir' replied Paynton. 'I took Samuel. A good lad. He got us to within fifty yards of the beach and I walked from there.'

'Big crowd?' Brathby asked.

'Several hundred, maybe as many as a thousand. A group from *Uminco* were there, half a dozen or so. They were in a sort of small temporary grandstand to which I was directed, which had been reserved for foreigners. The *Uminco* group had obviously had a few drinks and were passing a bottle around. It was not a pretty sight. Frankly I was disgusted. They cheered when they saw me, offering me a drink and inviting me to sit with them. The police had allocated them places at the front. I gave them a friendly wave but did not choose to go over to them; instead I joined the few others from the Diplomatic Corps who were present. The Swedish Consul was there, doubtless gathering details for some human rights protest, and a man from the Turkish Embassy, I can't imagine why. Also a Ghanaian, presumably out of respect to the *Uminco* guards, both Ghanaians, who were killed.'

'Nobody else?' It was Brathby again.

Until then Paynton had been speaking quite calmly, almost sadly and reluctantly, but he now gave what, in any one else, Cardenas would have categorised as a snigger. Cardenas sat up, looking at him carefully. Had the mask slipped? And if so, what was behind it?

'Yes, an Attaché from the American Embassy, God knows what he was there for. To see what make of gun the firing squad was using perhaps. Or else …'

Brathby, who had noticed nothing untoward, interrupted him: 'Who made up the firing squad?'

'Members of the Presidential bodyguard, sir. Usually on these occasions a detachment from the local police is sent but apparently in view of the seriousness with which this government viewed the offence they, the prisoners that is, were upgraded …'

He was breathing a little heavily, though the mask – if mask it was – was back in place, Cardenas noted. 'It was intended as some sort of compliment, or apology, to us; or so it was strongly hinted by the Ministry of Foreign Affairs *Chef de Protocol*, who came over to speak to the diplomatic contingent, such as we were.'

'Did the robbers appear to have been ill-treated?' Typical Brathby to be concerned with that. 'How close were you to them?'

'Close enough to see there was no facial bruising, broken noses or the like, and no other obvious signs of their having been beaten. But the condition of their lower clothing, if you get my drift, sir, showed that they weren't too … er … that they took a dim view of the situation! Sorry, sir.' He suppressed what seemed like a nervous laugh. 'Don't mean to be flippant.' He paused for a moment. Cardenas waited, watched. The manner, tone, and language of Paynton's reply to Brathby's innocent question had suddenly opened up the clear possibility that behind Paynton's mask was – what exactly? – *Relish*? Had the man actually *enjoyed* it? Yes, this was clearly a possibility and one which must be investigated.

'Francis, I think you need a drink,' Brathby was saying. 'There's scotch in that decanter over there, if you wish.'

'Thank you but no, sir.' He smiled rather vacantly, first at the Ambassador, then at Cardenas. 'Shall I continue?'

He was under control again now, but the experienced Cardenas knew which signs to look for, and where he would find them.

'Yes, do go on', the Ambassador said. 'When you're ready. Tell me, Francis did you find all this distressing? Perhaps it was unreasonable of me to have ...' Brathby was looking anxiously at Paynton as if he were more concerned for the man's welfare than in exploiting the moment to assess his calibre.

'No, not "distressing" exactly. It was of course an unusual experience, and in principal I deplore capital punishment. It was very ... how shall I put it ... educational. It was strange, so very strange, I mean the way they actually carried out the executions.'

Paynton took a further long drink of iced tea and continued: 'You see they were disposed of in batches, if I may use that term.'

For a moment Cardenas thought that Paynton was going to lose his composure again but he went on normally:

'What they did was to bring on five at a time and tie them to separate posts. Then the firing squad shot each one in turn, starting with the man on their left. But they wouldn't shoot the second man until they were sure the first one was dead; this often involved the officer administering the *coup de grâce*, and then the same with the next one, and so on until they'd finished all five. Those in the group tied to the posts while waiting their turn were pulling like mad on their cigarettes, some of them with four or five in their mouths at the same time.' His mouth began to twitch at the corner. 'Must be awfully bad for their health ... oh, sorry, sir ... perhaps I'm not feeling quite as calm about this as I should.'

'That's understandable, Francis. And "our" five were the last. Anything special in connection with them?'

Could that fool Brathby not see that this was exactly the moment to put pressure on the man? What else was there to come? What distasteful trait, what crude quirk of personality was behind the unstable mask? Cardenas resisted the urge to intervene, and waited for Paynton to continue. He now felt more confident that his earlier guess was right. Had Paynton got a *thrill* out of the occasion? A bit of close covert surveillance, his own Service's *métier*, was called for. He watched.

'Well, the police commander came over to the stand and asked the *Uminco* group if they'd like to come and rough them up a bit before they were shot.' Paynton was continuing his story. 'That turned the

Uminco men quiet, they shook their heads, one was sick – I could smell it from twenty yards – and another shouted that he'd seen enough and left.' He moved a little uncomfortably in his chair. 'Yes, there was one other … er … shall we say peculiarity about "our" group. Are you sure you want me …?'

'Yes, Francis, go on.'

He hunched forward, as if keen now to continue. 'Well, sir, by this time the accuracy of the shooting was deteriorating, and the officer had been very busy with his revolver. Maybe the marksmen were getting bored, or the hashish which I'm told that they're issued with on these occasions was wearing off. Anyway the first three were dispatched reasonably quickly, and in the usual way had been cut down and were lying on the sand by their posts, with the flies beginning to move in on them. Very different with the fourth, however.' The pitch of his voice had risen and he was dabbing his forehead with a handkerchief.

'In what way?' the Ambassador asked.

Before Paynton could reply Cardenas, who had been watching him as a cat watches a mouse-hole, suddenly stood up and said abruptly: 'I shall start on the food, Bernard, if you don't mind. Francis it might do you some good to stretch your legs.'

Brathby was clearly puzzled by this interruption but was obediently on his feet and following Cardenas's lead in getting a plateful of sandwiches. 'Yes, do help yourself, Francis,' he called.

Paynton half made to rise but then subsided into his seat saying that he was not yet hungry. But not before Cardenas had spotted the physical manifestation of what he had begun to suspect. How very interesting. But perhaps it was coincidental, not necessarily stimulated by recounting his story? If so he should be able to suppress it easily enough.

Ignoring Paynton's protestations, Brathby had brought him some sandwiches and the three were seated again as before.

Paynton, remarking that after all he did fancy something to eat, was fast demolishing what Brathby had brought him.

'You were saying that things were different with the fourth man in the group.' Cardenas prompted, to Brathby's obvious disapproval.

'Yes. They fired at him, the fourth man, that is. He was wounded, in the chest it seemed, and his head fell forward; unlike some he had only one cigarette alight – he'd been pulling on it strongly and with his eyes shut. As his mouth opened the cigarette must have fallen inside his shirt, which then started to smoulder and burn.'

'Very strange that it caught fire in that humidity,' Cardenas commented.

'I thought so too, Richard,' Paynton said. 'But perhaps the soldiers had been sprinkling him with petrol beforehand ... the American attaché said that it's a game they sometimes play with the prisoners ... they start snapping their lighters and ...'

'Yes, I can imagine it, Francis.' Brathby looked shocked.

'Bit of a muddle really. The officer went over to finish him off, at the same time shouting at his men to beat the flames out. The prisoner was screaming. It was all fairly chaotic, especially as the officer's revolver was empty and he was fumbling around in his pocket for more ammunition. Then he dropped the rounds on the sand and had to wipe them before loading the gun ... it all seemed to take a long time, the man at the stake, burning, writhing, screaming. When that was all over they went through the normal procedure with the fifth man in the group – he'd been fairly unhappy, as you can imagine.'

'But you saw it through to the end?'

'Oh yes, of *course,* sir. Then the American and I accepted the offer of a beer from the *Chef de Protocol*, who had a cold box in his car. The Swede refused and left, muttering darkly, and the others didn't seem to have been invited. I took my leave after ten minutes. I hope that was about right, sir.' His mouth was twitching again. 'I was uncertain how long protocol dictates that should be spent over unofficial post-execution drinks with a medium-level Foreign Affairs official. Perhaps', he went on chattily, almost cheerfully, 'he and the American are still there, toasting friendship between those peace-loving countries who like guns and the death penalty. They certainly seemed to be getting on well. I suppose ...'

'Francis, would you be so very kind as to fetch me another tonic from the table behind you?' Cardenas interposed, at the same time laying a restraining hand on the Ambassador's arm.

'Of course', Paynton replied, at first hesitating then suddenly taking an interest in a newspaper on the coffee table and carrying it with him, holding it in a curious fashion in front of his body, almost like an apron.

'Ice and lemon?' he mumbled with his back to the others.

His last doubt now removed, Cardenas felt both disappointment and triumph. And almost certainly Brathby had noticed nothing out of place.

'I think that's as far as we can profitably go for the moment,' said Brathby, standing up. 'I am in your debt both for attending this unfortunate event, Francis, and for your vivid account of the proceedings. If you were distressed at what you observed, that is to your credit – it was clearly a scene of cruelty, and bungling cruelty at that. You have done well.'

The simpleton had missed the point.

'Thank you, sir.' He did not look at Cardenas.

How diminished Paynton was – but did he know that Cardenas knew? When it sunk in – with all its implications, for the man was no fool – would he react with shame, or with anger?

'Thank you once again for your work this morning, Francis.'

'May I take this newspaper away with me, sir?' He gestured to the one he had picked up from the coffee table. 'There's something in it which took my eye earlier.'

A brilliant cover-up, Cardenas appreciated, but in vain.

'Of course, Francis, do take it.'

As Paynton left Cardenas caught his eye for a moment, and nodded very slightly. The freeze – no other word for it – that gripped Paynton's face in that brief instant told Cardenas all he needed. The man certainly knew that he had betrayed himself irredeemably, and was appalled at the possible consequences.

So, my poor friend, it's goodbye to that sensitive UN Post you so coveted and seemed tailor-made for. And I had such high hopes of you.

8

The door closed behind Paynton, and the Ambassador walked over to the window. Were those tiny flickers of lightning that he could see in the Northern sky? Perhaps.

'Are you sure you've had enough to eat, Richard? Or another tonic perhaps?'

'Yes to the first question, no to the second,' Cardenas replied. He was at the other window, with at least half his mind elsewhere, Brathby thought. Not that that excused him.

'I thought Paynton did well to see it through this morning,' said Brathby. 'Not easy for him. Wouldn't have been for anyone. He was a little upset while recounting it but then that was perfectly natural: who wouldn't be? In my view he did an adequate job in difficult circumstances.' But for all the response he was getting from Cardenas he might as well have been talking to one of the posts the tiefmen had been tied to.

'So what are your plans for the rest of the day, before supper at Bill's, that is?' asked Brathby, changing tack. Cardenas must know perfectly well that he was anxiously waiting for the promised news of the *Stuffing* investigation; but he was damned if he was going to beg for it.

'This afternoon I am going to Police Headquarters, to call on Zalomo. Elias has an appointment there and has asked me to accompany him.'

'Oh, *has* he?' said Brathby, taken by surprise. 'Perhaps he hopes to glean any last minute information about tomorrow's demonstrations. But I'm unclear why you agreed to go with him, Richard.' Yes and uneasy too, and unconvinced that the initiative for the visit had really come from Elias.

'I'd have thought that you, as Ambassador, would see the point,' Cardenas said. 'The Deputy Under-Secretary will doubtless want to hear my views on the Police Training Scheme and it will be helpful to me, in speaking to him, to have met the Commissioner. You too, Bernard, may also find it useful to have my opinion of Elias's relationship with Zalomo.'

This was so unsatisfactory and threatening that Brathby was at a loss to know how to respond. At the most rudimentary level nobody with the faintest respect for common sense, let alone protocol (and very often the two coincided, Brathby reflected), would have made such an arrangement without consulting the Ambassador. More importantly, once there, Cardenas was quite capable of saying something to upset the relationship between the Embassy and the Commissioner. It was indeed not unthinkable, Brathby realised – an unwelcome thought but one that must be considered in the light of the evidence building up – that Cardenas was even *aiming* to upset the relationship, though God alone knew why. And there was something sleekly self-satisfied about him. What else could be in that notebook?

He could in theory forbid Cardenas to accompany Antoun. But that would risk stimulating him to report adversely on the scheme to the DUS. The Embassy had always had problems in justifying the funding, the benefits being so unquantifiable; the last thing Brathby wanted was someone in London stirring up old doubts. Also a last minute change of plan could cause problems for Antoun. Strange, incidentally, that *he'd* not mentioned the visit when he called on the Ambassador this morning and had spent so long saying so little.

'I interpret your silence as having accepted the points I have made,' Cardenas continued. 'After that visit I shall return to the Embassy to check out one or two other matters and make some final notes for the reports I shall submit in London. This evening, as you know, I shall be with the Consul and his staff.' He paused and added, 'I *do* hope that satisfies your curiosity concerning my movements.'

'Richard, I didn't ...' he stopped short. He had nearly apologised to the little rat for nothing. Meanwhile, when was the bloody man going to talk about *Stuffing*, if ever?

'No, I'm sure you didn't ... whatever it was.' Cardenas moved away from the window and towards the door.

For a moment Brathby thought he was going to leave.

But with his hand on the door knob he turned and spoke: 'Oh yes, I nearly forgot. The *Stuffing* investigation, of which you may wish to hear the details.'

'If you *are* actually going to tell me about this, then perhaps we could sit down comfortably.' His hands were mentally around the man's throat.

'You sit by all means, Bernard. It won't take me long. Not a very

213

creditable story. These things seldom are, are they?'

Cardenas had his back to the window and for a moment it seemed to Brathby as if the distant flickers of lightning were actually emanating from the man's body. This suitably Mephistophelean vision gave Brathby a moment's relief from his churning anger. God had a sense of humour, after all.

'Seldom creditable …?' He said as lightly as he could.

'My dear Bernard, I doubt if you'll be as casual as that when you've heard what I have to say.'

Brathby was silent. His curiosity was drowning in a fresh surge of anger at this insufferable man's insolence. Then he recovered himself, feeling a new strength, the strength of knowing that he himself had nothing to be ashamed of, nothing to apologise for, least of all to Cardenas. Despite all his faults, he knew that he was an honest man, who cared for others. Perhaps too much for his own good, he reflected; here he was now, for example, automatically concerned in advance for any of his staff whose shortcomings might be exposed, instead of thinking primarily how the report might threaten him personally.

'Given the security fault lines in this Embassy', Cardenas began, 'the microphone attack could have happened at almost any time, and unless remedial steps are taken may indeed be repeated, and perhaps more efficiently. What happened was disappointingly easy to work out.' He consulted his black book. 'It started when …'

Coldly, almost expressionlessly, Cardenas explained step by step how the microphone had come to be planted.

Brathby listened, the implications rapidly sinking in as Cardenas went through the story. If reported to London in an unbiased way it would go down as a regrettable but not too serious a breach of his Embassy's generally sound defences, and one which had been swiftly neutralised. No great harm had been done. But Cardenas, for some inexplicable reason, seemed intent on painting it in the most damaging colours possible. Why? Bernard, mystified, could only conclude that Cardenas needed to justify his own existence. Sad. But the consequences for himself and his loyal staff could be serious.

'Now, Bernard', Cardenas was saying briskly, looking at his watch as he finished, 'I must join Elias for our expedition.'

'Yes, indeed. I hope the Big Rains don't start while you are out this

214

afternoon.' Despite everything, the thoughts racing through his head, and the threat hanging over him, Brathby would maintain his standards of behaviour– rather like Jack, he thought, fighting his way through the hangover of the century to report to his Ambassador and to keep a business appointment. He even managed to add: 'I hope to be finished with my engagements quite early this evening. If you're not too late perhaps we could have a cup of coffee together when you get back from the Consul's party.' Yes, and he might then learn from Cardenas how he intended to present the *Stuffing* story to the staff next morning. Which could be useful.

'Perhaps.' He returned the black book to his pocket and spoke again: 'Incidentally I shall only be imposing on you and your Steward for this one night. A relief to you both, no doubt. I leave by tomorrow's flight to London. I have instructed the Administration Officer to arrange the formalities. Elias will accompany me to the airport and through the controls.'

He left the room.

9

Cuthbert hobbled towards the fruit market, clutching his string shopping bag. Twice he had tripped on the broken pavement and nearly fallen; an arm had come off his spectacles when Berridge had pushed him aside and a crude repair with a strip of his Master's elastoplast had not worked well.

He was tired but resolute. The warmth of his love for Eventide and the cold of his hatred for the evil one were flapping like two big birds in his heart. But soon he would be able to rest. From the special feel of today's wet heat and the pattern of the bunching clouds Cuthbert knew that the Big Rains were nearly ready to come. Their work, he knew, was to clean the world. In doing this there were things they destroyed. It was natural.

A few steps beyond the fish market shelter – closed today and deserted save for destitutes, who would be moved on sharply when the mammies returned – was Adewole, the one-legged fruit man. His stock was piled high in splintered wooden boxes, with the choicest items displayed on ground sheets. All the fruit – even the oranges – were a monochrome green. He waved his crutch at Cuthbert and called out, laughingly: 'Why you back so soon, old friend, eh? Dat fruit so sweet your Master done chop um one time?' He turned aside to shout down a customer who was complaining about the price of bananas.

Until his accident – a battlefield wound, he sometimes claimed, but everyone knew he'd fallen in front of a lorry when drunk – Adewole had been an Army cook. Now he made a living this way, helped by his brother Benson, a mortuary attendant, whose occasional contributions of ice helped to maintain Adewole's reputation for the freshness of his fruit and also served to chill the bottled drinks which he sold as a sideline.

'Two pineapple I beg you, Ade', Cuthbert asked, 'de ripe one.'

'De last ones no good?' Adewole wrenched open a crate. 'Make you take two for free.'

'No, last ones dey fine.' He handed over some coins. 'Just plenty guest for house. Dis one sweet?'

'Ah lah.'

'Make you greet your brudder from me.' said Cuthbert, turning to go. 'I fit go now.' He plodded on towards the Church of the Rivers where, sandals in one hand and the heavy bag of pineapples in the other, he made his way to the corner pew. He sat and the ache in his spindly old legs began slowly to drain away.

'Holy Mary, Mudder-of-God, oh I too tire.' But she knew of course – knew everything – so why was he telling her? 'I come to tank you for answering my prayer. You done finish half de job; oh yes, I savvy proper what you do, oh yes. De bad man under my woof. Now I beg you, Mary, give me power for dis ting I mus do.'

He remembered the Angala proverb: *Who spits on me enters the jaws of the crocodile.*

10

'Come in Tom and sit down. Sorry about this morning, I was running a bit late.'

The Ambassador was trying to give Muckle his attention but couldn't prevent Cardenas's account of *Stuffing* replaying in his head. Of course he wouldn't lose his job, certainly not for this alone, but he'd have to get rid of Cuthbert and perhaps even struggle to ensure the man's pension. Then there was Eventide to consider. Of the Embassy staff it would of course be the Head of Chancery, as responsible for security, who'd take a good deal of blame. Although, he must remember, Paynton had actually recommended having Sodham sent home.

Brathby wrenched his mind back to Muckle, who didn't look his usual cheery self. Not a problem with Cardenas he hoped. Anyhow he must first get tomorrow morning's business sorted out; he explained the sweeping and monitoring requirement to Muckle. 'I know it's not your responsibility, Tom, but I would be very grateful if you could stretch a point and do this for me.'

'Oh, Buster, of course. Very pleased to help out.' He paused. 'I'll need to get my kit into the Residence and set up quite early. Where would you like me to be based?'

'Wherever is technically the best. And comfortable for you too if possible.' He paused. 'One other thing, Tom. Did you go to see Dr Bux as we discussed?'

'Oh yes,' Buster. 'Just bit of wear and tear,' he said. 'Gave me some magic ointment and told me to give it a rest for a while.'

'Good. I'm pleased that your ... that things are on the mend.' He paused. 'Now there was something you'd wanted to bring up this morning?'

Muckle hesitated and then said: 'Yes, Buster, you see, well things have been a bit hectic on the operational front. New opportunities and that. So I've asked my office to ask The Brain ... er ... to ask Philippa if she could come back a bit early. Just wanted to tell you that, Buster, maybe should have asked you first. Sorry.'

'No, Tom that's fine. I'd be very pleased to have Philippa back early.' He knew very well that she was known in her service as The Brainbox. And the name suited her. Pity she's not here now, he thought

– if anyone could neutralise Cardenas it was the Head of the Intelligence Station.

Muckle thanked him and left. Was that really the matter which had seemed so pressing before lunch?

Brathby returned to the Ayumba despatch. But two minutes later Violet came in: 'I'm so sorry, sir, it's the Consul. Says it's urgent and he must see you.'

'Come in, Bill and sit down.' They'd spoken only this morning. If it was about manning for his section again he'd have to sort it out with Paynton. .The man was in his shirt sleeves and sweating heavily. He slumped into the chair opposite the Ambassador, clenching his fists as he sought the right words. Brathby had never seen him quite so agitated.

'Sorry, Bernard, I can handle most things, as you know, but this is the limit, the absolute limit. I got back just now from that Commonwealth immigration *ram-sammy* – had to stay on for lunch too which was a pain – and found Jane Paige in a right tizz.'

'What had happened?' The Vice-Consul was new and young but Brathby had thought her pretty level-headed.

'Berridge, that's what happened. I could throttle the bastard.'

'Tell me,' Brathby croaked weakly, before regaining his voice, and his grip. Bill needed his support, maybe advice. This was not the moment to go soft.

'Bloody man had said he wanted to look over my department – in practice that meant looking over Jane, it turned out. Clearly he knew I wasn't going to be there. Asks her about visa applications, pressure of work and all that – damn all to do with this confounded microphone investigation he's supposed to be doing, as far as I can see – and even gets her to show him the queue of applicants. Goes back to her office with her. Has the downright effrontery to say that his views are being sought in London on whether the new man, this Cypriot fellow they've got lined up as my main reinforcement, is really needed out here. It's quite out of order.' He was banging his hands on his knees.

'Yes, appalling, I agree. How did Jane react?' He gestured towards the refrigerator. 'Bill, do help yourself to water. Or beer if you prefer.'

'Water's fine, thanks.' He got up and poured some before flopping down again in his chair. 'Well she, poor girl, was naturally flummoxed by all this, just told him that in her view we *need* more help. "And just how long have you been out here my dear?" was his patronising response to that, which made her furious, as you can imagine. Told me she wished afterwards she'd asked him the same question.'

'Sounds as if she did her best, anyhow. That was it then, was it?'

'No, it bloody wasn't, Bernard.' He was banging his knees again. 'This is really hard to stomach but I'm quite sure she's telling me the truth: the dreadful man made a quite unambiguous and heavy pass at her. Not just a chat up either.'

'My God, the poor child … and that foul man. What did she do?'

'Luckily she knows how to handle herself. Pretty girl like that has to, I suppose. Anyhow she half turned, ran the outside of her shoe down his shin bone as hard as she could and walked straight out, cool as ice.' Bill was breathing heavily. 'We've got to do something about this man, Bernard, we really have.'

'What do you suggest?'

'What worries me most is that she might tell Harry Fieldhouse. He's sweet on her, that's obvious, and if he found out, I couldn't answer for the consequences. He might do *anything*. Anything at all.'

'Then he mustn't find out. Not till Berridge is gone – he leaves tomorrow evening, incidentally.'

'You're right Bernard.' He finished his water. 'What sticks in my gullet is that the bastard is due at our place for a buffet supper tonight.'

'Will you go ahead with it?'

'Difficult. I can't cancel the whole do; there are twenty or so people coming round.' He was thinking. 'Better leave things as they are. Jane won't be coming now of course. But as for what he did to her this morning, what do you think?'

'His word against hers, that's the problem. Anyhow, Bill, would Jane want to go through the hassle of making an official complaint?'

'I'll speak to her but I'm sure you're right.' He sighed. 'Now what about my Cypriot reinforcement; could Berridge screw that up, do you think?'

'I'm afraid it's possible. He *does* seem well-connected back home. We'll just have to keep the pressure up from this end, Bill.'

'Right. He won't have sent off any signals about it yet, will he?'

'No. When he arrived he said he didn't need telegraphic facilities.

220

What he's been doing here is all in his head, to be precise in his black notebook and in his head, and he'll write it up when he gets home, he says.'

As the Consul was leaving the Ambassador added. 'My commiserations to Jane and please tell her that I too would be grateful if she kept it to herself until Berridge has gone. Also that I hope she did him some damage with her shoe.'

It was even more difficult now for Brathby to concentrate on his despatch; but he eventually held his intrusive thoughts at bay long enough to make some progress. He worked away steadily.

'I had Polly on the phone about half an hour ago, sir, but didn't want to interrupt you. I hope that was right.' Violet had brought in the tea.

'Oh Polly called, did she?' He tried to sound neither too keen nor too casual. 'What did she have to say? Is she feeling better? What was her news?' He must stop burbling like this.

'She says she's feeling a lot better and may come into the office sometime this evening to write up some shorthand notes. Oh yes, and she looks forward to seeing you tomorrow.'

11

Commissioner Zalomo took the well-worn stone steps two at a time, strode down the whitewashed corridor and entered his office. Squash at lunchtime was definitely better for him than sitting around with beer and sandwiches, a deplorable habit learned at Hendon and now abandoned for ever.

'You're looking pleased with yourself, sir.'

'I am, Ferdie'.

'Because you beat that Records Office Inspector again?'

'No, because I narrowly lost to him.'

'Lost …?'

'Yes, lost. After I played him the first time I sussed out that he'd let me win; quite narrowly – three games to two – which was clever of him, but not clever enough'.

'So what does he want, sir? Apart from promotions, praise, medals, all the usual stuff?'

'He wants out of Records – where, incidentally, I'm told he's doing a good job – and into CID, which he no doubt sees as glamorous and the fast track to fame'.

'So, thinks him, if I get half-way up the Commissioner's …'

'Just so. But he got the wrong man. I told him so, and made him a proposition'.

'Which was?'

Zalomo laughed: 'I awarded him what I christened a transfer score of ten. If he gets it up to twenty, I said, I'll move him to CID. Each time he beats me, best of five games, he adds one to his score – each time he loses he subtracts one.'

'Brilliant'.

'He tried like billy-oh today, I can tell you, Ferdie, and although I was on excellent form he still pipped me. So now his transfer score is up to eleven. I'm going to have some tough games, I know that'.

'And if you get him down to zero?'

'Hadn't thought of that. Maybe move him to the Riot Squad?'

Zalomo practised a back hand drop shot into the corner, where the smallest permitted portrait of the President was hanging, and sat down. 'Right, Ferdie, let's get on with the war. What have I got this afternoon?'

'Lecture to new entrants at 4.30. Before that, friend Elias from the British Embassy.'

'Oh God, the Greaseman again. *Surely* he's not still checking up on the demo arrangements?'

'Probably, sir. He *says* he wants personally to deliver the visas for the Minister's young ladies, as he put it; and also may he please have the honour of introducing an Embassy visitor.'

'That'll be a man named Berridge I expect, who flew in from London on Wednesday. Anything known, Ferdie?'

'Word is that he's some sort of Investigator. Recently there was an incident of some kind – no details I'm afraid, some internal security matter apparently – and this man's arrival may be connected with it. Anyhow nothing that need concern us, I concluded.'

'You're probably right.'

Inspector Ferdinand consulted his notes. 'At a quarter past five you attend briefing for the Riot Squad – I've made a few notes here. Incidentally …' He hesitated.

'Yes?'

'A cousin of mine dropped in at lunchtime, sir. He's got a friend in Egushi Village. Apparently agents of a certain Minister whose identity would be no surprise to you' – he raised his eyebrows – 'are spreading money around there, the message being that there'll be plenty more for those who turn up for tomorrow's demonstration, and don't forget to stock up on rocks and the odd petrol bomb.'

'Serious, d'you think, Ferdie?'

'Could be if it developed. I took the liberty of briefing my friend to find out the names of the likely ringleaders in Egushi. Then we can arrest them tomorrow at dawn, perhaps?'

'Excellent, arrange it. Issue what orders you need to, in my name. Anything else on the demo?'

'The new consignment of rain capes has been "mislaid" somewhere. I've told the Quartermaster Inspector that if they're not unmislaid by six o'clock this evening you'll use his balls for your next squash game'.

'Anything else?'

'Sergeant Omobi reported in. You remember him, the man who slightly overdid the cook's interrogation?

223

'Vividly. Had he got the receipt for the compensation?'

'It's in your in-tray. He sent his grovelling apologies for what had happened and volunteered for the demo reinforcement for tomorrow.'

'All right. Tell the Riot Super to use him. But strictly as missile-fodder and for head-cracking. He mustn't be allowed anywhere near the British Staff, or he'll be off arresting the Ambassador.' He paused. 'Ask Efemi in, will you Ferdie.'

'Coffee?'

'More important than that'.

The Commissioner had signed off a dozen letters and started on a pile of petitions when Efemi arrived.

'Sit down, old friend. How are you?'

'Fine, tank you.' He sat. 'Not coffee you want, den?'

'No, Efemi, information. The Big Rains. When will they come? It's important to know.'

'Tomorrow.'

'Yes, I can see the signs. But what time tomorrow?'

'In de morning. Maybe three, four, hours after de sun come up.'

'Many thanks, Efemi.' He knew he could rely on this prediction. The old man had an almost magical attunement with nature. Every year the date for the Police Sports Day was chosen only after he'd had been consulted over the weather.

'One ting more, Zed', the man added, unthinkingly addressing him by the name he had used when the Commissioner was a young man.

'Yes, my friend?

'Dis year de Big Rains will be *very* big. Big pass ever before. And will start very heavy. Pity dem poor people in de bush house.'

'Thank you, Efemi, thank you.' He stood up. 'Oh and please help me by taking these cigarettes away. I don't want to start again. Bad for my squash.'

Efemi smiled his toothless smile and left, two packets of *Lucky Strike* clutched in his thin old hand.

12

In the refuge of his study Bernard Brathby swallowed half his beer, eased the tension in his shoulders, closed his eyes and sank back in his favourite chair. His jacket and tie lay on the table where he had thrown them, his shoes where he had kicked them off.

The reception he had just returned from, although boring and entailing two hours of standing around on aching feet, had been light relief after a day poisoned by Cardenas. And tomorrow would be even worse, no doubt, when the man held forth to the staff about *Stuffing,* exposing in the process their Ambassador's weakness and negligence.

With luck Cardenas would not take up the offer of coffee this evening– what had they to say to each other, after all? If he wasn't back from the Consul's in the next hour Brathby would go to bed – meanwhile he had a chance, perhaps, to relax. He really ought to talk seriously to Cuthbert, now that he knew what had been troubling the poor fellow these last few days. But in the kitchen just now it had been clear that this wasn't the moment to confront him with the matter. So he'd tried to send him off to bed, but Cuthbert insisted on staying up in case he was needed to make coffee.

Brathby was summoning the energy to fetch the latest volume of his diary from the storeroom when the door bell rang sharply, once, twice, three times in quick succession. Who on earth could that be at this time? His self-invited house guest, having forgotten to take his key? Improbable. Duty Officer or Duty Security Officer perhaps? But either would have phoned first.

The bell rang a fourth, fifth and sixth time as above the quiet air-conditioning he heard the slap, slap of Cuthbert making his way down the stairs.

Brathby was hardly out of his chair, conscious of weird, confused voices, when the study door opened and Cuthbert stumbled in: 'Sah, it's missy Polly, sah. She fall down, by top of stairs.' He added, as Brathby darted forward. 'She in trouble, sah.'

Polly was collapsed to her knees on the floor, weeping, babbling, something like 'unk … unk …' Together they gently got her on her feet, helped her into the study and onto the sofa. 'Quietly now, and drink this,' Brathby said, putting her hands round a glass of brandy that Cuthbert had poured out, and guiding it to her lips. 'Whatever it is, you're safe now, you're safe." She looked at him like a confused and terrified child, not swallowing the liquid, which was dribbling down her chin and mingling with her tears. 'It's my unk ... unk ...' Her hands grasped his fiercely for a moment and then returned to cover her face.

'Thank you Cuthbert.' Calmly, Bernard, calmly, he commanded himself. 'Please stay up in case I need you. When Mr Berridge returns tell him that I'm busy and must not be disturbed.'

As Cuthbert left the room Brathby, turning back to Polly, half heard him mutter something that sounded like: 'dat man, I go kill um.'

Brathby, shocked, puzzled and almost overwhelmed by a confusion of emotions, knew that he had to grapple with the situation rationally. First he must calm her down, and *then* find out what had happened. He coaxed her to take a few sips of the brandy and for a moment she was quiet, although her shoulders soon began to heave again, and then again until she burst out: 'He tried, he tried ... oh no, oh no.' She was digging her fingernails into his arm. He welcomed the pain as a form of communion with her. Slowly the spasm seemed to pass and she sat just quietly weeping.

Then she pushed back her hair from her eyes and focused on him. She seemed to be through the worst. She took another sip of her brandy, swallowed, and then spoke. 'I'm so sorry to be like this, sir, it was so ... so awful. I never thought ... oh what can I do ...?'

Brathby forced himself to remain silent, just to smile at her and squeeze her hand. She would speak when she was ready. Alongside his love and his pity was fast forming the cold determination that whoever had done this thing, whatever it was, to his Polly, would pay a dreadful price. *Tiefmen*, rapists – they would be tracked down and when their turn came to die he would himself watch them suffer. It gave him a measure of comfort as he waited for her to explain.

'I ... I need to wash my face and hands, sir. Could I have a wet flannel and a towel? I'd ... I'd rather not move from here because ...'

'Of course, of course.'

He was quickly back with what she needed. To give her a moment's privacy he walked over to the window, gazing out sightlessly and commanding himself to be patient.

'I'm ... I'm a bit better now, sir. You're so kind. It's – it's hard to explain.' She was huddled into the corner of the sofa, hugging her knees, her head hanging and eyes half-closed.

He longed to hold her, comfort her, but sensed that this was not the moment, although earlier she had seemed to welcome his touch.

'Take your time, Polly, and tell me in your own way.' Banal words, to be sure, but perhaps helpful.

'I went to my office – you see – stuff in my safe – needed typing up, notes about the Inspection – don't know how good Vi is – you see my shorthand, and I didn't want you – all the bother of dictating it again. I couldn't sleep – dozing off during the day – so I thought, well, might as well come in.' She smiled almost apologetically.

'I see.' He didn't, but that was unimportant.

'When I went in the SO was on the phone – just gave me my key – didn't say about anyone being in the building. Went to my room – just about to open the safe when …' She was losing the colour from her face again and her voice was beginning to tremble. She appeared to falter and then to regain control. What on earth could have happened just next door in the Embassy and with the SO, that competent Fred, on duty?

'And then …?' The gentlest of cues.

'Noise – from your room – I opened the door – He – *He* was there – Just as if …'

Her breathing was heavy again; she was distractedly twisting her hair.

'*Who* was there?' With a ghastly certainty he knew the answer.

'My unk …' she retched; 'my … uncle,' she spat out the word.

'Uncle?' What *could* she mean?

'My Uncle Richard – standing there – the same man, the same evil … oh, I was so frightened … I *am* so frightened.'

'Polly, I'm here with you. Nobody can harm you now. But I don't understand what …'

'May I have some more brandy? Thank you, sir.' She sat up a little but stared straight down at the floor, still trembling. It was two or three minutes before she recovered and began to speak again. She had regained some control over her voice.

'You see, when I was very young, only five, my parents died. Killed in a plane crash. I went to live with my mother's sister, my aunt Althea,

a widow. Then when I was just nine she married that … that … man.
I know now he only wanted her money, he never loved her. Left her
years ago, not officially, just never sees her any more. A weak and stupid woman, I'm afraid – bit like me.'

There must be more to come but she had gone quite silent. He
sensed that she wanted to talk but hardly dared. It was a delicate moment; he must help her across the threshold. 'You said he was an *evil*
man.'

She was leaning forward and had grasped the table. 'Yes,' she said
eventually, 'evil'. She took a deep breath and continued quietly.
'Funny but at first I quite liked him. He worked and lived mainly in
London and didn't come home often; but when he did he would read to
me and help me with my school work. In fact he took more notice of
me than of my aunt.'

Brathby had a sense of what was coming.

'But when I was eleven he started to come to my room at night and
wake me up. At first he just wanted me to … to, well, play with him
… you know.' Biting her lip, and eyes now closed, she went on, 'and
then … then … the other thing started.

'I knew it was all wrong. I hated it but who would believe me? And
she, *she* must have known especially as he would shout … you know,
when …'

'Oh poor Polly, poor, poor child. How terrible – how terrible for
you!' And this vile animal, this rapist, would at any moment be returning to this house. He thrust away the thought.

'And – oh God how can I say it – but I must get it all out now, sir –
even what he did … you see … what he did, even that wasn't normal,
not natural, even if I'd been grown up. You see he turned … you understand, sir?'

Brathby immediately grasped the implications. 'Yes, yes, Polly, I
do. There's no need to say any more. I understand. You poor dear
child'.

'It seemed to go on forever, three long years. Then he seemed to
lose interest; and anyhow he came home less and less frequently.'

'And your aunt?'

'She was just weak, pathetic. She knew, must have known, about
… about *him* … though I never told her. But when I was sixteen I left

home, went up north, couldn't bear to be with her any more. I had a bit of money from my parents. I had a friend who'd moved there, let me share her place. I got a clerical job and went to night school. Secretarial. Tried to forget the past. Wrote to my aunt once or twice a year but made her swear never to let him know where I was.'

'And then eventually you came to work at the FCO, of course.' She seemed to be happy to talk now. Why did he know so little about her background? He remembered that she'd never volunteered much about her past and had gently deflected him when he'd asked questions.

'Yes, eventually. You know I was once married?'

He did; it was in her file. 'Yes, but divorced I believe?'

'No, the marriage was annulled, although for convenience I kept my husband's name – he was a nice, kind, understanding man – camouflage really in case *he* ever looked for me however unlikely but ..., annulled because of ...'

She took another small sip of her brandy, ' ... because of non- ... you understand, don't you?'

He did. And also the cause of it, as she was now confirming. 'I've never been able to let go, you see. It's all right if I'm dancing, which I adore, so long as it's not too close, or sometimes having my hand held as you did just now. Oh ...' She was crying again, but softly and sadly this time. 'You see, I *can* love, I *can* feel, as indeed I do for ... and I know you like me too, but when it comes to anything more, then ... well, even at the thought of it his face comes back. I can feel him breathing over my shoulder and I seize up with fear and disgust. He's there – and as long as he lives he'll still be there.'

She looked infinitely sad, and his heart wept with her. He was also fighting to contain an almost overpowering rage. If Cardenas arrived back now at the Residence, could anything stop him from trying to pound him to death?

He shook himself back to the here and now.

'You knew of course from the telegram you unbuttoned that it was your uncle the FCO was sending out? So you decided ...'

'Yes, to keep out of the way until he'd left. I was so shocked to see his name. I'd heard from my aunt that he'd joined MI5 some years ago, but I'd no idea he'd been seconded to the FCO, let alone that he could appear out here. It was too much for me.'

Yes, too much indeed. And he'd badly misread the situation at the time. 'Did you think he knew you were here, working with the Embassy?'

'I thought it unlikely, sir; I'm on the list as Penelope Pym, no reason for him to make the connection.' He saw her wince as the significance of the words bore in on her. God damn and blast the man to hell.

'But you were going to come in tomorrow, to help me at the meeting. You knew you'd meet him then, of course.'

'Yes, I thought that if I screwed up my courage to see him just once again, then it might break the spell; and of course with you and all the others there he couldn't do anything to me. I just hoped … to be … to be cured … so that I could be …could be like other women.' The tears came flooding again.

It made sense, he realised, for her to try to exorcise the demon. 'And this evening, in the Embassy; what happened then, Polly?'

She was grasping the table again, knuckles white, just about in control. 'It all came sweeping over me again – vividly – a sort of flashback I suppose. I felt sick, paralysed. And then … then he took a step towards me and stretched out his arm to … to grab me I knew, I just *knew*. He must have recognised me, and it was starting all over again, just like in my nightmares. I could think only of escape. I panicked. Ran down the corridor. I must've pushed the button to get out – then I was here, Cuthbert letting me in.' She released her grip on the table and looked at Brathby, her face white and anguished. 'Oh what a useless mess I am.' She fell back into the corner of the sofa, weeping and drained.

What sick irony, Brathby thought, his sense of balance still active even at this moment of acute emotional turmoil: it was highly improbable that Cardenas in one quick glance would have recognised her as the child he had abused and his gesture towards her could have meant nothing more than friendly reassurance to some unknown person he had surprised. He must have been mystified by her reaction and abrupt flight from the Embassy.

Brathby had the sense not to say any of this. And besides it was unimportant: by his evil actions in the past he had ruined Polly's personal life – and consequently Brathby's own, for that matter. And *this piece of filth* was the same man who had been causing trouble in his

Embassy ever since his arrival – could it be only two days ago? Outraging Jack Squires and provoking him to drink and insults; identifying Bill's deepest concern and stirring up his anxiety about it; treating Elias with contempt and assaulting Jane Paige. Cardenas was eating his way into the place like a fast-growing cancer. Doubtless others had received his attentions (Muckle clearly still had something on his mind) and Brathby himself had been treated, both personally, and as Ambassador, with an astonishingly arrogant lack of consideration.

But Brathby disciplined these thoughts. Surely it was sheer paranoia to imagine that the man had deliberately set out to ruin him and his Embassy. He focused on the immediate problem of what was now best for Polly. Who was no longer crying but clearly exhausted, giving an occasional nervous glance towards the door.

As he was opening his mouth to reassure her, they heard Cardenas's short confident step as he reached the top of the stairs. Polly clutched convulsively at Brathby's hands. The man was coming towards the door. Brathby shook off Polly's grip and stood up to shield her, grasping automatically at the nearest weapon, a paper knife.

Suddenly it was clear that Cuthbert was saying something, and quite loudly, to Cardenas. Then a moment's silence and Cardenas was moving down the corridor in the direction of his bedroom.

Brathby gave Polly's hand a reassuring squeeze and opened the door. 'Thank you Cuthbert. Has Mr Berridge gone to bed?'

'Yes, Master. He want see you. I tell um no. He vex. He go to room.'

'You did well, Cuthbert.'

'Master, I too tire. Go bed now?'

'Of course, Cuthbert, of course; and thank you again.' Once Polly was safely off the premises he could deal somehow with Cardenas. All the better if Cuthbert were out of the way.

Polly was calmer, Brathby could see, but needed rest, and plenty of it. She readily agreed to leave her car in the Embassy compound and be taken home by Ogolo, the Ambassador's driver. Despite his pleas she refused to let him come with her. Nor would she agree to let him phone Vi to look after her when she got home.

'You've been wonderful, sir. But I just need to sleep now. I'm so tired that I can't think what it all means.' She hesitated. 'There is one thing I'd like to ask of you …'

'Anything, Polly, anything.'

'Tomorrow morning. I'd like to be here. I can't come to the meeting itself of course because that …that man'll be here, and you've got Vi to help you but …

'Yes Polly?'

'But I'll feel safe, in a corner out of the way, with you nearby; and perhaps you'll need me afterwards. Perhaps … perhaps I can catch up on some of my typing even.' She gave a half smile.

'Fine Polly, of course. You can work here in my study.' He rather clumsily squeezed her shoulder. 'I'll install you when you arrive and then come to see you when we've finished the meeting. Cuthbert will bring you coffee. You'll probably see Tom moving around as well. Yes, a good idea of yours.'

He held her hand for a long moment. There was so much he wanted to say but she was clearly exhausted. 'Now I'll ring down to Ogolo, and he'll bring the car round here to take you home. You must try to get some sleep, Polly. I'll see you through this, I promise. You've nothing more to fear.'

Part 4

1

'Good Lord, Harry, you *are* early,' the Ambassador greeted him as he entered the Residence reception room on Saturday morning to find the Third Secretary putting chairs round the long dining table. 'Though I'm pleased to see you of course. Had any breakfast? I'm sure Cuthbert could rustle you up something.'

'Grabbed a bite earlier on, thank you, sir. Thought I'd try and get ahead of the game. Used my Duty Officer key to get in.' The Ambassador looked rough, Harry thought. Not surprising really, with Berridge as a houseguest on top of everything else.

'Popped into Chancery on my way here, sir, to look at the overnight traffic and get your copies; once sleepy Sodham had deigned to open the door, that is. Tom Muckle was already there gathering various mysterious pieces of kit. Told me he'd had to wake up our ever-vigilant SO to open the door for him.'

'You're right about Mr Sodham's slackness, Harry. Report the incident to Francis on Monday, will you? Meanwhile we've more pressing matters to attend to.'

As if to underline what the Ambassador was saying a flash of white lightning bit across the sky, followed by a long but distant grumble of thunder.

'Spot any demonstrators on your way here, Harry?'

'A few, sir, although of course it's still very early. But the chaps that Zalomo promised to reinforce the gatehouse are here; also a couple of his men to protect the entry to the Consular/Commercial building, and a Sergeant Omobi, apparently assigned to the back wall of the Residence. At least that's where I found him urinating when I did my tour of inspection.'

The Ambassador smiled but it clearly took an effort, Harry could see. 'Now', he said with what seemed forced briskness, 'I'll take that folder of telegrams off to my study and work there for the next hour or two. When Polly arrives – she's a little better but won't be at the meeting – Cuthbert has been asked to bring her through to me. But if you see her first will you please do that, personally escort her, that is?'

'Of course, sir. I'm glad she's better.' Was the Old Man going off his head? It wasn't exactly a secret that he was sweet on her, but did he think she was going to faint, or somehow disappear between the front door and his study?

'So I'll leave you here to get things organised and to receive people as they arrive. Keep a seat for Violet on my right – she'll be taking notes – and put Mr Elias on my left. The remainder more or less as they tumble.'

'And Mr Berridge, sir?'

'Oh yes, of course, Berridge'. Brathby paused wearily as if making the decision was almost too much for him. 'Well, since he's going to address the meeting I suppose he'd better be at the foot of the table, directly facing me.' He stopped again and looked round. 'I think that's all. Make sure everyone has coffee or cold drinks or whatever they need. Cuthbert will be along soon with the trays.'

'And if anyone wants to see you, sir?'

'Send them along the corridor, if you think it can't wait until the meeting. All right?'

'Fine, sir.'

As soon as the Ambassador had left the room Harry plonked himself down at the head of the table, addressing his talented and devoted staff of twenty-five years hence. He dazzled them with his witty, lucid and comprehensive summary of the current threat to Anglo-American relations and how he proposed, with their loyal support, to neutralise it. Meanwhile in the Washington Residence itself the beautiful Lady Fieldhouse would be putting the final touches to the planning of this evening's dazzling reception, which the President himself had graciously agreed to honour with his presence. As he bowed over the First Lady's gnarled and heavily-bejewelled hand he …

The door opened slowly and Antoun Elias, panting slightly, slid tentatively into the room. 'Oh it's you, Harry. Good morning.'

'Good morning, Mr Elias, all our defences in position?' He liked the amiable rogue. He also thought that Paynton, as well as being insufferably rude to the man, badly underestimated his value.

'We must hope so, Harry. I've already seen the Commissioner this morning, and the Riot Super and some of their men.'

'What a busy fellow you've been. I suppose you now want to see the Ambassador?'

'If His Excellency can spare a few moments, yes indeed. Is he …?'

'He's in his study down the corridor. I'm sure he'd like to see you.'
As Elias turned to go Harry asked. 'By the way Antoun, how did you
get in? I didn't hear the bell.'

'No, the door's propped open. I wondered about the security aspect of that but the Commissioner has got a man stationed there and
there are also three tough-looking Englishmen on the door, some reinforcements the Head of Chancery has organised without informing me
no doubt.' He smiled thinly and left the room.

Reinforcements? Englishmen? What was all this about? He should
go and have a look.

But before he could move the door opened and Jack Squires came
in. Looking worried but determined, he thought. He was carrying what
appeared to be a heavy briefcase.

'Good morning, Colonel.' Harry came to mock attention. He knew
that Squires liked him. Had even gone so far one evening as to say that
he'd make a damned good Subaltern. That was serious praise indeed,
coming from him.

'And good morning to you too, Harry. Still Duty Officer are you?'
He glanced around. 'One could do with a spot of coffee …?'

'Coming up soon, Colonel, no doubt. In fact if you could hold the
fort here for a while I'll go and check with Cuthbert.'

'Thanks, but on second thoughts I'd better attend to my guts first.
A touch of the old Montezuma's Revenge. Bogs in working order, are
they? Saw some workman chappie out there. Not a plumber, is he?
That's always a bad sign.'

'No, just a man come to look at the roof.'

'Right, I'd better be off. Please put this case down where you think
I should be sitting.' He plonked it on the table. 'Thanks. Right, quick
march.'

Squires disappeared. Fieldhouse lifted the briefcase onto one of the
chairs and went over to the window. The sky was so black that he could
hardly make out the trees. Distant lightning was playing. *Surely* the
rains must break soon – within the hour he guessed. Peering through
the murk he could just make out a couple of cars turning in towards the
Embassy compound accompanied by a growing crowd of demonstra-

tors, placards and banners to the fore. What fun it all was. Dramatic storm in the making, Embassy potentially under siege and this weird spook from London about to reveal all about the planted microphone. All he needed now was the presence of the delicious Jane. Ah, another arrival - her perhaps?

But it was only a rather pale-looking Polly. 'H.E. in the study, is he?' she asked.

'Yes, pop along there. No, no, hang on. I'm supposed to escort you.' He smiled at her. 'You okay, got over whatever it was? We've all missed you.'

'Yes, I suppose I'm all right, Harry,' she replied slowly, and they went down the corridor.

Polly safely delivered, Fieldhouse put his head in the kitchen, bade a cheery good morning to an unusually dour-looking Cuthbert, patted Eventide on the head and admired his football. Then having elicited that the cold drinks would be brought in 'soon, soon' and coffee at some later indeterminate point, he returned to the reception room. Who would be next to arrive, he wondered.

'I do hope everything is quite in order for the meeting,' was the Head of Chancery's greeting. He was standing behind the chair on which Fieldhouse had placed Squires's briefcase, tapping on a clipboard and looking around critically.

'Good morning, Francis', Fieldhouse replied firmly. 'I can't say that *everything* is in good order but everything for which *I* am responsible is in good order.'

Paynton paused, looking cross. 'And yet it seems that Singleton has taken it into his head, unasked and without prior consultation, to bring three of his men to help guard the Embassy.'

'Jolly decent of him, I thought.'

'But unnecessary and irregular. Think of the problems if one of them were injured or if the British press got hold of the story.'

This was fussy nonsense even by Paynton's standards. Fieldhouse forbore to point out that if the men's presence was unnecessary it would be highly unlikely that any of them would be injured. He felt that his unlovely Head of Chancery had more serious worries. Or perhaps he was having withdrawal symptoms from having gone nearly a day now without seeing anyone shot.

'I'll check in with H.E. In the study, is he?'

Fieldhouse nodded and Paynton left, clipboard clasped importantly under his left arm, almost colliding with Tom Muckle and failing to acknowledge the latter's greeting.

'Cheery bugger, your boss,' Tom remarked when they were alone. 'Wouldn't swap places with you for a season ticket to *The Welcome Pussy*.'

Although this was Tom's usual cheery tone, Fieldhouse thought he looked under strain. Woman trouble perhaps, more likely *women* trouble, plural. Funny really – such a rough fellow but he had to fend them off with cattle prods, it seemed. Not that Harry was jealous. Might have been a year or two back, but now that he'd discovered Jane and love (tra-la-la-la), well who wanted a string of cheap conquests? Nevertheless …

He wrenched his mind back. 'Sorry, Tom, I was day-dreaming. Do you want help of some kind?'

'No, just taking a breather.' Idly Tom picked up the MA's briefcase. 'This yours then, Harry? Quite a weight.'

'No, it's the Colonel's. Hope it doesn't leak.'

'Right, well I'll be back to my magic machines. I'll sweep from all angles I can find. Bloody place is like a rabbit warren.' He turned to go. 'You haven't seen that Berridge around have you? I've a question for him.'

'No, no such luck.'

'Okay boyo, on my way. When comrade Cuthbert produces the coffee ask him to send me a mug via the little football fan, would you. If he can find me, that is, I'm in and out of the building a good deal. 'Bye now.'

Suddenly there was a crashing sound in the corridor and Fieldhouse opened the door to investigate. This was turning into a circus … no, he thought, amused, more of a shambolic farce …

It transpired that the Admin Officer Cyril Ellison, and a young Embassy driver who had offered to help him, had successfully got into the roof-space through a trap door near the top of the stairs, in a last minute attempt to fix some loose tiles before the rains arrived. But on the way down Ellison had fallen off the ladder, bruising his cheek and hurting his arm quite badly. Muckle had apparently gone to telephone for Dr

Karim-Bux, Paynton was trying rather bad-temperedly to establish exactly what had happened, and the driver in the roof was wondering how he could get down without adding to the fuss. Cuthbert was unsuccessfully offering brandy to the shocked but teetotal Admin Officer, and Jane, who had just arrived, was calmly arranging for him to be helped to one of the spare rooms where he could be properly examined when the doctor arrived. Colonel Squires, very pale, was approaching the group from one of the corridors. Joe Singleton, who was just at that moment coming up the stairs, clearly recognised that there were enough helpers on the scene already and called over to Harry and followed him back to the reception room – the calm spot at the centre of tumult, it seemed.

'Tried to get your Ambassador on the phone last night, Harry, to offer some extra men in case things turned nasty but the lines were down – so I've brought them anyhow. Hope that's okay? We'll take our pay in beer at the Club later if it hasn't been burned down.'

'Very kind of you to do this, Mr Singleton. I'm sure H.E. would like to see you and thank you personally. He's in the study, if you'd like to go there now.'

Harry hoped that Jane would be along soon. The door opened but it was only Bill, the Consul. 'Where's the boss, Harry? In the study, I expect.'

As he turned to go Harry tried to explain that the Ambassador was very busy at the moment and perhaps Bill could hang on for a minute or two.

'Yes, it can wait, I suppose. It's very disruptive to routine work you know, demonstrations and police all over the place. Not to mention this damned *Stuffing* business. I've managed to arrange for a couple of dozen visa applicants to be interviewed by the locally-engaged staff but I had to send the others away. If we weren't so short-staffed we wouldn't have to be working Saturdays anyhow. But we can't risk the poor devils queuing in the open with trouble brewing. Not to mention the Big Rains about to break.'

Bill walked wearily over to the chair at the far end of the table, and closed his eyes for a moment before speaking again. 'Come to think of it, Harry, I don't need to burden H.E. with all that, do I?' He yawned. 'Incidentally Edith and I were sorry not to see you yesterday evening.

You'd have livened us up. Still, being Duty Officer of course, you couldn't come. Jane cried off as well.'

'I'm sure that my absence was more than compensated for by the attendance of our visitor, Mr Berridge,' Harry offered with a straight face.

'Have you seen him yet this morning?' Bill's teeth were almost audibly grinding.

'No, but I've contained disappointment,' Harry smiled. Did everyone feel that way about Berridge? 'Ah' he said as the door opened again and Joe Singleton signalled that he'd finished with the Ambassador, 'that means H.E.'s probably free now if you still want to see him.'

'I won't now, thanks. But I'd better look into Registry to pick up my telegrams. Be back for the meeting. Damned waste of time it'll probably be.' The Consul slipped away leaving him alone in the room.

'Jane, at last, at last.' As she entered he rose, then sank on one knee, gracefully doffing an imaginary plumed hat and bowing his head low.

'Harry, you clown, do stand up,' she said laughing. Violet was also in the room by now, and giggling.

'Cabaret over,' Harry said, 'and good morning to both you fair ladies. Did either of you see Cuthbert by the way?'

'Yes,' said Jane, 'he's about to bring in the cold drinks. I'll just dump my bag and papers and go and help him.'

'Me too,' said Violet, and they left, to be immediately replaced by the Commercial Counsellor.

'Good morning. What a lot of files you've brought with you,' Harry greeted him.

'Never know what delays to expect. Remember that, young man – always have work with you.'

'Thank you. I shall never forget.'

'Where do you want me to sit? Down this end here where I can spread some papers, that all right?' And receiving a smiled assent he opened the top file and began to study it.

What a bundle of fun you are, thought Harry.

The door opened yet again and in crowded Cuthbert, Jane and Violet with trays of cold drinks. Eventide, clutching his football, was observing wide-eyed from the doorway.

As Harry hastened forward, unnecessarily, to help, Woodley, the Information Officer backed in, a massive umbrella in one hand and a thick pile of newspapers under the other arm.

'Morning, Bert,' Harry greeted him. 'Sit anywhere at the far end. Cold drinks now, coffee available any moment. Roll up, roll up, any more for the *Skylark*?'

'Did I hear the word coffee?' Another arrival.

'Yes, Lydia. You're looking very beautiful this morning. Do you really need the uplift – if that's the word I want – of the dangerous drug caffeine? And where are your files? Your boss, over there, seems to have brought plenty.'

'Good morning to you, Harry, you awful man.' Lydia paused. 'Let me tell you that I've just this minute driven in and I'm not at all sure this demo is going to be as peaceful as everyone was thinking. In fact …'

'Why not pop in on H.E. in the study and give him the details?' he replied, adding in a stage whisper, 'and if you see Tom skulking in the corridors tell him I'll be sending him some coffee.'

As he looked up his eye was caught by Colonel Squires squeezing his way in the door. 'Well, one feels a good deal better now. Ah, coffee I see. Cup for you, Harry?'

'In a moment, Colonel, thank you. I must …'

Elias was in the doorway and beckoning him to step out for a word. 'Just spoken to the Riot Squad Super, Harry. There's been a nasty incident by the gatehouse – Amoni, one of our drivers, has been roughed up. The Super thinks the situation will get worse. Would you pass that on to His Excellency for me, please, Harry – I've looked for Francis Paynton but I think he's gone to the Drivers' Room; perhaps he already knows of the incident. I must get the Commissioner on the walkie-talkie. Will be back for the meeting.'

All this had come out in a rush. Was Greasers really worried that a riot might develop, or was he enjoying the excitement? Both perhaps. But he was certainly hyped up.

Other staff members were arriving, some finding themselves a seat at the table, others bustling around the coffee tray. Most people must be here by now, surely. Harry totted them up; though they kept slipping through his fingers – Paynton still outside in the compound somewhere it seemed, probably chastising the driver for having been beaten up.

Greasers of course had just gone off to contact Zalomo. Commercial, Information here, Bill working on a file oblivious of all around; but Jane *not* here any more. She'd probably gone to check on the Admin Officer, or to help Cuthbert.

So where was bloody Berridge? Saving himself for a dramatic entry? Pop up through the floor in a black cloak perhaps. Time the little shit was here anyhow. Perhaps he was in the study with H.E?

In fact he should go along and fetch the Old Man now; it was nearly time for the meeting. And anyhow he'd got to give him Greasers' news about the incident. But that was outdated now, he realised, as he saw people crowding at the window, staring out into the gathering gloom. It was getting serious; a group of demonstrators were now inside the compound itself. The police – uncharacteristically – were trying to persuade them to leave peacefully. The tactic was not succeeding and another gang, waving banners demanding *Send Us Back the Criminal Ayumba*, had now also got past the gate and was approaching the Embassy group of buildings. A car had just screeched up in front of the Residence – it had narrowly escaped being caught by the rioters.

Colonel Squires had picked up his briefcase and was saying over the hubbub: 'Harry, time one took command at the front door. Will report back.'

He almost collided with Dr Karim-Bux, who stood aside as the Colonel left the room, making for the stairs.

'Morning, doctor' cried Fieldhouse. 'Come and join the party.' Party? It was Bedlam. A junior diplomat's nightmare. A laugh, in a way.

'Will you be directing us please without delay to the patient? The getting here was not easy you know, nasty locals banging on our windows and saying unpleasant things to us.'

'*Us*, doctor?'

'Yes, Nurse Tayla is here for doing any dressings. Hurry please, Mr Fieldhouse.'

Someone on his way past nearly fell over the doctor's medical bag. Chaos now reigned supreme, it seemed to Harry.

Jane was just coming back in so he asked her to take Dr Karim-Bux and his nurse to the Admin Officer. He himself went off towards the Ambassador's study.

Just about to knock, Fieldhouse saw Muckle approaching the door from the other long corridor. 'Hello Tom' he called out. 'Looks as if the natives are a bit restless, but the gallant Colonel has taken charge so the Empire will be saved. Your bit going all right?'

'Yes, yes, quite all right, thank you for asking.' Muckle moved down the corridor, as if in a daze. Where was his kit, Harry wondered?

That didn't sound like the usual Tom. Definitely off-colour. All this close liaison with the Commercial Section must be getting to him.

'Come in', called the Ambassador. 'Half-past already?' There were a number of papers out on his desk and he and Polly had clearly been working away peacefully. Or something. They both looked pale and nervous. What had happened to everyone in the Embassy – some sort of *plague* going round?

Fieldhouse started to recount what Elias and Dr Karim-Bux had reported about the demonstrators and what he had seen from the reception room window but Brathby interrupted: 'Thanks, Harry, we've seen bits of what's going on from the window and Mr Elias has been in to report. Apparently the Commissioner is not too happy about the situation and is sending reinforcements. There's a small group of armed men in place but they're under orders not to open fire unless the situation becomes critical – deaths could be politically difficult for him.'

'Quite.'

'Anyhow, Harry, let's go to the reception room and see if we can get the meeting started. Is everyone there?'

'Not sure about Francis Paynton, sir. At last sighting was heading back to the Chancery.' Desperately he tried to keep a mental tally of who was where.

'I see. Anyone else missing?'

'I haven't seen Mr Berridge yet. Thought he might be here with you.'

'No he hasn't been here. He's probably with the others by now. Right, let's go.' The Ambassador turned back to speak to Polly. 'Lock the door after us, as we agreed. Let nobody in until you know who it is.'

'Yes, sir.'

'I say, sir', Fieldhouse said as they walked down the corridor, 'does that mean you really think they might get in to the Residence?'

'Er … probably not … but better to take no risks.'

'Shall I get the Colonel up here, I mean for the meeting? And should we all just sit here with the lights on and the shutters open?'

'Let's see what the situation is like first.' The Old Man was worth a bottle of valium.

'Ah, our missing Head of Chancery,' stage-whispered Harry. Paynton was mounting the stairs from the compound and the three of them entered the Reception room. Those at the window turned to greet Brathby and those seated rose to their feet.

The situation in the compound now seemed calmer, as Harry could see for himself, and Elias was telling H.E. that he'd just spoken by phone to the Commissioner, who now appeared more confident that the trouble could be contained.

Then Colonel Squires re-appeared, briefcase in hand – the fastening strap now hanging loose, Fieldhouse noticed. Addressing Brathby, the Colonel announced that one was a good deal more sanguine about the situation now and it was better, one thought, to leave the locals, plus Singleton's men, to guard the front of the Residence themselves now that the immediate danger seemed to have receded.

All sat. Silence prevailed as they waited for their Ambassador to speak. It was just after 9.30. The first big drops of rain, heavy as lead shot, were slowly plopping in the compound.

'Does anyone,' Brathby enquired mildly, 'happen to know where Mr Berridge is?'

2

Yes, where *was* Mr Berridge, Violet asked herself? She'd heard he was a nasty piece of work, and she hadn't liked the little she'd seen of him herself; but his being late for this special meeting which the Ambassador had called – well, that really was the limit. What's more he was actually staying in the Residence, so couldn't claim to have been delayed by traffic or anything like that.

'I'm sorry you're being kept waiting, ladies and gentlemen,' the Ambassador was saying, 'but I'm sure Mr Berridge will be here shortly.'

The Ambassador left the table to look out of the window, then returned to his seat. 'Still only the early drops. I'm told that it can continue like this for hours before the heavy stuff starts. Then suddenly - is that not right, Colonel? - it just explodes?'

'Most definitely, sir, but it gives the place a good hose down.'

He was brought up short by a knock on the door. Violet was thinking that she'd better answer it, but Harry was already there, and had disappeared into the corridor.

He was back a minute later. 'That was Dr Karim-Bux, sir, reporting that the Admin Officer is now resting, no serious damage done. I advised that he and Nurse Tayla should stay here until we give the word that it's safe to leave. I've put them in the waiting room.'

'Quite right, Harry, thank you.' He paused. 'You didn't see Mr Berridge, I take it?'

'No, sir.'

'Right.' The Ambassador glanced at his watch. 'Harry, take a good look around the Residence for him, please. He can't still be sleeping, surely. He turned to the Information Officer. 'Bert, go down and check he's not anywhere in the Chancery; and on your way you might check with Joe Singleton and his merry men in case they've seen Mr Berridge go out into the compound. That would be a bit worrying.'

Not that the Ambassador looked all that worried, Violet thought.

He turned to her next. 'Violet, please go and ask Cuthbert when he last saw Mr Berridge. Thank you.'

In the corridor outside Harry turned left for the bedrooms; Violet veered off towards the kitchen. She opened the door gently, calling out hello to Cuthbert. No sign. He seemed to have washed up from breakfast and everything was neat and tidy. Oh well, he might just be in his quarters. She knew where they were – she'd helped out when Eventide's room had been done up – and was soon tapping on his door. No response. After a moment she tentatively opened it. Not there. Nor was Eventide anywhere to be seen. Not even his football. She also checked the shower and lavatory. She wondered where they could be. Surely he couldn't have gone shopping, not when he knew he'd be needed in the Residence and with the area crawling with demonstrators.

She arrived back at the Reception room as Harry was reporting that Mr Berridge was nowhere to be seen. 'It seems that his bed's been slept in, and he's had his breakfast.'

Woodley, the Information Officer, had also drawn a blank. Not only was Mr Berridge not in the Chancery now, but the Duty SO - 'Sodham, unfortunately, sir' - thought that he hadn't been there at any time this morning. 'People coming in and out like rabbits, sir, the SO told me, but he's kept some sort of sketchy record. He said that Mr Berridge is not a man one forgets.'

'You can say that again', Violet heard Harry murmur gently behind her.

'And you, Violet?' the Ambassador asked her.

'Me, sir? I couldn't find Cuthbert anywhere, to ask him. He seems to have gone out.'

'*Out*?' Now the Ambassador did look worried.

'Well, he's nowhere in the Residence, sir,' she replied. 'Nor Eventide. I looked in their quarters, everywhere.'

'Your Excellency?' Antoun was wringing his hands in that funny way of his.

'Yes Mr Elias?'

'May I suggest, Your Excellency, that I ask the Police Commissioner about Cuthbert? I'll need to use the walkie-talkie downstairs.'

'Yes, do that please.'

'Shall I try the gate guards, sir, see if they've seen Mr Berridge – or indeed Cuthbert?' It was Head of Chancery speaking now. He'd been very quiet since he arrived, Violet realised. Hadn't even said good morning to her yet for goodness sake. Nothing unusual about that, Violet admitted, but he did seem unusually nervous, almost depressed. Or was she imagining things? Perhaps the *Stuffing* report would blame him and he knew it. After all he was the one responsible for security, wasn't he?

'Thank you, Francis. I'd rather thought that would already have … yes of course, go ahead. If you can get through.'

Colonel Squires had been at the window to check on what was going on and now spoke: 'There seem to be more demonstrators inside the compound now, sir. I ought to look over the defences downstairs.' A nod from the Ambassador and he was off, swinging his briefcase. What he wanted that for, Violet couldn't imagine. Bang the rioters over the head with perhaps!

'Thank you all for your patience,' the Ambassador addressed the remaining staff, 'we'll get the meeting going as soon as possible. We'll aim …' He stopped as the noise level outside rose steeply. 'Harry , Bert, shutters closed now please. Immediately. But leave a small gap for observation. The main lights off please, Lydia.'

Violet felt the general air of excitement, of suppressed alarm. But everyone seemed so calm. Commercial Counsellor still ploughing his way through the files as if he was sitting at his desk on a normal day. Bill quietly making notes – probably trying to work out a new roster for the part time visa officers. Others quietly chatting among themselves, ready for whatever the Ambassador might ask of them.

Her train of thought was interrupted by Francis Paynton coming up to the Ambassador: 'The line to the gatehouse is working, sir. One of the men there thinks he saw Cuthbert going out about a quarter of an hour ago but can't be certain.'

'And Eventide?'

'Sorry, sir, I didn't think to ask.'

'Well, please do so, as soon as you can get through again.'

'Of course, sir. And Mr Berridge …'

'Oh yes, and Mr Berridge?'

Funny, Violet smiled to herself: it was almost as if the Ambassador had forgotten about him.

'No sign of him, they said. But they could have missed him – they've probably been skulking in the corner of the gatehouse or lying

246

on the floor and so could easily ...'

'I don't think we should assume that, Francis' – the Ambassador sounded sharp with him, Violet was pleased to note – 'and anyhow it seems rather unlikely that Mr Berridge will have tried to leave the compound ...'

At that moment there was a great roar of anger from outside and the sound of downstairs windows smashing. Head of Chancery should have had the shutters put up there before now, Violet thought.

'Better take a look, sir,' Harry was calling out. 'Hundreds of them seem to be getting in to the compound.' As he spoke a barrage of stones hammered against the woodwork.

The Military Attaché had come in and was reporting breathlessly. 'Getting ugly down there, sir. Couple of hundred, something like that, most with sticks, a few with *machetes*. Don't seem interested in the Consular/Commercial building. Nor Chancery - no lights on there, grilles in place and the SO sensibly keeping his head down. All attention on us here, the Residence.' He gasped in some air.

'Joe Singleton and his chaps?'

'Brought them inside, sir. Sight of white faces ... could inflame the mob ...'

'Good.'

'Problem there, sir. Riot Super only has some two dozen men at the door. Half are armed but one doubts he'll give the order to open fire even if the front door is attacked.' The Colonel seemed to have his breathing under control now. 'Says Zalomo has issue instructions to do that only if the lives of Embassy staff are in obvious danger. Political sensitivities and all that. By the time he decides to give the order the mob could be in here.' He paused. 'What one needs now is for the rains to break.'

'One second, Jack.' The Ambassador turned to address the Information Officer. 'Bert, bring Polly in here from my study. Also Tom Muckle, wherever he is.' He paused. 'Francis, start keeping a timed log of what is happening. Minute by minute please. I'll need it for the report to FCO when this is over. Is that clear?'

What a fine man the Ambassador was and how calmly he was handling this dreadful situation. Violet was glad the Colonel had brought the *Uminco* volunteers inside. And then suddenly she realised what must be wrong with Francis – he was just plain scared stiff.

The Colonel had left the room again and the noise of the mob was steadily increasing. Angry chants of *'Ayumba He Take Too Much Dash, Send Him Back For Us To Lash'*, interspersed with volleys of stones. Even the Commercial Counsellor had looked up from his papers. Perhaps he would die defending his files, Violet giggled nervously to herself.

Oh good, here were Polly and Tom Muckle. She saw the Ambassador smile at Polly and briefly touch her arm before speaking to Tom: 'The Colonel's at the front door. Ask him if he thinks it would help if I went out and spoke to the demonstrators.'

'Oh, no,' she heard Polly exclaim in dismay as Muckle left the room.

'Listen carefully, everyone, please.' They were all listening to the Ambassador; even the Commercial Counsellor was looking up from his files. 'If, and it is still unlikely, the demonstrators break into the Residence, we shall barricade ourselves in this room, with the furniture. Head of Chancery will organise the defences. And ...'

As they listened Tom Muckle appeared at the door and called out: 'Colonel said to tell you, Buster, that unless the Super gives the order to fire warning shots the mob will storm us in minutes. The signal is one pistol shot but the Super won't fire it.'

'Anything else, Tom?'

'Yes, Buster. He reckons there are over five hundred now in the compound.'

'Right, Tom, I'm coming down to talk to the Super. Bill, I'll leave *you* in charge here. This is where Consuls earn their keep!' he added with a smile. 'Get Head of Chancery to move the barricade – tables, bookcase, whatever – into place when you judge it necessary, even if we're not all back. All right? ... No Harry, you can't come. I need your cool head in here to help look after the others.'

As the Ambassador moved to go there was a sickening crash of windows smashing on the ground floor, and ominous thuds, like a battering-ram at work.

Oh God, Violet thought, are they breaking in? As if in a dream, she saw the others in slow motion. Harry putting his arm around Jane, the two of them together moving the large table towards the door, Bill giving quiet, clear orders. As she went over to help with the barricade she noted uneasily that Francis Paynton seemed shocked and ineffectual. Even the hair he was so vain about was dishevelled. Yes, he *was* a coward as well as a bully.

She'd thought the noise couldn't get worse but now it did, a horrible, shrieking, threatening din and a splintering sound that must be the front door about to give way.

Then, quite clearly, there was a shot. One clean crack.

Immediately the hubbub checked. Peeping through the shutter Violet could see the mob swaying back and forth, as if undecided where to go.

Then a volley of louder shots, over the heads of the mob. The crowd, almost solid from the gatehouse to the Residence, was now apparently uncertain whether to go forward or back.

Then, just as it seemed as if they were on the verge of moving forward again, there came flash after flash of vivid lightning. The myriad faces of the mob, gazing heavenward in awe, appeared to her to form one surreal mass, like a leaderless tribe awaiting a signal from its gods. Then came a series of terrifying explosions as crashes of rolling thunder shook their world.

Suddenly everyone in the room was silent, Violet noticed, waiting for that moment when the Big Rains, just now so dramatically announced, would actually begin.

Yes, slowly, slowly, then a little faster and heavier and then – Violet was almost sorry for the mob who were now, God be praised, beginning to slip away from the Residence - the Rains were turning into a steady, pounding, remorseless, solid wall of water, accompanied by unrelenting thunder and lightning. Down, down, down, heavier and heavier, crashing to the ground in a deafening, earth-shaking deluge. Their placards abandoned, the rioters were running desperately towards the trees, sliding in the mud, losing their shoes, falling, struggling to get up again. Dimly visible to her was a line of police, well protected in their waterproof capes, methodically bashing retreating skulls. The danger was over. Relief swept through her. The air already smelt sweeter, and was deliciously cool.

After gasps of relief the room suddenly went quiet again until Harry spoke: 'I say, if Comrade Berridge is anywhere out there, he must be awfully wet.'

*****

'Going to see if H.E. needs me', Harry called out to the Consul and bounded off down the stairs, leaving the others crowded round the window. Some of the younger elements were removing the shutters to get a better view.

The Ambassador gave Harry a welcoming nod as he joined the group under the storm porch; he, the Colonel and Greasers were huddled round the Riot Super, who was shouting to make himself heard against the pounding rain. A little distance away Joe Singleton and his men were talking cheerfully together.

'Yes, a near thing, Ambassador', the man was saying, 'but not as near as all that. I always knew the thug element would run at the warning shots. I delayed until the last very moment, as Commissioner Zalomo had told me, but there was never any serious danger.'

Colonel Squires's eyebrows seemed to have disappeared into his hairline, Harry observed. So what *had* really happened, he wondered. Squires had been so certain that the Super would not give the order to fire until it was too late.

'Well, Superintendent, whatever the finer points of timing we are clearly very much in your and the Commissioner's debt. Thank you.' The Ambassador paused briefly while a roll of thunder temporarily obliterated all other sounds. 'Now, I understand that you and Mr Elias have agreed on what would be a sensible level of police protection for us for the next few hours – incidentally I fully accept your assessment that the demonstrators are most unlikely to return.'

'Unless they can swim,' Harry murmured in Elias's ear.

The Riot Superintendent nodded vigorously.

'I know that Mr Elias has already asked you,' the Ambassador continued, 'so please forgive my mentioning it to you again …' – Harry saw the Super glance rapidly at his watch – '… but my Steward, Cuthbert, accompanied by his young assistant, appears to have left the compound some time in the last hour. I've no idea where they've gone or why they left; but I *am* concerned that they may have been caught up in the violence. Would you please tell Commissioner Zalomo that I am asking him as a personal favour to allocate resources to finding Cuthbert and the boy?'

'Of course, Ambassador. Anything else, sir?'

'No, not immediately …'

Harry butted in. 'What about Mr Berridge, sir?' Not that he was any great loss, Harry thought, but the Ambassador surely hadn't just forgotten about him!

'Yes, indeed, thank you, Harry.' The Ambassador was frowning as he explained to the Superintendent. 'Mr Berridge is a Foreign Officer visitor to the Embassy – in fact the Commissioner met him yesterday.

'Yes, I heard about him. Is there some problem, sir?' The man was clearly anxious to be away.

'I hope not, Superintendent. Except that we don't know where he is. He slept in the Residence last night but failed to attend a meeting at half past nine this morning. We haven't yet had time to mount a full search for him.'

'Worrying for you, sir. Perhaps when the demonstration started he took refuge in Chancery or in the Consular/Commercial building?' Another look at his watch.

'We think not, Superintendent.' He paused as flooding water drove them all back deeper into the porch. 'But I'll have a more thorough search made before asking the Commissioner's help. Mr Elias will be in touch if Mr Berridge doesn't turn up soon.'

'Very well, sir.'

'Until then I'd be grateful if the fact of his … er … absence went no further than you and the Commissioner. I particularly wouldn't want the Press to learn about it before I know the facts.'

'Right, Ambassador. We'll wait to hear from you. Meanwhile we'll look out for your Steward and the boy. I must be off now and make my report. You've got these two fellows here,' he indicated the two nearby constables, 'for the front door and Sergeant Omobi round the back, and four or five others, with an Inspector, based in your gatehouse, to be available as needed.'

'Sorry about that, sir,' Harry said when the Superintendent had left. 'Mentioning Mr Berridge, I mean.'

'It was just that we'd look a bit stupid in the Office, Harry, if the media reported Mr Berridge's disappearance, if indeed he has disappeared, before we'd done so ourselves. Which we won't do, before

251

we're sure. He could turn up at any moment, couldn't he?'

'Yes, of course, sir.' Steep learning curve this morning.

'Now,' the Ambassador said, 'it's time we rejoined the others upstairs.' He led the way.

*****

'Please sit down everyone. I think we're all here now?' Harry did a quick headcount and nodded.

'First, what news of casualties?'

The Ambassador had addressed the Head of Chancery, who didn't react immediately, and it was Polly who answered. 'Tom and I saw the Admin Officer just now, sir. He's comfortable.'

'Yes, apparently Dr Karim-Bux has given him something to help him sleep,' Paynton eventually contributed. 'Otherwise nothing to report.' No mention from Paynton of the driver who'd been hurt, Harry noticed. Not important enough for a mention, it seemed.

'Good.' The Ambassador smiled gently. 'Now despite the slightly unusual events this morning' – from the general laughter at this mild attempt at humour Harry realised that a number of his colleagues really had been quite frightened – 'despite that, I still intend to hold the meeting concerning *Stuffing* since you have all been so kind as to turn up.'

Old Man rather overdoing it, wasn't he, thought Harry? This morning he had been … how could he define it … perfectly clear in his actions, but now he seemed … well … light-headed was the best way he could think to express it.

The Ambassador continued: 'I take it that nobody has seen Mr Berridge? No?'

'No, sir', they chorused.

'Nor Cuthbert and Eventide?'

A similar but more concerned response.

'Although the police authorities are confident that even the strongest swimmers among the rioters are unlikely to return' – more laughter – 'I think it would be prudent if we all remained here in the Residence for a while.' He looked along the table. 'Now, immediate duties.' He paused for a moment. 'I think it would be helpful if Colonel Squires and Mr Elias, while it is all fresh in their minds, were to prepare an account of how the police handled the situation. That will be for use later.'

The Ambassador turned to Paynton, who seemed numbed by events, or perhaps just indifferent to them, Harry thought.

'Francis, would you have a first crack at a brief telegram to London, please. Just cover the essentials: background to the riot, a few shots fired above the rioters' heads, unlikely to be a recurrence, rain stopped play! Emphasise, mentioning Mr Elias by name, that our close relations with the police were most valuable.' That at least put some expression, albeit a sour one, on Paynton's face, Harry noted. 'Don't mention Mr Berridge's apparent disappearance. I suggest you work in my study, taking Violet with you. Clear the draft with me as soon as it's ready; we need to get it off to London within twenty minutes.'

'Bert' – the Ambassador turned to the Information Officer – 'the British press will be onto this business soon, no doubt. So please prepare a brief statement, for use when needed, and clear it with me before the *Stuffing* meeting. Harry, prepare a preliminary physical damage assessment please – it'll probably be the first thing the Office asks for.' The Ambassador was certainly taking a grip. 'Polly, please ensure that the doctor and his nurse and our *Uminco* heroes are invited to the club at lunchtime. Thank you.' He turned to the Consul: 'Bill, would you organise an immediate search for Mr Berridge and also have someone phone the American Embassy in case he went for a walk and took refuge there.'

'Hospitals as well, sir?' asked the Consul.

'Yes, by all means.' He looked round and addressed Lydia: 'Would you conscript a couple of volunteers to organise some more coffee in time for the meeting; thank you. Right, I'll see you all back here in twenty minutes. I hope that by then Mr Berridge will have been located and available to speak to us.'

3

'So no information about Mr Berridge's likely whereabouts from anyone?' A shaking of heads. 'Very well, we'll start without him. I know that he was very keen for us all to know the facts and draw the necessary lessons from them. He gave me the details yesterday.' Eventually, Brathby added silently.

The Ambassador, conscious that what he was about to recount reflected badly on himself, wished that Polly were there to lend moral support; but he'd sent her back to the study with instructions to lock herself in again, 'just in case your uncle returns to the Residence.' It had seemed the best thing to do.

'D'you want me to organise a further search, sir? One is beginning to think he may have been kidnapped.'

A possibility that didn't seem to alarm any of those present, Brathby noted. 'Thank you, Jack; we'll talk about that after the meeting. In fact, I'd like you, Jack, Mr Elias, Harry ... and yes, Head of Chancery of course ... and you, Violet, please to stay behind afterwards; we shall then discuss the best course of action.' Paynton was not looking well, and in fact rather nervous. Disappointing: Brathby would have expected him to react more robustly to pressure...

'Now', he continued, '*Stuffing.*'

All looked at him expectantly. 'You will remember that five days ago, on Monday morning, Tom Muckle discovered an active radio microphone in my room in Chancery. The Office sent Mr Berridge to investigate, with the brief to find out *how* the device had been inserted there, rather than what organisation was behind the operation.' He paused for a moment and then asked: 'Can you all hear me properly despite this light shower we're having?'

Assured that he could indeed be heard, and rewarded with light laughter at his weak joke, he told them the tale.

Some time ago, he said, a man claiming to be a kinsman of Cuthbert's, a cousin in the extended family sense,, had turned up at the Residence, pleading destitution and asking for food and shelter. Cuthbert was not really convinced that he was a relative but he gave him something to eat, out of kindness. The so-called cousin claimed to have some kind of magic powers and promised he could keep the evil spirits away from young Eventide. That was clearly a well calculated argument. Cuthbert didn't trust the man but, well, you don't fool around with magic, particularly when it might affect Eventide, so he allowed the "cousin" to stay in his quarters for a few days. The man then went away but he returned some weeks later, apparently prospering and bearing gifts for Cuthbert and for Eventide.

'Last week he came back for a third time. He told Cuthbert that a bad spell had been put on Eventide but that he, his devoted "cousin", could lift the spell. To do this he required a special magic power which could only come to him by standing alone and motionless in the office of the great Oga Oga, Cuthbert's Master, Her Majesty's Ambassador. He was evidently well aware, from his previous stay, that Cuthbert had a key to my office in Chancery and was responsible for keeping the fridge there stocked with beer.

All eyes were fixed on the Ambassador. Reactions varied from the amazed to the amused to, in Paynton's case, the apparently uninterested.

'How far Cuthbert believed this nonsense, I don't know, but dreadful threats were made about what would happen to Eventide if Cuthbert refused to cooperate; and the man had promised to leave immediately once he had acquired his "magic power".' Brathby paused, lost for a moment in the inherent absurdity of his sitting here in the middle of a torrential downpour, recounting this unlikely story.

'The rest is farce, but serious nonetheless. Early on Sunday morning Cuthbert went into the Chancery to check the beer supplies in my office. The Duty SO was Mr Sodham. Cuthbert then left the Chancery, propping open the security door. The SO would have assumed that he was going to fetch some beer. Minutes later a man, apparently Cuthbert but in fact his "cousin", came back into the Chancery. He was holding a box on his right shoulder, thereby concealing his face from the SO, if he should bother to look up. That was when, alone in my office, Cuthbert's "cousin" planted the listening device behind the bookcase. Then he left the building, quite openly but with the now empty box on his left shoulder, again concealing his face. He returned to Cuthbert's quarters in the Residence, collected his few belongings and vanished.'

'Risky operation, sir,' commented Colonel Squires. 'Very bold.

Very clever. But one wonders what it achieved and who was behind it.'

'Yes indeed, Colonel. The answers must be that it achieved little and that we may never learn who instigated it. What is important is to focus on any shortcomings that may have contributed to the security breach. I am sure you will agree that is important, Head of Chancery?' The man seemed to be half asleep, in marked contrast to Antoun Elias who was leaning forward enthusiastically to catch his every word. 'Yes, sir, clearly it is.'

'Good. In that context you will realise that my allowing Cuthbert a key to my Chancery Office was a serious breach of security, for which I accept full responsibility. I can fairly say that it was the major enabling factor in this matter.' Was he really thinking in this pompous language, or was it just coming out that way?

'But, sir, it surely couldn't have been done without an SO who was blind or asleep, or both?' Harry interposed.

He was right of course but this was not the place to examine Mr Sodham's shortcomings. 'You have a point there, Harry, which will be dealt with separately.' He looked over at Paynton, now slightly more awake. 'I should also say that if I had earlier followed advice from Head of Chancery about that particular SO then the planting of the microphone would almost certainly never have occurred.' Yes, there was no doubt that Paynton had, as so often, been right. That he was now apathetic, ill or – but why? – frightened, did not nullify that. But had he got what was needed to cope with a crisis? On the evidence of this morning it seemed doubtful...

The Ambassador stood up. 'Well, that's it. You've all been put to a great deal of trouble, for which I am largely to blame.' Against the murmurs of polite disagreement, he added: 'Well, sufficiently to blame for me to insist that all drinks at the Club today are to be put on my account.' Acknowledging the thanks he added: 'I shall be over later to ensure that my wishes in that respect are being carried out. Now would those I mentioned earlier please remain to discuss what we do next about Mr Berridge. Violet, would you kindly arrange for Polly to be sent home in my car, and then rejoin us here to take notes. Francis, on second thoughts, perhaps you ought instead to check up on our *two* casualties and look in on the Duty SO and at the gatehouse.' In his condition he was certainly not going to be useful for anything much more than that.

'All we can do now is hope that Mr Berridge will turn up. If he hasn't done so by the time his flight has left for London this afternoon I shall inform FCO. Thank you all; I shall see you at the Club.'

As they left he signalled to Elias to stay back. Extraordinary how, despite the morning's excitements, he remained neatly groomed and smelling slightly of sandalwood. 'Tell me, Antoun' – he saw his olive skin glow pink with pleasure at being thus addressed – 'would it be helpful if we were to press the police further about Cuthbert and Eventide. I really am most worried about them.'

'I think it would be useful, Your Excellency, if I called on the Commissioner at his office. I think I could arrange that by speaking to his secretary, Ferdie, something along the lines of our wishing to report to London on the riot in such a way as to create the best climate for possible expansion of training programmes … something like that, Your Excellency.'

'Admirable. Might even be true.'

Elias laughed. 'True? Yes, what a good idea, Your Excellency. Then I'll come over to the Club to report.'

Yes, where he'd be sipping a beer and wishing that instead he were with his beloved and tormented Polly.

Joe Singleton was at a corner table at the Club with Bernard Brathby, Bill and Edith. The Consul's wife always came along on a Saturday lunchtime and she'd just remarked, to general laughter, that she was jolly well not going to be deterred today by an extra drop of rain and a few ill-mannered demonstrators. Funny old trout, Joe said to himself. But one of the best. Good one for the trenches, Squires would say. And Goodness how she loved to dance - one of the main reasons she came along. She'd never get Bill on his feet but Joe would always give her a whirl or two once he'd had another couple of beers.

There was a blast of humid air as the door opened briefly to admit a couple of late-comers, who added their storm umbrellas to the general pile and disappeared to the toilets in search of towels.

Joe loved this place although it was really no more than an old army barrack room, tacked onto the side of the Consular/Commercial building. The furniture was basic and the floor-covering a mixture of strange-smelling lino and ancient worn carpet. But there was a long solid wooden counter that served as the bar, where there was room for the much-used sandwich toaster and also an ancient record-player. At the moment this was scratching out the dated quick-step *If You Knew Suzie*. It was still a bit early for much dancing although Harry had already persuaded Jane onto the floor, and he reckoned that it wouldn't be long before his deputy, who was knocking back the beer, screwed up his courage to ask Vi to dance. Joe, who'd seen him in action at a company party, hoped she had resilient feet.

Manning the bar, as usual, was Bert, the Information Officer, assisted today by Lydia from Commercial Section, whose toasted cheese sandwiches were being snapped up as fast as she could make them. She threw frequent glances towards the door.

Antoun Elias, that pleasant rogue, had looked in very briefly a couple of times to report that neither Berridge nor Cuthbert and Eventide had been found. Francis Paynton – a cold fish that one and looking very queasy today, Joe thought – had stayed only for one dutiful drink, saying that if needed he'd be in the Chancery catching up on work.

'How's Polly today?' Joe asked the Ambassador quietly. 'I caught a glimpse of her this morning. She's not coming in for a drink?

'No, she's gone home,' Brathby answered briefly, his thoughts apparently elsewhere. 'Excuse me a moment, Joe.' He signalled Harry to come over and spoke to him.

'The gate guards do know that I'm to be informed immediately if Cuthbert and Eventide come back? You're quite sure they understood?'

'Absolutely, sir, but I'll have another quick check round anyhow. Back in a few seconds.' He grabbed an umbrella and disappeared out of the door.

Moments later the door opened again and in came Tom Muckle. It was immediately obvious whom Lydia had been on the look-out for but Muckle came straight over to the Ambassador's table to report. 'Sorry, Buster, tried all my contacts, but not a dickey bird, no Cuthbert, no Eventide. Not even that Mr Berridge, I'm afraid.'

That was on the cusp of insolence, Joe thought, but Bernard either hadn't noticed it, or didn't care.

'Thank you anyhow, Tom,' said Brathby, and away the man went, to be swept onto the floor by Lydia before he could even get himself a drink.

Then Harry was back again, to make an apologetic nil return, before joining the increasingly noisy crowd round the bar, where the attractive Nurse Tayla, an infrequent visitor to the Club, was getting a good deal of attention from the men. The drink intake seemed double that of a normal Saturday - understandable after this morning's excitements.

Joe finished his beer – God, it must be his fourth or fifth – and went to empty his bladder in preparation for getting Edith on the floor for a foxtrot. Staring at his reflection in the mirror Joe furrowed his brow and asked himself what it was that was puzzling him, something that wasn't quite right, some false note.

Yes, that was it. There was a lot of activity connected with the missing Berridge, comings and goings, but none of them, not even Bernard, seemed *genuinely* concerned about him, despite the obvious possibility that he'd come to some harm. So all right, maybe he'd made himself unpopular, but he *was* a British official. And they were looking hard for him, weren't they? But nevertheless…

Too much beer, he told himself, directing a final squirt at the back of the bowl, too much bloody beer. Dancing time.

*****

A few minutes later, just as Joe and Edith returned to their table, flushed from dancing, Elias came back in and was waved to a chair by Brathby.

'The British Caledonian flight to London has just left, Your Excellency. Mr Berridge was not on board, and his booking was not cancelled. Nobody at B-Cal or among my contacts at the airport has seen him. Nor, Your Excellency, has the Commissioner any news of him – or of Cuthbert.'

'Thank you, Mr Elias, you've done everything you can and I'm very grateful. It's time you went home to rest.'

Brathby signalled to a relaxed but watchful Harry to come over. 'Right. Time to tell London we've mislaid Mr Berridge. Get over to the Chancery and start drafting the telegram; I'll join you in five minutes.'

Joe stretched. 'Come on, Edith, one more twirl for the road. What d'you say? Oh my Gawd, it's *Twist Again* – but I'm prepared to risk it if you are. If we can find space on the floor, that is. Place has gone mad.'

5

All night it poured down steadily, and Sergeant Omobi had been allowed to sleep on the gatehouse floor. But at dawn on Sunday morning the Inspector had kicked him awake and sent him back to his position guarding the far side of the Residence.

At least the rains had temporarily relented, the smell of carrion and garbage had been washed away and he even had an old chair to sit on out here, propped up against the Residence back wall, not far from an ancient door, long unused and painted over.

The pink plastic cover of the chair was badly torn and its innards were bursting out, but it was large and soft. That young man Herri had found it for him; and twice sent him some *chop*, which was more than his own people had done. Herri was one good man.

Sergeant Omobi, an old blanket wrapped round his neck and head against the sudden early morning chill and the mosquitoes, carefully lit his last cigarette. Then he selected a sharp stone from the pile by his chair. He was sure the dog would be back, despite two direct hits and a glancing blow the day before.

Yes, here it was now, coming within range; small, yellowish, ribs showing through its starving body. It came nearer and stopped, eyes fixed wetly on him, trying to wag its broken tail. It didn't flinch as Sergeant Omobi stood up, stone in hand and shouted: 'Why you no pees off? No *chop* here. I nuttin for you. Go *chop* de bodies in de creek. Dis *chop* I need for *me*.' He threw a stone, which narrowly missed. It moved nearer.

'Dis one brave dog,' Sergeant Omobi said to himself, reaching for more ammunition.

The next shot was on target. The dog yelped, retreated but then turned to face him again, tail still raggedly moving.

Why not dis crazy dog go look for *chop* some udder place? Why here and suffer de stones?

Anyhow time for his own *chop*. Time to finish the sweet potato and chicken mixture he'd saved from last night, wrapped tight in a cloth inside a yellow plastic box. He ate slowly, with his fingers, moulding the food into small balls, and taking each mouthful with a swig from his water bottle. It was good.

The dog was creeping closer, ignoring his shouts and raised hand.

He swore at it and tipped out the remnants of his meal onto the ground. 'Eat dat den and pees off, you stoopid dog.'

Part Five

1

'Good morning, Sergeant Omobi,' says Harry, appearing with *small chop* for him soon after dawn on Monday. 'Not much to guard here, is there? Expect they'll send you off today.'

'How you, Herri? You fine?' He was always smiling, this man.

'Absolute tops, thanks'. Whatever that meant.

Harry had spotted the dog lying by the old door. 'See you've found a friend, Sergeant. Can't say he looks frightfully well-nourished to me, poor chap, wouldn't you agree?'

'He hungry.'

'Yes, quite. Well just hang on here, Sergeant and I'll see what I can do.'

And in short time this amazing young Ingleesi was back with a bone, a bone with *meat* on it, which he tossed casually into the air. The dog clamped its teeth around it and limped away fast to hide in the long grass.

'Oh yes, Sergeant, and I thought *you* might appreciate a packet of fags. Bad for the wind and all that but … well, there you are.'

Then Harry went on his way and the Sergeant sank back in his chair and closed his eyes. He's had worse duties than this; and considering how cross the Commissioner had been with him over that small mistake with the cook – well, he'd been one lucky policeman. So far. But any more slips and he *would* be demoted.

*****

'Come in, come in,' Brathby sat up in bed and called out eagerly as he heard the knock. 'Is that you, Cuthbert?' He was scrabbling for his dressing-gown. A night of mixed worry and hope. But now perhaps…

'Afraid not, sir, only me.' A tray appeared beside the Ambassador's bed.

'Oh, it's you, Harry.' He couldn't keep the disappointment out of his voice. 'What on earth are you doing here?' He added hurriedly, 'Not that I'm not glad to see you, and grateful for the tea.'

263

'I'm still the Duty Officer, sir. Head of Chancery was due to take over yesterday evening but he's not up to scratch, he said, so I volunteered to carry on. Been jolly interesting too.'

'I dare say, but making tea for the Ambassador isn't part of the duties.' He lifted his cup for the first sip. 'Sorry if I sounded ungracious when I saw you, Harry, and the tea is excellent. It was just ...'

'... that you thought Cuthbert might be back? I'm afraid there's still no sign of him, or of Eventide. I checked again with the Police just now.'

'And no news about Mr Berridge either, I suppose?' He felt he should ask.

''fraid not, sir.'

'Any other news?'

'From what I've been able to pick up it seems most unlikely there'll be any more demonstrations. But the Commissioner will probably want to keep his chaps here for a day or two to be on the safe side.'

'Right. Anything else?' He was not looking forward to today, especially after being awake half the night.

'Dr Karim-Bux saw our casualties again yesterday evening. Amoni, the driver, won't be fit for duty for a few more days, but our gallant Admin Officer is recovering fast and will be in this morning.'

'Good.'

'Oh yes, one other thing, sir. I spoke to Colonel Squires last night and he's insisting on sending Octavius to look after you until Cuthbert is found. He'll be along soon.'

'Decent of him. Not necessary of course ...' He wondered if it had been Harry's idea in the first place.

'The Head of Chancery is unlikely to make it in today - some unspecified indisposition. Everyone else expected on parade, sir, as the Colonel would say.'

'Including Polly?' He was torn by his visceral need to see her and the complications that doing so would involve. God, it was all so difficult.

'Yes, Vi reports that she is much improved and hopes to be back at work by tomorrow.'

'Thank you, Harry, for everything. See you in the office later.'

He'd make a good Ambassador one day, that young man; he should be able to handle the agonising decisions between the greater and the lesser evil that sometimes went with the job.

*****

'You stoopid beast. Why you sniff-sniff at dat old door? Go chew de bone.' Sergeant Omobi yawned and closed his eyes again.

But the dog continued to sniff and slaver and began to whine repeatedly and then to bark. He cursed the animal, levered his way out of the chair and walked over. What *was* de problem?

Then he smelt it. No mistaking it; he knew it well. And definitely coming from inside the building, behind the door. The area around it had been washed clean by the rain.

What to do? The Inspector had ordered him to stay out there. 'Only come to gatehouse if you need to shit, or you on charge for desertion', he'd said.

So he'd have to wait until someone came, maybe that nice Herri. But no, surely he must report this thing quick quick. Worse trouble if he didn't.

When Sergeant Omobi appeared the Inspector was drinking tea in the gatehouse and turned on him angrily: 'Why you here? You know what I told you!'

Sergeant Omobi explained.

'You sure?'

'Course I sure. I know dead corpse when I smell um.'

'Right. We go check.'

*****

'What's the problem, Mr Sodham?' Harry asked cheerfully. The SO was arguing angrily with the Inspector and the Sergeant.

'Say they need to see a senior member of staff, just burst in here like …'

'All right, I'll handle this', Harry said. 'Inspector, Sergeant Omobi, can I help?'

'Please come with us, to the outside wall', the Inspector said. 'Something is bad.' Which could mean anything, Harry reflected, following them.

'De dog, it was de dog,' offered Sergeant Omobi as they made their way round to the side wall of the Residence. 'He smell um first.'

'Smell what, please?' They were approaching the Sergeant's chair.

'One body, we sure one body in dere.' He pointed at the door.

'Well, young Rover does seem quite excited. Let me investigate.' A buzzing of flies could be heard from behind the door. He put his nose to a crack in the woodwork.

Moments later he turned away to retch in the grass. 'Please stay here Inspector; I'll get the Ambassador.' He moved off quickly. He wanted to get away from that sweetish, cheesy smell – whatever it was.

With Head of Chancery not in today Harry didn't even need to consider informing him first. Straight in to see the Old Man.

'Right', said his Ambassador, when Harry had finished speaking, or jabbering rather. 'You've no doubt that there's a body there?'

'Well, the police say it smells like one, sir, and they should know, if you see what I mean. And it could be both of them ...' Surely the Ambassador had thought of that. Otherwise where was the boy?

'Yes, of course, there is that possibility.' Harry waited, heart still thudding, while Brathby marshalled his thoughts. Admirable how he kept his nerve and spoke so calmly.

'Harry, find Mr Elias and ask him to come outside and handle liaison with the police. Also the Colonel, who should recognise the smell of death if that's what it is. Brief the Head of Chancery – no he's not around, so the Admin Officer – to prepare to break down the door. Meanwhile I'll go and see – or smell – for myself. We'll meet in the Residence in a few minutes.'

'In the Residence, sir?'

'Yes, wait for me there.'

*****

Harry had been right. Brathby recognised the unmistakable gamey smell from his Congo days. Squires concurred: 'No doubt about it, sir. One remembers ...'

Brathby spoke to Elias. 'I'm going to investigate from the inside. Dissuade the Inspector from bringing in the Commissioner until we know for certain that there's a body in there, human or otherwise.'

He took the Colonel aside: 'Jack, keep things calm for me in the Embassy please. Word will soon get out. Thanks.'

2

The Ambassador and Harry Fieldhouse each took a torch from the hall table in the Residence and moved down the corridor towards the old storeroom.

'Did you say the key is kept "under the elephant's foot", sir?' If it weren't that the bodies of Cuthbert and young Eventide might be lying rotting somewhere down there, the situation would be downright comic, Harry thought.

'Yes. Here it is.' The Ambassador unlocked the door to the storeroom and immediately they were conscious of a disturbed humming. 'Careful of these four steps', he said and then switched on the light, a single, dim bulb on its ancient flex.

The smell was getting worse, but still part of Harry's mind took in the extraordinary variety of rubbish, from mildewed old cricket balls to the venerable wrought iron umbrella-stand containing old hockey sticks and other sporting equipment.

They gagged and held their handkerchiefs over their noses.

'It – they – must be down there.' Brathby pointed to the far corner. 'There are the remains of an old staircase over there. Not fit for use but …' He hesitated, trying not to breathe.

'*I'll* look,' said Harry. He didn't want to look but felt that Brathby wanted to even less. 'Give me your torch, sir, it's better than this one.' He moved slowly towards the opening in the floor.

'Oh, sorry about that.' He had had to retreat for a moment while he controlled his stomach. 'I don't trust the floor here. I'm going to lie flat and shine the torch down.' He held the handkerchief over his face for a few moments and was soon able to continue. 'Will you hold my ankles, sir?'

Forcing himself to take only occasional, and shallow, breaths he moved the torch beam around until eventually he saw it, almost at the foot of the stairs, or rather where the bottom steps presumably used to be. A body. Definitely a body, face down. But … but not Cuthbert, not Eventide. He felt a spurt of joy. A white man, almost certainly, yes a white man, though now half black with huge flies. Of course! Of course! It must be the missing Mr Berridge. Yes, he could now make out enough to be sure. He shuffled quickly backwards and stood up moving quickly towards the door. Not trusting himself yet to open his mouth he found himself giving a thumbs-up sign to his Ambassador.

Just as he left the room Harry glanced back and saw the Ambassador reach down to pick up a small black notebook that was lying in the middle of the room. He wondered why he hadn't seen it himself when they first went in.

'I think this must have belonged to Berridge' said Brathby, slipping it into his jacket pocket. 'I'd better look after it for the time being'.

Back in the corridor, with the door locked behind them, they looked at each other.

'I'm much in your debt, Harry.'

'Sorry about the thumbs-up, sir, bit disrespectful of the dead and all that, but you knew what I meant, didn't you? That's it's only Mr Berridge.'

'Oh yes, I understood. He must have fallen and broken his neck. But what on earth was he doing there in the first place?'

Yes, and what thoughtful person had locked the door after him and replaced the key under the elephant's foot, Harry wondered.

*****

Zalomo arrived while a kneeling Dr Karim-Bux was completing his preliminary inspection. The old disused door, which the Inspector had told him about on the telephone, had now been forced open giving access to the body from outside.

'Thank you for coming, Commissioner', the Ambassador greeted him. 'I think you know everyone here? Mr Elias of course, my Military Attaché Colonel Squires, and the Consul. But perhaps not my Third Secretary, Harry Fieldhouse.'

The young man shook his hand.

'And Dr Karim-Bux?'

'Oh yes indeed.' It would be interesting to see the doctor in action. Zalomo knew a lot about him.

'Good morning, Commissioner,' said the doctor. 'Will you also be wanting a police doctor to be looking over the deceased before he is moved? Your photographers of course have been busy here already.'

'No,' he answered shortly, and then spoke privately to the Ambassador. 'If I am right, Your Excellency, this man is a British subject on British government business and appears to have died on British territory.' And behind a sealed and guarded door, he could have added.

'Yes, Commissioner, absolutely right.'

'Then my government will not wish the Police to be officially involved. That would only be a complication for you.' As well as for us of course, thought Zalomo.

'I understand.'

'But of course, Your Excellency, you are very welcome to use our civil mortuary for a post-mortem, if you intend to have one. Also you could house the body there until you can arrange repatriation, or local burial of course if you prefer.' He'd had time to think this through on his way from Police HQ.

'Most helpful, Commissioner. Many thanks.'

They rejoined the group in time to hear the doctor summarise:

'From this first looking I conclude that your Mr Berridge met his demise from a comminuted fracture of the skull with rupture of the left middle meningeal artery leading, it is seeming to me, into bleeding in the brain, causing unconsciousness followed by respiratory failure and demise. Or, in the language of you laymen, a bang on the head causing death.'

'An accident of course?' the Consul was asking. They had retreated a yard or two from the body.

At that moment the yellow dog, sensing its opportunity, rushed forward out of the grass and before anyone could react, it sank its starving teeth into the corpse's arm and was tearing out a great mouthful.

While the others looked on stunned, Zalomo moved quickly forward and gave it a massive kick in the ribs. It yelped and ran away, a substantial morsel firmly clamped in its jaws.

'My preliminary view', replied the doctor, as if this interruption had not happened, 'is that unlawful killing must be behind this decease. The contusion is too precisely localised to have been caused by his falling on any sharp object which is being close to him in this place. And there is nothing of that kind close, is there?'

Which was true enough, as Zalomo had already observed.

'I'm afraid the good doctor may be right, Your Excellency,' he said, and expanded on this as the Ambassador walked him to his car. 'By the way we're still looking for your Steward and the boy; I haven't forgotten them.'

Interesting, the Commissioner thought, as he was driven back to his office. Elias had looked guilty as hell and had, he recalled, a strong personal motive to kill the unpleasant visitor. Well, if he *had* done so, bully for him. Berridge had clearly deserved what he'd got. He'd not only humiliated Elias but, much more importantly to Zalomo, it was obvious that he'd been opposed to the Police Training Scheme and might have caused problems when he returned to London. So good riddance.

*****

'Should make for an interesting telegram to London, sir.' Harry whispered in the Ambassador's ear as the latter rejoined the group near the body.

'Yes, and you can help me draft it. Now.'

Private and Personal
FLASH, London

My Earlier Private and Personal Telegram

With deep regret I must now report that the person concerned has been found dead in an obscure and closed-off corner of these ancient buildings. My Medical Adviser's opinion, pending full post-mortem, is violent death, i.e. foul play. Police Commissioner Zalomo has given me his unofficial view that, in his jargon, it was an inside job. Zalomo has not asked me to waive diplomatic privileges to enable him to carry out a criminal investigation nor, sir, do I think you would wish me to do so. The Commissioner seems content not to be involved further.

You will of course take into account that the visitor entered this country under a false identity, i.e. technically illegally, albeit under official auspices and with a diplomatic visa. I may perhaps be able to fi-

nesse this aspect with the Foreign Minister but you will be well aware of my current difficulties with the administration here over Ayumba.

BRATHBY

MINUTE

From: *Deputy Under-Secretary*
To: *Permanent Under-Secretary*

Mr Richard Cardenas. HM Ambassador's Telegram, attached.

This officer, evidently a sort of secret-policeman seconded to us from Another Government Department, seems to have had the effrontery to get himself done to death on British official premises.

I understand he was visiting the Post in a false identity and, for all I know, in a false nose as well. This was of course entirely on his own initiative and unauthorised by me.

I quail from the thought of drawing up a brief for the Secretary of State should the Press get hold of the story or, worse, should Questions be asked in the House. Diplomats in disguise? Hon members rolling in the aisles.

Rather HM Ambassador should, I suggest, be invited to respect, posthumously, Mr Cardenas's evident desire for incognito status, and dispose of his remains accordingly, in compliance with Standing Instructions for Death of British Subjects Abroad. A discreet in-house investigation by HM Ambassador to ascertain whether disciplinary proceedings are called for in respect of a breach of Regulations on the part of any member or members of his staff, would satisfy Mr Cardenas's parent Department, keener (if possible) than even ourselves to see him – like Sir John Moore at Corunna – "buried… darkly at dead of night." I attach a Draft Telegram to the Post in this sense.

3

'Right Harry,' the Ambassador said, once they were installed in the sitting room, he at a desk and Harry at a small table in the corner. 'We'll start our investigations with the Security Officer who was on duty.' He inserted a marker in Berridge's black notebook.

Harry was chuffed that Brathby had asked him to help in the enquiry. He was also nervous in case he screwed up; after all, difficult though it was to grasp, this was serious business. Someone in the Embassy had committed murder, or at least manslaughter – unless the doctor and local fuzz had got it all wrong.

The Ambassador had chosen him, he'd said, because he was certain that Harry hadn't, as he had so ponderously put it, 'been personally involved in any illegal act or acts that may have been perpetrated'. Also, as Duty Officer on the Saturday morning - i.e. when Berridge had disappeared - he'd been best placed to observe what had been going on. Brathby was especially interested, he'd said, in what Harry could remember about the movements and behaviour of the Head of Chancery, the Military Attaché, Mr Elias, the Consul, Tom Muckle and the Duty SO. He didn't specify why.

'Only those six, sir?'

'Yes, unless you noticed anything particularly suspicious about any of the others', he'd said, and then turned back to further study of Berridge's black book. Harry felt somehow that Brathby's chance of solving the problem lay in that book rather than in anything that Harry could remember as Duty Officer.

But it would certainly be useful, Harry pointed out to him, if they had a rough idea of *when* Berridge had gone to the storeroom. The Ambassador couldn't help on that point. All that was known, he'd said, was that Berridge had breakfasted on a slice of pineapple and a cup of coffee; but whether Cuthbert had taken the tray into him or left it outside the door for him to collect, was not known, and maybe wasn't important anyhow.

Had Cuthbert volunteered any information about Mr Berridge, Harry asked, pursuing the matter, either when bringing in the Ambassador's early tea or when serving him breakfast in the dining room? No, and nor, it seemed, had Brathby even asked after his house guest that morning. Which was slightly unusual, Harry thought.

So no progress there. They'd have to see what the various suspects - not that his Ambassador would like that word - had to say for themselves. Brathby seemed oddly ambivalent about the task, as if he found it a distasteful imposition, yet not without its fascination.

A tap on the door and an unhappy Sodham presented himself, looking hungover, none too clean and fighting a losing battle to keep his shirt fastened.

'I am enquiring into Mr Berridge's death.' The Ambassador was looking at Sodham closely. 'Yes, sir.' He was sitting on the edge of his chair, still struggling with his shirt. 'Can't 'elp, sorry, sir.'

'Did Mr Berridge come into the Chancery on Saturday morning while you were Duty SO?'

'Er, no, sir. Nor after. I stayed at the desk after my relief came. Too early for the Club you see, and too dangerous to go 'ome.'

'Very sensible, I'm sure. Did you come up here to the Residence at all, Mr Sodham?'

'No, sir. No cause to, 'ad I?'

The Ambassador had the black book open in front of him. 'You were earlier interviewed by Mr Berridge, of course.'

'Yes, sir. Of course, sir. Couldn't 'elp it, could I?'

'Quite. What did you think of him?'

'Doing his job, I suppose. Wasn't a very polite man, I must say.'

That was one to treasure.

Brathby tapped the black book. 'Of course you realise that Mr Berridge worked out that it was your negligence that had enabled the microphone to be planted?'

'So 'e said, sir.'

'He made a number of notes against your name, Mr Sodham.' The Ambassador glanced at the black book. 'What does *Camberwell* signify?'

'My 'ome in London, I s'pose. Was going to 'ave me sent back there, I shouldn't wonder.'

'And *Penthouse*?'

Well it didn't refer to the location of Sodham's luxury flat, Harry chuckled to himself.

'Well, sort of magazine, sir. You know what I mean …'

'Yes, yes. I understand. Why should he write that in his book, though?'

'P'raps thought I'd been reading it on duty when that black feller came in with the beer on his shoulder.'

That would make sense.

'Yes, well. The other entries here seem to be personal comments on your appearance and attitude, and this isn't the time to go into that.' He paused. 'Is there anything else you'd like to say, Mr Sodham?'

Scarcely the Spanish Inquisition, thought Harry. Clearly the Old Man didn't consider Sodham to be a serious suspect. Moreover, on the evidence so far, he seemed to have no idea how to conduct this sort of enquiry. But perhaps the black book held the key to the Ambassador's methods …

*****

A few minutes later the Consul arrived, armpits stained with sweat and dabbing at his face and neck with a huge handkerchief. He sat back in relief on his chair, smiling, and nodded his thanks to Harry for a large glass of water.

'Good to see you, Ambassador', he started. 'Just got back from the so-called mortuary, more like an ice-factory actually. Zalomo had put the word in all right and we've got a place for this Berridge man: a special area where there's emergency generator back-up during power cuts.'

Harry tried not to dwell on the fate of those in the less privileged sections.

'The other good news is that Jane Paige – bright girl that one – has tracked down a lead-lined coffin, left over it seems from the days when we were sending bodies home all the time. It was on an old inventory, you see.'

He had never known Bill so enthused about anything that didn't concern visa applications. The man was positively glowing.

'Appropriately enough it was in a corner of the room he was found in, underneath a mass of stuff, old bedsteads, an ancient wardrobe – there's even an old thunder-box in there. Fascinating, some of the rubbish. Now …'

275

'But Bill, it's not yet been decided to send him home for burial. We may well finish up needing to find a spot for him here.'

'Never mind, it won't go to waste; the coffin I mean. I'm having it taken to the mortuary this evening. We'll pop him in: apparently it preserves a body even better than in a cold store. Then we can use it to bury him here, if so decided. What do you think?'

'At the moment I'm concentrating on how Berridge actually died.'

'You mean you didn't send for me just now to discuss …' Harry could see the comprehension dawning. The Consul seemed amused that he'd got it wrong.

'No, sorry Bill. Of course I'm interested in how we're going to dispose of the … er … remains, and we'll go into that in detail later on. But right now …'

'Ah, I see. Local Court of Enquiry is it?' He held out his water glass for a refill. 'I thought London might have allocated the incident a codeword and be sending out another investigator. They could go on like that indefinitely I suppose.'

Harry had never seen him in such high spirits. Exuberance, or a near-hysterical guilty reaction? How was the Ambassador going to deal with it?

'You see, Bill, I have to question all those who had the opportunity and motive to have done away with Berridge – after all the man didn't commit suicide and no outsider could have got in. So …'

'Yes, yes, I understand.' He seemed more normal now. 'Fire away, sir. Ask whatever you need to.'

'Well Bill, I can't quite visualise you as an assassin, but I must ask …'

'Of course I'll help if I can. Although I can't pretend I'm not heartily glad the bloody man is dead – and that whoever did it deserves a medal.'

'Bill, I'm hardly desolated myself. But I've been instructed to do what I can to clear up the mystery. You'll understand that'. The Ambassador looked into his black book. 'These are notes which, ah, Berridge made while he was here. Now, against your name he's got *AM Really necessary? Section coping adequately.* What does that mean?'

'*AM* are the initials of the young man being sent out here, a visa specialist. We've discussed him before, Bernard. Berridge, damn his eyes, intended to sabotage the posting. That's what that entry must mean.' He thought for a moment and asked nervously: 'He didn't send any telegrams, did he, about the Visa Section, do you know?'

'No', Brathby responded, 'everything was recorded in this book, it seems, and in his head of course.'

'Excellent', said the Consul, 'in which case no damage done.'

'Well, I suppose …'

Was the Ambassador losing what little control of the proceedings he might have had? Harry found his approach increasingly enigmatic.

'Anything else about me in that book?'

'No, but there's an entry about Jane.'

About Jane. Harry was startled. What…

'Yes, it says *Jane Paige, V-C, seems competent but over-sensitive.*'

'What the devil did Berridge mean by that?' exclaimed Harry. And why was Bill looking at him like that?

'Well, no harm now I suppose, now that he's dead,' Bill replied, 'He must have been referring to that … er … complaint Jane made to me.'

'Oh yes of course, that must have been it', the Ambassador said.

'Could you please explain?' Harry asked.

The Ambassador turned to answer him. 'What happened, Harry, was that Jane told Bill that Berridge had made a pass at her, and not a subtle one at that.'

'Bloody man!' Harry burst out. 'If I'd known I'd have …' He stopped talking just in time.

'Just so, Harry', his Ambassador said quietly. 'Which was why Bill asked Jane not to tell you. It was difficult for her but she handled it well.'

That was good to hear. 'I understand, sir, and, well, it seems as if someone else's saved me the trouble.' Then as another aspect bore in on him he added hurriedly: 'But not Jane, I'm sure she wouldn't do anything like that and she was busy most of the time looking after the Admin Officer. And she didn't even …'

'All right, Harry, she's not a suspect. We'll leave it there.' The Ambassador paused. 'Now Bill, is there any way you can help with this mystery? Of *course* I don't think you really wanted him dead, however strongly you felt about him. But *someone* did the deed.'

'Sorry, Bernard. Could be almost anyone, I suppose, if he dealt with others as he dealt with me, and with Jane.' He stood up. 'If you're finished with me I'll get back to my desk. Work piling up as usual.' He paused: 'And now if I've understood you correctly I'd better be looking out for a local resting place for Berridge's bones, just in case. Perhaps the Church of the Rivers would take him. They're not too picky I'm told.'

As the door closed behind the Consul the Ambassador said. 'One more, Harry, and then we'll take a break. Who's it to be? I don't mind admitting that I can't quite believe *any* of our colleagues are responsible. However please now ask Mr Elias to come up, will you.'

*****

'Thank you, Your Excellency. Oh, good afternoon, Harry.' Elias sat down carefully, his powerful sandalwood perfume wafting across the room. 'First may I report to Your Excellency that the police are continuing to be most co-operative; Dr Karim-Bux has been offered various forms of support for the post-mortem, at a technical level you understand, Your Excellency. Help with the analysis of specimens, access to police medical instruments, that sort of thing. Moreover, the Commissioner has been kind enough to send us two sets of photographs of the deceased which were taken after the discovery, one set for our Dr Karim-Bux and one for Your Excellency's files; also …'

When was the man going to draw breath, Harry wondered.

' … he, the Commissioner that is, Your Excellency, has sent us the negatives of those pictures, saying that since they'd been taken on British official premises it seemed to him to be the correct form of action under the circumstances. He also pointed out, wishing especially to draw our attention to this, Your Excellency, that the police photographer and the technician who produced the prints had both been trained in the United Kingdom and …'

'Yes, thank you, Mr Elias. What I really must ask you …'

Was the Old Man now going to get a grip on Greasers? Or would the latter, like Bill, call the tune?

Seemingly oblivious of the Ambassador's interruption, Elias continued:

'I am also very conscious, Your Excellency, that we were all so busy this morning, following the discovery, that I have not previously had the opportunity to express my sorrow to Your Excellency for the loss of this fine Foreign Service Officer in his prime. I can only hope that his family ...'

'Yes ... er ... thank you, Mr Elias, but there are a few questions I must ask you.' Was he now going to take control? 'You heard Dr Karim-Bux's preliminary view that Mr Berridge met his death through foul play.'

'One can only hope, Your Excellency, that with closer examination of the deceased he may come to a different conclusion. It's ...'

The Ambassador raised his voice slightly. 'Despite your expressions of regret, Mr Elias, would you not agree that Mr Berridge's death was welcome to you?'

Harry could only stare: by the Old Man's standards this was going for the jugular.

'In some ways, Your Excellency, I suppose ...'

The Ambassador interrupted. 'This is Mr Berridge's notebook which I found after his death. It is open here at the section about you. Please read it aloud.' He handed the book to Elias.

'Well, Your Excellency, I see ... er ... you want me ...'

'Just read it out please. Slowly, clearly and with no comments of your own. There'll be time for that later.'

'Just as you say, Your Excellency. Well it says: *1. Pension irregularity. Cannot be allowed full UK-based rights. Discuss with Departments. 2. Undeclared and untaxed income from Intell work – obtain tax office opinion. 3. Zalomo relationship – almost certain corrupt. Probably keeps Z informed re Emb activities. 4. Sensitive re relations with Soviet bloc officials. 5. Extension for one year. Why so keen? Nest-feathering, presumably. 6. Clandestine visits to AE's house by corrupt Embassy contractors – wife might testify.* He looked imploringly at Brathby. 'Your Excellency, the things written here are quite false. Mr Berridge could twist anything to make it look bad. And Bertha ... really! Now, to take these lies in turn ...'

Harry admired the adroit way in which the Ambassador quickly assured Elias that he certainly didn't want to discuss these 'insinuations' now, and maybe never would. Their relevance, he said, was simply that Elias must have known that Berridge was planning to do him very serious harm once he had returned safely to London. Could Elias explain why on Saturday morning he'd been seen heading down the corridor towards Berridge's bedroom?

Was that bluff, or information which Brathby hadn't shared with Harry, or was it based on Harry's own assessment that Greaseball seemed to be everywhere at once? Almost certainly bluff and, to Harry's surprise, it worked.

'Your Excellency, you know I am a completely truthful man,' – another one to treasure – 'and I wish to tell you why I was there.'

Probably he assumed he'd been seen there, reflected Harry, by any one of those odds and sods who'd been milling around the passages at that time. Who *hadn't* been?

'You see, Your Excellency, I had the strong impression from Mr Berridge that he was going to make trouble in London about my pension. I thought, Your Excellency, to make one last appeal to him, so I tried to find him, but he was not in his room.'

'When was this?' the Ambassador asked.

'Soon after the driver was hurt by the demonstrators, Your Excellency. I came upstairs to report that incident.'

'Did you enter his room?'

'No, Your Excellency. I knocked several times and his finished breakfast tray was outside the door. But I never saw him.'

'You went looking for him?'

'Yes, Your Excellency.'

'Including towards the old storeroom area?'

'Yes, Your Excellency, but there was no sign of him.'

'Was the door to the old storeroom closed?'

'Yes, locked, Your Excellency.'

'*Locked*! You tested it?'

'Yes, Your Excellency, I had thought Mr Berridge *might* have gone in there … but …'

'Why did you think that?'

The Old Man was putting the boot in and old Greasers was sounding suspiciously honest.

'Well, he was that sort of person, Your Excellency, looking into dark corners as it were; and he had to be *somewhere*.'

'And the key?'

280

'In its usual place, Your Excellency, under the elephant's foot. So of course I didn't look any further for Mr ...'

'How did you know where the key was kept?'

'It's always been kept there, Your Excellency.'

Quite, thought Harry.

The Ambassador stood up to stretch his legs.

'Is there anything else you can think of to help me in this enquiry, Mr Elias? It seems we have a locked-room mystery, like in the best detective stories!'

Now that *was* wet, thought Harry. The Old Man had been doing well but had now lost it. He was a damned good Ambassador, Harry was sure, but no ace at interrogation. Unless he was being super-subtle?

'Well that's another one done,' said Brathby when Elias had left without offering any further information.

Harry was beginning to wonder if the Ambassador was really interested in finding out who among his staff had murdered that little shit. Or was he just ticking off the names on his list?

'I intend to see Head of Chancery next, at his flat, Harry, but I shall go alone. He is your line manager, so it wouldn't do for you to act as my assistant when he is questioned.'

'Yes, sir, I can see that.'

'But maybe you can help on this here. There's a long entry on Francis in Mr Card ... er ... Mr Berridge's black book, much of it complimentary. But there are one or two notes that I can't understand. What are *Exec Account* and *Tum Pen*, do you know? And here: *BB unaware.* Also the word *Sad*, heavily underlined. Sad about what?'

'May I see, sir?'

The Ambassador showed him the entry.

'Well, the *BB* could refer to you, sir.'

'Yes, Harry, I'd got that far. But the other entries?'

He thought hard but had to admit that he couldn't help.

'Right.' Brathby stood up. 'So, Harry, could you please organise my car and let Francis know I'm coming to see him.'

'And if he says he's not well enough?'

'Then I'm still coming to see him.'

That was more like it.

4

How disagreeable that his Ambassador insisted on visiting him, presumably in connection with this morning's discovery. Fieldhouse had informed him of the details by telephone. The bumbling Brathby doubtless fancied himself as Grand Inquisitor. He could think of nobody less suited to the role.

'Sorry, sah, Master not well,' he could hear his Steward saying. 'Come dis way. You like drink?'

'Just iced water please, Moses.'

Paynton leant forward slightly in his *chaise longue*, languidly indicating a chair for Brathby to sit on. He did not feel at all well, and if he was thought discourteous – he mentally shrugged – well, did that really matter?

'I'm sorry you're indisposed, Francis.'

How typical of Brathby to maintain the civilities so scrupulously. Or perhaps he really was sorry. Anything was possible with him.

Paynton nodded in reply and closed his eyes.

'Francis, I'm afraid I have to ask you some questions.'

'Do you?' He kept his eyes closed.

'Will you please read these entries from Mr Berridge's notebook and tell me what they mean,' Brathby said and put the book in front of him.

Paynton looked at the notes. A bad moment. He made no immediate response. He'd expected some routine questions concerning the alleged murder, but these entries seemed to confirm his worst fears about the other matter. His brain was working furiously. Think man, think. Brathby wasn't the brightest, or worldliest, of men, was he? Yes, he might just get away with it. Perhaps all was *not* lost.

'Let me have another look, sir, if I may,' he said, sitting up and deciding to sound more accommodating. He must get this right. 'Yes, I think I know what is probably meant here …'

Later Brathby asked him a number of distinctly soft questions about his movements on Saturday morning, and then took himself off. God, how ineffectual the man was, Paynton thought, reflecting how differently he would have gone about it if their positions had been reversed.

5

'Useful interview with the Head of Chancery, sir?' he asked politely when Brathby returned, although bursting with news of his own.

'Yes, fairly, Harry. But the whole situation remains complicated and I'm not quite sure where ...' He paused as if searching for the right words.

'Sir.' He could contain himself no longer. 'Sorry to interrupt you, sir, but it's Cuthbert and Eventide. They're back – back here in the Residence. Isn't that great?' He'd meant to be so controlled about telling his Ambassador, but in his excitement the words came tumbling out. What a day! So far one corpse, indeed a *Corpse Diplomatique*, he muttered irreverently. Then the questioning of murder suspects (were they *really* that?), and now the return of the runaways.

Harry's news about Cuthbert lit up the Ambassador like a beacon. 'Back!' he was exclaiming. 'Back! But that's wonderful. How, when ... where is he now? I'll ...'

'Soon after you left, sir. The Commissioner sent them back in a police car. They'd been hiding out with a friend of Cuthbert's. He's just getting Eventide to bed – the lad looked absolutely done in – and then he'll come in and report.'

'They all right? Not hurt or anything?'

'No, they're fine, sir. Just tired.'

'And did Cuthbert say why ...?'

'I didn't ask, sir. Thought it better to wait until you got back.'

'Quite right, Harry. Thank you.' There was a knock at the door. The Ambassador was on his feet.

'Would you like me to leave, sir?'

'No no, Harry, stay here.' He was opening the door.

'Oh, sah, I so stupid, so stupid.' Cuthbert had grasped the Ambassador's hand and was kissing it, to Brathby's obvious embarrassment. 'Forgive me dat I run away. Forgive me please, I beg you.' He was trembling, torn, Harry thought, between relief at being back home, fear of what the Ambassador might say and embarrassment at the fuss which he, a mere servant, was causing.

And then Brathby, at a stroke, put Cuthbert at his ease: 'Cuthbert, I am very relieved to see you, very relieved, and I want to hear your news. But first please bring beer for Mr Fieldhouse and me.'

On his return with the drinks Cuthbert was persuaded to sit on an up-right chair by the door and tell his tale. Harry noticed that although he himself had to work hard to make sense of Cuthbert's disjointed ac-count his Ambassador seemed to have no such problem, gently teasing out the story from the still confused old man. Harry's admiration for H.E.'s style grew though he still seemed to be playing a curious game.

*****

On Saturday morning, Cuthbert said, he had taken Mr Berridge's breakfast tray along, knocked to alert him and left it outside the door. He hadn't carried it in because 'I no want to see dat man at all.' The Master must know by now, Cuthbert said, that he had done a very stu-pid thing; he'd helped that bad man, the one who claimed to be a cousin, to visit the Master's office in the Embassy. Cuthbert was very ashamed of this and knew he ought to have told the Master; but he was frightened because the cousin had made threats about Eventide. Then Mr Berridge had found out about the cousin and what that bad man had made Cuth-bert do. He had threatened horrible things for the boy if Cuthbert re-fused to help him. Also, Mr Berridge had asked bad questions about the Master; no, he could not now remember what these questions were. Yes, that was a really bad man. He was sure that he was the one who make Miss Polly cry the night before. Very bad man.

A little later that morning, he explained – it was after Mr Tom and a few others had started to arrive – Cuthbert happened to be in the area of the old storeroom ('I dere by chance, Master'). The door was shut but not locked and the key was in the door. Cuthbert said he'd peered in, found the light on and, when his dim eyes focused, could see Mr Berridge lying there – 'on de floor, dead.'

Cuthbert would be accused of killing him, he knew. He was only a servant, and after the way the man had spoken to him about Eventide he had good reason to hate him. Not knowing what else to do he had just left the room immediately, locking the door behind him and putting the key away in its usual place.

Then he went about his duties in a daze, Cuthbert said, automatically tidying up and getting coffee and cold drinks ready for the meeting, all the time wondering what to do about Mr Berridge and becoming more and more frightened. The body would soon be discovered and he knew he would be blamed. He must escape while he could. So he fetched Eventide from the quarters and went out through the gathering rain storm. 'We go hide at de house of Benson, my friend who work in dat place where dey go put dead people.' When the police came today he'd thought they'd come to arrest him for the murder.

All this had come tumbling and stuttering out in pidgin but it slowly became clear to Harry what he was saying, although Cuthbert's chronology was somewhat confused to say the least. It probably wasn't important that Cuthbert made no mention of the menacing crowds which must have been there when he and the boy left; could it be that in his fright he hadn't even noticed? But something seemed wrong about his account of how he had found the body and then immediately left again, locking up behind him.

Surely the Ambassador was going to probe a little more deeply?

But it seemed not, and by now Cuthbert had moved on, saying how shamed he was of letting the cousin get into Master's Embassy room; and if Master sack him, well so. Only please to help Eventide, he begged. As for the small Master, although dis be bad ting to say, he too glad de man done die. But he no kill um, he swore. Perhaps Mr Berridge was so sick at de bad tings he had done dat he kill himself, Cuthbert suggested.

The Ambassador reassured Cuthbert, now so exhausted that his head was nodding and his spectacles kept falling into his lap, that if he had not killed Mr Berridge then he had nothing to fear. But in future he *must* be sure to bring problems like the cousin thing to him. That's what the Master was there for, to help. Cuthbert had been stupid about that matter, but not wicked. He was forgiven. Now he must have something to eat and go and rest. The Master would send Octavius back to the Colonel. Cuthbert would not be needed any more now but morning tea at the usual time tomorrow, please. And it is very good to have you back here safe and sound.

And if that constituted thorough questioning of the person who must surely be the chief suspect then Harry was Eskimo Nell's big sister.

'Poor old chap', Brathby said to Harry when the door closed. 'It was too much for him. I can understand how he acted as he did. Dear old Cuthbert. I'm quite sure it happened just as he said about discovering ... um ... Berridge – it must have been a dreadful shock for him. As for the *Stuffing* business, well he was out of his depth. I suppose we'll eventually have to produce a report on that business for London but I don't see any need, shall we say, to emphasise Cuthbert's involvement.'

'No indeed, sir'. Harry got the message.

'Yes, he's had a really raw deal. Poor old fellow.'

Harry felt reasonably sure that what Cuthbert had told them about the cousin, and about Berridge's pressure on him to talk, was absolutely straight. But, without knowing quite why, he was deeply sceptical about Cuthbert's account of discovering Berridge's body in the storeroom. But it was clear that the Old Man had swallowed every word, and was generally satisfied.

*****

Which was more than could be said of the next interview. Harry had hoped that he'd now hear about the Ambassador's visit to the Head of Chancery, but instead he'd been sent off to dig Tom Muckle out of his room.

'Afternoon Buster. Bad business this with Mr Berridge.'

'Yes indeed, Tom. Sit down. Harry is here as my assistant in this investigation. You can speak freely in front of him.'

'I see, sir.' Muckle looked distinctly uncomfortable, Harry thought. Probably worn out by Lydia's demands. No, don't be flippant, he reprimanded himself. After all this is a murder enquiry. He wanted to see how the Ambassador would handle Tom, a trained question-deflector by profession.

'Now to get straight down to business, Tom. I've been instructed by London to investigate the circumstances of Mr Berridge's death.' He paused. 'Dr Karim-Bux's preliminary view is that he was assaulted – banged on the head. If that is correct it seems certain that his assailant was one of us, that is from the Embassy staff. You understand that?'

'Yes, Buster. Stands to reason.'

'So I have to ask you some questions Tom. Purely a formality, I hope.'

Muckle nodded. 'Tom, did you see Mr Berridge at all on Saturday morning?'

'No, never.'

'But at some stage you were down in the corridor that leads to the old storeroom?'

'I were everywhere, Buster, with my kit. Taking readings and all that.'

'But you didn't see him?'

Muckle shook his head.

'Was the key in the lock of the old storeroom door?'

'No, Buster.'

'How can you be so sure?'

'Just am, Buster. I *notice* things like keys.'

Had he seen anyone else from the Embassy in that area of the Residence? He didn't think so; oh yes, he'd seen the Colonel, he thought. Where? Apparently coming out of the old toilet, in the corner down there. Had Tom seen Cuthbert at all that morning?

Yes, once or twice, but he couldn't remember when or where exactly.

The Ambassador was clearly making no progress along these lines and picked up the black book.

'Seen this before, Tom?'

'No Buster.'

'It's where Mr Berridge kept his notes about us all. One of the entries for you reads: *TM Intell Clerk. Obstructive. Admitted noisa BM racket. Very big scale or major unclop. Needs removing.* What does that mean Tom? Firstly why does he label you "obstructive"?'

Eventually, Tom replied, rather woodenly. 'He pushed his way into the Station, by force like. There's rude, isn't it? I tried to get him out.'

'But failed presumably … so what did he see there – what is this *noisa BM racket*?' Could *BM* stand for black market?'

Another long pause. 'Yes, probably does.'

'Are you telling me, Tom, that you're personally involved in something like that?' He was clearly shocked.

'Sorry, can't say any more. Sorry, Buster.'

'You mean in case you incriminate yourself, is that it?'

'Sort of.'

'Very well, Tom. In that case I'll have to discuss this with Miss Brainbridge at the first opportunity. She's due back some time early evening, isn't she?'

'Yes, Buster. I'm meeting her at the airport and taking her to her flat.'

'Please ask her to give me a call if the line's working, and if not to drop in here at about eight.'

'Right, Buster. Sorry.' He didn't say about what.

Harry had never seen Tom at a loss before. Could he have killed Berridge? Well, if he'd told the truth about Berridge uncovering his involvement in currency trading then he certainly had a strong motive. And probably he'd had the best opportunity of everybody. But why *immediately* admit to the *noisa BM racket* – did he think Berridge had already reported it to the Ambassador, or to London? In which case what was the benefit in killing the man? And anyhow Tom's ready admission of what Berridge had supposedly discovered didn't feel right; Tom was quite capable of murdering the man but he wouldn't get himself mixed up in some grubby money racket, Harry felt.

'All very puzzling,' said the Ambassador after Muckle had left; 'I don't know what to make of it. He could hardly have acted more guiltily but …'

'Yes, sir. Something strange there. Er, sir, about the Head of Chancery…'

'Yes, Francis was very helpful and explained the entries satisfactorily. What's more he's feeling a bit better, I'm glad to say. Now, next, I think we need to speak to the Colonel. Fetch him please, Harry.'

At the door, Harry turned. 'Sir, when you see the Colonel …' He felt a bit awkward but H.E. *had* asked him to mention anything suspicious.

'Yes?'

'He had a briefcase with him on Saturday morning, sir. It sort of swung around, difficult to describe, as if there was something loose and heavy in it. Almost certainly an innocent explanation but well …'

'You mean it could have contained a weapon, something like that?'

'Well yes, sir, could be.'

Or a bottle, he told himself as he went rapidly down the stairs and out into the compound.

He savoured the freshness brought by the Big Rains. For once it was almost pleasant to be in the open air. So how would our gallant Military Attaché stand up to the relentless grilling of the Examining Magistrate? Poor chap would probably confess immediately. And how disappointing that Paynton had satisfactorily explained those curious notes about himself in the black book.

In through the front door to the Chancery, a smile to Fred the Duty SO, and then he was striding down the corridor to clamp the handcuffs on the criminal Colonel.

6

'Good afternoon, Ambassador.' Colonel Squires sat down. 'Interesting times we live in, as my old friends the Chinese say when they slit your throat. So it's a Court Martial, eh, with young Lieutenant Fieldhouse as Prisoner's Friend?'

H.E. laughed lightly but was looking a little uncomfortable, presumably not relishing having to question his good friend about something so distasteful as murder. 'It's more like a Court of Enquiry, Jack, with Harry as scribe and coffee-wallah. Which reminds me – can we give you a cup?'

'Not yet thanks. Maybe when one gets dry-mouthed from the interrogation.' Squires was clearly nervous. 'But I say, what excellent news about Cuthbert and the young Eventide. Think how one would feel if it'd been the pair of them lying down there with their skulls smashed in and the ghastly Berridge returning to the Residence like an evil spirit! Which is what he is now, no doubt.'

'I don't suppose that anyone in this Embassy here feels that Berridge's death is a personal loss,' the Ambassador admitted, 'but he was a *British* official,' he added firmly, 'and *I* am under orders to enquire into how he died.'

Colonel Squires looked suitably chastened. 'May I smoke?' he asked. 'Many thanks.' He tapped his cigarette against the packet several times before lighting it. 'Sorry about the flippancy. It's obviously a serious business despite one's personal view that his removal was an act of Pest Control, for which one must be grateful. So fire away with your questions, Bernard. Clearly one must help as best one can.'

The Ambassador took him through his movements during the Saturday morning, occasionally glancing Harry's way for confirmation. 'Did you at any stage go into the old storeroom, Jack, or anywhere in that area?' he eventually asked.

'No, don't think so … No, wait, yes of course. One had a spot of the old gippy tummy – curry at *The Republic* with Armitage the night before, you know? Symptoms disappeared once the rough stuff started, often the way, isn't it! So yes, wandered down there to visit the bog, the one this end being occupied, one remembers.'

'See anyone down there, Jack?'

'Yes … yes, it's coming back. Tom Muckle was lurking around with his kit taking readings or sweepings or whatever it is those chappies do.'

'Did you have your briefcase with you?' the Ambassador asked.

'To visit the bog! Good Lord, no. Left it in the reception room; Harry will remember that, won't you, Harry?'

'Yes, Colonel, I can confirm that.'

'As a matter of interest, Jack, what was in the case? Something loose and heavy, I'm told.'

Sounds like Lydia, Harry was reflecting, when he realised that the Colonel was giving him a cross look. He must have worked out that Harry had supplied that information. He was also looking a little shifty.

'Can't imagine how anyone got that impression, Ambassador. Just a few papers and … er … well …'

'A bottle perhaps Jack?'

'Well … er … yes, as a matter of fact. I mean, one didn't know what the day might bring.'

A heavy bottle, Harry thought, and a robust one too from the way the Colonel had confidently plonked down his briefcase on the table that Saturday morning.

But the Ambassador seemed satisfied; and after all if the Colonel hadn't taken the briefcase to the storeroom area how could its contents be significant? So what did it matter if Squires was lying on this point?

Brathby then opened the black book and pushed it across the table. 'These entries here, Jack – this notebook belonged to Berridge – they obviously refer to you. Can you help me make sense of them?'

Colonel Squires stubbed out his cigarette and studied the page. 'Well *Malt* is no great mystery, one would have thought. *Washington* with a line through it? Probably meant that the creature intended to scupper any chance one had of being sent there. *Metropole* – well that's the MOD building where the Attaché postings are administered from – same line of thought presumably.'

The Ambassador leant forward and pointed. 'What about this *Fins critical*? Any ideas?'

'*Fins* abbreviation of finances presumably. Man had no doubt cottoned on that things are a bit tight for me in that department and hence one's extra need for the posting.'

'And further reason for him to sabotage your chances perhaps; if he had it in for you, that is?'

'Probably. Bloody man. He needed killing all right. Not that I did it – but then I would say that, wouldn't I, ha ha?'

'What about this *Arms dealers – k-b's*?'

'Preposterous.' He growled. 'Evil swine. He was clearly going to insinuate that I was taking kick-backs from fellows like Armitage. Can you imagine it? Me doing that. Can you?' He stood up, clenched his fists angrily and sat down again. 'I mean, *can* you?'

'Calm down, Jack.' The Ambassador said. 'That's one thing I'd never believe of you, you must know that.' He paused, before adding, 'but you must agree that you had a very strong motive for doing away with him.'

Colonel Squires looked straight into Brathby's eyes. 'One couldn't agree more. The man was poison. But …'

'But you didn't?'

'No, but whoever did deserves a medal.'

'Excuse me, sir, Colonel', Harry interposed a little tentatively. 'But could you help on one small point? When you saw Tom Muckle down that corridor …'

'Yes?' He was frowning.

'Can you remember what, if any, instrument, or other object, he had in his hand or was working with?'

'Er … well, as a matter of fact, no, one can't. Only saw the chap briefly, was concentrating on getting to the bog – matter was getting urgent you know. Why, is it important?'

Harry wasn't sure if it was or not. But it seemed somehow unlikely that the Colonel had no memory of what Tom had actually been doing when he saw him.

*****

'What were you getting at, Harry?' the Ambassador asked, when Squires had left.

'Not quite sure, sir. But didn't Tom tell you that he saw the Colonel coming *out* of the bog?'

'Yes, so he did. But it's probably not significant. Just a slip of mem-

292

ory by one of them, I expect.'

'Yes, I expect so, sir.'

The Ambassador stood up and stretched. 'Well, Harry, very many thanks. We've now seen everyone who could reasonably be called a suspect, though really I can't believe it of any of them. I'll run it past Philippa this evening and see if she can help.'

'Just one thing, sir.' He was feeling uncomfortable but it had to be said.

'Yes, Harry?'

'I wondered whether perhaps you ought to interview Polly as well, sir. Just to round things off, as it were.'

'You really think so? Why?'

'Well, Cuthbert made that curious comment about Mr Berridge having made her cry – it would be interesting to know what that was about – and then of course she *was* on her own for part of the time on Saturday morning, *and* not far from the store room.'

'And you really think Polly capable of such a deed?' The Ambassador was clearly not pleased.

'No, sir, of course not. But …'

'But what?'

'Well if you don't question her, sir, it just might be construed as … as favouritism. Her being your PA, you see.' He paused. 'Or if you preferred, sir, I could go on my own to see her. She might have something useful to tell us anyway.'

'No, I don't think so, Harry. If she's got to be questioned we'll deal with her in the same way as the others. She can come here.'

'And you'll want me as well?'

The Ambassador seemed undecided. Then he said; 'Yes, of course. Sometime early evening perhaps, just before I see Philippa. Meanwhile you might call in on any of the others we haven't seen just to check whether they've anything useful to contribute. Make it clear they're not suspects but you want their views, that sort of thing.'

'Yes, sir.' He left.

The Old Man certainly hadn't liked the suggestion about Polly. But Harry had been right to bring it up. And it was intriguing that the dreadful Berridge had apparently been offensive to Polly as well as to all the others they had interviewed. But when could the two of them have met? Perhaps Cuthbert was wrong. But if he *wasn't* wrong then Polly might also have had a motive to dispose of the man. Not that it could be a serious one, surely. Or could it?

On his way down the stairs Harry decided to use his roaming brief to call in on Jane and ask her a few questions. Like whether she'd partner him in the tennis tournament, for openers.

7

'Thank you, Polly', the Ambassador said, standing up to bring the interview to a close. 'I'm sure all this has been as much of a shock to you as it has been to the rest of us. But you've been extremely helpful.'

Which in Harry's firmly-held, but wisely unexpressed, view was complete bollocks. What *was* the Old Man up to? From the moment she'd come in he'd treated her in an exaggeratedly gentle manner. Fair enough, perhaps, but it was also in an unmistakably *stilted* manner. And Polly herself? Well she'd behaved like an under-rehearsed actress fumbling with her lines.

While they'd been waiting for her to arrive the Ambassador had firmly instructed Harry to leave it all to him. On no account was Harry to throw in any questions; Polly was only just recovering her health and would be nervous about being questioned. Great care must be taken not to upset her. He hoped that Harry had got that quite clear.

No, Polly had said quietly when the Ambassador had at last finished asking her how she was, and assuring her that she had nothing to fear; no, she hadn't seen anything suspicious that morning. No, she hadn't seen Mr Berridge. No, she hadn't been down the corridor leading to the old store room. As they both knew, she'd been working most of the time in the study, as earlier agreed, and with the door locked. Only later had she come to the reception room.

But *when* had it been agreed that Polly would work in the study, Harry wondered? And did it make any sense, since when the trouble outside actually became serious Polly was brought *out* of the study to join the others in the reception room? It was also unclear to Harry whether Polly had in fact *ever* met Berridge. If so, then *when*? Because if there was anything behind what Cuthbert had said about Berridge making her cry, there must have been some sort of encounter. When did it happen, and what was it all about? Was it like Berridge's pass at Jane, or something else? And why did the Ambassador make no reference to the matter?

Was it fanciful, Harry asked himself, to conclude that his Ambassador *knew* that Polly had relevant information, perhaps even incriminating information and that he did not want her to come out with it in front of a third party? And that she understood that and was trying not to fluff her lines?

Moreover the personal relationship between the two of them seemed different, more intense. Had the Old Man at last summoned up the courage to reveal his ill-concealed desire for her and swept her into the Ambassadorial king-size? No, he didn't think so. Yet *something* of significance had recently passed between them, Harry believed. But what?

Or was all this just his romantic imagination running riot? Perhaps the excitement was addling his brain.

*****

'Thank you, Harry,' the Ambassador said when Polly had left. 'I think I can release you now. You've been a great help.'

In what way, Harry wondered, as he walked across to the adjoining building? He certainly hadn't contributed much to the Polly interview. Hadn't been allowed to. The Old Man was so sensitive about her. More than that, plain potty about her.

Just as he was about to enter the Chancery a car drew up near the Residence and Harry saw Philippa's gaunt, authoritative form emerge. He watched her stride in an ungainly but determined fashion towards the door. He imagined that he could feel the power radiating from her, even at this distance. Perhaps *she* would solve the mystery? But could she do so without creating shock waves throughout the Embassy?

It was impossible to imagine a happy ending to all this. Not even Philippa The Brainbox could conjure that from nothing.

Part Six

1

Philippa didn't so much mind having her leave cut short – she was anyhow beginning to feel a little bored – as finding that instead of being able to buckle straight down to her own work she'd first got to sort out Tom. The lad had really got his Y-fronts in a twist. And also until her Ambassador could find an acceptable solution to this Cardenas mystery, the Embassy would be in turmoil – which was not conducive to her cracking on with a number of projects she had in mind.

Tom had met her at the airport and had lost no time on the journey to her flat in explaining the real reason – as opposed to the pretext of needing help on Antoun's *Blunderbuss* project - why he'd asked for her to come back early. That dreadful Berridge man had burst into the Station – literally burst in, look you - and so to protect *Carrot* he'd told Berridge the money was his own, that he was dealing on the black market, though whether the man believed it or not he didn't know. Then after he had … er … died, the Ambassador, because of some notes Berridge had made, had come to believe the black market version too, and he hated that because Brathby had always been decent to him. Although - so sorry, Philippa - there was an abbreviated reference in Berridge's notes to a possible *Uncleared Operation* so you see it was on the cards that the man had sussed out what was really going on.

Tom knew what a dreadful cock-up it all was. And now he was shitting himself because the Ambassador apparently suspected that it was he who'd murdered Berridge and he couldn't prove that he hadn't. Especially as he'd got form as it were, having sorted out that intruding *tiefman*. Oh God, there's a ghastly mess and what a relief that she was back. Oh, Philippa, help this boyo out of trouble, and please don't send me home.

Poor worried Tom, she reflected later as she wound down the windows to return the greetings of the Embassy gate guards. But also bloody careless Tom to have allowed that prime shit Cardenas to barge in on the Station premises; she couldn't just ignore that, whatever else happened. *Carrot* had been at stake – an operation of extraordinary delicacy. Such a pity, as otherwise Tom had coped well in her absence.

It seemed that he'd handled Antoun cautiously and sensibly over this potential new source across the border, the so-called *Blunderbuss*. He'd also told her about a number of other possible intelligence leads he'd unearthed during her absence. All good stuff: but could she save him from the consequences of his security breach? She fervently hoped so but it wasn't in her hands. The Director would have to be told and Tom would have to go back to UK to explain to him in person. There was no avoiding that.

Meanwhile she could at least clear him of the black market suspicion. It would entail briefing Bernard about *Carrot*; that was overdue anyhow and she'd now got the green light from her Head Office to do so. Unlike his predecessor as Ambassador he was discreet about Intelligence matters. As for the suspicion of murder hanging over Tom? Well, she knew that if Tom *had* done it – and goodness knows the protection of a supremely delicate operation was worth an undeserving life or two – he'd somehow have avoided being in the frame. Also, she felt, he'd have told her he'd done it, and why, and thrown himself on her know-how to protect him. Which she'd have set out to do, as a matter of professional honour if nothing else.

She didn't yet know what Bernard expected of her in connection with Cardenas's death but she certainly wasn't going to carry out any protracted investigation.

She parked her car – which Tom had kept in perfect working order during her leave – and strode towards the Residence, welcoming the clammy stickiness of her body and glorying in the stink of Africa. She thought with pity of those of her colleagues serving in Europe, living in predictable comfort and safety but with bloody Head Office breathing down their necks. At least here she did more or less what she wanted, subject to the eleventh commandment of course.

Yes, she confirmed to herself as she approached the door, she'd confine herself to briefing Bernard about *Carrot*, thus clearing Tom of suspicion of currency dealing at least; and she'd offer to have a look in at the old store room, in case she spotted anything obvious that had been overlooked and which might get Tom off the suspect list. And if someone else had killed Cardenas, then bully for him.

And now here was dear old Cuthbert opening the door for her, and Bernard at the top of the stairs, with a smile on his face. A smile which betrayed relief as much as pleasure, thought Philippa. The poor chap clearly expects me to sort out this whole Cardenas affair. He certainly looks weary and harassed.

'Hello Bernard', she said, 'help is at hand'. She gave him the kind of kiss normally reserved for small children in distress and led him into his own Residence.

2

Francis Paynton brushed his hair carefully and then came through to inspect the cold supper which had been laid out for him. Smoked salmon and tinned oysters – imported of course, as indeed were the bread and the butter to accompany them – to be followed by local bananas and imported tinned raspberries. And, most satisfactory, a good wedge of Brie, bartered for a bottle of Dimple Haig with a friend in the French Embassy. Not a bad meal really, considering he was in this unsavoury corner of West Africa.

'You may go to your quarters now, Moses. I'll call if I need you.'

'Thank you, sah.'

Paynton didn't reply. As the door closed he poured himself a glass of white Burgundy and sat down. He was hungry, almost voraciously so. It seemed certain now that what Cardenas had learned about his proclivities had died with him. Until Cardenas had so fortunately been disposed of, Paynton had had to assume that his chances of the UN job were in peril. Even after the man's death he had feared that Cardenas might have told Brathby, or the FCO. But apparently not, it had finally emerged.

He smiled as he recalled how that clown Brathby hadn't been able to make sense of Cardenas's notes. *Exec Account* he'd asked about, and been happy to have it explained that Cardenas had been very interested in Paynton's *Account of his Executive Duties*. Amazing that Brathby couldn't see that it far more probably referred to Paynton's *Account* over lunch of the *Executions*. And the note, in close proximity to *Exec Acc*, of *Tum Pen*! It was, of course quite clearly a reference to Paynton's visible state of sexual arousal when recounting the story, i.e. *Tumescent Penis*. But Brathby had readily agreed with Paynton's hastily imagined suggestion that the entry must derive from some talk they'd had about <u>*Taking Up the Matter*</u>, *TUM* in Berridge's shorthand, of his, Paynton's FCO, <u>*Pension*</u> rights, if seconded to the UN. But what about *Sad*, the Ambassador had pressed on, having accepted that preposterous explanation without a murmur; *Sad* about what? This also probably referred, Paynton had silkily suggested, to the possible UN job. Although he would like to have the job and would accept it if offered, he had told Cardenas that he was *Sad* because it would entail cut-

300

ting short his present Post, where he was settled and happy and learning a lot under his Ambassador's guidance. Any thought that the word could be an abbreviated reference to the Marquis de Sade had clearly never entered the naive Ambassador's head.

Amazingly Brathby had swallowed this hogwash. Then he'd just reiterated his best wishes for Paynton's swift recovery and departed. Slightly worryingly he'd said nothing about actually supporting Paynton's nomination for the UN post; but then the poor man had so much on his plate that he probably couldn't face up to the prospect of losing him from his staff. No, there really shouldn't be any problem from Brathby. The man was so weak. He couldn't even sort out his own love life.

Secondment to the UN Post would certainly be a tonic after his current drudgery. It would be an important and well-paid position. The responsibilities even included, he had learned, overseeing all UN investigations of prisoner mistreatment, torture allegations etc. in the Middle East. He'd be busy.

Paynton polished off the oysters, started on the smoked salmon and poured himself a second glass of wine. What an excellent meal.

The urgent demands of his stomach now assuaged, Paynton found his mind returning to the executions which had so nearly been his undoing. Some of the details were really quite bizarre; that business with the clothes catching fire for example ...

3

'I'd forgotten what an interesting view you have from your window, dear Bernard,' Philippa Brainbridge said as she entered the Ambassador's office the next morning. 'So how *is* the body count going these days?' Philippa Brainbridge felt tired but relaxed and also quite justifiably pleased with herself.

She turned as the door opened and a worried-looking Polly, with whom she had earlier exchanged greetings in the outer office, brought in the coffee tray. She gingerly placed it on Brathby's desk, accepted their thanks with a half-smile, and retreated wordlessly to her own room.

'May I have beer instead, Bernard?' she asked, gesturing towards the fridge and going across to help herself. 'It's nearly noon and my feet don't seem to have touched the ground since I saw you yesterday evening.

'I'm so sorry, Philippa, if you've been overdoing it on my behalf, and only just off the plane too. But you so kindly …'

'Bernard, you misunderstand me.' How typical of the man to be so considerate when he must be desperately anxious to know about her investigations. She crossed the room and closed the adjoining door to Polly's office.

'I haven't been on your case all the time, you know. As you're aware I had a glance round the supposed crime scene once yesterday evening. And I've been there again just now, and also had a word with dear Cuthbert. Oh yes, and I looked in this morning on Dr Pox for a word about the injuries sustained by the late unlamented. He seemed quite happy about a couple of points which I checked out with him, and which I'll come to a little later. Incidentally, he asked me to do what I could about getting his contract renewed. Otherwise I've been mainly busy on other things. Rather boringly the Commissioner had heard I was back and asked me to see him last night. You know, stuff like that.' No need to tell Bernard that Zalomo had assumed that it was Antoun Elias who must have killed Cardenas, and clearly thought the better of him for it.

'So about Cardenas, have you come to any …?'

'Oh yes it all looks quite straightforward to me. You see …' She

302

paused to smile at her Ambassador and take a swallow of beer. She really oughtn't to tease him, she knew; he was looking quite strained.

'How do you mean, "straightforward"? Do you really know, I mean how *can* you know who …?'

'Bernard, I've studied Harry's notes of your "interrogations", I've talked to Cuthbert and I've carefully examined Cardenas's poisonous little black book. I *do* so hate to be a spoilsport but the simplest solution to your "murder" mystery must be that Cardenas died by accident.'

'Accident?' She could see hope flare up in his face and then rapidly subside. 'But surely not. I mean how …?'

'Bernard', she said, watching his face closely, 'it seems to me that everyone's been far too quick to take as gospel the peremptory pronouncements of Dr Pox and our chum Zalomo that this was (a) an obvious case of "foul play", and (b) an "inside job". I'm tempted to say "Men, typical", but I forebear.'

She took a sip of beer and continued.

'Did you never for a moment consider that this could have been just an accident – an Act of God?'

Brathby's tense and worried face relaxed slightly at this. Following up her advantage, she went on: 'There is no evidence that anyone *else* was in the storeroom at the same time. Perhaps it takes a woman's intuition, or perhaps just common sense, to see the obvious answer …'

'That …?'

'That Cardenas just fell off the ladder and cracked his head open on the umbrella stand, finishing up where old Cuthbert says he found him. In fact the stand's still got traces of blood on it. Incidentally a fall from the top of the ladder like that would explain how his notebook, which he must have had up there with him, finished up where you found it.'

'God knows I'd like to believe it, Philippa,' he burst out, 'but it doesn't add up. I mean first of all …' He got up and started to pace around the room.

'Before we come to that, Bernard, there's one point still puzzling me. Perhaps you can help. Why was Cardenas up the ladder at all? What could he have been looking for, do you think?' She followed his progress round the room.

'Of course' – the Ambassador stopped pacing and sat down abruptly behind the desk – 'my *diaries*. I keep my personal diaries up there, on

top of the cupboard. He must somehow have found out about them and
…'

'And been snooping around for something he could use against you,
no doubt.'

'Yes, that would be in character. Yes, yes, that makes sense, all
right. About the snooping, I mean.'

'But …?'

'It's the other things. God knows I want to believe you're right,
Philippa, about it being an accident I mean. But it's hard to visualise
how Cardenas could have tripped, fallen or whatever against the umbrella stand hard enough to have injured himself so badly, yet without
knocking the thing over. And if it *had* been on its side then Harry and
I would have certainly have noticed when we went in.' He was drum-
ming his fingers on the desk in agitated fashion.

'Moreover,' – she knew he was coming to the most serious of his ob-
jections – 'when Harry and I went into the storeroom the ladder was
standing in its usual place, neatly against the side of the wardrobe. If
Cardenas had fallen from it, which he might well have done, then it
would either have been leaning against the wardrobe where he'd put it
or, more likely, have been lying on the floor.' He was on his feet again.
'But equally impossible to explain is how a dying man got himself from
the floor of the storeroom down to the lower level, where we found
him. There's no answering those points. Is there, Philippa?' His face
sagged miserably. 'It just doesn't make sense.

'Cuthbert', she said softly, 'Cuthbert.'

'What *do* you mean?' He was on his feet again.

'Cuthbert told you, didn't he, that he came in, saw the man sprawled
on the floor, assumed he was dead – as indeed he *may* have been –and
left in a panic. But not too panicked, it seems, to have found the key,
which was presumably in Cardenas's pocket, or otherwise how could
he have locked up? I'm surprised you didn't ask him about these points
when he returned from his walk-about.'

She leant forward and continued: 'And what else does a good servant instinctively do, whatever the circumstances? He *tidies up*! So
Cuthbert moves the ladder off the floor and puts it back where it be-
longs; he heaves the umbrella stand upright and restores its contents.
Does this almost automatically, while in shock from finding Cardenas's

body and without necessarily understanding the significance, either at the time, or indeed later, of what he was doing. Just domestic acts, routine and soothing, while he tries to pull himself together and decide what to do. Certainly he wouldn't be thinking, like you or I would, of the forensic implications.'

'Yes, yes.' He was allowing himself to hope now, it seemed. 'Yes, it could have happened like that. But …'

'But …?'

'It still doesn't explain how the man got down to the floor below.'

'No, not for certain, but there are two likely explanations.' Philippa stopped and gave him an affectionate frown. 'Bernard, you're making me giddy. Do please sit down.'

He did. 'Yes, two likely … you were saying …?' He looked at her with dog-like hope. She really was a most striking woman, most convincing; he desperately wanted to believe her.

'Well, one explanation is that when Cuthbert found Cardenas the man was not dead, just severely stunned. But some time after Cuthbert had left the room, having tidied up as we have deduced, Cardenas could have recovered consciousness, staggered towards the old staircase and gone crashing down, finishing up where you and Harry found him. So either a second fall, or delayed trauma from the first fall, finished him off.'

'Or else?'

'Or the ladder and the stand weren't the only things that Cuthbert tidied away.'

It seemed to take Bernard several seconds to hoist in what she meant.

'Who knows what was going on in Cuthbert's head at the time?' she continued, 'shocked as he surely was? Anything at all. He could even have believed that it was *you* who had killed Cardenas, if indeed he was quite dead when he found him, and have had some muddled idea that he was protecting you by hiding the body. And it's even possible that his subsequent disappearance had some element in it of aiming to divert suspicion from you.'

'Philippa, you could be right. It all makes sense.' His face was alive with hope. 'We must ask Cuthbert exactly what happened, straightaway.' He made to stand up. 'Get the details, get it sorted out.'

'Must we, Bernard?' She laid a restraining hand on his arm and looked him straight in the eye. 'Whatever Cuthbert did, he did for the best of motives. Do you really want to upset the old boy any further? It could simply confirm any fears he may have that you believe him guilty of the extermination of that rat. Or stimulate him to tell us other things that could never be checked and which we probably don't want to hear. You see, if Cardenas were still alive, even though mortally injured, when pushed down the hole, then strictly speaking Cuthbert would be guilty of his murder. Would he not? Best to leave things as they are, don't you think?' She leant forward and put her hand on his.

For a moment Bernard seemed bewildered, almost in pain, but then sank back in his chair, evidently convinced. She could feel the tension draining out of him. When he did get up it was only to get her another beer and pour one for himself. He closed his eyes for a moment and sat quietly as if reviewing all they had discussed, allowing himself to accept her solution.

'Philippa, let me get this quite straight, my dear, quite straight. You're saying that Cardenas, while reaching for my diaries, just fell off the ladder onto the umbrella stand, killing or fatally injuring himself in the process. That it was as simple as that?' His relief was almost pathetic. His hand felt very cold.

'Just so, Bernard, just so. Unless of course he was *pushed* – by person or persons unknown. On purpose or otherwise. But we've no reason to think that, have we?'

Brathby jerked his hand away and made as if to leave his seat before subsiding again. He was regarding her warily.

'But you know, Bernard', she went on, 'I was particularly intrigued by one or two small details of the case.' Philippa reached into her briefcase and pulled out the familiar black notebook which Brathby had used as an *aide memoire* for his own investigations.

'The repository of our departed friend's secrets', she smiled, 'which you lent me yesterday evening. You discovered it, I think you said, just after you and Harry had found the body on Monday morning.'

As Brathby nodded she leaned back and took a sip of her beer. 'Shall I tell you an interesting thing I discovered about this little item?' asked Philippa with a curious smile.

'Of course, fire away', Brathby replied with unconvincing enthusiasm. He must be wondering what she was going to come out with.

'The most interesting thing about this notebook has nothing to do with its contents', said Philippa quietly. She got to her feet and with the toe of her shoe flicked the switch of the Ambassador's document shredder. Brathby watched open-mouthed as his Intelligence Officer slowly and deliberately began to tear pages from the notebook and feed them into the machine. For a full minute the low hum of the motor and the satisfying sound of shredding paper filled the room as Philippa slowly and wordlessly consigned Cardenas's notes to oblivion. She tore off the last page with a dramatic flourish and leaned conspiratorially towards Brathby.

'No Bernard, the most interesting thing about this notebook is that there are fingerprints in blood on the front and back covers.' She held up the disembowelled book for Brathby to see more clearly.

'Virtually impossible to make them out isn't it? The dried blood is almost invisible against the black cover of the book. In fact, to see them properly I had to use the ultra-violet light that we keep in my office for checking counterfeit currency. For Operation *Carrot* which I told you about last night.'

Brathby's expression changed from puzzlement to shock. Philippa watched the colour drain from his face as she put a reassuring hand on his shoulder.

'Leaving aside its obvious potential for professional forensic examination, it occurred to me that whoever handled this notebook must have had blood on their hands at the time - presumably fresh blood from the corpse. And yet the notebook was discovered almost at the same time as the body, long after Cardenas's head wound had stopped bleeding. Discovered by you, Bernard.'

Unable to speak, Brathby sat gripping the front of his desk.

'The inescapable conclusion, therefore,' Philippa continued, 'is that Cardenas did not die immediately from his wounds and that *he himself* handled the notebook while fatally injured. The blood and the fingerprints must be his. That is the only logical answer, wouldn't you agree, Bernard? I mean the facts do not allow any other interpretation, do they?'

Before Brathby could answer, Philippa forced what remained of the notebook into the jaws of the shredder. The machine protested briefly but completed its task of destruction, spitting little strips of cardboard and leather into the collection bin.

'Yes, of course… that must be the way it happened, Philippa', Brathby said hoarsely. 'Thank you for clearing it up for us.'

'Not at all, it was my pleasure,' said Philippa, 'but there is just one thing I'd like you to do for me, Bernard.

'Of course, whatever you want.'

'Have your suit dry-cleaned, Bernard'.

She drained her beer and with a wry smile left the Ambassador alone with his thoughts.

TO: Priority FCO
Confidential

After further careful investigations, with the help of my local Friend, into my visitor's unfortunate demise I now record a verdict of death by misadventure. My full report follows by bag but I can tell you now, My Lord, that the deceased was undoubtedly alone at the time, in a notoriously dilapidated and dangerous part of this historic and picturesque building (a matter about which my Administration Officer is corresponding separately with the appropriate Department). What my visitor was looking for there has not been determined.

HM Consul is making funeral arrangements. I presume we need expect no relatives of the deceased to attend. BRATHBY

4

'It doesn't matter, my love, really it doesn't matter. It'll come right soon, Bernie my darling. I'm happy just to be with you, really *with* you at last. The other can wait. It's not important.'

Now he was sitting on the edge of the bed, with his head slumped forward. 'I feel so useless, Polly, so stupid. All this time I've longed ... and now. It's as if some part of him is still present in the house. I wonder, Polly, can this work out for us?' His shoulders were beginning to shake.

She had to get this right, for both their sakes. And she had no useful experience to guide her. Perhaps it had been a mistake to come to bed together for the first time like this, straight from the funeral. But he'd wanted her so much, he'd said. And there could surely be no doubt that he loved her; well, not after doing that for her, as she was fairly sure he had.

She knelt facing him and kissed his hands. 'Listen to me, my dearest. You know I love you and we've come through so much together. We don't *need* to try again yet, not until you want to. You see Bernie – I nearly said "sir" – this, this is only a part of you. I love all of you.' Although she was powerfully aware that, for the first time in her life, she wanted a man – this man – physically, while at the same time being nervous how she would cope.

He stroked her head. 'I'm sure you're right, Polly my love. It's just that ... oh ... I can't explain.'

'Perhaps what you need now is a good shot of scotch. Me too perhaps, as well. Yes?' She stood up. 'You did send Cuthbert off, didn't you? Wouldn't want to shock the old boy, would we?'

'He'd probably be delighted it's happened at last.' He paused. 'Not that it has though, has it? Oh damn, damn, damn. Oh Polly.'

She silenced him with a gentle kiss.

Through the kitchen window she could see and hear the monotonous rain beating down relentlessly. Orphans of the storm, she thought; what shall I do? God knows it was never going to be easy for her but for *Bernard* to have problems – she hadn't expected that.

She must use her brains as well as her instinct. She thought hard. Was there anyone she could ask? Just possibly Violet, if she could bring herself to do so. Could she? Why not?

Meanwhile she must get him his scotch. She found the bottle and two glasses. Man does not live by … she blushed as that four-letter word came unbidden to her mind – by … that … alone. Not that he'd had that yet. Oh dear, it was all so difficult. But she'd get this right. She would. She must.

On tiptoe she could just reach the ice trays on the top shelf of the fridge. She pulled one towards her.

What was that funny little leather pouch doing there she wondered, tucked away right at the back? Something of Cuthbert's no doubt, nothing of interest to her.

Say after me Polly, slowly – this man loves me; find a way to get it right.

5

The occasional thud of a dart, clink of glassware, a general hubbub of chatter, denoted the regular Saturday session in progress at the Club; more cheerful than usual perhaps, as though some baneful presence had been removed.

Doctor Karim-Bux looked up from his seat by the bar as yet more people piled into the Club. How kind of Miss Brainbridge to be inviting him to celebrate the renewal of his contract. But he wouldn't be here next Saturday, he lamented, that damned annual leave having come round again. What a rotten nuisance. And he couldn't decently be taking less than three weeks, oh no. A long time to be away from his demanding practice; not to mention to be holidaying with that tiresome woman and those fat, stolid children of his. He took a deep draught of his Lahore ginger.

*****

'You did well, Bernard, really well.' Joe Singleton looked affectionately at the Ambassador. 'You too, Bill of course', he added, standing up. 'Got to pay a short call and then we'll have our dance, shall we, Edith? Jolly old Africa. Everything's going to be the same here, isn't it? I do hope so.'

'What did he mean, Bill that we'd done well?'

'Got that beastly man buried, I expect', said Edith.

'Did I tell you, Bernard', asked Bill, 'that everything's clear now for my young Cypriot fellow to come out next week?'

'Wonderful news, Bill, wonderful news.'

*****

Violet winced as her partner trod on her feet again. He was a very bad dancer. But he seemed a good bloke and obviously fancied her. Not too many of those around.

She hoped her advice would do the trick. Pretty basic stuff – though not for Polly? She gave an inward giggle. Not that it wasn't a serious matter and a serious suggestion.

*****

'Of course, Commissioner, this year's extension will enable me to continue helping you with the Training Scheme.' They were standing in a corner of the room, heads together, glasses in hand, the noise level an adequate protection against their being overheard.

'And …?' Zalomo knew that Elias had something else to say. A devious little sod, but not to be underestimated, he was even more certain of that now. He drilled an imaginary backhand drive towards the bar.

'Well, Commissioner', Antoun gently stroked his nose in the timeless Levantine gesture of a shared confidence. 'I think you would agree that the successful outcome of the various problems that have beset us recently in the Embassy has been strongly influenced by the assistance you have so kindly provided.'

'Yes? And of course it has been made easier for me by having an insight into the background.' Zalomo knew where this was going now; he'd heard it all so many times.

'Exactly, Commissioner, exactly.' Elias's eyes sparkled and he lowered his voice to a confidential murmur. 'And it would not be useful, I feel, to deprive you of background to any such problems as may arise in the future …'

'But of course your motives in confiding in me might be misunderstood by your superiors, and hence there is a need for discretion. That right, Elias?' Zalomo too was speaking very quietly.

'Yes indeed, Commissioner. And I have recently had my confidence in my superiors' trust severely shaken. I was more or less accused of murder; yes, believe it or not, *me*! But nothing must go wrong in this final period at the Embassy while I am saving hard for my retirement.'

Zalomo played a delicate drop shot while he pondered how to test this oleaginous hypocrite, who should be *proud* of having done away with his persecutor. 'Funds are tight at present – I couldn't pay cash for such … ah … background.'

'My dear Commissioner, never in a thousand years could I accept money!' he exclaimed, looking more disappointed than scandalised, Zalomo noted. Perhaps he'd gone too far? A glancing backhand…

'However, Mr Elias, I *could* introduce you – indirectly of course,

312

and anonymously – to a well-connected official from across the border who has regular access to important information about that country. As a matter of fact this man offered me an arrangement of sorts a few days ago. But I declined. Mind you, he'd doubtless be very demanding financially. But, if you wish, I could bring the two of you together. Which might prove profitable to you both, if you follow me?'

'I understand completely, Commissioner, this is most interesting. So if you could arrange ...'

'I'll do that, Mr Elias.' He paused. 'Tell me, meanwhile, has your Ambassador heard anything recently from London about our lost sheep Ayumba? Copies of any relevant telegrams would be useful.'

No point pissing about with a man like Elias. Miss Brainbridge's secret business would come on the agenda in due course.

'Oh yes and finally, you might do me a small service, my friend, by passing on my condolences to the Ambassador's Steward. A cousin of his, who visited him recently, was found dead by the side of the road last night. The funeral took place this morning.'

*****

Refusing the offer of another game of darts, Squires took his drink into a corner of the room, sat down and gazed sightlessly at an old newspaper. Difficult. The Ambassador had this morning shown him the Honours-in-Confidence telegram from London offering him, the Colonel, the CBE. That was very gratifying indeed. And Squires had himself also had a personal telegram this morning, from the MOD. It said that the Washington job, with promotion to Brigadier, was his if he wanted it – but the Post was now strictly *Married Accompanied*; and also (the message was dressed up but unmistakable) he would be on probation for a year and must be teetotal for at least that period. A somewhat poisoned chalice, it seemed.

Alternatively, he thought, he could resign from the Service, when he'd finished here in a few months, and take up an offer from Armitage's people. That would entail six months' training in UK before returning here as their area salesman to exploit his excellent contacts in the armed forces. Fat salary and generous expenses and no bloody nonsense about resident wives and laying off the booze. But what a come-

313

down for a man of honour which – let's face it – he knew himself to be.

He was agonising over this when he realised the Commissioner had slid into the chair next to him.

'Forgive my disturbing you, Colonel Squires.'

'Not at all, Commissioner, one is always glad ...'

'I wanted to thank you for using your pistol last Saturday to activate the warning volley from my men. That stupid Riot Super should have done it himself. You saved the day.'

'Really, most kind, but nobody ...'

'Don't worry Colonel I'll keep it to myself. Expect you haven't got a licence for it, or Mr Brathby doesn't know about it. Something like that.'

What a good chap Zalomo was. He'd be a useful friend if he did return here to flog instruments of death. Definitely. Or would he? There'd be a price no doubt: like passing on news of any potential trouble in the Army.

*****

Elias could scarcely believe his luck. He would not now need to fabricate information from an imaginary *Blunderbuss*. He was being offered the real thing – a genuine, live, secret source. And one who'd be immensely profitable.

*****

Tom was packing to go home and face the enquiry. May as well throw in Dr Pox's special penis unguent, he thought. Don't know how long I'll be away or even if I'm coming back at all. Bloody Berridge. It was nice to know the little shit was dead. There's happy indeed. And bless Philippa for sorting that bit out, removing any suspicion from him. Only she could have worked out that Berridge's death was an accident. That took real brains.

*****

Polly was at home. She couldn't face the Club. She turned over Violet's suggestion. Could she really bring herself to do that? It just wasn't her, not in her character. It was outrageous. But something unusual was needed. She wasn't sure she could do it. But as she rejoiced again that Richard Cardenas was dead she felt her courage welling within her. Yes, she would try it.

6

It was midnight and at Polly's suggestion Brathby was sitting at his office desk, fully dressed. He pressed the buzzer. As the door opened he stood up, a seething morass of desire and inhibition, lust and guilt.

She approached the desk, shorthand notebook and pencil at the ready. 'Was there something you wanted, Ambassador?'

She was wearing her spectacles. Only her spectacles.

Brathby sat down again, trembling. 'Take a memo, Miss Pym,' he said severely; 'Subject – "Well-conducted popular demonstration leads to spectacular revival of dormant native passions."'

Good God, he thought in the few seconds before his senses were totally overwhelmed, what *am* I getting myself into?

*****

'So praise you, praise you, Mudder-of-God. Make you take dis fine candle and de tanks of dis your servant. Tank you, tank you, I too tank you.'

Cuthbert left the church and hobbled through the rain, across the road and down to the fetish-festooned and fly-buzzed hut by the river. His little leather bag clutched in his bony hand, he stepped carefully between puddles of chicken blood - if it was chicken blood - and unidentifiable scattered bones. He spoke to the straw mask, within which the Doctor sat concealed.

'De man done die and dis your payment. Wot ting dis? Dis be de gentles of dat bad white man. My friend in mortuary done gettum. Dey small but maybe you fit use um for piccin medcin.'